Be Your Forever

Natalie Knolls

Contents

To the ones who were made to feel that the size of their body defines their worth.
Fuck that and fuck them.

Content Warnings

This book may contain content that may be sensitive to some readers. While the characters and story are fictional, the struggles they deal with are very real. As an author and therapist, your mental health is important so please take care of yourself first. These topics include:

Off page drunk-driving car accident; Mention of Alcoholism and drug overdose (not by MC's)

Mental health rep; Body image issues; Panic Attacks

Explicit open-door sex scenes & Use of vulgar language

Temperature play; Wax play; Breath play; Bondage play; Cat and mouse fantasy

Salirophilia & Katoptronophilia

Degradation play/kink; Blindfold kink: Daddy/ Brat kink

Praise Kink; Blindfold kink

Edging

Brianna

Somewhere lost in the atmosphere

Smile. Pretend you aren't slowly dying inside. This is your best friend's wedding for fuck's sake. The least you can do is pretend. My smile has been permanently plastered on my face since this morning. Me, Avery, and Cas' grandmother, Evelyn, have been in the bridal suite for hours with the two of them sending worried glances my way. You'd think I'm dying.

Dying. Death. Accident. Max.

I went a solid five seconds without thinking about him, about that day. I feel the familiar panic bubbling up my throat, and I run into the adjoining bathroom.

It's hard to breathe, but I can't let Avery see me like this. It's her special day. She's marrying her best friend, the love of her life, and I'm here ruining it with my bullshit. *You're the worst. Avery should have never chosen you as her maid of honor. What kind of friend are you?*

A soft knock on the door halts my thoughts before my best friend's buttery voice sounds from the other side. "Bri? A-Are you okay?"

Am I okay? That's a loaded question, one I don't have any real answer to. The day of the accident changed so much, dousing me in numbing cream from head to toe. I can't seem to get a grasp on how I feel, and I'm left figuring out how to do life like this.

The sound of knocking shakes me out of my thoughts a second time. *Avery. Wedding. Maid of honor.*

I swallow the panic as oxygen slides down my lungs, soothing the anxiety like a warm mug of tea when you're sick. My jittery fingers allow the cool, smooth sensation of the doorknob to center me before I plaster a smile on my face and swing it open.

"I'm great. I just needed a moment to fix my makeup. I don't want to look like a raccoon in your wedding photos. What would people think?"

Avery blinks up at me, face scrunched with concern. She doesn't believe me—I know she doesn't. She opens her mouth to speak, but I interrupt her.

"Anyway, it's not about me. It's your day, so let's get you into your dress. Let's go! Cas is going to faint when he sees you."

With her hand in mine, I'm dragging toward her floor length, mermaid style wedding dress. She takes off the white robe the venue supplied and I, along with Evelyn, help her into the stunning gown. It fits her like a glove. Seriously, when we went shopping, she tried it on and needed zero alterations. It's an off the shoulder dress with lace trim and a small train, and she's absolutely beautiful. Even in my haze-filled mind, I can appreciate her beauty. Her usual ivory skin gives off a subtle tanned glow, illuminating her freckles like diamonds. Her soft, wavy hair is in a low ponytail resting over her right shoulder with pearls woven throughout. She's an absolute vision.

"You look beautiful, Avery." Evelyn has been a blubbering mess the entire time. If I wasn't so lost in my head, I'd be joining her. We all stare in the mirror as the photographer takes a million and one photos. I make sure my smile is a permanent fixture on my face. The last thing Avery needs is to look back on these memories and see my dead expression.

After another hour or so, it's time to get everyone lined up as I prepare to walk down the aisle. My body might be physically here, but emotionally and mentally? It's lost somewhere in the atmosphere. My guess is it never left the hospital.

Cas and Avery decided to do things non-traditionally. Yes, they have a bridal party, but we all get to walk down the aisle by ourselves and then sit in the designated front row. That's where I find Asher. He's already sitting down, his eyes glued to me. I don't pay much attention to him, but I take my assigned seat and stare at the altar. If I keep my focus there, then I don't have to see the crowd of concerned faces I'm sure are burning holes into my back. Despite my better judgement, my eyes flicker to the empty seat next to Asher.

Panic surrounds me like an early morning fog, a thickness so intense I can barely see a few feet in front of me. Instead of watching the celebration of love, visions of that day assault my brain, taunting me mercilessly.

January 2026

I love hanging out with my brother. Max and I have always been super close, pretty much attached at the hip since we were little. Since becoming adults, however, we haven't had much time to get together as much as we used to. So it was nice having him here with me. Our usual sibling banter is in full swing, tossing jabs at each other left and right. Just like old times. Conversation flows easily. We talk about Avery and Cas' upcoming wedding next month.

Everything's perfect. Until it isn't.

Squeal.

Crash.

My body jolts forward, slamming against something solid and cold. I can't hear anything besides the ringing in my ears.

What happened? Why does my head hurt? Questions plague my mind, but I'm discombobulated. Despite the pain, I shift my head toward Max's direction, only to have a dreadful cold overtake my body. It feels as if I stepped into a walk-in freezer. The faint sound of sirens is like the ominous music that plays in scary movies when something is about to happen.

But all I can see is him. Max. Slumped over. Immobile. Every rational thought evacuates my body as black flecks dance across my vision.

I hardly remember how I got to the hospital, only that I'm here. The doctors and nurses say I'm lucky to walk away with only a few stitches and a mild concussion.

Lucky? How am I lucky when I learn shortly after that my brother is in a coma? They try to get me to focus on myself and not worry about my brother. It's not until I'm screaming at the top of my lungs that they finally cave.

Coma.

That word is a dagger straight to the heart. The doctors are hopeful he'll make a full recovery, but they're wrong all the time, right? They tell me it's to reduce swelling so they can operate on him, but my mind attaches to the word 'coma' like a tick on a dog. There is no shaking it off.

Everything is different now. I'm different. A familiar, deep, masculine voice sounds from the hallway. My feet carry me before my brain has time to process. That's when I see him. My heart seeks his like a bee chasing after nectar.

The feel of Asher's warm, calloused hand on my thigh grounds me to the present moment. His soft, blue eyes stare into mine, and a calmness washes over me. I can't explain it, but I feel safe. As quickly as I look into his eyes, I'm turning away. I don't want to see his soft expression turn to pity. And I can't bear to look at the empty chair anymore. I keep my gaze trained forward, focus on breathing through my nose, and continually blink back the tears that threaten to blow my cover.

I somehow manage to get through the ceremony, smiling and laughing like I should. Like I'm supposed to. I've successfully dodged my parents like they are the plague. I can't look into their grief-stricken eyes anymore, knowing I'm the cause for their pain. After everything happened, I hid within the comfort of my own home. For about two weeks, I tried to pretend like everything was fine, when on the inside, I was rotting away. The irony of it all is that my bedroom is a perfect representation of that. I clung to my couch like a barnacle on the side of a ship. I couldn't look my parents in the eyes and pretend everything was okay. In the comfort of my own home, I could shut out the outside world, crawl into my hole and wallow—something I've exceeded expectations on.

On the outside, I'm smiling, shaking hands, and expressing gratitude for being here. On the inside, I'm counting down the hours until I can change into my favorite pair of sweats, crawl under my covers, and pretend life outside the four walls of my bedroom don't exist.

I've been glued to my seat, repeatedly checking my watch.

Twenty more minutes. It's socially acceptable to stay for twenty more minutes, then you can pull an Irish goodbye and leave.

I glance up, trying to place where Cas and Avery are so that they don't see me leaving. I don't want to hurt their feelings. I just...I can't be here. But instead of finding them, I see a familiar pair of baby blue eyes next to me. *Asher.* He hasn't left the table all night. Many people have asked him to dance, and he's politely declined every time.

"Y-You don't have to babysit me, Asher. You can go dance and have fun. I'm probably bringing down your vibe."

Asher's hand finds my thigh again, squeezing just hard enough that I'm forced to look into his eyes. "There's nowhere else I'd rather be than next to you."

His kindness is something I don't deserve. I mean, Max is his best friend. I'm just...the sister of said best friend. I nod my head, choosing not to entertain the conversation I don't have the energy for. After the allotted twenty minutes is up, I make the excuse of needing to pee. If

Asher notices that I'm bringing my jacket and purse to the bathroom, he doesn't comment on it. I call myself an Uber, and within five minutes, I'm hightailing it out of here. Thank you to my driver, Geo, for being two minutes away. Easiest five star rating ever.

I'm so happy for my best friend. She deserves all the good things in life, but I just can't let her down. I once called her my little Eeyore, but now I've taken on that role, and I don't want her to be dragged down into the pit of darkness I've found myself in.

Brianna

Dressed for my funeral

Cold, heavy chains cut into my wrists as I try to break free, but my nightmares hold me captive, forcing me to watch everything in slow motion with an evil smirk written across their faces. Ear-splintering sounds of glass shattering and tires squealing are a broken record in my mind. All my desperate attempts to change the direction of my dreams fall flat.

Tires squeal.

Glass breaks.

People shout.

Max lays lifeless beside me, red blood oozing from the side of his face. My screams and shouts fall silent. No one can hear me. I reach for Max, but I'm yanked from what's left of my car. My head is pounding, and I assume my face is scratched and bloody from the glass. I watch as they pull Max from the car seconds before it bursts into flames, illuminating the scene in its red-orange glow.

I've been living this nightmare for months now, a former shell of myself with zero energy to do the basics like shower or change my clothes. My outfit is falling apart, with random chocolate ice cream stains on my sweats and my pink, oversized hoodie fraying at the hem. A perfect representation of my life. My clothes may be tattered and worn, but they've become my home. My safety blanket. They don't judge me for my lack of energy or personal hygiene. They allow me to hide from the world, but more importantly, they allow me to hide from myself.

I'm dressed for my funeral. Here lies Bri. She was bold, brilliant, outgoing, and charismatic. The girl that everyone once knew and loved is dead. In her place is a zombie. Someone who goes through the motions just to get through the day. Gone are the days of hanging out with friends, getting drunk, and hooking up. Her free spirit has been snuffed out like the last remaining candle in a dark room. Any attempts to reach out and comfort her are half-assed. She doesn't deserve to be happy. She doesn't deserve to live life like nothing happened.

Guilt and I have entered a toxic, codependent relationship. Without Max's chaotic energy, what's the point of anything? Why should I carry on with my life the way I used to? I miss the old me, but the old me is the reason Max was in the hospital in the first place. I'm the reason he spent months completely immobilized and helpless in a sterile hospital bed. He may be on the road to recovery, but I'm still trapped in the past, still trapped beneath the rubble of my shame and no energy to remove the excess weight.

Electricity licks and buzzes down my spine, the tiny hairs on my arms standing to attention. My heart beats at a dangerous speed, and no matter how much I gasp for air, I can never get enough. I glance toward my dresser and see the orange bottle with a white cap glaring at me, mocking me. *You are useless. You are weak. You can't do anything right.* Mental health medications aren't something to be ashamed about. My best friend, Avery, takes them for her anxiety. In no way am I calling her weak—in fact, she's one of the strongest women I know. But I'm learning firsthand that we don't always practice what we preach. While Avery is strong, brave, and incredible, I'm useless, a failure, and defective.

The panic feels like I've become a wolf in one of my shifter romance novels, scratching beneath my skin, hoping to gain control over my body. I frantically shake my hands in a desperate attempt to rid myself of the anxiety while pacing my bedroom floor. My face feels hot. Hot...just like the flames from the accident.

Max lies unconscious on the floor. Blue and red flashing lights. Glass everywhere.

I'm warring with my mind to cling to the present moment. Scenes from the accident flicker across my brain without any warning. I'm blinded by my own images, my mind and body yearning to head in different directions. My brain wants to bully me into replaying what happened on an endless loop. My body is determined to remain in my room.

Focus, Bri. Don't go back there. Nothing good comes from reliving that experience. You're not dying. You are in your room, not at the scene of the accident.

I force my gaze to look around the room, a pathetic attempt at regulating my breathing. I see my twinkly lights dangling behind my earthy-brown colored four-poster bed. My blush comforter is soft to the touch, with little wrinkles from another restless sleep. My pillows are scattered throughout my room, ranging in different shades of pink and white. Already, my heart has slowed down immensely, my breathing more regular.

I glance out of my bay window and focus on the Pacific blue sky and the white, cotton candy-esque clouds in the sky. It's a particularly chilly morning. The trees are a collection of sticks and twigs bound together, completely void of life and color. I walk toward the small bench to open the window, allowing the bitter winter air to slap across my face, leaving a faint stinging in its wake.

Breathe in the calm serenity of the morning.

Breathe out panic and shame.

I repeat this mantra in my head. Slowly, the tingles evaporate from my body, my mind returning to its resting ground. Well, as much as it can with how chaotic it's become.

I've never been this much of a hot mess express. Outside the normal levels of anxiety everyone experiences, I never had an issue with my mental health. Yeah, I struggled with inadequacy from time to time, but I've always prided myself on being an open book. Sometimes too open. But that was something I loved about me. Now, the very thought of sharing my internal dialogue makes my skin itch as if tiny ants are crawling over me.

The accident did a number on me, especially because I wasn't alone in the car. It was me who wanted to go out and have fun. A little sibling bonding time, if you will. It was me who planned everything out. It was me who ended up in that car wreck, and it was me who put my brother in harm's way.

My skin twitches with discomfort. I hate who I've become, but I don't know how to fix it. I don't know if I even want to fix it. So instead of dealing with everything head-on like a mature, responsible adult, I slink back under my covers and hide from the world. It's become my new norm.

The sound of my front door unlocking has me bolting upright. I know without looking in the mirror that my wavy hair is a rat's nest and my eyes are puffy. In this installment of my nightmares, I prayed it was me who got injured and not Max. Maybe if it happened to me in the dream instead of him, it would relieve me of my guilt. Spoiler alert—it did not.

"Brianna?" The soft, soothing voice belonging to Avery calls from downstairs. I love Avery to pieces. She's my soulmate, my person, but I just can't face the disappointment on her face when she sees what I've become. Especially after I pulled an Irish goodbye at her wedding and ghosted her. So I shrink back under the covers, hoping she'll give up and leave. I should have known that wouldn't be the case.

Her normally soft footsteps are drumbeats as she makes her way toward me. My room is usually organized and clean. You could swipe your finger along any surface and there wouldn't be a speck of dust. Now, it looks as if a tornado and hurricane flew through it. Empty bags of snacks and candy wrappers decorate my floor. Clothes are tossed haphazardly. It's so bad that I can't recall what the actual floor looks like anymore. Do I have carpeting or laminate flooring?

My blanket still covers my head, and I brace myself for judgment when she peels the layers back. It isn't fair to assume she'll judge me; she's my best friend, for fuck's sake. Avery and I have been attached at the hip since we met in college. We've had our fair share of messy moments without any judgment. We accept each other as we are—flaws and all. Yet, it feels like I'm a disappointment to her. I haven't been a proper friend, which only adds fuel to my fire of shame. My mind is a master manipulator, excelling at spinning webs of lies.

"Bri?" Avery asks again, her voice much closer now. Despite hiding under my blanket cocoon, I know she's standing in the doorway to my room. *She is going to run for the hills. You can't even clean up your room. You're such a failure. She's going to take one look at you and walk away for good.* My thoughts buzz in my brain like wasps. Stinging me regardless of whether I bother them or not. I've prepared for the worst, so when I feel the bed shift next to me, I squeeze my eyes shut. If I don't see her, then she can't see me. I cling to that hope like a child clutching their favorite teddy bear. It doesn't work, and Avery just crawls under the blanket with me.

Breathe in. Breathe out.

I repeat that mantra five times before gaining the courage to open my eyes and shift to look at her.

All the preparations for what I thought I would see evaporate. Avery doesn't look disgusted with me. Her eyes shimmer with empathy, opening her arms and inviting me to crawl into her embrace. I feel like a puppet on strings, my life no longer my own. I can't fully register how good it feels to have a choice. Avery just lies there, her arms outstretched and a smile on her face. Her body language screams comfort. Her eyes say *I've got you. I'm here for you and I'm not going anywhere.* I know that even if I reject her warm gesture, she won't go anywhere. Despite the toxic sludge my brain tosses at me, that's a fact I know to be true. Avery will always support those she cares about, even when said person doesn't give two shits about themselves.

The second Avery's arms wrap around me, I lose it, clinging to her like a lifeline as I soak her shirt with my hopelessness. I let it all out. Since everything happened, I've shut everyone out—including Avery. Yet, here she is, acting as if we just hung out the other day. My radio silence hasn't deterred her from being my friend. She's here in my room, giving me everything I know I need, but don't have the courage to ask for.

Avery begins to hum the tune of *Stand By You* by Rachel Platten. She's always communicated best through song. And while she isn't singing the words, I know the lyrics enough to understand what she's trying to say. She knows that Rachel Platten is my all-time favorite artist, so it means a lot that she chose this song. My head rests against her chest and I focus on the buzzing sensation from her humming to radiate through my body. Right now, I'm protected, I'm loved, and most importantly, I'm safe. I'm not fully committed to accepting all those feelings, but right now, I can keep the fire of hope inside my heart simmering.

Avery massages my scalp, and I feel my body become heavy with sleep. Just by being here and comforting me, Avery has planted a seed of faith. And maybe with time, that seed can blossom into a beautiful, thriving plant that can withhold even the toughest of storms. I fall asleep with a soft smile on my face, and it's the first time in months that nightmares aren't the star of the show. I can't help but think that maybe I'm not so damaged after all.

Asher

I'll be her anchor

My FINGERS CURL AROUND the cool glass, the squeaking sound falling faint against my ears. I'm staring into space, numb to my surroundings. It could be busy as hell, but I couldn't tell you how packed we are. This happens after visiting Max's house. No matter how many times I see him, I'm left feeling drained. Visions of him unconscious in the hospital are burned into my brain. Seeing anyone covered in bumps and bruises lying lifeless on a hospital bed can traumatize a person. Seeing your best friend, though? Double the trauma.

Despite everything that's happened to him, Max is still Max. He's still the goofy, outgoing guy who will stop at nothing to make you laugh. I don't know how he manages to stay so positive, but he does.

"Hey, Ash?" Gage, my business partner and friend, asks.

"Yeah?"

"That glass is pretty clean, don't you think?" I frown at his question before glancing down. The glass is, in fact, in pristine condition, so I place it down carefully before grabbing the next one.

"You've been at that thing for almost ten minutes. What gives?"

Gage isn't one to engage in small talk with people, typically responding in grunts and nods. I'm one of the lucky few who gets more than three words out of him. Gage O'Reilly is my polar opposite: covered in tattoos, has gauges in his ears, and a permanent scowl on his face. Our female customer base triples anytime the man is behind the bar, with muscles any man would never admit to envying and eyes that stare straight into your soul. Like, seriously, the man can fish out a lie from across the bar. He's a total ladies' man, and whenever he decides to smile, if you listen close enough, you can hear the hearts of women—and even men—break. Despite the attitude, Gage is a total charmer.

I met him during an intro to business class in college. At first, I never planned to go to college. During my senior year of high school, I had zero idea of what I wanted to pursue. The only things I cared about were baseball, reading, my friends, and Bri. Being my high school's all-star pitcher, everyone thought I'd go pro, but that never really interested me. To me, baseball was just a hobby, a great way to channel all that excess energy in a healthy way. So when I enrolled at Brookestone University, I was undecided, remaining that way until I met Gage. We were paired together during a project where we had to come up with a business idea and a plan. At first, we seemed like an unlikely duo with him being more reserved, but somehow, we worked. We bonded over our mutual dream to own our own bar, so coming up with a business idea was fairly easy.

In that oversized, bright college classroom was where Aces was born. Gage and I were so eager to open up our own bar that we dropped out of college to pursue our passion. It's been one of the best decisions I've made in my life so far.

"Ace?" Gage asks, using the name Max gave me in high school. Hearing Gage use the nickname pulls me out of my thoughts and into the present.

"I went to see Max earlier today. I guess I've been distracted." I shrug.

"Ah damn. How is he doing?" One of Gage's redeeming qualities is his empathy. I guess it's inevitable when you grow up with three younger sisters. There's more to him than meets the eye, but for some reason, he keeps a huge part of him under lock and key.

"He's doing okay. He has most of his range of motion in his arm, but Max being Max tends to overdo it. He's struggling with not working right now, and it fucking sucks seeing him like that. And then when I think about seeing him connected to what looked like hundreds of tubes, my mind falls down a rabbit hole." The image of seeing my best friend hooked up to medical equipment will forever be burned into my brain.

January 2026 (The day of the accident)

It's my favorite day of the week: crunching numbers and making sure the bar is in the green. I am knee deep in receipts and paperwork when I hear my phone buzz. I glance at the caller ID, and when I see Max's mom's name, Colleen, flash across my screen, something in my gut tells me to answer it.

"Hello?" My tone quivers ever so slightly. Panic is a snake that slithers its way up my throat, threatening to wrap around my neck and squeeze the life out of me.

"Hi, sweetheart. I-I'm so s-sorry to call, but there's been an accident." Loud buzzing fills my ears, and I barely make out what she said.

Accident.

Drunk driver.

Max.

Bri.

I have never hung up a phone so fast. I snatch my keys from my desk, and the second I am behind the wheel, I break about a dozen laws. I don't give a shit. I have to get to my best friend and my...my Bri. This hospital is so damn familiar to me now that I hardly need the nurses' guidance. With the amount of times I had to pick my brother up from the many times he had to get his stomach pumped, I could walk these halls with a blindfold. Then there was that time Cas was shot by his father. I really don't want to be back here so soon, but I push back the trauma tied to this place. My best friend and love of my life are here. I curse the slow elevator, attempting to rid myself of my anxiety through the incessant tapping of my foot. Normally, I'd be the person who holds the door open for anyone needing to get on, but not this time. My finger hurts from how hard I repeatedly press the third floor button.

After the elevator's snail pace-like climb, I run right into Colleen and Liam's arms. It's hard to tell who's more upset because we are all a combined shaky, hot mess. I squeeze a little harder before I pull back and guide us to those stupid maroon chairs before asking what happened.

"What? H-How?" I stammer out.

"They were hit by a drunk driver running a red light. Bri has a few stitches and bruises, as well as a minor concussion. The doctors are finishing up with her now." Liam's normally steady voice is rough and shaky.

"And Max?" Colleen and Liam exchange a look before expressing the extent of his injuries.

"Max suffered the most. He has some minor internal bleeding from a punctured lung caused by some broken ribs. His entire left leg will require surgery from the multiple fractures. He'll also require surgery for his right arm as well as his shoulder and collarbone. The doctors said he also suffered some grade two soft tissue damage and has a severe concussion. He's currently in surgery now, and we're just waiting until we can go see him."

Fuck. It's a miracle they're able to somewhat function with both of their babies being checked on. A door from one of the rooms opens, and without even looking up, I know it's her. I've been in tune with Brianna ever since I met her—I just didn't realize what that meant until it was too late. Shit, I still don't know what happened the day she went from wanting to be around me to despising my entire existence. My blue eyes meet her gold-rimmed amber ones, and I freeze. Just looking into her eyes puts me in a trance. The rich honey color reminds me of those videos where they make caramel. Even with gauze covering her left temple and a pretty significant bruise on her collarbone, she is radiant.

I freeze like a deer in headlights when she sees me. I stand up, ready to leave and allow her space to grieve, but she surprises me. I thought she'd lay into me like she has in the past. But she runs at me like a puppy greeting its owner after being gone all day. The wind is briefly knocked out of me, and we're seconds away from collapsing onto the ground. With Bri's legs wrapped around my waist, I somehow manage to get us on the floor with minimal clumsiness as we sit together while she weeps in my arms. I hug her tight against my chest while peppering soft kisses on the crown of her head. Her clinging to me is as much for me as it is for her. I love to be needed, it gives me a sense of pride and accomplishment—probably one of the reasons I love bartending so much. But there's nothing like being needed by her. Being needed by the one person whose entire existence makes your heart beat with purpose. We stay like that until it's time for me to leave. I offer to take her home, but she insists on staying put. The drive home is a dissociated blur, unable to feel anything but the lingering warmth from her touch.

I think about that day often. I swear, my heart stopped for a moment when I got that call. I'm still grateful that Gage was there that night, because one look at my panicked expression and he knew. Anytime I mention my appreciation to him, he just shrugs it off. He isn't much of a talker, so it makes sense for him. My arms tingle at the memory of Bri in my arms. I sometimes have a hard time believing that she chose me to run to. I've had about a dozen scenarios in my head as to why she'd want to seek comfort in my arms. *She was in shock. She didn't realize it was me. She actually doesn't hate me, and this was her way of showing me.* Okay, maybe that last one is wishful thinking, but remembering how distraught Bri was that day still sends shivers down my spine. Then I think about Cas and Avery's wedding a few months ago, and how she let me touch her. It was a simple touch, a gentle squeeze of her thigh, but she didn't shrug me off. Both of those incidents might seem small to most, but to me they are everything.

The wedding was the last time I saw Bri. Normally, I'd find an excuse to see her whether it's suggesting to Avery that they have a girls' day at Aces, or I'm "accidentally" crashing a sibling hang out. Just being around her bathes me in a sense of calmness. I've desperately wanted to reach out to her many times, but I'm not sure if she wants to see me. If I'm being honest with myself, I'm desperately holding onto the tiny glimpse of a vulnerable Bri. She isn't one to ask for help, claiming it makes her look weak. And letting me touch her like that? She's probably hating herself even more. As for me, I'll take any vulnerability Bri is willing to give me. She also needs time to recover—I'm just not sure if that healing journey includes me. However, if she asks, I'll do anything to be her anchor.

The door to the bar opens, and in walks Avery, Bri's best friend. She looks around the crowded bar, searching for someone when her eyes lock with mine. She gives me a sad smile before walking toward me.

"Avery. Hey, what's up?"

"Can we talk? Somewhere private?" Avery fiddles nervously with her fingers, clearly worried about something. My mind blanks at what could be troubling her, but I nod toward the office before responding.

"Yeah. We can talk in my office." I wave in the direction of the tiny space, signaling for her to go first. I turn toward Gage, but I don't have to say anything. He understands.

"Have a seat. Do you want any water or anything? I can easily go and grab something from the bar," I suggest.

"Oh, no thank you. I'm good. How's Max? His parents have been telling me you've been stopping by." Avery's voice is soft with an undertone of pain. I know her and Max go back a few years, so I can imagine how painful this must be for her.

"He's hanging in there. He's still in the boot, but the doctors are weaning him off of it. He still has his sense of humor and often compares himself to Iron Man. So given the circumstances, I'd say he's doing better than most would in his situation. How are you handling everything? I know you have a complicated relationship with hospitals, given every-thing that happened with Cas." Cas, my friend and Avery's husband, has been in the hospital twice—once because of an overdose, and the other when his father shot him in the stomach. Having more people you care about struggling with injuries has to be hard.

"It's been tough. I hated seeing Max and Bri in the hospital. I'm glad they're okay, but it was still a shock when it happened. Speaking of Bri, have you seen or talked to her lately?" Avery's eyes fill with concern, and my gut instinct tells me I'm not going to like what she tells me next.

"I haven't. I didn't know if she wanted me around, or if she just needed time to herself. Why, what's wrong?" My voice cracks at the end, giving way to fear that something is not okay.

Avery confirms my suspicions. "She's not doing good, Ash. I hadn't seen her since the wedding. She's been holed up in her home for months. She ignores most, if not all, of my texts and calls. I was so concerned that I went over there using the spare key she gave me, and what I saw was..." Avery sniffs, so I offer her my hand for her to hold. Her smile doesn't reach her eyes, but she squeezes my hand and doesn't let go.

"Asher, she's a mess. When I went into her room, there was just so much stuff everywhere. Clothes, candy and chip wrappers littered her entire floor. It looked like she hadn't moved from her bed in days. And when I crawled under the covers with her, you could tell she hasn't been taking care of herself. Her hair was matted, and her sweats were days old. My heart broke for her. She's not taking this well, Asher, and I don't know what to do for her. The second my arms wrapped around her, she lost it. She cried herself to sleep, and then I cried myself to sleep. I just...I don't know what to do."

I put a hand to my chest, and I can feel my heart break. Who knew Bri was struggling that hard? She's always so fun and outgoing, so this behavior is a total one-eighty for her. I get up from my chair and move around the desk to squat in front of Avery. I have no plan as to what I'm going to say to her, but I have to say something. What comes out of my mouth surprises us both, but it feels right.

"Let me help. I'll do whatever it takes to bring our girl back."

What I don't say is that I'll do anything and everything to bring *my* girl back. Avery gives me a grateful smile before hugging me.

"Really? Oh, thank you, Asher. I knew you'd be the perfect person to help her."

"Well, I don't know about that. I'll do what I can. You can count on me."

Avery squeezes me one more time before pulling away from the hug and walking out the door.

I clutch at my heart again, feeling it crack even more thinking about how Bri's light has been snuffed. I'll do whatever it takes to bring her back to life. I just have to work up the courage to go to her. I have to be able to brush my own feelings for her aside and be whatever she needs from me. I make a mental note to call my therapist so she can help me sort through my emotions before I see Bri. When I do, I want to be able to have a clear head on my shoulders. Honestly, this is probably something I should have done the day after the accident happened. Regardless, I'll do whatever it takes to share my light with her, because she's too amazing to fade into blackness.

Brianna

Resurfacing from the darkness of my own guilt

TODAY IS THE FIRST time in months I feel like I've resurfaced from the darkness of my own guilt. I stand underneath the showerhead and focus on the hot water beating against my skin. The steam hugs me like a long, *long* lost friend. My scalp, which is in desperate need for some love, tingles from my tea tree shampoo. I scrub my body, focusing on the gritty slide of the exfoliation beads on my skin. I forgot how therapeutic and grounding a shower could be. Anytime I have the energy to do the basics, I cling to it like a lifeline.

I finish all my skincare steps before exiting my ensuite bathroom to jump back into my uniform of sweats and a hoodie. I may be feeling better right now, but I'm not ready to give up the sweats. They don't hug me like my old clothes used to, which I guess is the purpose. Since the accident, I've put on more weight. *Thanks, emotional eating.*

I used to be so proud of my body. I had an hourglass figure, toned stomach, and a firm ass. Now? My stomach has rolls, my thighs are thicker and full of stretch marks, and I have no one to blame but myself. So goodbye cute, sexy, skin-tight clothes, and hello pullovers, joggers and leggings.

Jeans? I don't know her anymore—nor do I want to. She's so judgmental, tending to put your flaws on display.

Yeah, no thanks. I think I'll stick with hiding my body. I still can't look in the mirror for longer than the few minutes it takes to tame my rat's nest hair. Looking at myself for extended periods of time leads to me outlining my flaws like art on a canvas. And then *boom*, emotional breakdown. And I've had enough of those. I seem to cry at the drop of a hat nowadays. Last week, I couldn't get the damn cap off a jar of pickles. I ended up on the kitchen floor, hysterically sobbing.

The sound of my phone pinging brings me out of my self-loathing only to dive right back into it when I see who it is. My throat thickens with emotion and my eyes sting with unshed tears.

> **Mom: Hey sweetie, I wanted to check in on you. I know you need your space. I'm thinking of you always. I love you, Lovebug.**

You thought you could get rid of us? You are nothing but a failure.

I haven't seen or talked to either of my parents since the wedding. After the accident, I was able to keep up the ruse of being okay. But like in the game of Jenga, one wrong move and the whole structure comes tumbling down. Small spikes of anxiety turn into full-fledged panic attacks, and I just can't do it. I love my parents, but I can no longer look them in the eyes without feeling an intense amount of guilt for everything that happened.

The rational, healthy response would be to talk to them about my feelings. But the rational train left the station ages ago. Instead, I've isolated myself from everyone I love. Misery, party of one.

My throat feels tight, and my eyes sting when I see my mom's recent text. And, because I'm masochistic, I scroll through every previous message from my parents, knowing it'll only cause me pain.

You're a shitty daughter. Look at how hurt your parents are. All. Your. Fault.

> **(February 20th, 2026) Mom: Hi, lovebug. I wanted to see how you were doing. You left the wedding without a goodbye. I tried to call you, but it went straight to voicemail. Please give us a call soon. Love you.**

> **(March 3rd, 2026) Mom: Hey, lovebug. Your father and I miss you so much. I'm not sure what's going on, but please call or text us back. We're worried. Love you.**

(March 14th, 2026) Mom: Hey bug. I hope all of our messages are going through. I was looking through my camera roll and I came across a few of you. You looked stunning in your maid of honor dress. I love and miss you so much. Please call or text your dad and I, let us know you're okay.

(April 5th, 2026) Dad: Hey, bug. I wanted to check in and see what's going on with you? You haven't reached out to your mother and I. We're really worried about you. Love you

(April 28th, 2026) Mom: Hey sweetheart, we understand you might need some space. After a lot of discussion with your father, we've come to the understanding that you probably need some time alone. Just know we're here for you when you're ready. We love you so much.

(April 28th, 2026) Dad: What Mom said. We love you, kiddo.

Because I'm a glutton for punishment, I scroll through *every* unanswered message.

Avery: Hi, Bee, I just wanted to say I love you. I know you're struggling right now, but know I'm always here for you.

Avery: Babes. My heart breaks for you and Max. I hate seeing you both in so much pain.

Avery: I know you're lost in your own space right now and I can't do much to help, but maybe a few memes will help?

Avery: *meme attached*

Avery: *meme attached*

Avery: *meme attached*

Avery: Okay I love you so much. Please take care of my bestie. She means the world to me. xoxo

Avery's texts are one thing, but Max's? Those are a knife straight to my heart.

> **Max: Hey, Breezy. Where the hell are you? This hospital room is absolute ass without you here.**

> **Max: Hey Breezy, Mom and Dad finally talked to me about everything that happened. It's not your fault, you know that right? Love you, sis.**

> **Max: ...?**

> **Max: Okay, so maybe you don't know that what happened isn't on you. I know I can't convince you otherwise, but I will keep trying. I miss your stupid face. Please talk to me.**

I place my phone in my pocket...I think I've tortured myself enough. I have no real reason to ignore everyone, but tell that to my brain. She's very good at being the villain in my story, gaslighting me into believing I'm the awful person she makes me out to be.

So, instead of trying to fight through the rubble, I activate my turtle shell, hiding myself from the world—especially the ones I love most.

In the past, when I needed a break from reality, I turned to reading. There's nothing like getting lost in a book—preferably a smutty romance. Real-life men can be so disappointing, but fictional book boyfriends? They never let me down. But now, when I think about HEAs and green-flag fictional men, it doesn't hold the same appeal. I don't deserve to escape into the pages. I deserve to live with my mistakes.

I walk toward my library, hoping it'll give me the joy I once felt. My fingers wrap around the cold brass-colored doorknob, and I freeze.

You don't deserve to read books. You can't even take care of yourself, so why do you think you should do anything that makes you happy? You don't deserve to be happy.

My inner demons screech in my head, drowning out the rational angels telling me that's fake news. I shake my head before turning around and walking down the stairs.

I gather everything needed to make my go-to meal: cereal. It's not a five-star dish, but it brings me comfort. A perk of making cereal? You can't really fuck it up. Cocoa Puffs have been a staple in my diet for these last few months. I mean, it's chocolate. Who doesn't love chocolate? Plus, it gives me a small boost of serotonin. And when I get even a sliver of happiness, I clutch it in my grasp like a squirrel with its nut.

I put the bowl aside to make some much-needed coffee. I pop a sugar cookie coffee k-cup into my Keurig, the smell of rich, buttery vanilla filling the kitchen. I add the necessary amount of creamer to my mug, grab my cereal bowl, and head to my dining room table. I don't even really taste the food, another symptom of whatever the fuck is going on with me. Food is no longer for survival, but a way to numb the pain. It's a temporary glimpse at happiness—even if it's not authentic. I feel a vibration in the pocket of my sweats, and the sensation alone has my heart dropping at my feet. I should ignore it...I've already drowned in enough guilt today. But do I do that? No. Because I apparently like to torture myself.

> **Max: Hi, Bri. I know you're reading these texts. I wish you'd let me in, tell me what's going on. I can't help but think I did something wrong. Just...Can you please talk to me?**

Fuck. Why did I look? I *knew* the text would only make me feel like shit.

You're an awful sister. You're so selfish. You abandoned him when he needed you.

The sound of a doorbell pulls me from my downward spiral. *Who the hell is that?* My parents and Avery have keys to my place and usually let themselves in. Not that they would be visiting, anyway. Why would they when I've been ignoring them? And Max...Well, I've been ignoring him ever since the accident, so it's not him. Do I have any rationale for leaving my brother on read? Nope.

So I did what any sane person would do...I Googled my symptoms. It's probably the *last* thing I should have done, but I needed answers. So I typed in 'trauma after accident' and 'ignoring family' and, well...my results were an affirming slap in the face.

Depression.

That word is still a punch to the gut, leaving me wheezing for air whenever I think about it. That one Google search led me down a rabbit hole of information that made my head spin. But one tidbit has always stood out to me. Turns out, my isolation from everyone is due to my newfound chemical imbalance...Thank you, trauma. And what mental health article isn't without tips and tricks to help you work through it? The word *therapy* felt like it was written across every document in big, bold, black ink. Underlined. Italicized. It screamed at me from every page, encouraging me to talk to someone, but I wasn't ready...I'm still not.

Your friends and family blame you for the accident. They're disappointed in you for putting your brother in the hospital.

I've entered into an abusive relationship with my internal dialogue, their words like knives to my now shattered self-confidence. I never used to be this anxious and insecure. I had amazing parents who always instilled self-love and confidence in Max and I. Anytime we made a mistake, they gave us the space to process our feelings before creating a game plan to do better the next time. I envy that version of myself. I crave the presence of the bold, confident Bri. Now, I'm a tsunami of anxiety and self-doubt. That's probably why I've cut myself off from everyone I care about. I don't want them to see how far I've fallen.

The doorbell rings again, and I pray that whoever it is takes the hint and leaves. I hold my breath and make no move to get up. If I remain frozen in place, they'll go away. The logic isn't there, but it makes sense to me.

Knock. Knock. Knock.

Dammit. I heave a frustrated sigh and get up from my chair so aggressively that it scrapes against the floor. The shrill cry pierces my eardrums, but I'm too annoyed to care.

I bypass the hallway mirror, knowing I'm sure to be a hot mess. Maybe that'll scare away whoever's on the other side. My lungs fill with air in an attempt to control my irritation before gripping the door handle. When I open it, however, I'm not expecting the person on the other side.

Asher Larson.

My brother's best friend, the bane of my teenage existence. Asher and Max have been attached at the hip for as long as I can remember. You'd think with Max being the oldest of the three of us, he wouldn't want his little sister tagging along. It was quite the opposite as the three of us were always hanging out. Somewhere along the way, my crush began, and I'd find any reason to be close to Asher. His genuine kindness was what drew me in initially. But it's the moments when we were alone that I cherish the most.

"Bear?"

My eyes snap to attention as I take in the man before me. My brother's best friend. A man I spent most of my adolescent years pining after. My crush on Asher was all-consuming. But when I finally gathered up the courage to act on my feelings, *she* had to go ahead and ruin it. After that, I made it my mission to give him the cold shoulder. I was good at holding a grudge...up until the accident. Now? Well, it takes all my energy to get out of bed. Self-hatred spams my mind, leaving little to no room for anything other than self-pity.

Yeah, I've despised Asher for years, but I can still appreciate his beauty. I am a woman, after all, and he's hot. Asher stands at about six-four with hair the color of sand. Gentle hues of gold and muted earth blend effortlessly together, falling like crested waves against his forehead. My fingers twitch to sink into the golden silk, to scratch my nails across the shortened sides. What some men would do for a mane like his. And his eyes? They're a blue unlike anything I've ever seen, reminiscent of a hot spring, inviting and comforting. When his captivating irises collide with mine, a sweet serenity washes over me.

Today, he's wearing a dark gray Henley with three-quarter sleeves and dark wash blue jeans with his favorite pair of Chucks. He's wearing the shit out of that shirt. It looks like his muscles are being suffocated, which makes sense. Being the top pitcher throughout high school will do that to you. Seriously, the man is built. It's no wonder women threw themselves at him in high school. They still do. I've watched hundreds of women throw themselves at him, which only added fuel to my hatred. Some might have called it jealousy. But I knew better...at least I wanted to believe I did.

The sound of a throat clearing pulls me from my ogling. *Shit.* I shouldn't be checking out Asher. Isn't there, like, some rule against your brother's best friend dating your little sister? And even if there aren't, I'm *supposed* to detest the man. Even if my heart swells remembering how attentive he was with me at the hospital and the wedding. But then I think of the text from Max earlier, and any sort of affection I was feeling is gone, leaving shame masked as irritation in its place.

"Why are you here?" I bark at him, not bothering to play nice.

He's here because he pities you. Look at him, a man like that would never want to be with you. He doesn't actually care about you...no one does.

See? Anxious thoughts leave no room in my brain for any other feeling.

"Hi, bear." Asher doesn't even flinch at my abrasive tone. No. Instead, he offers me the most panty-dropping smile known to man. Not my panties, though, *definitely* not mine. The thought of anyone seeing me in my underwear has my body breaking out into hives.

Asher's smile is mesmerizing, displaying dimples I want to lick. *Gah no, Bri. Stop that. He's only here out of obligation and not because he wants to be here. Also, he's Max's best friend, which means he, too, blames you for the accident. Get rid of him and go back to bed.*

"What are you doing here?" I repeat, harsher than before. Everything about this situation is embarrassing. No one, especially Asher, should be seeing me like this. The sooner he leaves, the sooner I can crawl back into my self-loathing cave.

"I was in the neighborhood. I wanted to check in, see how you're doing." Asher shrugs nonchalantly.

He only feels sorry for you. He's only here because your brother asked him to check on you. He's going to report how sad you look to your brother.

I'm a puppet on a string that's controlled by my internal villains, their cackles playing on an endless loop inside my mind. *Now is not the time to have a breakdown, Bri.*

"I'm not some sad, pathetic loser, you know!" I shout at him, my voice breaking at the words *sad* and *pathetic*.

"I-I never said—"

"Don't bother. I know why you're here. Max sent you. I don't need your pity, Asher. I'm fine."

I'm fine...The biggest lie anyone can ever say.

"Max didn't send me. I'm here because I c—"

"Don't lie to me, Asher. You don't care about me, you never have." I'm projecting...I know I am, but I can't seem to stop the words from pouring out of me. It's not *Asher* who doesn't care about me. It's *me*. I don't care about myself.

"You know that's not true. I've always been there for you. You're going through a lot right now. I can't fully understand what you're feeling, but I want to try. I want to be here for you, Bri, because I want to. Not because Max sent me here."

I want to be here for you because I want to. The words poke small holes in my armor, and I want nothing more than to run and hide.

"Please just go, Asher." I don't even wait for his response before I close the door.

Wait, stay. I need you. I push that small voice aside and fall to the floor. Panic grips me by the throat, restricting my airflow. I'm gasping for air, desperate to fill my lungs, but black dots begin to dance across my vision. I'm seconds from passing out, so I lay on the floor. The cool texture is a welcome sensation. I hyperfocus on the feel of the laminate against my cheek as I focus on my breathing. By the time I'm back to normal, well, my *new normal*, I'm tired.

Emotional exhaustion is a bitch. It's the middle of the day, and I'm already making my way upstairs so I can sleep. The second I enter my bedroom, I crawl under the covers where no one can find me. Under these covers, I can hide from everything and anything that makes me feel like a failure. It's under these covers that I'll stay for the next fourteen hours. I fall asleep to the daydream from moments ago, and if I cuddle the blankets a little tighter, I don't notice.

Asher

Mental ping-pong

"ASHER, DUDE. WHAT GIVES, man? You've been distracted since the moment you walked in. I've had to bring you back into the conversation several times." Max gives me a questioning look.

Where do I even begin with answering his question? I've been lost in my head, replaying my interaction with Bri. I've had enough therapy to know that the hateful words she was spewing had nothing to do with me. I know she's struggling, but not knowing how to help her shreds my heart into a million pieces.

I remember when I used to be the person she'd turn to for comfort. There's always been this unspoken connection between the two of us. But of course, nothing ever happened because it was never just the two of us. Max was always with us. Max—my best friend and the number one reason I couldn't do anything to act on my attraction toward his sister. In the rare moments it was just Bri and I, there was a raw vulnerability to us sitting together in the silence. I was too naïve to cherish the moments back then, but I yearn for them now. She always gave the best hugs. It's the reason for her nickname.

SIXTEEN-YEAR-OLD ASHER

I stand outside her bedroom door, my stomach tied in knots. I can do this. She's just a girl. She's your best friend's sister. Shit. I should just leave now and she'll never know I was here. I turn to leave, but the sound of a door has me stopping in my tracks.

"Asher?"

"Hey...Hi." I mentally facepalm my forehead. Real smooth, Asher, real smooth.

"You want to go to our spot?" Bri asks, and it takes me longer than I would have liked to respond. She's beautiful, always has been. Her long, chestnut curls lay untamed against her face, and her amber eyes pierce straight through to my soul. God, she's breathtaking.

"Yeah, let's go, bear."

Bri rewards me with one of the most beautifully mesmerizing smiles. One that burns my entire body like the whiskey shot I was dared to toss back by none other than the woman beside me. The first time I slipped out that nickname, I remember Bri getting all up in my face, asking if I was calling her fat. I swear my entire stomach dropped to my feet as I floundered up the word "no" about a hundred times, only to have her toss her head back in a full-bodied, villainous cackle. After my heart stopped threatening to beat out of my chest, I oh so graciously reminded her of our first ever interaction. Instead of shaking my hand like any normal person would do when meeting someone for the first time, Bri charged at me and wrapped me in the biggest hug known to man. I couldn't explain it then, but returning the embrace felt as essential as breathing. The nickname, however, didn't come until I really got to know Bri. Like a bear, she's protective and soft. But not too soft that she'll let anyone bulldoze over her and her loved ones. I was always good at sticking up for myself, but during one of our many neighborhood baseball games, someone on the other team purposely tripped me, causing me to tumble before I reached the base. Nothing was sprained or broken, but Bri stomped her way toward the boy and punched him in the nose before going off on him. I stared up at the situation, stupefied for a few seconds before leaping to my feet to pull her back.

"Easy, bear, I can handle myself."

Bri, in turn, growled at me, which only solidified the nickname.

I'm so wrapped up in everything about that trip down memory lane, that I about topple over her when she stops walking. I reach out to grab her shoulders so neither of us falls over.

"You okay, Ace?" Bri asks, tossing a sly smirk over her shoulder.

"Yeah, just got lost in my head. I'm good."

We sit down side by side. Our shoulders are barely touching, but I feel the contact everywhere. I attempt to swallow past the sawdust that seems to fill my mouth as I sit next to her. This has been our thing lately. I sit next to her while she reads, and I couldn't be more content. One would think I gain nothing from this type of interaction with her, but they're wrong. While she reads her book, I'm playing on my phone. Well, that's what Bri thinks I'm doing. Yeah, I play a few games, but I'm also compiling a list of everything she's read so that I can add it to my list. Maybe one day I'll work up the courage to talk books with her...one day. For now, I'm content sitting next to her, bathing in her beauty.

What gives, man?

Max's question reels me back into the moment. I feel torn. He's my best friend and deserves to know what's happening. I mean, I've sat by his side as we wait for texts he knows won't come. He's hurting, and I hate seeing him in pain, but this isn't my story to tell. Bri, for whatever reason, wants to shut herself off from the world. And sharing any intimate detail with him feels wrong. So I settle for sharing something else that's been plaguing me.

"I've just had a lot on my mind, is all. Things at the bar have been really good, but I feel like something is missing. And no matter how hard I think, I can't quite figure it out. Enough about me, how are you feeling?" I nod toward Max's right leg.

"I have moments when it feels a bit stiff, but otherwise it's back to normal. Physical therapy is kicking my ass, but I'd like to think I'm crushing it. I think I've annoyed my therapist with how many Iron Man references I make, but she goes with it now. I'm glad I'm out of that damn thing, but my parents—more so my mom—has been hovering. She still thinks I should be in the boot—even after the okay from the doctor. I love my parents, and it's been nice having them stay with me, but they need to go, man. They're retired, for fuck's sake. They need to get back to traveling the world, not babying me." A sigh seeps from Max's lips, his hand aggressively scrubbing his face only to be replaced by a bashful look. I know what he's going to ask before he asks it.

"So...How is she?"

She could refer to anyone. I could play dumb and talk about someone we know, but I'm not sure that'll fly right now. Max might still be working through the final stages of his recovery, but Bri's still a wreck emotionally. She has yet to answer his texts. At first, I was confused as to why she would ignore him. But from my understanding of depression, isolation is one of the biggest indicators that someone is struggling.

But I still want to protect Max from the pain that having that knowledge will bring, so I decide on a half-truth...sort of. A little white lie won't hurt, right?

"I don't think I'm the right person to answer that. I haven't really seen her much. Avery would probably be a better person to ask."

It's not a complete lie. I *haven't* seen her that much. I resist the urge to rub the back of my neck, knowing it's one of my tells that Max will call me out on. Having a best friend you practically grew up with is a blessing and a curse.

Max's face screams I *don't believe you*, but he lets it go for now. Who needs a lie detector when you have a best friend? What he does say, though, takes me by surprise.

"I need a favor from you. Before you say no, I need you to hear me out."

Déjà vu is like a punch to the stomach, knocking the wind out of me. I know what he's about to ask before he opens his mouth, but it doesn't stop my heart from pounding against my ribcage.

"Anything," I murmur.

"I need you to watch over her. I'm not getting the full story. From you, from my parents, and even from Cas and Avery. She used to always answer my texts and beg to hang out with me, so I know something's going on. If I can't be there for her, I need you to be. I trust you to take care of her, Ace."

I *know why you're here. Max sent you. I don't need your pity, Asher. I'm fine.*

Well fuck. When I went to see Bri earlier, she accused me of doing exactly what Max just asked me to do. Damn. I already had every intention of helping Bri, before Avery or Max approached me about it. I know that if she decides to let me in, I'll need to do a damn good job at convincing her that I didn't help her out of obligation.

"Of course I'll help her. But I'll be honest, I'm not sure she'll want my help. She can't stand me." I shrug it off like the hurt isn't oceans deep, but we both know that's bullshit.

"I don't buy that. Bri just gives you a hard time because she hates herself for liking you." Max smirks at me.

"You're delusional, Max. What Bri feels for me is hatred."

It wasn't always this way between us. Bri and I got along great, joking and laughing with each other. I honestly thought our friendship would turn into something more, but then that stupid fucking high school party happened. We were flirting one minute, and then all of a sudden, she was giving me the cold shoulder. I'd give anything to time travel back to that day and figure out what the fuck happened. Maybe one of these days I can ask her, but for now, helping Bri heal is my main priority.

"There's a thin line between love and hate, my friend. And I'm leaning toward the former. I think it's all an act. Hell, she—" His eyes bug out of his head, and he slams his mouth shut.

"Care to finish that sentence?" I tease.

Max just grins while shaking his head. "Nope. You'll have to ask her."

"Yeah, let me get right on that. I'm sure she'll be 100% open with me." I roll my eyes at him and bark out a laugh.

I so desperately want her to share her pain with me. I can only imagine how heavy the load is. Deep down beneath her *leave me alone* exterior is my bear, craving the comfort she's too embarrassed to ask for. As much as I want to have something more with her, that ship, for whatever reason, has long since sailed. But I can easily put my feelings aside for her. It's not about me...It's about her. Well, I *think* I can put these feelings aside.

Max and I continue to reminisce about the shit we got into when we were teens. After a while, I notice Max yawning more frequently—probably from a more intensive day of physical therapy—and I take that as my cue to leave. I tidy up his room before getting ready to leave. I'm at the bedroom door before I turn around and whisper, "She's in good hands, Max. She's like the sun, bathing people in her warmth. I'll stop at nothing until she's glowing like the goddess she is."

Max is all but passed out, but I *swear* I hear him whisper, "Oh, *this is gonna be fun.*"

Bastard.

Brianna

Mourning the death of my teenage dream

> **Max: Hey, Breezy. Asher came to see me today and we talked about you a little. I know our parents and friends are hiding something from me. I just wish I could hear your voice again. See your face. I miss you, Bri. Please talk to me.**

SEE? WE TOLD YOU Asher was only there because of Max. You're such a selfish person. Who doesn't even go visit their own brother in the hospital? You can't even text him back. He probably hates you, ya know. Everyone does.

Another unanswered text from my brother throws my anxious thoughts into a frenzy. They're right. I couldn't fathom sitting with him in the hospital, knowing I'm the reason he was there in the first place. It's not like I didn't try, though. I went to the hospital when I knew my parents wouldn't be there. Shoutout to Avery for her help—she didn't ask for an explanation, she just did it. I rode the painfully slow elevator before standing in the fucking doorway, taking in the scene before me.

Cuts. Bruises. Scars. And tubes. So many goddamn tubes.

Then I ran. I ran to the nearest bathroom, withdrawing all the contents in my stomach into the toilet.

He's in this hospital because of you. You survived with little damage while he's in a coma.

Your fault.

Your fault.

All. Your. Fault.

I squeeze the doorknob, hoping the cool texture will shock me out of my toxic thoughts. I'm standing outside my office door for what feels like the millionth time, struggling to gain control over my anxiety. Everything feels so big. Everything hurts. I hear the faint buzzing of my intrusive thoughts in the corner of my mind, but I push forward.

Breathe, Bri. It's just a room. Who cares if you and Max worked on building an entire wall of floor to ceiling bookshelves? You can do this.

The door creaks when I open it from the lack of use. The air smells stale, almost stiff. Can air smell stiff? I flip the light switch, watching as tiny dust particles glitter against the midday sun. It's a breezy spring day, so I open the window to let in some fresh air. The sun hits my face, the wind whispering promises of a light at the end of the tunnel. Trees sway in the breeze, and if I listen closely, I can hear classical music coming from my neighbor's house. What once used to drive me insane now provides a sense of security I didn't know I needed. Tears prickle behind my eyes, but I wipe them away and return to the task at hand.

My eyes flicker to the worn cherry bookshelves covered in a thick layer of dust. I've always been meticulous about keeping my shelves in pristine condition, dedicating every Sunday to making sure the wood shined so bright you could see your reflection. And my books? I worked hard to ensure that each book was immaculate. Now grime and what looks like spider webs coat every crevice. I *should* tidy them up, make them sparkle. But shame is a wet log in a fireplace, refusing to light up, leaving me feeling useless and frustrated. It doesn't matter anyway; these books aren't going to be sitting on the shelves much longer.

There's something about diving into a story and falling in love with the characters that always brought me joy. My list of book boyfriends was ever growing. Now, the place in my chest that reading once filled is completely void. I miss getting lost in a story, but I just can't scrounge up the energy to do it.

I have to have at least a hundred or so books to donate, and I've put it off for far too long. I scan my shelves in its entirety, and I'm reminded of a dream I once had...emphasis on *had*. Opening my own romance-only bookstore has been a fantasy of mine. Watching someone's face light up when they're matched with their perfect book? Priceless. Ever since then, I've been building my collection to add to my future store. Now? I can't even fathom following through with that dream. Now, I just want to get through the day without a breakdown.

I mentally log everything I need to get so I can pack everything up while mourning the death of teenage me's dream. Fuck, this is overwhelming. I walk over to the white papasan rocking chair in the corner, grab my grey, weighted throw blanket, and snuggle beneath its warmth. I'll just sit down for a few minutes and rest before tackling such a big project.

The sound of my phone ringing has me bolting upright, my heart still racing from my favorite recurring nightmare. Who the fuck is doing a drumroll with my heart right now? I wipe the grogginess from my eyes and reorient myself to my surroundings. My phone rings again and I answer it without glancing at the caller ID.

"Hello?" My voice comes out dopey and slow.

I wasn't planning to sleep, but that's all my body wants to do nowadays. Which I guess is another reason for my current figure. I grab the fallen blanket off the floor and cover my body like a shield. What do I need protection from? Me. I need protection from myself. Because whenever I look at my figure, I get all—*no*. Don't go there. I fight a full body shiver, and the sound of my name on the other line of the phone jerks my focus back to what woke me in the first place.

"Hey, Bri. Everything okay?" The masculine timbre is a blanket fresh out the dryer, its heat curling around me, bathing me in comfort. I rub my eyes, attempting to rid myself of the grogginess associated with a midday nap before looking down and seeing Asher's name across my phone screen.

"I, um...yeah. I'm sorry, I just woke up from a nap. W-Why are you calling me?"

I've felt awful for how I treated Asher when he came to visit me. I said some god awful things. Things that my anxiety was feeding me through an invisible earpiece. After a long and surprisingly restful sleep, I immediately wanted to take it back. With all the hurt that I'm carrying, I don't have room for anything else, let alone a silly grudge. Something I've taken away from the accident is that life's too short. It can be ripped away from you fast and hard, shattering your world within mere seconds. Was teenage me valid in her anger toward Asher? Yeah. But did she have to ice out someone who had meant the world to her? No. What can I say, adolescent me was a tad dramatic. Okay, more than a tad. Asher's presence has always been my pillar of strength. My flashlight in the dark, guiding me through my darkest moments.

I pull my phone back to check the time. 2:30 p.m.

I cringe at what Asher must think of me, which of course gives my inner demons the green light to cause chaos.

You're lazy. I mean, look at you. You don't work out like you used to. All you do is eat and sleep. No one's gonna want you looking like that.

Stupid fucking intrusive thoughts. They're a tornado determined to destroy everything in its path.

"I hope it was a good nap. I could use one myself. Things at the bar have been crazy, and I've been talking to Gage about hiring someone else. The best I get out of him is a shrug and a grunt. I'll wear him down eventually. I was calling to see what you were doing. I've had a craving for some Uncle Tito's tacos. Wanted to see if you were down. You hungry, Bri?"

Why is he so nice to me? I yelled at him, pushed him away.

Despite all that, my mouth waters at the thought of stuffing my face with tacos. Then, almost immediately, my mind steers itself into self-hatred territory when I think of the body underneath the blanket. I really shouldn't be stuffing my face with tacos—no matter how much I want them. Just the thought of being seen in public has me panicking. DoorDash and Uber Eats have been the real MVPs over the last several months. In person grocery shopping? Don't know her. But for whatever reason, Uncle Tito's isn't on either delivery service, which is the one thing I'm craving.

"Bri? Don't feel like you have to say yes. We can just go another time. Or not at all, whatever you want." Is it just me, or do I hear a hint of nervousness in Asher's voice?

"Um it's not. I'm not—" I ramble when I'm anxious. Wait, why am I nervous? It's not a date or anything. I mean...it's Asher. And he's *off limits*. I mean, he could get any woman he wants. Tall, beautiful, *thin* women. I used to check those boxes. But because I was fueled by hurt and embarrassment, given the choice between sleeping with Asher and remaining celibate, I'd have chosen the latter.

"Bear?" Asher asks, shaking me from my thoughts.

"I—thank you, but I'm not really up for going out. I'm also not dressed to go anywhere." I'm not sure what I expect to come out of his mouth, but it isn't what he says next.

"Oh, well I'll just bring it to you instead. You still like shrimp with extra cheese and hot sauce?"

The man has the memory of an elephant, rendering me speechless that he remembered such a small detail. I can count times on one hand that we've gotten tacos together, and I've known him for over ten years. And said instances always involved Max. I mean, before I entered high school, I was always hanging out with them. Not because my parents forced my brother to include me, but because both Max and Asher wanted me around.

My order has always been the same: three shrimp tacos with extra cheese and hot sauce. My heart soars at both the sweet gesture of offering to bring me food and that he remembered my order. The sound of my name being called for a second time has me jumping out of my head and into the present.

"Bri? Just tell me what you want, and I'll give it to you."

Is it me, or is there a double meaning behind that statement? Maybe I'm hoping there's one? Wait, I don't want there to be one...Do I? I glance at my now uncovered body and wince.

Even if you wanted him, he'd never go for you.

"Oh, you don't have to—"

"Bear." My nickname comes out as a growl. I could just give in, comply. But my internal demons are allergic to kindness, spewing venomous vitriol my way at any given opportunity.

"But I—" Again, he interrupts me.

"Answer the question. Do you want food or not?"

"Yes, please."

"Good girl." *Oh, my.* My stomach erupts in flutters and...is that? No. It can't be. There's a dull ache between my thighs, something I haven't felt in so long. And now I'm squirming in my chair, my desire choosing this moment to come out of hibernation.

And of course, my stomach chooses this moment to growl, so I ask him to throw in an order of chips and guac. I'll probably regret it later, but right now my focus is on fueling my body. Despite how I feel about my image, I need to eat. Regret peeks around the corner, waiting for her chance to shine, but I refuse to let her in.

I quickly get dressed, run a brush through the tangled mess that is my hair, and splash my face with cold water. I have to look somewhat presentable. About thirty minutes later, the doorbell rings, and then it hits me.

Oh, shit. I'll have to eat in front of him.

Old me wouldn't give two fucks. Current me cares way too much. I don't want him to feel disgusted by me. It doesn't help when I scroll on social media and see people who look like me eating food. The pictures aren't what bother me; it's the comments saying something along the lines of *damn, that girl needs to go on a diet.* Then I click on someone who's thin and appears "healthy" eating, and underneath the posts are endless congratulatory words and endless praise. The comments get to me more than they should, but it's hard when they're a direct hit to your self-confidence.

The doorbell rings again followed by three consecutive knocks. It's now or never, I guess. I head downstairs, mentally preparing myself for his reaction while taking grounding deep breaths. *You can do this, Bri. It's just Asher. No need to get all worked up.* Despite what I tell myself, it's easier said than done. I let out a slow deep breath before opening the door and facing my own inner demons.

Asher

There's something about eating them out

MY STEPS FALTER, MY once wild beating heart drums a low, steady rhythm inside my chest, almost as if it knows something I don't. My palms are slick and prickly, itching to reach out and touch her. My gaze lazily sweeps over her body, and it takes everything in me to keep my jaw from hitting the floor.

Bri's in a pair of black leggings and a faded, dark gray Brookestone University hoodie. Her face is free of makeup and her wavy, chestnut hair is in a messy bun atop her head with a few stray curls framing her face. My fingers twitch with the urge to tangle my fingers in her wild mane. Can curly hair be a kink? Possibly. But for me, it's not curly hair in general that does it for me. It's *her* hair. The soft breeze whips her curls around her face, assaulting my nose with her vanilla scented shampoo. I reminisce on all the times I used to tug at her hair, annoying her being my main goal. But as I got older and began to understand what attraction meant, I knew it was much deeper than that. I was merely obsessed with the feel of her hair between my fingertips, the silky strands gliding through my fingers effortlessly.

I shake myself from the trip down memory lane, basking in the glory of the stunning woman before me. It's such a simple look, but she's anything but. I could get lost in her honey-colored eyes, but if I keep staring, she's going to think I'm weird. *Dial it back, man. Don't scare her with your intensity.*

"W-Why are you staring at me like that?" Bri asks while fidgeting with the hem of her hoodie.

She looks at her outfit as if she'd like to disappear inside it. I'm used to the fearless, confident Bri. The girl who's never afraid to call you out on your shit. But the woman who stands before me is clearly lost. She's like a deer in the forest; any sudden movement and she'll bolt. My heart aches at seeing her struggle, my body buzzing with the incessant need to fix it.

But if I learned anything from my brother's issues with addictions, she has to do this on her own. Regardless of all that, I'm going to do everything in my power to help her.

I clear my throat before answering. "Um nothing. I got the food. I'm starving, so lead the way."

Bri cocks her head and raises a brow like she doesn't believe me. My cheeks ache, a telltale sign of a smile as I catch a small glimpse of the real Brianna. Underneath all the rubble is the sparkling, sarcastic girl waiting to be pulled out. Bri turns and heads toward the kitchen, and I silently groan at the sight of her ass. *Hot damn, her body.* I only get a glimpse of her ass, but my imagination runs wild at how it would look bent over my desk as I—*shit.* Fuck. And now I'm so fucking hard that I need to adjust myself with my other hand.

When I enter the kitchen, Bri is on her tiptoes trying to grab something from the top shelf. Her hoodie rides up just enough to get a peek at her back dimples I just want to sink my teeth into.

Like the masochist I am, I place the takeout bag on the table and walk up behind her to help her grab the plates. Bri gets spooked, her back slamming against my front. My hands grip her hips to steady her, and I have to breathe through my nose to steady the fire burning inside me. This has the opposite effect on me when I get a strong hit of her vanilla-cinnamon scent. It's like stepping into a Cinnabon store; the sweet, savory aroma assaults my nose and my cock hardens, pressing against the fly of my jeans.

"Fuck," the curse slips out. Bri glances over her shoulder, and I'm absolutely gutted at the look of hurt and shame swirling behind her beautiful eyes. Before I can open my mouth, she's wiggling out of my arms, looking like she wants to shrink within herself. Before she can get too far away, I reach out to grab her wrist.

"Hey, what happened? Did I do something wrong?" I'm genuinely con-fused. Is she upset that I touched her? Did she feel my hard on, and she's uncomfortable?

"I'm sorry." Bri looks everywhere but my eyes. I furrow my brows and cock my head to the side, wracking my brain as to why she's apologizing.

"Why are you sorry?"

"Uh—" She still won't meet my gaze, so I grab her chin and force her eyes to meet mine.

"I want you to look me in the eyes when you tell me why you're apologizing." I wait for her eyes to meet mine. She looks so small, and it breaks my heart.

"I'm not who I used to be."

Her body squirms beneath my touch, itching to do whatever it takes to get out of this conversation.

"Who you used to be?" I ask, clarifying.

"I...Well, look at me, Asher." Bri gestures to her body, which leaves me even more puzzled.

"I have eyes, Bri. I need you to tell me what you mean."

Her jaw drops at my words, her expression baffled. I choose to remain silent, waiting to see if she'll explain further.

"C'mon, Asher. Don't tell me you haven't noticed."

I can feel my face contort with confusion, yet I still say nothing.

"I've..." She sputters the words, cheeks and neck as red as a fall sunset. "I've gained weight, and I hate how I look." Her voice clogs with shame. "I-I'm sorry you have to see me like this. I—"

Her words whoosh out of her the second I grab her by the waist and place her on the counter, forcing her legs open so I can step between them. My hands move to grip her thighs, her body shivering beneath my touch.

"Brianna. Eyes on me." I wait her out, and eventually, she looks at me with tears in her eyes. "Baby, no. Listen to me. I'm not upset at seeing you like this, so I don't know what you're apologizing for."

"Listen, Asher, I don't need you placating me."

"I'm not just saying that to say it. I mean it. What do I need to do to prove it to you?" I demand, but she just blinks at me, mouth agape. I need to be quick on my feet with a way to convince her.

"Take the hoodie off." My hand shoots upward to grip her throat.

"W-What?" Bri stammers. My head cocks to the side as a playful smile spreads across my face. She's cute when she's flustered. The hand on her throat squeezes, and I watch her eyes flutter before they become hooded with pleasure.

My girl likes my hand wrapped around her pretty neck. Interesting.

"You heard me. Take. The. Hoodie. Off. Either you do it or I will."

Bri pulls her bottom lip between her teeth, contemplating her next move. As for me, I want to take that supple, pink flesh in between my teeth, and bite down before soothing the sting with my tongue. What she says next takes me by surprise.

"Take it off yourself. But I'm warning you, it's not pretty."

How can someone be so insecure and bold at the same time? Bri lifts her arms over her head, giving me her consent to take it off. My lungs fill with a slow, calming breath before my hand leaves her throat to move toward the bottom of her hoodie. My thumbs rub soothing circles on her bare skin as I groan at the feeling of goosebumps that break out on her skin.

The hoodie glides up slowly, and I take in every inch of her upper body. She's in nothing but a lavender bralette, and my mouth waters. What I see are perfect, full tits and curves I want to dig my nails into. She's a walking wet dream, and I'm salivating like a dog on Thanksgiving hoping people will accidentally drop food.

"Fuck," I repeat my sentiment from earlier. She looks good enough to eat.

"See? I told you. Can I have my hoodie back?" She makes a grab for it, but I toss it across the kitchen before turning back to her.

"No. What you did, bear, is lie. I don't appreciate liars, Bri." I smirk at her.

"W-What?" Bri asks.

"You heard what I said. A liar. You said I wouldn't like what I see, but you're wrong. Do you have any idea how fucking hot your body is? It's ridiculous how sexy you are. These tits? These curves? I'm having a hard time not devouring you whole right now."

I lick my lips while staring at her with animalistic hunger burning behind my eyes.

"You're just saying that. If you were into my body, you'd do something about it. I find it hard to believe you're that into me." Bri shrugs. Is she serious right now? How can she not see what I see?

The hand returns to her throat and tightens with enough pressure to not cause too much pain. Bri's eyes widen not with fear, but lust. I need her eyes on me when I say what I wanna say. I loosen my grip, but keep my hand firm around the base of her throat.

"I want to...so fucking badly. It's not because I don't find you hot as hell, but because you don't find yourself sexy. No amount of me fucking you will fix that. Men don't define your worth. You do. And until you see just how stunning and amazing you are, we can't go there."

She stares at me, jaw on the floor, her cheeks painted with the prettiest blush on them. I'm going to kick myself in the balls for this later, but I have to stick with my plan.

I back away from her embrace, and before she can grab it, I tie her sweatshirt around my waist. I decide to forgo dirtying dishes, deciding to use the now soggy taco wrappers as our makeshift plates.

"Are you joining me, bear? These tacos aren't gonna eat themselves. There's just something about eating them out that satisfies me."

I wink at her, knowing she catches onto the double entendre. She walks over to me in nothing but her bralette and leggings, but instead of digging in, she stares at her food before looking down at her stomach.

"Brianna." Her name comes out like a command that has the desired effect when her eyes snap up to meet mine.

"Eat or so help me God, I will find a better way to fill that pretty little mouth of yours."

Bri's eyes flicker down toward my painfully hard cock while wetting her cherry-red lips. I watch her eyes flutter a few times before lowering the temperature on her desire.

Even though all I can think about is her lips wrapped around me, I watch her *finally* start to eat her food. *Good girl.*

I refocus my attention on my half eaten food, but my appetite is gone. Watching Bri this worried about her weight...Well, it kills me inside. The Bri I used to know would go to town on her food—the same way I planned to go down on her.

I have a long way to go with helping her, but I wouldn't have it any other way. Brianna is worth the long haul.

She's worth forever.

Brianna

You'll always be safe in my arms

CRASH. THE SOUND OF glass shattering pierces my ears. People are screaming and crying. It's pure chaos. The nightmare jolts me awake. It feels like the walls are closing in around me, and I can't breathe. My bedsheets are tossed haphazardly on the floor, and I'm lying in a pool of my own sweat. *Breathe in, breathe out, Bri. It was just a dream.*

The clock on my nightstand reads 1:00 a.m., and I can feel the telltale signs of a panic attack begin to emerge. The last time I had one this intense was after Asher came to check on me. My head says deal with it in silence, don't let anyone see you. Especially him.

He's Max's best friend, for fuck's sake, Bri. Could you be any more pathetic?

My phone weighs heavy against my palm while my head and heart declare World War III against each other. And no matter how hard I try, I cannot remain a neutral party. I scroll my phone to find his contact and hit call before my brain has time to overanalyze my decision.

One ring.

Two rings.

Three rings go by, and I'm about to abort the mission when the sound of muffled sheets accompanied by a groggy voice carries over the line.

"Hello?" Asher's raspy, sleep-filled voice does something to me.

"Hi." The sound is merely a whisper in the quiet of my room. I try—and fail—to hide the pain in my voice.

"What's wrong?" Ruffling sounds come from the other end of the phone, and I hear the faint click of a lamp turning on. Given my current state of mind, everything takes longer to process. I woke him up. Of course I did. Not everyone is up at one in the morning.

"I-I'm sorry I woke you up. Don't worry about it. I'm not even sure why I'm calling you right now. Just forget it. I—"

"Hey. You can always call me whenever you need. I need you to find the confident Bri inside you and ask for what you want."

What *do* I want? When did I get so needy? I used to be a badass bitch who thrived off her independence. Now? I've become a stage-five clinger, and I hate it. But I'm way too tired to make rational decisions, seeing as how sleep and I are two passing ships in the night. The last time I got a decent night's sleep was when Avery crawled into my bed. I couldn't possibly ask Asher to come sleep with me. Could I?

"It's gonna sound so stupid. I—just forget about it. I'm sorry, I—"

This is Asher, Bri. You're supposed to hate him. And now you're asking him for help? This is what rock bottom must look like. Too weak to do anything on your own.

"Asking for help doesn't make you weak, Bri." It's like he jumped inside my brain, reading my every thought. How does he *do* that?

That's exactly how I feel, though...weak. I used to ask for help and never think twice about how others viewed me. Now, when I even *think* of asking for what I need, it feels like people are judging me. *Poor, helpless Bri. Look at her, she can't do anything for herself. How pathetic.* I wish I could talk to my best friend about how far I've fallen, but I can't. Not after all the times I've left her on read. I don't have to look at my phone to see her most recent slew of texts. I have them damn well memorized by now.

> Avery: Bee. I was scrolling through TikTok the other day and I came across that book you were telling me about. The new Kennedy Ryan book? So I splurged and bought it. I had to tell you. I know you won't respond, but I still wanted to tell you. I love you. Please take care of my bestie.

"Bear? You still there?"

Oh, shit. Asher. So I *did* call him then. A part of me hoped this was just a vivid dream.

"Y-Yeah. I, um. I really shouldn't have called you so late. I mean, we aren't, like, together or anything. I mean, who would want to date someone like me? I'm a fucking mess. No one would ever be attracted to someone like me, especially not—" *Fuck. Get a grip, Bri. He doesn't want to hear all that.*

"Especially not who, Bri?" Asher interrupts my nervous rambling.

"Y-You know exactly who I'm talking about."

"I need to hear you say it."

"E-Especially someone like y-you."

"You're saying that I don't find you attractive? That's a complete load of bullshit, but we'll put a pin in that for later. What do you need from me, bear? Be that confident badass I know you can be."

"I need you to come sleep with me." The silence on the other end is deafening. OH SHIT! I just asked my brother's best friend, my former—yes, *former*, because I can no longer say I hate him anymore—nemesis to sleep with me. Ground, swallow me whole, please.

I need to clarify what I meant...ASAP.

"NO! Not sleep with me as in have sex with me. I, um...I mean actually sleep. Like, in the same bed. Our clothes would be on, and we can each take a side. My bed is big enough..." Ugh, and now I'm rambling like a madwoman. Surely he thinks I'm crazy. "Okay, just ignore everything I said. Forget I called. Goodni—"

"I'm on my way," he says before hanging up without commenting on my word-vomiting.

Great, there's no turning back now, and the desire to text him a *haha, I was just kidding* text threatens to take hold of my body. I remove myself from my sweat-slicked sheets and make my way downstairs. I highly doubt I'll be getting any sleep. Especially since Asher is on his way to sleep over. In. My. Bed. If my overly anxious mind won't let me sleep, the sheer proximity of Asher fucking Larson lying next to me with all his intoxicating masculinity will surely do it.

A buzz shakes against my palm, and I look down and notice I have my phone in a tight grip. An eerie awareness radiates down my spine, and somehow I *know* without looking at my phone who the message will be from. Does that stop me from looking? No.

> **Max: Brianna Mae. Why are you ignoring me? You leave me on read and I can't figure out why? Please just answer my texts. Or even better, come over. I miss you.**

My blood freezes, and dark black spots flicker alongside my peripheral vision.

You are the worst. Look at you. You're a cold-hearted bitch for ignoring your brother.

My breathing turns shallow as I desperately gasp for air. But no matter how much oxygen I take in, it's not enough to fill my lungs. I'm faintly aware of my feet guiding me to the living room, but barely. I can't focus on anything behind the sound of blood rushing in my ears. The world begins to tilt on its axis. That, or I'm collapsing to the floor. When I wanted the ground to swallow me whole, this isn't what I meant.

A soft beat sounds somewhere in front of me. Wait, is it in front of me? Behind me? I can't really tell; my eyes are slammed shut in an attempt to ward off the spinning. The sound repeats followed by a deep voice saying...something.

Crash. Glass shattering. Piercing cries.

"Bri?" The sound of what I *assume* is a door opening followed by my name is somewhere in the distance.

"Shit, baby, what happened?" The ground disappears beneath me, and my first thought is I'm dead and on my way to heaven.

The smell of cinnamon and leather collides in the best kind of sensory explosion. Yes. I have died and gone to heaven. That's the only logical explanation I can conjure up with how potent and delicious this smells.

"Breathe, bear. I got you."

Wait, I know that voice. His deep vibrato reverberates against my cheek. It's my own form of serotonin as I feel my breathing begin to slow.

Asher.

"H-How did you—" How I manage to form a somewhat coherent sentence is beyond me. But if I had to guess, it has everything to do with the man next to me.

"Your door was unlocked. You really need to stop doing that, bear. Now keep breathing. That's it, Bri. Just follow the rise and fall of my chest. My arms are wrapped tightly around you. I'm here, baby. I'm not going anywhere."

Following his direction is like second nature, and soon my breathing begins to match his slow, even breaths. I feel his arms squeeze me tighter, but not in an uncomfortable way, in a *I know I'm safe and protected* kind of way. Even if the thing I need protection from is my own remorse.

Asher and I sit in comfortable silence. My heartbeat and breathing have since regulated, but I'm still cradled within his arms. His fingers brush through my hair, sending tiny pinpricks of calm that can be felt from the top of my head to the tips of my toes.

"You doing okay?"

"Mmmm." I nuzzle against the crook of his neck as if I'm scent marking him. When my eyes pop open, reality is a cruel slap in the face.

Who would want to be with you now? Look at you. So pathetic. You just nuzzled your brother's best friend. A friend who just saw you at one of your lower moments.

Asher stops my frantic attempt to scramble from his grasp. He just hugs me tighter, refusing to let me go.

"Oh no you don't. I told you I wasn't going anywhere. And neither are you. Tell me what's going on in that pretty head of yours." His fingers resume their scalp massage, and my body melts even further into his body.

Do I tell him my thoughts? Maybe if I lay them all on the line, he'll leave me alone. If he spent one second inside my head, he'd go running for the hills.

"No I wouldn't."

My face scrunches in confusion as I blink up at him. "What?"

"You said I would leave you alone, that I'd run for the hills. I wouldn't, bear. No matter how many times you've pushed me away in the past, I'd never just walk away from you. You mean too much to me."

You mean too much to me.

Click. Those words seem to heal a part of my wounded teenage heart, washing away my resolve to hate the man. In its place is confusion. *Why doesn't he hate me? Why is he here? Why...me?*

I let out a long, exaggerated yawn as my mental exhaustion has finally caught up to me. Asher notices and, with minimal effort, lifts me up bridal style, my head resting against his shoulder. It isn't until he reaches the landing that I begin to squirm in his arms.

"Asher, you can p-put me down. I'm too hea—" The look in Asher's eyes is fierce enough to stop me mid-sentence.

"Don't you dare finish that sentence." His words come out as a growl, and I can't help but jolt within his embrace. Asher notices my shock and winces.

"I need to have you close to me, bear. I just...Please?"

His pleading tone has me nodding my head in agreement. Somehow, I don't fully believe he needs me in his arms. But I'm too tired to care, let alone dissect what he truly means. Asher pushes my door open with his shoulder—I guess I didn't close it all the way—before putting me down on my feet.

"Thank you." My tone comes out so softly that I'm surprised he hears it. But of course he does...He always does.

"You don't have to thank me. I'd do just about anything for you." His gruff, whispered confession slams into me, threatening to knock me off my feet. With my eyes trained on the floor as if it's the most interesting thing ever, my head nods with the quickness of a damn bobblehead.

A soft groan has me turning to attention, and I notice Asher's eyes are trained on my thighs before his tongue darts out to wet his lower lip.

What the—then I look down and freeze. *Shit.* I'm in nothing but an oversized t-shirt. In my nightmare-filled daze, I must have taken off my sleep shorts. Not that they would have covered much—they're practically glorified underwear with my thunder thighs.

He's probably disgusted by you. Don't think for a second that he wants you. No hot, muscular man wants to fuck the fat girl.

"I-I'm...um." I pull at the hem of my shirt, hoping it'll cover my bumpy skin. My eyes blink at an alarming rate as I try to stop the tears that threaten to spill down my reddened cheeks.

He's sure to run in the other direction now. There's absolutely no way in...

"Beautiful," Asher whispers.

"Bea—What?" I stammer. Does he not see what I see?

Asher stalks toward me, and I instinctively take a step back. We continue this pattern until the backs of my thighs graze against the mattress with enough force that I sit down.

Asher's smile can only be described as pure sin, and his gaze like liquid fire. He kneels in front of me, gripping my chin in his hands before leaning in to whisper, "I said beautiful. You, Brianna, are so damn beautiful."

"But you...No, you don't mean that. You can't."

"And why not?"

"Well, for starters, you're my brother's best friend. Aren't there, like, rules?"

"Fuck the rules. What else ya got?"

"Look at me, Asher. I have fucking stretch marks on every inch of my body."

Asher glances down at my thighs before meeting my eyes "And?"

"I'm embarrassed by the marks on my skin. They're an ugly reminder of everything that's happened. So you paying attention to them so closely, it makes me feel gross." Tears begin to form behind my eyes.

His rough thumbs gently brush the tears off my face. Great. I had to go and vocalize my insecurities, and he's now going to leave any second now. I brace for the inevitable coldness that comes from his absence. He does, in fact, get up, but it isn't to leave. He makes his way over to my bed, laying down without any regard to the sweaty sheets. I'm completely dumbfounded, especially when he pats the space next to him.

"What are you doing?"

"You asked me to sleep with you. That's exactly what I'm doing. So get over here."

"Y-You don't want to leave?" I ask.

Asher unknowingly holds my hope within his strong hands. And when he pats the side next to him again, this time with a smile, I crawl over to him. He pulls me in so we're face to face as he brushes the hair from my face. Our foreheads touch, and that clicking sound from earlier returns. This time, it feels like a piece of my tattered soul clicks into place.

I feel Asher's fingers trace the jagged lines with the most delicate, loving touch. Our eyes meet, and years of deeply buried yearning rises to the surface.

Safe.

In his arms, I feel safe.

"You may see these lines as a bad thing, but I don't share that opinion. Your stretch marks are a roadmap to your story, to everything you've had to endure. And I find it *incredibly* sexy," he growls.

Desire pools between my legs, and I have zero time to hyper-fixate on any negative thoughts with him staring at me so intently.

"Seeing them illuminated beneath the moon? You have no idea how badly I want to trace my tongue along every single line. But we'll save that for another time. Right now, you need to sleep. You've had a long night."

He presses a chaste kiss to my forehead, but it feels anything but. My toes ache to curl and my heart skips a beat.

"Goodnight, Bri. Close your eyes. I've got you."

"Thank you, Asher."

"Anything for you, bear. You'll always be safe in my arms," he whispers, kissing my forehead again before pulling me even closer to him. With my head nestled against his chest, I fall asleep with a smile etched across my face.

Asher

Addicting. Tempting. All mine.

LIGHT SHIMMERS THROUGH THE windows, bathing the room in a kaleidoscope of golds, pinks, and blues reflecting off the butterfly window chime that hangs on her bedroom window. My eyes drift closed as my face stretches into a lazy smile, allowing the morning sun to brush warm strokes against my cheek. Early spring mornings are my favorite. The world is quiet. No one's rushing around frantically trying to get from place to place.

It's just calm. Peaceful. Perfect.

Speaking of perfection, I suck in a deep breath, and my senses are overcome with the warm, sweet aroma of vanilla coffee. Sugary notes dance around me as I breathe deeper, filling my lungs with the smell of *her*.

Addicting. Tempting. All mine.

Bri.

I shift my body, glancing at the woman next to me. Bri must have shifted in her sleep, as her back is now pressed against my front. My hand that's sprawled across her stomach is interlocked with hers. Chestnut hair cascades chaotically down her back, rendering me speechless. The sun's got nothing on her radiant glow. Seriously, she could be dressed in a garbage bag with yesterday's makeup smeared across her face, and I'd still find her incredibly sexy.

The rhythmic rise and fall of her chest might have an outsider believe she's at peace, but I know her. And if what happened last night is any indication of what's happening beneath the surface, then my girl's pain is multilayered. And how she talked about herself yesterday? It left a gaping hole in my heart. She's so goddamn breathtaking, always has been. And it's not just her looks; it never has been.

Bri's beauty is beyond skin deep. Her body houses a heart so pure and generous it warms even the coldest of souls. The aura around her is so powerful, you can't help but be sucked into the orbit. Her love is a force to be reckoned with. She'll stop at nothing to make sure her loved ones are happy. If only she could turn that outward love inward. But her body? Fuck, I could explore her for hours and it'd never be enough.

My lips brush ever so softly against the nape of her neck, which in turn has her wiggling further into me...into my morning wood. *Fuck*. That wasn't so smart. I grip her hip to prevent her from doing it again, but her ass accidently grinds against my painfully hard cock. *Now is not the time. And definitely not how I should be thinking about Max's little sister. Although, if I'm being honest, anytime I'm around Bri, I forget all my reasons why I should stay away. Better to ask forgiveness than ask for permission, right?*

I hear the sheets rustle, and I can feel her shift in my arms. But am I looking at her? No. My eyes are glued shut, breathing through my mouth and willing my dick to chill the fuck out.

"Asher?" Bri's husky voice does little to no favors to my situation. But I'm a sucker for her soulful eyes, so I meet her gaze. When our eyes meet, her smile widens.

I want to take a picture of this moment, blow it up, and put it on my wall. I simply return her stare, and when she squints her eyes at me and purses her lips, I realize I must be hardcore staring.

"What?" Bri asks, her voice still coated with sleep.

"You're gorgeous, Bri."

Bri gasps and bites her lip, a sign that she's nervous. I rub my thumb against her lower lip, attempting to free it from its captor. About a million different emotions flash behind her honey-colored irises.

"What's going on in that pretty head of yours?" I ask, not expecting an answer, but surprised when she lets me in.

"I'm embarrassed about yesterday. I, well...I don't like people seeing me like that, so..." She averts her eyes, and I give her a moment to process what she wants to say.

"So weak and defective," she finishes.

Well damn. Her words are a mallet to my heart, shattering it into a million pieces.

"Brianna, look at me," I demand. When she refuses to do so, I grip her chin, forcing her eyes to meet mine.

"You are *not* weak or defective. You are possibly the strongest woman I know. You went through something that could so easily destroy a person beyond repair. But you? You get up every damn day and carry on. That is one of the strongest and sexiest things you could do."

"But sometimes I can't even take a shower, let alone brush my teeth. I make cereal for just about every meal, and sometimes I wear days old sweats. How is that sexy or strong?"

"Bear, you're healing. I know this is easier said than done, but you need to allow yourself some time. Some grace. But if you can't do that, then let me help you carry some of the load. No one should have to carry the heaviness all on their own."

She searches my face for what I assume is bullshit, but she won't find any there. I mean every damn word I said. She's quiet for a moment before she presses a gentle kiss on my chest, and I feel it everywhere.

"I might just take you up on it. Since you said you'd help carry some of the load, I was wondering if you could help me with something."

"Anything," I murmur.

"I need to go through my office and clear out all the books I have."

Well, that wasn't what I was expecting her to say.

"But you love to read. Why are you getting rid of them?"

That's one of the things Bri and I have in common. It may have started out as me reading books to find a way to connect with her, but I've fallen in love with the hobby. Bri's face always lit up whenever she would talk about a book she was currently reading. My Amazon recommendations have never been the same, and honestly? I love it. Who knew smut could be so informative?

"I don't anymore. Well, that's not entirely true. I just can't bring myself to pick up a book. Not after everything that happened with Max and I—" Her voice tapers off, and there's a look of pure horror written across her beautiful features.

"What does Max have to do with wanting to get rid of your books?"

"You don't really want to hear all that." She waves her hands in a desperate attempt to dismiss her feelings.

"I *always* want to hear what you have to say. If you're open to sharing, I'm open to listening."

Bri's eyes begin to water, and my body shakes with how hard she's crying, so I let her get it out. Whatever she's holding onto has been building for months, and I'm glad she's letting it out with me. She doesn't have to share everything with me, but I feel like she's letting me in. And that's a gift I plan to cherish with my whole heart.

I hear her let out a shaky sigh, and I don't let her go until she pulls away from me.

"Hey, you don't need to tell me anything. This is your story to tell. You're in control here."

"No. I want to tell you. I just don't want you to think I'm stupid. Logically, I know that how I'm feeling is irrational, but emotionally, I can't wrap my head around that fact."

"I will *never* think you're stupid. Screw logical thinking. You're allowed to feel how you feel."

"Right. Well, you remember the accident?" When I nod my head, she continues.

"So, I'd been pestering Max to go axe throwing with me. It's been on my bucket list for, like, ever. It took him a minute to agree, so when he finally caved, I booked the room right away.

"On our way to the place, Max and I were jamming in the car, reminiscing on our childhood memories. Despite his resistance, Max was excited to do this with me. He's great that way. He's always doing things for others just because it makes them happy. It's one of the things I love most about him." Bri's face distorts with emotional pain, and it guts me.

"Baby, you don't have to keep going. We can stop here." I trace patterns on her arms, hoping to give her some comfort.

"No, I need to get this out. We were at a stop light singing at the top of our lungs and laughing our asses off. The minute the light turns green, I step on the gas. Within a matter of seconds, my car is struck on the passenger side. I guess a drunk driver blew through a red light and slammed into Max.

"Cut to us in the hospital. Max is unconscious in the operating room, and I have a minor concussion and some scrapes and scratches. I barely had anything wrong with me, while Max was fighting for his life. I wanted to go fucking axe throwing." She sucks in a breath, darkness shrouding her features with how difficult this has been for her.

"Bri..." I whisper her name, tracing slow, soothing patterns across her cheek with my thumb.

"It was because of *me*. I wanted to go, he didn't. I begged. He agreed." Regret swims in her gaze. "He needed all of those surgeries because of *me*."

Bri hides behind her hands, looking like she wants to crawl into a hole and disappear. The breath I've been holding rushes out of me. Here is a woman who's been holding onto this unnecessary guilt. The amount of weight that Bri has been carrying on her shoulders is unfathomable.

"Bri. That's some heavy shit you're carrying. The only person who should feel any guilt is the person who decided to drive drunk. I know that believing what I say is easier said than done. It kills me to know you've been battling these demons by yourself. I know I haven't been your favorite person, but I'm here for you. Whenever you need."

"I...I don't hate you. Well, not anymore, I don't."

Her words feel like a lullaby to my soul, providing soothing comfort and healing a part of my younger self. My younger self who so desperately ached for her.

My fingers brush her silky tendrils away from her face, the smooth texture reminiscent of the highest quality cashmere sweater. A thought pops into my head, but I'm not sure how she'll take it. I try anyway in hopes that her lack of hatred for me will remain intact.

"Have you thought about talking to someone? Therapy has been really helpful when I had to work through my issues with my brother."

"I've been so consumed by my guilt and shame that I haven't thought about it much. I feel that because of everything that's happened, I have to suffer the consequences."

"Baby, you never have to suffer alone. Going through so much trauma alone is too much for anyone to handle. Promise me you'll think about going?"

"I don't want to be a burden—"

"You couldn't be a burden even if you tried. Just promise me."

"I promise." I'm not entirely convinced, but I'll take it for now.

"Great. If you really want to get rid of the books, I'll help you. I'll even donate them to a thrift store."

"I—Yes, that would be great. Thank you."

"Of course. Now, let's get to work." Little does she know that I won't be donating shit. I plan to keep these books in pristine condition until she's ready. She deserves the world, and I'm the guy to give it to her.

Brianna

Fall in love with what?

I'M SITTING AT MY kitchen table, iced coffee in hand, thinking through everything Asher said to me this morning. It makes sense logically, but emotionally? Well, I might need more weapons to battle my inner demons.

I'm nowhere close to who I used to be, but I felt something shift last night curled up between Asher's strong arms. It's true what I said to him—I don't hate him. He's been amazing with me ever since he showed up on my doorstep. But sometimes, the poisonous snakes bite, my self-doubt the venom that pulses through my veins. If I keep this up, I might never find the girl I once was. Sometimes, I wonder if I'll ever be.

But the way he caressed my stretch marks last night as if it was the sexiest thing about me was exhilarating. And the desire I felt? It's a sensation I'm craving a repeat of. His touch quieted every negative thought I've had about my body since I've gained weight. Now that I've had a hint at what freedom tastes like, I want more. And I think that Asher is the perfect person to help me.

While Asher's at the store picking up storage boxes, I try to come up with a plan of things I want to work on. The first thing that comes to mind is my negative body-image. I still only look in the mirror when necessary, and it's only for a brief second or two. I'm not the size eight I used to be, and it's been a struggle coming to terms with my curvier shape. It's not that I want to lose weight—or need to— to feel beautiful. I just want to fall in love with the body I'm in.

I want to fall in love with sex again.

Sex for me was a way to celebrate my body, my femininity. I mean, yeah, I'll admit I loved the attention from men, but it was more than that. Having every inch of me explored and appreciated was exhilarating. I am a firm believer in being both a giver and receiver, so I made sure to find partners with the same mentality. Now, when I think of sex, I'm hyper-focused on how I look to my partner, and it just takes me out of the act altogether. So, really, I guess sex and body image are one in the same.

I want to start living outside of the comfort of my own home. I was always the social butterfly, and I miss it. Besides Asher, Avery is the only other person who's seen me, and I feel like that's only fueling my insecurities. Plus, I miss my best friend. We used to have so much fun together, and I've been stuck in this fear that I'd bring the mood down. Which makes zero sense because Avery would never feel that. It's just something my mind has created.

After my talk with Asher this morning, I want to conquer my shame and guilt. He's right in the sense that I don't need to carry this trauma alone. Asking him to help me pack up my books was a huge deal for me. I want to get comfortable with asking for help, which includes going to therapy. I hate to admit it, but I need help. Even though he says I can lean on him, I don't want to put all my trauma on Asher.

I also want to conquer my newfound fear of driving. There's something about getting in the car—no destination in mind, just driving. I'd blast the music and belt the lyrics at the top of my lungs. I'm the worst singer known to man, but I couldn't care less. Putting on Grammy winning—well, in my head they were—performances for just me and no one else was intoxicating. I want that back. Not sure how that's going to be possible, because anytime I even think of stepping foot in a car, my panic renders me useless for the rest of the day.

And lastly, I need to find my purpose. I've worked at the hair salon for almost a decade, and as much as I love it, it just doesn't fill my cup like it used to. Immediately after the accident, I threw myself into my job. It worked for a bit, but then my depression got so bad that I couldn't leave my bed. Thank God I work for a huge salon, because my boss talked me into FMLA to give myself time to recoup. And I've been on that until recently when it ended, but instead of feeling happy, I feel empty.

Salon.

That word triggers a Pavlovian response, transporting my mind back to a particularly hard day.

January 2026

The eggshell envelope weighs heavy and rough against my palm. Inside, its rectangular shape holds tainted money.

"Name a number—any number, and it's yours."

"How much will it take to avoid a lawsuit?"

Those were direct statements from the parents' of the person who hit my car. She came from money, and while they could do nothing to stop the police arrest, they could do whatever it took to prevent a lawsuit. I had no interest in dragging the case further than what the cops had in mind, so I took the money–and it was a substantial amount. Enough to cover both mine and my brother's medical bills, as well as living expenses for a while. Must be nice to come from money.

The envelope lays unopened in my palm, but I already know what the contents of the check will say. Yet, I can't bring myself to open it. With the money I also received from the insurance, the solid nest egg in my savings from the salon, plus the continuous help I've received from my parents, I'm set. Despite my lack of communication with them, they still send money from time to time. And every time, guilt threatens to pull me under as if I'm stepping into quicksand.

It's always the same. Guilt takes me hostage, setting a ransom I can never pay. Tears sting behind my eyes, and panic climbs up my throat. Guilt turns to panic, and by that time, I'm already wrapped up in the vine as it squeezes the breath from my lungs.

"Uh, ma'am. Are you planning to get out?"

The trance that's overcome my body shatters like glass, and my eyes snap to the mysterious voice. A man in what seems to be his late forties, early fifties glares back at me from behind a pair of wire-framed glasses. His lips are pursed in a displeased scowl while the hand wrapped around the steering wheel taps in an annoyed rhythm. I shift my focus outside the window to find I'm in the parking lot of the salon.

Right. The salon.

"Oh, um yes. I-I'm getting out. Thank you."

I gather my purse and my phone before climbing out the car, but not before I hear the Uber driver huffing and puffing about dumb chicks. I have zero energy to pick a fight with him. So, I thank him again before closing the door and watching him speed off. I leave him a generous tip for the wait and head into my job. Could you really call it a job if you aren't actually doing any work? Alison has been amazing with everything, giving me busy work to keep my mind off the chaos that is my life. But I haven't been operating at one hundred percent.

I bet this is why she called for a meeting.

You're getting fired. God, can you do anything right?

I swallow the hard words down my throat, their bitterness churning in my stomach.

It's now or never.

I push open the solid-glass door, ignoring the sympathetic looks from my coworkers. I can't take their pity. I want to get this meeting over and done with so that I can crawl under the confines of my comforter and hide from the world—where no bad things happen.

I knock on her solid-wooden door, and the minute she opens it, I'm hit with a strong patchouli and rosewood scent.

Alison, my eccentric, fun-loving boss, greets me with a smile and a warm hug, the type of embrace only a grandmother is capable of giving. Alison is in her mid-sixties with neon purple hair styled in a hawk-fade. Both of her ears are decorated with piercings, and she has a full length tattoo sleeve decorating her right arm. She is a complete badass on the outside, but sweet like butterscotch candies on the inside.

She greets me with a warm smile and her arms outstretched, leaving me no choice but to walk into them. Not that I'd ever deny her. Alison's hugs have some sort of healing power, and anything that is going wrong in my life melts away. She leads me into her office, choosing to have one arm wrapped around my shoulders.

"So, I think it's time we talk."

Alison is also known for her waste-no-time attitude. The moment I sit down, she gets right to the point.

"I-I'm sorry, Al. I'm—I can...I can do better. I promise, I—"

Alison holds out her hand, a soft smile splayed across her face.

"Bri, you need the time off." She smiles at me sweetly, a tender hand on my shoulder. "We will all be here when you're rested and ready to come back."

"But I—wait, you're not firing me?"

"Why would I fire one of my best stylists? That would be stupid." Alison leans over her desk, laying a comforting hand on mine. "You've been through a lot. I think you need to take some time, really prioritize yourself. You can't function on an empty tank, my dear. Your job will still be here when you're ready. Because of the size of our salon, you can partake in the Family Medical Leave Act. I highly encourage you to take FMLA, Bri. And if you need more time, then you take it. No questions asked. No consequences."

"I-I...um...thank you. I, maybe I will. I just...thank you."

The chair squeaks when I stand up. Alison meets me halfway and pulls me into another hug. My vision becomes fuzzy, but I hold in the tears for when I get home.

As soon as I exit the salon, I'm pulling up the Uber app and requesting a ride. Soon enough, I'll be in the comfort of my own home. I can, albeit barely, manage to get into a car with somewhat manageable anxiety. I put my headphones on to block out the noise. My eyes are shut so hard, it borders on painful. But thoughts of driving again? That causes a full-fledged panic attack.

Where I can let the tears cascade down my face.

Where there's absolutely no way I can disappoint anyone again.

After my allotted time was up, I sent a text to my boss letting her know I needed more time. I didn't want to meet with her in person, so I messaged her. I am so thankful I have an amazing, understanding boss. She put me on temporary leave and told me to contact her when I'm ready.

But working at the salon doesn't call to me anymore, not like opening up my own bookstore would. Or, should I say, did. My heart hurts too much to follow through on that dream without my brother. Max and I used to plan everything together, especially with his work as a carpenter. I had everything planned out. I even went as far as creating a full business proposal and was planning to ask a bank for a loan. But my dream shattered the day my car did, dead and useless. I just want to fall in love with something again.

And speaking of falling in love, that's also something I want to do. After watching my bestie find her forever partner, a part of me yearns for that. I look at my parents' relationship with envy and longing. I grew up in a loving household, watching my parents be sickeningly affectionate with each other. I want the fantasies I read about in books to become my reality. I want a real life book boyfriend.

I scan my surroundings looking for a scrap piece of paper to write all these down so I don't forget.

Fall in love with my body

Fall in love with sex (again)

Start living for myself (aka take risks)

Asking for help (go to therapy)

Find my true purpose in life

Get over fear of driving

Fall in love

I'm so involved in scribbling things down that I don't realize Asher has snuck up behind me.

"Fall in love with sex, huh?" he chuckles. Out of all the things he could have focused on, he chooses that one. I turn to look at him, and his laugh instantly falls from his face.

Way to go, Bri. You think this silly little list will get rid of us? Think again. How desperate are you if you have to create a list?

"Shit, Bri. I'm sorry. I wasn't making fun of you. I...um...That was just the first thing I saw. God, that was such a dick move. I'm so sorry."

I pull the piece of paper against my chest as an embarrassed blush creeps up my neck. "You don't have to be sorry. It's just something I was thinking about since our conversation this morning. It's just a silly little list." I force a smile on my face that I know he doesn't believe, and change the subject. "Did you get the boxes?" I ask, hoping he'll just drop the subject altogether—which, of course, he doesn't.

"It is not a silly little list. I'm proud of you for making it. Can I...Can I read it?"

His palm is outstretched toward me, allowing me to make my own decision. I mean, I did say that Asher was the perfect person to help me. This could be my first risk: ask Asher to help me with my goals.

I stare into his stunning blue eyes, and I feel no judgement. He's genuinely curious, and I trust him. Not only to help me with each task, but I trust he won't make fun of me for it. I want him to know what he's getting himself into before asking for his help. My shaky hands loosen their death-like grip on the now crumpled piece of paper and place it into his waiting hand. I'm mentally playing a game of tennis with my anxious thoughts. My self-confidence holds the racquet and swats away any negative thoughts that try to sneak their way past my defenses.

He's gonna think you're dumb. It's because you are.

It's only been a few seconds, but it feels like an eternity. My fingers tap out a nervous rhythm on the table up until Asher places his hand over mine. He meets my eyes and smiles. His smile exudes pride and some other feeling I can't quite decipher. Before I know it, he's pulling me up, and his arms wrap around me.

"This is incredible. You created a rediscovery list."

"A what?"

"A rediscovery list. You put things on there so you can relearn who you are. I'm so fucking proud of you for wanting to do this. And before you say anything, it has nothing to do with what I said this morning and all to do with you. Our conversation might have sparked something, but this is all you. I hope you feel as proud of yourself as I do."

I look down at my list as the words *rediscovery list* rattle around in my brain. I grab the pen and add the words *My Rediscovery List* on top of the notebook paper. I stare at it a moment as satisfaction and joy swirl in my body like the Northern Lights. It's bright, and brilliant, and it's all me. I want to cling to this feeling for as long as I can, and I think this list will help me. I'm basking in my bravery, so I decide to ask the difficult—well, difficult for me—question.

"Will you help me?" I'm surprised at how strong my voice sounds, not a quiver in sight.

Asher cups my face with his hands, and we remain locked in an intense, slightly sexual staring contest. I refuse to allow self-doubt to slide through the cracks, so I keep my eyes locked on his.

"It would be an honor to help you. I do have one question, though. About the sex thing—" His sentence trails off at the end, and my eyes widen with mortification. Oh, shit, why didn't I think about that one? I know exactly how it looks to him.

"Oh, yeah, that one. Um, I don't expect you and I to have sex. I don't want to put you in an awkward situation. I mean, you're my brother's best friend. This has to break some sort of, like, code—" I'm interrupted when his lips crash into mine.

The kiss is beyond passionate. It's raw. Hungry. It's pure desperation, and I'm craving more.

I open my mouth, giving him the invitation to deepen the kiss. Our tongues dance together, and I can feel my blood begin to boil. My arms snake around his neck until my fingers grip his hair. The second I pull, he's lifting me up and walking me to the counter. I flinch briefly from the cool contact of the granite against my thighs. Asher stops, thinking he's maybe taken things too far, but I'm pulling his lips back to mine. I'm dehydrated, and the only solution is to kiss him. I tug his bottom lip between my teeth and suck. His groan stirs some primal need inside me. A need I haven't felt in months—if ever. Has kissing always felt like this?

I feel the sensation from my head to my toes. I'm dizzy with want, and if I pay close attention to my feet, they'll probably hurt from how hard my toes are curling. Asher taps on my thighs—a silent invitation for me to spread my legs. The second he's between my legs, I lock him in by wrapping my legs around his waist. Asher's response is to thrust his hips into me, and that's when I feel it. His dick is pushing against his jeans, and I can only imagine how painful that must be.

I remove one of my hands from his hair. My fingers slowly glide down his chest, feeling the rock hard body underneath. I don't stop until I reach his cock. My fingers lightly brush against it, coaxing Asher's hips to thrust forward again, which in turn has my grip tightening.

Holy shit, he feels big. Like, *I won't be able to walk normally for the next twenty-four hours* kind of big. It should be illegal to have a dick that huge. I squeeze him through his jeans, and Asher pulls away from my mouth and utters a *fuck*.

"Bear, if you keep doing that, I'm going to come in my pants, and that's the last thing I want to do." Asher lets out a breathy chuckle.

We sit in silence, foreheads pressed together as we gasp for air. Holy shit. Did I just play with his dick? While I'm disappointed he stopped us from continuing, I can't help but smile at the glimpse of the old me. That was hot as fuck. Maybe I've just needed to put shit I want to do on a list for it to actually happen. Good to know.

"Baby, I've already said fuck the rules. Fuck whatever damn code you think there is. I think it's great you want to fall in love with sex again. You should enjoy it, but if you use any other man to help you with that task, we'll have problems. I'm not violent by nature, but being around you has me throwing caution out the window. No man touches you. No other man will help you with that item. No one but me, understand?"

Asher's hand wraps around my throat, squeezing with just enough pressure to have my nerve endings go haywire. Asher is giving me a hand necklace. I repeat, Asher fucking Larson is giving me a hand necklace. And now my panties are soaked. Who knew possessive men would be such a turn on for me? Who are we kidding, I used to live for morally grey men.

I channel my inner brat and remain silent, testing the waters of just how possessive and demanding Asher will be.

Asher squeezes my throat even more before fusing our lips together. The kiss is everything I hoped it would be, but he pulls away too quickly. His stare is so intense I could come just from looking.

"Answer me. No other man gets to touch you. Only me. Do I make myself clear?"

I lick my lips before responding, "Yes, sir."

A growl comes deep from Asher's chest at hearing the title. "Good girl. Now, let's get to work. I'll prepare the boxes down here while you get the books ready. I need the space before I say screw it and fuck you right here." Asher squeezes my hips before gently lifting me off the counter.

I briefly lose my balance, but Asher's grip on my hips prevents me from falling. He looks at me like I'm his favorite meal, making my knees tremble.

He's off before I have time to process that look. As I make my way upstairs, I can't help but think about our arrangement. We should probably come up with some ground rules, but honestly, why not live a little dangerously? Afterall, it's a part of finding myself again. I daydream of all the possibilities, and I can't help but smile.

Asher

Staring at her with hearts in your eyes

It took all of my willpower to stop myself from fucking her on the spot. That list? Goddamn, my head is dizzy thinking about all the things we could do. I put it all aside for now so I can focus on my visit with Max. My phone chimes with an incoming text.

Cas: Hey

Me: Hey. What's up?

Cas: Nothing much. Wanted to see what your plans are for today. I have some news to share with you.

Me: I'm actually about to head to Max's house. You're more than welcome to tag along if you want.

Cas: Yeah. I actually have something to tell the both of you, so that makes it easier.

Me: Cool, want me to swing by your place on the way?

Cas: Yeah, that'd be cool, thanks man.

Me: You got it. I'm headed out now.

I ARRIVE AT CAS' house to find him cuddling with Avery on their porch swing, looking at her with stars in his eyes. My heart aches for what they have. Their journey hasn't been easy, but their love is something to admire. My mind drifts to an item on Bri's list: fall in love.

Out of all the goals on her list, that's the one thing I can already check off on my end. We only talked about the sex item on her list, so I'm not sure I'm the one she wants to fall in love with. Thinking of her falling in love with another man physically hurts, but it's her journey to take. I'll help her regardless, even if I'm not the one she calls hers.

"Get a room." I roll down my window, harassing the newlyweds.

Their heads snap in my direction, Avery's cheeks turning cherry red. Cas just laughs before kissing her forehead and heading my way.

"Thanks for picking me up," Cas says while buckling his seatbelt.

"No problem. How's married life treating you?" I ask, trying to hide the jealousy in my tone.

"It's incredible. I honestly never thought I'd get to marry my best friend."

"Your best friend? I thought Max and I were your best friends. I'm wounded." I place a hand to my chest in mock hurt, and Cas punches my arm.

"Whatever. So, Avery told me about how she asked you to help Bri. How's she doing?" It doesn't surprise me that he knows about Avery's request, but it still catches me off guard. It's not my story to tell, so I opt to give him a shortened version of the truth.

"She's doing good, given the circumstances. She's a lot stronger than she thinks she is. I just want her to see her true potential, ya know?"

"Yeah, I get it. It's hard to watch someone you love struggle."

"Yeah. Wait, what do you mean? I don't love Bri." Shit. *Play it cool, Asher. Feel it out first before you admit anything.*

"Asher. Remember when you and Max called me out for liking Avery? And how y'all came at me for denying it?" Cas...using my own words against me.

"Yeah..."

"Well, I'm telling you that you're just as obvious. Especially at my wedding."

"What are you talking about?" I ask, my attempt at playing it cool betrayed by the slight waver in my voice.

"You were glued to her side all night, holding her hand and staring at her with hearts in your eyes. And that one time when we were hanging at Aces, you accidentally slipped up and called her your bear. I had a feeling then, but I knew for sure at my wedding. You're head over heels for her."

"Fuck."

"If it makes you feel any better, I don't think she knows."

"Oh, thanks. That totally helps," I say sarcastically.

"For what it's worth, I think she's into you as well. She's just in denial," Cas says matter-of-factly while shrugging his shoulders.

"Um. How do you know?"

"Well, she's letting you help her. Bri is very headstrong, and despite whatever she's going through, she's not pushing you away. That, and the fact that both of you have been in the longest game of foreplay known to man. I think she didn't like the fact that she had some sort of feelings for you. I mean, given how things went down in high school—"

"Have you been talking to Max? I swear, I had the exact same conversation with him. Wait—what aren't y'all telling me?"

"Avery told me some shit, and I wasn't supposed to say anything. Forget I mentioned anything." Cas' panicked look has me on edge. I wrack my brain, trying to figure out what Cas is referring to. I can only think of what she whispered in my ear, and then she gave me the cold shoulder the rest of the evening. Could that have something to do with it?

"Dude, you can't just say something like that and tell me to forget it." Frustration blooms in my chest, soaking my words. Being left in the dark fills my mouth with a sour taste. First Max alludes to something, and now Cas? What the fuck!

"Hey, I told Avery I'd keep it a secret, and I plan to do just that. Just ask Bri, man."

"Yeah, cuz she'll tell me the truth," I scoff.

"She just might. Communicate with her, it never hurts to try."

"Communicate with her? Where did you get that bullshit advice from?" I can't help but smirk at Cas.

"Some dick who called me out on my bullshit with Avery. You should listen to him, he has some good advice." Cas is just full of jokes today.

"I'll think about it." And by think about it, I mean obsess over it until I cave in and ask her myself.

We arrive at Max's house, and all Bri talk is put on pause. Max greets us with a slower gait, and I know without asking that he had physical therapy. It's killing him that he isn't operating at 100%, but getting him to admit it has been a struggle. Still, the fact that he's still going to PT and working his ass off is a good sign. I know there were times when he wanted to give up. To stop going. After multiple conversations with Cas and I, we managed to talk him out of it. But, like myself, Max is a people pleaser. So, our pleading for him to continue was the motivating factor for him to keep going. Well, that and his love of carpentry. If it means he'll show up to his sessions and work on himself, then I'll nag him all damn day.

By the look on Max's face when he saw Cas with me, he's not all that surprised he's here. Max and I have been buddies for years before adding Cas into the mix. I'll admit, when Cas came into the bar years ago, I was hesitant. I'm one to admit to my faults when they happen. And yes, Cas burned a lot of bridges with his addictions, but I, too, fucked up by assuming he was back to his old tricks.

Years of vicarious trauma from dealing with my then alcoholic brother tends to cloud my vision from time to time. With lots and lots of therapy, I've learned a lot about triggers and how they can pop up at random times. Cas coming into the bar in the beginning stages of trying to win Avery back had my trigger alerts flashing neon red. The day after that happened, I called my therapist to get me in for a session to help me unpack it, because sometimes you just need that third party.

With her help, I was able to shift my perspective, and I ended up having a very therapeutic conversation with not only Cas, but my brother, as well.

"Ah. If it isn't Thing One and Thing Two. What's up?"

"I was already on the way when this one begged and pleaded to join us." I gesture toward Cas with my thumb.

"Begged and pleaded my ass. You all but got on your knees for me to tag along. It was really sad." Cas smirks at me, and I respond by flipping him off.

"Jackass." Then I point at Max before calling him out. "Always trying to start shit. You and Bri are the same in that way."

"Speaking of, how is she doing?" Max's voice is full of concern and sadness for his little sister.

What a fucking question, one I still struggle with answering. I'm smack dab in the middle of two siblings. Max and Bri have always been attached at the hip. Max has reached out to her numerous times, and all communication has gone unanswered. I know he doesn't understand Bri's sudden ghosting. They've always been each other's go-to when things get rough. Not knowing what happened is *killing* Max. On the other hand, Bri feels immense guilt for the accident, and I know she's harboring a lot of guilt over what happened. And if I had to guess, I'd bet Bri hasn't been by to see her parents, either. Max is my best friend, and Bri is my...something. So, I do what I think is best and change the subject.

"She's okay. Enough about Bri, though. I'm guessing by your current scrunched up expression that PT kicked your ass?"

Max looks defeated, and his wounded expression destroys me. I watch him shut down the disappointment and paste a fake as shit smile on his face.

"Yeah. Today there were a lot of resistance band exercises and some new stretches. My muscles are weeping. And my hand still hurts from having a band snap back at me. PT hurts more than being kicked in the balls."

"Oh, Max, always the drama king," Cas interjects, leading Max to flip him off without even looking in his direction.

"Anyway, enough about you. Not everything's about you, Maxwell." I hear him curse at the use of his full name, my cheeks hurting with how hard I'm smiling. He hates when I full name him.

"Cas told me he has something he needs to tell us." We both turn to Cas, and he has the biggest smile on his face.

"Avery's pregnant!" Cas exclaims, choosing not to beat around the bush.

"Holy fuck, are you serious?" I ask.

"Damn, y'all aren't wasting any time," Max says directly after me.

"We knew we wanted kids, but we weren't expecting it to be this soon. I'm excited, but terrified I'll be like my dad. Given my history—"

"You're afraid of turning into your dad," Max finishes his thought.

"Yeah. I'm back in therapy to work through some of my shit. I don't want to stress Avery out by bringing my trauma into fatherhood." Cas clears his throat. "I hope you know you'll be a huge part of this baby's life. They'll have so much love and support."

"I'm going to be the best uncle ever. I can't wait to spoil the fuck out of that kid. And Asher here will be one hell of a godfather," Max says, stirring up shit like he always does.

"Why do you assume I'd be the godfather? Hate to break it to you, but I think Cas and Avery are the ones to decide that, right?" I look at Cas, and I don't like the smirk on his face.

"Cas?"

"We haven't confirmed it officially, but Max is right."

"Told you," Max says at the same time I say, "What the fuck?"

"It's obvious Bri will be the godmother. And since you're most likely going to marry my sister, it makes sense for you to be the godfather." Max just shrugs like he didn't just say I'd be marrying his sister.

"What the fuck makes you think I'd be marrying your sister? For all we know, I could marry...I don't know, Giselle." Max glances at Cas before they both burst out laughing.

"You and Giselle? Yeah, good one." Max is laughing so hard he starts to wheeze.

"Nah. You and Bri are endgame. You both know it, yet don't do anything about it." Max is too observant for his own good.

"I mean, do I like Bri? Yeah, of course I do. But will I marry her? She doesn't think of me in that way."

Max and Cas look at each other again before speaking simultaneously, "She does."

My heart flips in my chest when I think of a future with Bri. I'd love to be her forever, but I can't get my hopes up.

Max, Cas, and I spend the rest of the time talking, laughing, and just hanging out. It's nice to just be with the guys. But if I'm being honest, I miss hanging with a certain curvy brunette that's taken my mind and heart hostage. She can hold onto both for as long as she wants, because truthfully? I don't want either of them back. My heart and soul are hers to keep.

When I'm at home and alone in bed, I replay all the events from today. *Bri and I.* God, I'd give anything to make that a reality. The day she chooses me to be the one she falls in love with will be the second greatest day of my life. The first being the day I fell for her. Because if she does give me her heart, I'll treat it like it's the most important thing I've ever been gifted. Because she's the most precious person who has ever entered my life.

Brianna

Now is not the time for self-deprecating

May 2026

I stare at Avery's contact photo for what feels like forever. It's a photo of both of us, cheeks pressed together with matching, cheek-splitting grins. Fuck, I miss my best friend. I miss our sleepovers and our at home spa days. But what I yearn for the most is talking to her. My head is a complete clusterfuck, and I need my bestie's help. Of course, whenever I gather the courage to reach out, intrusive thoughts pull me back into their darkness.

She hates you. Who ignores their best friend?

Why does my mind have to always kick me when I'm down? I already feel like shit ghosting my best friend, but my anxiety likes to constantly remind me. I tug at the loose collar of my sweatshirt, overcome with the feeling of being suffocated. My heart gallops like a wild stallion inside my chest.

Be brave, Bri. You can't keep letting your anxious thoughts win.

I hit the call button, our faces illuminating the entire screen. There's no time to contemplate what I want to say because the sweet, musical voice of my best friend sounds through the other end of the phone after one ring.

"Oh my God, Bri. H-Hey, how are you?"

How am I? I'm not sure how to answer that question. I don't want to lie to her nor am I wanting to tell her the ugly details of my current mental status. So, I go with a basic ass answer.

"I-I'm doing okay." I take a slow, deep breath to collect myself. "Aves, I'm so fucking sorry. I've been the worst friend. You probably hate me. I mean, I would hate myself, too, if I was being ghosted. I—"

"Brianna, stop. I don't hate you. I could *never* hate you. I just...Well, I miss you."

Avery's tears set off a chain reaction, and now we are both a blubbering mess of *I'm sorry* and *I miss you.*

I don't know why I expected anything else from Avery; empathy oozes from her pores. But my mind hasn't been the kindest to me as of late. Despite my toxic mental health, I'm able to admit how I've been feeling, and I'm damn proud of myself.

If I had a dollar for every time I've lied saying everything was great, I could put a nice downpayment on a new car. Speaking of driving, I need a new car since mine was totaled. I have the means to get one. My car wasn't fully paid off, so the insurance company issued a decent size check for a future new car. But thinking about driving still has my brain spiraling.

Getting a new car feels like a fuck you to my brother. And then getting a new car means actually driving said car. And then if you drive, then you'll have to drive past the scene of the accident.

Yeah...Driving is still a no for me. I'll tackle that item on my list...eventually. Maybe this is something my therapist can help me with.

"Bri?" Avery asks, interrupting my downward spiral.

"I'm here. Sorry, I got lost in my head, what did you say?"

"You don't have to apologize for that, I get it. I just said I'm so glad to hear your voice again. Y-You sound better." Avery's voice quivers on that last word.

"Avery? Are you okay? D-Did I say something to upset you?"

Silence fills the other end of the phone. I feel myself wanting to jump to conclusions, but I know she needs a moment to think.

"Huh? Oh, no, you didn't. My emotions have just been all over the place lately. A lot has happened, and there's so much I need to tell you."

I let out a sigh of relief and I drill it into my mind that what Avery is going through is not my fault. I repeat the mantra, *I didn't do anything wrong. She's not mad at you* over and over in my head. If I say it enough times, maybe it'll stick.

"Oh, well are you doing anything now?" There. I did it. I'm making progress with getting my old life back.

"Oh." Avery sniffles, and now we're both a hot mess for a second time during this phone call. These tears are the healing kind, letting out everything we've been holding onto. I guess what they say is true. Sometimes you need to fall apart before you can find yourself again.

"I, um, you can come over if you want. We can watch a movie while eating junk food. Just like old times."

"I'm already on my way. See you soon. Love you, babes."

"Love you, too."

Avery pulls into the driveway about thirty minutes later using her key to enter my home. The second we see each other, we're in each other's arms, rocking back and forth. Tears are a steady stream down my cheeks, and I can feel Avery shake with silent tears of her own. If I pay close enough attention to my heart, I can feel a small piece of the shattered organ snap back into place.

"I'm so glad you called." Avery lets out a watery chuckle.

"Me too. I've missed you so much. I promise to try harder. I'm, uh, also sorry about pulling that stunt at your wedding. I should have formally said my goodbyes, but I snuck out the back like someone sneaking out after a bad one night stand." My throat is raw from all the crying. I hug Avery tighter before letting her go.

"Bee. You've had a lot going on. You were there for me with everything that happened with Cas and I. Everyone heals in their own way. I'm just glad you called me. I don't care how long it took you to do it. As for my wedding, I was just happy to share my day with you. I don't care about how you left. I understood it then. I understand it now."

This is one of the reasons I love this woman. She's still here for me after an extended period of radio silence. Every person needs a best friend like Avery; she's absolutely incredible.

"I'm so glad you're my best friend. Now, let's load up on junk."

"I'm glad you're my bestie, too, now lead the way," Avery says, a grin plastered across her soft features.

"What did you bring us?" I reach down to pick up the bags, and when I look at what she brought, it's very...interesting.

"Um, Aves?" My eyes move from inside the bag to her face. Avery looks like she's holding back a grin. Wait—is she glowing?

Avery just shrugs her shoulders before brushing past me and into the kitchen.

"Avery!" I shout-laugh as I follow after her. But like, what the fuck? Inside the bag is a giant jar of peanut butter, a bag of pork rinds, a giant jar of pickles, and a bottle of red wine vinegar. The other bag has our usual silly face masks, purple and baby blue nail polish, and a few chocolate bars.

I enter the kitchen shortly after Avery and find her already sitting down at the dining room table, a giant grin on her face. I place the bags down, eyeing her suspiciously as I do so. I watch as she digs through her purse for a few seconds before pulling out a tiny, rectangular box. It's covered in a soft, dusty cedar wrapping paper with a white ribbon wrapped along both long ends and tied in a pretty bow in the center.

The paper feels smooth underneath my fingertips. I look at Avery with a questioning expression, but she nods her head while pushing the box closer to me. As much as I don't want to destroy Avery's impeccable wrapping job, curiosity gets the better of me, so I tear through it aggressively.

The moment I see it, I drop the box onto the table. My hands fly to my mouth as my gaze flickers from her to the box then back again. My eyes sting with tears, but I blink them back. We've already cried enough today. But oh my God.

My best friend is pregnant.

Holy shit.

The chair screeches as I pull it back to rush over to hug my best friend while we simultaneously scream. Everything in my life takes a back seat to the pure joy I'm feeling.

"Avery. Oh my God! I can't believe it. You're pregnant?" I shout at her.

"I am. I couldn't be happier. We couldn't be happier." Avery's ear splitting grin speaks for itself.

"How did this happen?" My voice shakes with excitement. My best friend is having a baby? The promise of a new life, a new beginning, dims the sadness that seems to cling to me.

"Well, Bri. When two consenting adults decide to get together and have this thing called sex—" I playfully slap her arm.

"Shut up. I mean, like, were you guys planning it? Was this a surprise? Forgive me, but my brain is trying to process everything. Y'all just got married."

You'd know if you didn't—Nope...Not going there. Now is *not* the time to be self-deprecating.

"We've talked about starting a family before. We just didn't expect it to happen this quickly, but we're happy. I'm only a few weeks along, but Cas is overly cautious. He tried to persuade me to have him drop me off, but after a long talk, he mellowed out."

I let out a watery chuckle, because that sounds like Cas. The man is a puddle when it comes to Avery.

"I'm just so happy for you guys. But wait, what about Cas' graduate program? He's so close to graduating. And your songwriting? What happens with that?" I've been a prisoner of my own pain, but that doesn't mean I'm not following my friends' lives.

"Cas will step back from his master's program to focus on work and our growing family. As for songwriting, I've been writing a lot more children's songs and lullabies. So being pregnant has inspired me," Avery says while glancing down, placing a protective hand over her belly.

"Oh, wow, that's amazing. You'll both be amazing parents. I bet Cas' grandparents are over the moon." I don't even have to fake the enthusiasm right now, everything is genuine.

"Thank you, Bri. That means a lot. His grandparents are ecstatic about the news. They've already started planning what to get the baby. I do want to ask you something, though."

"Okay, what is it?"

"Will you be the godmother?" Avery asks, her eyes shimmering with pure joy.

Godmother. I let that word sit on the tip of my tongue, and I can't help but wonder if I'm the right person for the job. My life is still a mess. My mental health has been absolute trash. I glance down at my best friend's belly and frown.

"I am honored you'd ask me, Aves. But I'm the right person to ask? My life is still in shambles, and I'm still crawling my way out of a dark hole. You don't want your baby looking up to someone like me."

"See, that's where you're wrong. Everything you just said makes you the *perfect* godmother. This baby is gonna see a strong, beautiful woman who's learning to overcome something painful. You're inspiring, Bri. I hope that one day you see just how incredible you are. So yeah, you are the perfect role model for the little babe."

Fuck. My throat feels like I swallowed my food without chewing it fully. When she puts it that way, it makes me feel less like a failure and more like a warrior.

"Well damn, Aves. Are you *trying* to make me cry? But you make a solid argument. My answer is yes. I'd love to be the godmother, and I'm gonna spoil the shit out of them. But wait, who's gonna be the godfather?" I watch Avery's face turn bright red and her lips are pursed—like she's trying to hold her laughter in.

"Avery?" I ask again.

"Take a guess." I study my best friend's face for a few seconds before things click into place.

"It's Asher, isn't it?" Avery's nod confirms my suspicions. Just saying his name out loud has my cheeks flushing and my body temperature spiking.

"Bri? What's going on? I thought you'd give me a snarl or sarcastic remark." Avery's hand waves in the direction of my face.

"Um..."

"No. Really?"

"It's not like that, Aves. We've been hanging out from time to time. He's helping me with some things."

"Helping you with what, exactly?" Avery's head rests on her hands as she looks at me with interest.

"I have this list and he's helping me work through it." I know Avery's going to ask about the list, so I share it with her before she has the chance to ask.

"Fall in love with sex, huh?" She waggles her eyebrows at me.

"You sound like Asher. He said the same thing. And, well...We might have kissed the other day."

"You WHAT?!? Wait, before you tell me everything, I'm hungry and I need my snacks. Let's get everything ready and go sit in the living room."

"Okay, but Aves, your snacks are disgusting. I'll stick with some chips with salsa, and popcorn." I gather everything needed on a serving tray and head to the living room. The second I sit down, Avery is on me.

"How did it happen? How was it? How do you feel about it?"

"It just sorta happened. One minute we were discussing how he didn't have to help me with the sex item on my list, and then before I knew it, he was kissing me. After that, everything became kinda hazy. And my God, can that man kiss. It was a toe-curling, hair pulling, frantic kiss, and it was amazing."

"Oh my God. Okay, but, like, how do you *feel* about it?"

"At first I was confused. I mean this is *Asher* we're talking about, someone I used to loathe."

"Used to, huh?" Avery eggs me on.

"Ugh yes, okay. I don't hate the man anymore. He's been incredible. He's patient, sweet, but dirty at the same time. It felt nice to be devoured like that, then I grabbed his di—" is all I manage to say before Avery interrupts me.

"Yeah...I called it. Y'all have been circling each other for years, so it's about time. Wait, did you say you grabbed his dick? Holy shit, Bri, way to bury the lead. How big was it? You should ask for a picture!" I gawk at Avery for asking for a picture, but then I remember doing the exact same thing with her in regard to Cas.

"Ha-ha, very funny. I only got a handful of it, but what I felt was huge and thick. So when we actually fu—"

"*When*, huh?"

"Yes, okay? When we do have sex, I know I'll be walking funny for days after. He's just...different, Aves. He doesn't look at me like I'm broken. He...just sees me."

I glance over to Avery who's looking everywhere *but* my eyes.

"Avery?"

"*Please* don't hate me, but I have a confession to make."

"Okay, what is it?" Avery's nervous energy has alarm bells sounding off in my mind.

"Well, I may have asked Asher to look out for you. I just, well, I knew you were struggling with letting people in, particularly those closest to you. I—um—well, I figured he'd be the perfect person to help you."

Avery's confession rattles me, alerting my internal beasts that it's time to come out and play.

Oh, you thought Asher wanted to be with you because he actually likes *you? Oh, honey... How sad.*

I—what can I say to that? I mean, she's right. I've held my friends and family at arm's length, so it makes sense that Avery would do anything she can to help me. But I can't help but wonder if it was all a lie. If things growing between me and Asher is a lie, a favor for a friend.

"Bri? Say something please. I-I didn't do it to hurt you. I just knew that if I couldn't be the person to help you, Asher would."

I search into Avery's piercing, green eyes and only see sincerity staring back at me. The smile that stretches across my face is weak, but I'm not upset with Avery. My hurt and confusion lies with the man who I thought genuinely wanted me.

"I know you didn't, Aves. I'm not upset. I just...Well, now I'm reevaluating every interaction I've had with Asher. I just feel so...stupid." My head falls in my hands.

Avery scoots closer to me, wrapping an arm around my shoulders. "Bri, I'm gonna need you to listen to me when I say this. That man worships the ground you walk on. I have no doubt in my mind that if I hadn't asked for his help, he would have found a reason to do so himself."

"Maybe you're right. I don't know, it's just a lot to process, I guess."

"I get that. Maybe you can talk to him? That's only if you want to. I support whatever decision you make."

"Ugh, this is making my brain hurt. Yeah, I guess I'll have to talk to him at some point."

"Take your time, bee. It's a lot of information to take in."

"Enough boy talk. You came here for girl time, so that's what we're gonna do."

"God, I've missed you. I love you, Bee."

"I love you, too, Aves."

The rest of the evening is spent laughing, snacking, and reconnecting. I know I'll have to talk to Asher eventually. But that's later Bri's problem.

Asher

You. I want you

I'VE BEEN HYPER FOCUSED on how to help Bri tackle her list, but it's been more difficult than I anticipated. I couldn't really ask Cas for suggestions with Max present. There's nothing more awkward than saying *hey, your sister wants to fall in love with sex again, and I plan to help her with that.* I think I'll pass.

Which is why I invited Cas and my brother, Xander, to lunch. About a year ago, I introduced the two, and they immediately hit it off. Given their history with substance and alcohol abuse, I thought it would be nice for them to lean on each other. I pull up to Porters Grille to see Cas and Xander chatting next to their cars.

"Aw, did y'all drive together? How cute," I tease.

"Don't be jealous," Xander retorts back before leaning in for a bro hug.

It's nice to see my big brother thriving. His drinking nearly destroyed our relationship. Growing up, he was my best friend, my idol. But then he tried to find himself at the bottom of the bottle, and everything changed. Xander is a few inches taller than me and is the spitting image of our father, Oliver, with dark brown hair and brown eyes. I took after my mom, Melissa, with my blond hair and blue eyes. Despite our differences and six year age gap, he's always been my go to confidant.

I greet Cas with the same hug before we make our way inside. We're seated pretty quickly thanks to the reservation I made this morning. I'm not much of a drinker, but when I'm around Xander and Cas, I'm mindful of my actions. Last thing I want is to make either of them uncomfortable. Xander has been sober for about six years now while Cas is still newly sober, but relapse is a sneaky bastard. So, instead of ordering my usual Manhattan, I order water.

Xander, unsurprisingly, is the first to break the silence. "What gives? Why are we here and not with Max discussing whatever you want to talk about?"

It's a valid question. I let out a sigh, knowing Xander is about to make fun of me.

"Well, it's not something I feel comfortable talking to Max about. See, I need your advice about Bri."

Xander grins and I just roll my eyes. *Here we go.* "Well, fucking finally. You've only been in love with her for years."

"Told you," Cas adds.

"Yeah, whatever. Anyways, she created this plan for regaining control over her life, and I need some help coming up with some ideas."

"It's like best friend boot camp 2.0," Cas remarks. Huh. I didn't think about it that way, but it makes sense.

"Yeah, I guess you could say that."

"What's on the list?" Xander asks.

Shit. I didn't think this far out. I should have assumed they'd ask, but this is personal for Bri. Well, they're about to get a vague ass answer.

"She just wants to feel like herself again...to feel beautiful again. The accident really affected her."

"The fuck? Does she not own a mirror? She's a fucking ten. I'd go after her if I wasn't happily married." Xander winks at me.

He'd never do anything with her, but jealousy doesn't seem to know the difference between a joke and something serious.

"Fuck off," I snarl, and out of the corner of my eye I see Cas smirk.

I turn to him and glare. "Just say it," I huff out.

"I've got nothing to say. It's just a strong reaction for someone claiming not to love someone is all." Dick.

"What Cas said. So, you've taken this upon yourself to help her?" Xander asks.

"Um, not really. She asked for help, and I agreed." We won't talk about what I agreed to. Some things should remain private.

"And I bet you so willingly agreed." Xander winks at me. I love my brother, but sometimes he can be ridiculous.

"Right. Well, now I have to figure out what to do to help her see how incredible she is."

"Bri is a bold and daring woman. And just based off of conversations with Avery, she has always been proud of her sexuality. Maybe you can do things to remind her of that? She probably doesn't feel good about herself, so show her what you love about her. Convince her of her beauty." Cas is wise beyond his years. I guess childhood trauma will do that to a person, but I appreciate his wisdom because this is the type of advice I'm looking for.

"Take her lingerie shopping," Xander adds.

Cas looks at him like he's ridiculous, but honestly? It's not a bad idea. She struggles with her body image, so this might be a good lesson in helping her love and accept her body. Plus, it's a win for me, too, because I get to see her in said lingerie. Will I tell him that, though? No, so I just roll my eyes and move forward.

"Yeah, sure. I'll get right on that one, Xander. Moving on. She also wants to start taking more risks and finding hobbies that she loves. Any ideas on that?"

This time, it's Xander who has the good ideas. "Well, you both love to read, so maybe you should do something like that? Honestly though, I think you might have to ask her what she wants, and then I think the ideas will come to you."

"Right, that makes sense, thanks." Our meals eventually come, and we spend the rest of our time catching up and giving each other a hard time. Xander ends up settling the bill, and I say my goodbyes before heading out to Aces for my shift.

The bar is busy when I walk in. There are not one, but two bachelorette parties...great. They are always a pain in the ass to deal with, but they tip well, so I just grin and bear it.

Gage is at one end of the bar flirting with who I assume is a bridesmaid from one of the parties since she's wearing a pink sash. He's a walking sex ad, but chooses not to use it to his advantage. To be honest, I don't recall the man ever really dating much. That didn't stop him from flirting with Bri when she and Avery came into the bar that one time. Granted, he was only doing it to get on my nerves. And something tells me Bri was doing it just to get on mine. I made him clean and mop the bathrooms as a punishment when we closed.

"Hey," a woman purrs.

I glance in her direction and notice she's practically leaning over the bar top. Her perky tits are hanging out, and I swear she's intentionally pushing them together. She has strawberry blonde hair with tan skin and hazel eyes. From what I can see, she appears thin, and her lips are full and plump. But she's not her. She's not Bri.

"What can I get ya?" I ask, purposefully leaning back and crossing my arms.

"Are you on the menu?" she asks. It takes everything in me not to gag on the spot. Desperation reeks from her side of the bar, and I'm not interested in participating.

"No. What can I get you?" I repeat, a little firmer this time, hoping she'll take the hint.

"Playing hard to get, hmmm? I like it. I'll take a drunken cherry martini. With extra cherries." She attempts to reach across the counter to put her hand on mine, but I'm quicker than her.

I prepare the drink for her, ignoring her blatant attempts of catcalling me. She's clearly already tipsy, so I hurry up and make the drink as quickly as I can. The faster she leaves, the better.

"That'll be fifteen. Do you have a tab open?" I hand her the drink and ignore her checking me out.

"I have cash." She rummages through her purse and pulls out a twenty. "Keep the change, handsome." I offer her a stiff smile before moving on to one of our regular patrons. Out of the corner of my eye, I see her frown, but I don't really give a shit.

Gage and I are working both ends of the bar, shouting out drink orders or asking for a specific bottle of liquor. We find our rhythm pretty quickly, and I'm grateful that I have Gage as my bar partner. He has zero tolerance for nonsense, and he knows what he's doing.

I'm in the middle of cleaning a few glasses when I feel a prickle of awareness at the back of my neck. I know without looking who has walked into the bar. But my eyes scour the bar anyway, looking for her. The moment our eyes lock, my jaw drops and my dick throbs behind my jeans.

Bri is a goddamn smoke show in black leather pants that hug her curves and a bright red bralette with her tits all but spilling over the top. She's in a pair of black heels and her hair is down in her natural waves. My mouth feels like I inhaled sawdust. My heart beats erratically in my chest and my hands are itching to touch her. Fuck, she's hot.

The look on her face tells me she doesn't believe it. Her brows are furrowed with worry, and she's nibbling on her lower lip. Bri's eyes ping pong around the bar until they land on mine. The second she sees me, the tension in her shoulders deflates before offering me the most blinding smile. Fuck, this woman will be the death of me.

She makes her way over to me, hips sway with each step. If I listen closely, I can hear the shattering sound of men's hearts breaking. What baffles me the most is she doesn't seem to notice all the men eye-fucking her as she walks past them.

Mine. Back off fuckers, this woman belongs to me.

Bri eventually stops in front of me and takes a seat.

I keep my eyes trained on her face, even though I want to scan her body and memorize every inch of her.

"Well, hello. What can I get ya?" I wink at her.

I hear the other girl from earlier scoff and attempt to whisper, "Seriously? Her?"

I feel Bri flinch, her shoulders hunching as she attempts to make herself small. I turn to the woman and glare at her before opening my mouth.

"Yup. If you have a problem with her, you can leave. Petty jealousy ain't cute."

My lip curls in disgust as I stare at the slack-jawed, insecure woman next to Bri. Something tells me she's used to men fawning all over her. Not me, though.

My eyes have been locked and loaded on the bombshell before me. My heart has been hers since I was seventeen, long before I truly knew what all-consuming love meant.

The girl blinks at me before running off to her party and complaining about how big of a dick the bartender is. I honestly don't give a fuck.

"Hey, Bri. Damn, you look hot. Let me know if you ever get tired of this tool, and I'll take real good care of you." Gage winks at her before shooting me a grin.

"You're fired, Gage!" I shout at him. I don't mean it. I even threatened to fire him when he flirted with Bri all those years ago. It's something we do.

"You wish, Ace. You need my ass." Gage turns to serve more customers while I bring my attention back to Bri.

"Y-You didn't have to do that. With that woman, I mean." She's tracing the grooves of the bar top, refusing to meet my gaze.

I lift her chin with my fingers and force her to look at me. "No one gets to treat you like you're below them, bear. I won't let anyone make you feel like you aren't worthy. So, if I have to put some jealous woman in her place, I will. Always. Now, what can I get ya?"

Bri chews on her lower lip while nodding her head. There's a look of uncertainty that passes behind her eyes. I open my mouth to ask her what she's thinking, but then she crooks a finger, signaling me to lean in. I'm hit with her vanilla and cinnamon scent, but what she says next renders me stupid. Blood rushes to my cock and my body feels like I'm covered in hot lava. *Mental note, ask Bri what that look meant.*

"You. I want you."

Fuck. I'm screwed.

Brianna

You heard me right

WHAT THE FUCK DID I just say? Did I...Did I just proposition him?

What the hell, Bri? You were supposed to confront him about his reasoning for hanging around you and then make your move.

I guess what they say about men thinking with their dicks applies to women, too. Because my vagina clearly has taken over my brain. That's the *only* reason why I've gone off script. It has *nothing* to do with watching his arms flex while he makes drinks. Nope. Not. At. All.

The ride over was spent rehearsing what I wanted to say, but the moment our eyes locked? I knew it was game over. Asher's checkered flannel is rolled up at the sleeves, leaving me with the most glorious forearm porn known to man. His blond locks are deliciously messy, like he's been running his hand through them.

I know of a better way to mess his hair...preferably while I'm on my back.

My pussy throbs at the visual of a certain sexy blond between my legs, my hands in his hair tugging while I ride his face. Yeah, I think it's safe to say I've lost all control over my mind. Okay...new plan. Fuck now...talk later. Yup, yeah that'll work.

"Could you repeat that? I could have sworn you said you wanted me, but I could have been putting words in your mouth."

Fuck now, talk later. Be bold, Bri. You can do this.

My fingers glide across the smooth, cherry wood before tiptoeing up his chest. Asher's stomach contracts beneath my touch, and his chest heaves quick, frantic breaths. When I meet his gaze, I'm met with dilated pupils, and I can see his pulse thrumming inside his neck.

My fingers curl around the collar of his flannel, tugging him toward me so that our lips are mere inches apart. The soft brush of our lips feels like a lighter to a stick of dynamite, my body on the verge of detonating with desire. I glide my lips along his jaw, cheeks, making my way up to his ear before whispering, "You heard me right. I. Want. You."

I enunciate each word by pressing quick, open-mouthed kisses inside the crook of his neck.

"Cool...cool. So, I don't need to get my ears checked." Asher quickly scans the bar before bringing his attention back to me. "I'm gonna ask Gage to take over. Give me a second to get my things and—" Asher attempts to leave, but my grip on him tightens, locking him in place.

"I never said anything about leaving. You have an office, right?"

"Y-Yes, I do," he stammers out.

"Is there a desk in there?" My fingertips trail along his collarbone, and then up and down his chest.

"Yes." His answer comes out as a half groan.

"Good, let's go." I pat his cheek twice before pulling away from him. I don't know who this Bri is, but I like her. She's feisty and goes after what she wants.

The sound of glass shattering followed by a muttered curse stops me in my tracks, and I glance over my shoulder. I watch Asher stepping over broken glass as he barks at Gage to clean it up. A sultry, seductive laugh slips past my lips at how distracted Asher is. Is this what it feels like to wield feminine power? It feels...liberating.

I step into the office, taking a moment to scan my surroundings. I expected to find the space very bland, but it's rather...cozy. The main centerpiece is a dark chestnut brown desk with neatly piled stacks of paper scattered across the smooth surface. The deep green of the walls feels like I've stepped into a forest. The black leather sofa off in the corner looks well-loved, with weathered lines etched into an intricate pattern.

This office screams Asher, comfy yet masculine. The sound of a door opening behind me pulls me from my perusal. I'm not prepared for Asher doing the BookTok trend of the door frame lean, a knowing smirk painted across his features.

Fuck. Me.

How the fuck does he know about this? Wait, does he know about that trend? Or is he just leaning because he knows it'll affect me? He cocks his head to the side before pulling the door shut. The turn of the lock is deafening against the erotically charged silence.

Asher stalks toward me, eyeing me like I'm his prey. *Goddamn cat and mouse fetish because fuck...This is hot.*

He steps forward, I step back. We repeat this dance until I'm backed up against the desk. I glance to my left and right before bringing my attention back to him. I feel the drumming of my pulse in my neck and between my legs. I...Is it possible to be *too* turned on?

I find myself caged in between his arms. He leans in, lips gliding alongside my neck toward my ear. My grip on the desk is borderline painful, but nothing compares to how painfully horny I am.

"Well, well, well, bear. You have me. Now, what are you gonna do with me?"

It's so hard to think as his tongue glides along the outer shell of my ear. *Wait, what was my plan again? That's right. Fuck now...talk later.*

Somehow, I manage to gain control of my limbs and push against his chest. Asher doesn't resist; he goes willingly. I feel my control slipping, but is that such a bad thing? Maybe letting him take over my body, pulling pleasure from every inch of my body, might be just what I need.

"I...I want to be fucked. Right here. Right now." *Fuck now...talk later.*

"Mmmm, you do, do you?"

"Y-Yes."

"Good girl. Now strip for me, baby."

Asher

I'll walk out of this office and find someone else to do it

BRI TAKES HER SWEET fucking time removing her pants. Her fingers graze the top waistband, drawing my gaze to the sliver of her exposed, tanned skin. I want to lick, suck, and bite just below her navel. I'm sure she tastes as sweet as she smells.

"Hey, Asher?" Bri asks with a slight hesitation in her tone.

I try, and fail, to assess the emotion painted across her beautiful face. "Yeah, baby?"

"Thank you," she whispers.

"For what?"

"This is a big deal for me. Sex has always been a way for me to let loose. I haven't even thought about being intimate with someone until you. You've awakened something in me. Something I never thought I'd get back."

Well, fuck. I knew it was a big deal for her, but I had no idea to what extent. Now I feel like I need to be gentle with her. Make sure she feels cherished and appreciated.

"You don't have to thank me. I'll admit, I had a plan to do filthy things to your body, but with that confession, I think I need to change the plan." I see a flash of disappointment in Bri's face before it morphs into a challenging expression.

Bri just smirks, eyes locked on mine as she steps out of her heels. She slides her pants down her body in a slow, torturous manner. The shiny, black material looks like heaven on my office floor, but my attention is pulled back to Bri as she puts her heels back on. Her red top quickly joins her leggings, leaving her in nothing but a lacy red bra, matching panties, and those damn black heels.

Bri saunters toward me, swinging her hips with purpose. The smell of her sweet aroma renders me momentarily speechless. Every rational thought or plan has evaporated from my mind, but then she leans in and whispers something I'd never expect her to say.

"That's fine. Plans change. I get it." Bri shrugs before walking toward the door.

I watch her finger the handle before tossing a smirk over her shoulder, a wicked grin stretched across her face. "If you don't want to bend me over that desk and fuck me like you mean it, I'll just walk out of the office and find someone else to do it. You aren't the only one who can help me fall in love with sex again."

Red blurs my vision, leaving Bri the only thing in vibrant colors. She knows *exactly* what she's doing to me. Bri's hand barely closes around the doorknob before I'm spinning her around and slamming her back into the door. I don't give a fuck who hears it. My hand wraps around her throat and squeezes.

"Mine," I snarl. "No other man touches you. I thought I told you that." I slam my mouth onto hers and kiss the absolute fuck out of her. My tongue forces its way into her mouth and dances with hers. She tastes like caramel and mocha—probably from her favorite iced coffee. I bring my knee in between her legs, forcing her to spread them for me, but I don't stop there. I rub my knee against her core, giving her just enough friction to have her entire body light up. I swallow her moan and increase the pressure on her neck.

Bri's grinding herself against my leg, trying to get herself off. But that just won't do. She'll come when I tell her she can.

I break away from the kiss only to make my way down to her neck and bite, tearing my name from her throat. Good. Let every single fucker in this bar know who she belongs to.

I pull away from her, allowing both of us to catch our breath. Bri looks sexually frustrated. Fucking hell, this woman.

"Go to the desk, grab onto the end, and bend over. I want your ass in the air for me." She moves quickly and gets into position. Bri's ass is spectacular. Round, and full, and absolutely mouth-watering. I rear a hand back before it connects with her ass in a loud smack. Bri gasps before she squeezes her thighs together. I smack her ass again, this time harder, and she lets out a moan.

"You really thought you'd get away with pulling a stunt like that? You think I'd let any man touch you, let alone look at you?" I smack her ass again, but this time I soothe the pain by pressing a soft kiss to the sore spot.

"What have you done to me, Bri? I'm not a possessive man, and yet, that's all I want to do. I'd drag you out into the middle of the bar right now and fuck you in front of every single patron so that they know who you belong to." Bri's thighs rub together, trying to create as much friction as possible. Her arousal flows down her inner thighs, begging for my tongue. For my cock.

"My little vixen likes that, huh? She likes to be shown off. But you're mine. No one gets to see this ass." For emphasis, I massage her sore cheek before leaning down and biting it.

"And no one gets to see this pussy. It's all mine." I move my hand and grip her cunt through her underwear, and she lets out a whimper. "You're all mine, baby. Do you understand that?" My two middle fingers rub back and forth, and Bri grinds against my hand. I allow her a moment before removing my now drenched fingers and flipping her over. I make sure to lock eyes with her while I take my fingers and put them in my mouth, allowing the taste of her arousal to coat my tongue.

"Fuck, you taste good. Makes me want more. But I'll be nice and give you options. I can fuck your cunt with my tongue, my dick, or my fingers. Which do you prefer?"

"I w-want your tongue," she whimpers.

"And what do you want my tongue to do to you?" I prompt.

Bri looks at me with pure determination in her eyes. "I want your tongue to fuck my pussy."

"Good girl. Your wish is my command. Now relax, Daddy's got you." I peel her underwear down her body with my teeth and wrap them around her ankles, locking her in place.

"Before I do, we need a safe word for if you need and want to stop. The second you say it, I'll stop, no questions asked."

"Sloth," Bri says confidently.

"Sloth?" I can't help but laugh.

"Yeah. Sloth. The animal is slow, so I figured that'd be a good safe word." Makes sense to me.

"Sloth it is. I need you to agree to use it if you need to. If you don't agree, this stops right now."

"I agree."

That's all the consent I need before diving in. My tongue flicks up and down her slit, tasting her, teasing her. Bri is absolutely drenched, and I can feel her slick dripping down my chin. She bucks her hips, grinding against my face, and I place a firm hand on her stomach, holding her down. She isn't in charge here. I am. I swirl my tongue this way and that, trying to find a rhythm that works for her. It isn't until my tongue dips inside of her that she lets out a cry. *There it is.* I want to spend some time on her clit, so I take my fingers from my free hand and curl them inside of her, hitting a spot that makes her squirm and moan. My lips close around her clit, sucking it like a lollipop. I feel her walls flutter around my fingers as I pump them in and out, increasing the speed with each thrust.

"ASHER. Oh my God, right there. Fuck. You're so good at this."

I decide to insert another finger inside her and push as deep as she'll let me. I let go of her stomach, allowing her to grind against my hand and face.

I let go of her swollen bundle of nerves for just a split second. "That's right, baby. Fuck my hand like the dirty girl you are. You want to come, don't you?"

"Yes. I-I need to."

"Then demand it. Ask for it. Beg for it."

"Asher, make me come, please? I need to." She screams when I blow and nip at her clit. She's getting close, I can feel it.

"You won't come until you address me properly. Do you want to come?"

"Yes, Daddy. I want to. I've been a good girl. Please let me come."

"Anything for you." I bring my attention back to her throbbing clit, moving my tongue in a circular motion while pumping my fingers inside of her. The second I curl my two middle fingers, she explodes on my tongue. I drink every last drop like a man dying of thirst.

"Asher." It's *my name* she screams when she comes.

"That's right. Scream my name. Let everyone know who owns this cunt, baby. You come so beautifully." Bri grinds against my face as she rides out the rest of her orgasm until she's a sweaty, shaky mess. I lick up every drop of her arousal before sliding up her body to kiss her, forcing her to taste herself on my tongue. We're both spent, but the kiss is intense and passionate. I could kiss this woman for the rest of my life.

Eventually, I break the kiss, and we both are panting from one of the hottest things I've ever experienced.

Without much thought, I pull her into my arms, needing to have her wrapped up in my embrace. Her legs are still in their makeshift restraints, locking us both in place. We both need this hug more than we realize. Yes, we just did some intimate shit, but I like showing her the affectionate, kinder side of me. Especially after what we just did.

"That was hot as fuck. I can't wait to do that again." Bri is quiet, which has me concerned. I pull out of her arms, expecting to see regret, but I see Bri looking completely satisfied.

"I need a minute. You literally tongue fucked the words out of me. I can't even process anything beyond you between my legs." We both start laughing, enjoying each other's company.

"Do you have to go back out there?" *There* meaning the bar. I don't want to, but I need to. But Bri's here, and I just want to stay with her. Talk to her. Fuck her some more.

"Yeah, unfortunately I do. But you are going to put your clothes back on and stay in the office. I don't want any men ogling you like they did when you walked in." Bri scoffs at me like she can't believe a word I said.

"They weren't ogling me, Asher. I think you need to get your eyes checked."

"Brianna. I saw at least three men choke on their beer the second you walked in the room. Two almost fell out of their chairs, and a few others practically had their tongues hanging out of their mouths like dogs. So, yes, they were gawking at you, and they liked what they saw.

"I gotta go, but you hang in here and chill until closing. I'm thinking of shutting down early so we can go home and do that again." I give her a quick kiss before I adjust my hard on. I lean down to look in the mirror, making sure I look somewhat presentable. I shoot a quick glance at Bri, tossing a wink in her direction. My hand is on the doorknob when I hear her sweet, sultry voice stop me.

"Uh, Asher?" She points to her own chin, her cheeks blooming a gorgeous shade of ruby red.

"What?" I feign innocence, knowing damn well what she's referring to.

"You have...um." Her shyness returns, her eyes darting away before meeting mine again.

"Baby, I'd happily wear your cum on my lips for the rest of my shift."

Her jaw drops as I leave her there, blinking back at me with a spot-on impression of a computer malfunctioning. Good, now she'll know how it feels to be stupid with lust.

I walk out of the office, ignoring all the eyes that are on me. I don't give a shit that they just heard us having sex. I go straight to the dirty glasses and begin washing them. I feel Gage walk up next to me and just stare holes into the side of my face.

"Not a word," I say.

"Wasn't gonna say shit, man." I glance at Gage as he winks at me before tossing the towel over his shoulder and serving more customers. The grin stays on my face the entire evening, because in my office is my person. The one I know I want to do life with. Who wouldn't smile at that?

Brianna

How does he know about tropes?

THAT. WAS. INCREDIBLE. THE way Asher just took charge and *dominated* me? New kink unlocked. But it's been thirty minutes, and I have to pee. I pull my bottom lip between my teeth, listening to the faint murmuring of voices from the other side of the door. I know people heard me—heard *us*—but I've held off for as long as I can. I either say screw the embarrass-ment and walk out of the office, or face the wrath of a UTI. Yeah, fuck that.

I get up from the desk, grabbing my clothes off the floor, and get dressed as fast as humanly possible. I open the door and peek around the corner to make sure Asher is occupied. He might not want me leaving this office, but I can't hold it in anymore.

Balanced on the balls of my feet, I hurriedly rush toward the bathroom, praying my heels don't make any noise. There's nothing more satisfying right now than emptying my bladder. I let out a sigh of relief before finishing up in the stall. I'm just pulling my pants back up when I hear the door open.

I don't think much of it, but the second I step out of the stall, I freeze. Standing before me is a five-foot-ten blonde goddess with the kind of curves a supermodel would envy. Her blonde tresses are styled in old Hollywood waves, resting against her mid-back. Perfect bee-stung lips any man would have wet dreams about, that also spit pure venom at anyone who dares to get in her way. Eyes so blue and sharp, she could cut you down to size with just one look.

Giselle. My friend turned nemesis. We used to be friends...a long time ago. Before Avery came into my life in college, Giselle and I were attached at the hip. Many summers were spent going to the community pool or spending all day at the beach. But then middle school hit and, well, it's a tale as old as time: girl dates popular boy, girl abandons friends. I no longer lived up to Giselle's newly curated image, so she left me high and dry with zero explanation. We were content to pretend the other didn't exist. I thought *maybe* we could be friends again. I had stupidly hoped we would, but then said boyfriend went and fucked it all up, leaving our friendship broken beyond repair.

I peer into my former best friend's eyes, and the hairs on the back of my neck stand on end. Of course she'd be here. It's where she stalks her prey.

"Brianna. It's sooooo good to see you." Her voice is coated with venom—get too close and you'll get poisoned.

"Giselle."

The whooshing of the water flowing from the sink isn't enough to drown out her shrill voice. The soap lathers between my hands as my focus becomes obsessed with watching the tiny bubbles pop. The warmth from the spout isn't enough to distract me from the sinking feeling in my stomach. Conversations with her are never good.

Her gaze feels like tiny spiders crawling beneath my skin. The blood drains from my face when her eyes trace every curve of my body, nausea clawing at my gut. My mouth feels like I ate a giant spoonful of peanut butter, and there's no water to cut through the thickness.

I can't stay in this bathroom forever. It's a decent-sized bathroom, but with Giselle being in here, it feels like it's been slashed in half. I dry off my now pruney fingers with a paper towel, making a beeline for the door, only to have her step in between me and the exit.

"That was quite the little performance you gave back there. I hope you got paid well." She smirks, and the insinuation isn't lost on me. Either I'm a porn star or an escort. Normally, I wouldn't let her get to me. The old version of me would refuse to let her lack of self-worth get the better of me. Now, I can't seem to muster up the courage to fight back.

"I don't know what you're talking about. Now, if you'll excuse me." I attempt to push past her again, but she stands firm in her spot.

"Asher really is good with his hands, isn't he? Has been since high school, especially at parties. You remember that one party, right?" Giselle's villainous grin turns my stomach sour.

How could I forget? It's the reason for my hatred for her.

And Asher.

Sophomore year of high school

Damn, Asher looks good. I stand up from the couch; my body sways and my head feels dizzy. How much have I had to drink? I look down at the red Solo cup, then back at Asher. If I'm going to follow through with my plan, I need as much liquid courage as possible. I toss the remainder of the drink back and paste on a confident smile before making my way toward him. I make sure to add an extra sway to my hips, hoping that he'll notice and want to pull me away from the party to do not so safe for work things. I search for my brother, making sure he's nowhere near his best friend. If I'm going to embarrass myself, I'd rather him not be around to witness it. And I don't think he wants to hear his little sister whisper dirty, dirty things to his best friend.

"Asher," I slur my words, throwing my arms around him. I can't believe I'm acting on my years-long crush.

"Woah. Hi, bear." Asher stumbles back from the force of my hug. I don't care. His arms are around my waist, and I feel his touch everywhere.

"How much have you had to drink? Maybe we need to cool it a little, huh?" Asher laughs.

"I'm not that drunk. There is something I want, though." I whisper in his ear, and I swear I hear him groan. Excellent, my plan is working.

"Oh, yeah? What's that?"

I lean in closer so that I'm right next to his ear when I whisper, "I want your dick inside me, painting my pussy with your cum." I feel Asher's arms tighten around my body as he takes a sharp inhale.

"Bri, I–" he starts, but I interrupt him.

"Hold that thought. I need to pee." I run to the bathroom. When I finish and come out, I am stopped by the queen bitch herself.

Giselle.

"I think it's cute, your little crush on Asher. Guys like him don't go for plain girls like you. I would know." Giselle grins at me as she wipes the corners of her mouth.

"That man sure knows what to do with his dick." Giselle winks, cackling as she walks away.

And just like that, my plan is ruined. And I'm now sober as fuck. I finish my business before I walk out. I notice Asher trying to capture my attention, but I ignore him. He thinks he can do shit like that and continue what we were about to do? Ha. Think again, pretty boy.

"What do you want, Giselle?" I ask, blinking back the tears that are threatening to come.

"Why would I ever need anything from you? You'll just take what you want anyway." Giselle finally steps out of my way, but not before sending her final blow.

"I hope you know we fucked the other day. He may call you when he wants a *good time*, but I'm the one they call when they want to be satisfied the right way. That shirt is a little *too* tight, don't ya think?" She wiggles her fingers at me before flipping her hair over her shoulders and walking out the door.

See? Everyone can see how pathetic you are. Asher only fucked you because he feels sorry for you. Laughter from outside the door briefly interrupts my internal dialogue, only to use it against me seconds later. *You hear that? I bet Asher is telling everyone about how gross your body is. If it weren't for Avery asking for his help, he wouldn't be hanging around you.*

Tears are freefalling over my cheeks now, and my breath lodges in my throat, suffocating me as if I swallowed a softball. I need to get out of here. I make it about halfway to the bar's exit, my phone open to the Uber app, before I feel a hand gripping my arm.

"What are you doing? I thought I told you to stay in the office." Asher. Of course he would spot me. I don't answer him, but any attempts to shake myself free are thwarted when he turns me around.

"Bear, what happened?" Asher's face is distorted with concern.

"Don't call me that." Hurt laces my tone. I really don't want him to see me cry. "Let me go."

"No."

"No? Asher, I-I can't be here. I n-need to go." My voice cracks with each word.

"No, you're gonna stay here and we're gonna talk about it. You know how dumb the miscommunication trope is in books. We aren't going to play those games when we can have a conversation. You can either walk into my office willingly, or I'll throw you over my shoulder and bring you in there myself. What's it gonna be?"

Asher is completely serious. Also, how the hell does he know about *book tropes*? I'll have to ask him about that. I have no choice but to talk to him, but I'm terrified of the answers I might get. I yank my arm out of his hold and walk back to his office, but not before hearing him murmur *good girl.*

"Give me a few minutes and I'll join you." I try not to flinch when he kisses my forehead by the door of the office, but I can't help it. Asher notices, and a hurt expression flashes across his face before he pastes on a smile. This is going to be a fun conversation.

Asher

The plans I have for her and that body

WHAT THE FUCK HAPPENED? When I left, Bri was purring like a content kitten. Now, she's one second from fleeing. I'm simultaneously serving a patron while wracking my brain as to what happened when Gage claps me on the shoulder.

"Hey, Ace. Just a heads up, Giselle is here," he informs me.

The hair on the back of my neck stands on end. Fuck...This won't be good.

"Okay, and?" I could give a rat's ass about that woman.

"Well, Giselle spotted your girl on her way to the bathroom and made a beeline for her. I saw Giselle walk out with a smile on her face, and Bri looked like she wanted to disappear."

Everything makes sense now. Giselle lives for drama. Rage bubbles like lava in my veins as I think about all the possibilities that could have transpired in that bathroom. Spoiler alert, none of them are good.

"Hey, do me a favor. Close down early. I need to talk to my girl."

"You got it."

Groans and curses erupt within the bar when Gage announces last call, but I couldn't give a shit. My priority right now is Bri.

I step into my office to find Bri curled in a ball on the couch, tears streaming down her face. Pain wraps around my heart like a noose threatening to squeeze the life out of me as I watch her body shake with hurt I'm determined to fix. I crouch down in front of her, brushing some of her wavy tendrils from her face.

"Look at me." Desperation seeps from my voice.

She shakes her head a few times, but eventually, her eyes meet mine. My stomach bottoms out and my heart threatens to fall to my feet. Bri peers up at me with bloodshot eyes, puffy cheeks, and fuck does she look beautiful. Even with tear-stained cheeks, she's stunning.

"What did she say?" I ask. Her eyes widen and a soft gasp escapes past her lips.

"H-How did you know?"

"Gage told me about her following you."

"It's stupid. We aren't even, like, together or anything. I mean, we never said we were exclusive. We haven't even had sex yet, so just for—"

"Let's get a few things straight. One, you and me? We're fucking exclusive. Two, I don't know what Giselle told you, but her and I have never happened. And three—" I grip her chin in my hand, my gaze burning into hers. I need her to understand that I'm serious. "And this is the most important part, bear. It's only you and me, baby. I'm fucking you, and only you. My cock belongs to you and *only* you. Just like your pussy belongs to me and *only* me. I'm not opposed to murder, so there better not be anyone else."

"N-No. There isn't anyone else. Giselle got in my head about high school, and my brain went wild after that," Bri admits.

"What are you talking about, Bri?"

"Remember that one party? Where I, um…" Bri's voice trails off, her gaze ping ponging around the room, looking for something to focus on. I gently cup her cheek, watching as her eyes flutter closed.

"Care to finish that sentence?" I know *exactly* what party she's referring to, but I want to hear her say it. I *need* to.

"Asher." My name comes out in a hushed whisper, caressing my body like a feather.

"Brianna." I refuse to let her cower.

"When I, um, asked you to fuck me."

Bri's chin lifts, her eyes sparkling with fierce determination.

"Bear, that's not something I'd *ever* forget. But if I remember correctly, I tried getting your attention later that night and instead received the cold shoulder."

"Yeah. I had the biggest crush on you back then. I had this plan to make my move only to have it ruined by Giselle saying y'all had sex earlier that night. When I saw you trying to get my attention, I saw red. I hated you so much at that moment. And I—"

"She lied."

"W-What?"

"She. Lied. I've never had sex with her, Bri. Not now, and sure as fuck not then. Not when I've only ever wanted one person. I'd rather take an oath of abstinence than be with her."

"Oh." She blinks up at me, astonishment flashing across her beautiful features.

"Yeah, oh. I've only had eyes for one woman. A striking, sarcastic, funny brunette. With the most incredible brown eyes and the most killer ass I've ever seen." I watch as recognition crosses her face.

"Me?"

"Yes, Bri. You. I've been gone for you for years. Why would I want to throw that away by sleeping with Giselle?"

"I'm sorry..." Bri hangs her head, her shoulders touching her ears. I cup her cheeks with my face and watch her body visibly relax.

"You don't have to apologize. I'm sorry she made you feel like I was messing with her when all I've ever wanted is you."

"But she's stunning. I wouldn't blame you if you—"

"Stand up," I demand.

"What?" Lines form in between Bri's brows as she stares at me with a startled expression.

"You heard me. Stand up." This time, I don't wait for her to move. I grab her arms and bring her over to the full length mirror in the corner of my office. I stand off to the side of Bri, but we are still both in the mirror.

"What do you see?" I ask her. Bri looks like she's seen a ghost. Her pupils dilate, and she looks as if she's ready to drop to the ground and curl up in a fetal position.

"I-I can't. D-Don't make me." I bring her back over to the couch. I lay down first before bringing her on top of me, but she resists.

"I'm going to squish you."

"That's what you're worried about?" I snort, knowing and hating the implication. "You can't hurt me." My fingers scrape across her skin, and I watch as gooseflesh ripples across her body.

"Now, come here," I growl at her, noticing her eyes widen like saucers and her spine snapping straight.

Bri hesitates briefly before laying on top of me. I open my legs so she can nestle in between them, and I run my fingertips up and down her spine.

"What happened there? In the mirror." I have never seen someone react so strongly to seeing themselves before.

"I don't like looking at myself. I still struggle with loving my body. It's why I put that on my list to work on."

"What do you see when you look in the mirror?"

"I see failure. I see ugly. I see someone I don't recognize—a stranger. I see someone I don't love." That last word—love—hits me right in the gut.

"Baby..." My voice is a husky whisper washing over her. "You're gorgeous." My eyes trails down her body, lingering on every inch I want to trace with my tongue.

"Your beauty radiates from that perfect, caring heart of yours. You push your friends to be the best they can be." I suck in a breath before continuing, "You push me to be the best I can be. And that body of yours?" I grip her chin with my fingers, hoping to drive home just how serious I'm being. "It drives me fucking wild. You drive me fucking crazy. I even started reading books because of you." That's an admission I didn't think I would share with her so soon, but to hell with it.

"Really?" She looks down at me with a sparkle in her eyes that I haven't seen in a while.

"Yes, really. It started as a way to get close to you. I figured if I started reading the books you were, I could talk to you about them, and that would be the start of something for us. Of course, I never followed through with that, but I still kept reading. I fell in love with it because of you. You inspire people, Bri, and to me, that's the most selfless and beautiful thing a person can do. You inspire me every damn day to be the best version of myself."

"Oh" is all she says. I laid a lot on her, so that's understandable.

"Yeah, oh." I let out a chuckle, our eyes meeting in the mirror.

"Now, this mirror and body image thing, my brother Xander gave me an idea earlier."

Her lips part, creating the perfect O shape. So perfect, my cock twitches in my jeans. *Focus, Asher. Now's not the time.*

"Don't worry, I didn't tell them about your list."

Bri sighs, tension quickly evaporating from her body.

"Do you trust me?"

Bri looks at me with a pained expression, her chin wobbling as she attempts to hold back her tears.

"Bear?"

"Why did you come over that day?"

I flip through every interaction we've had, trying to figure out what day she's talking about.

"Baby, what day are you talk—"

Bri interrupts me and my stomach drops. "Avery told me she asked you to look after me. I—Why did you do it? Am I really that pathetic that you feel like you need to look after me?"

Wait, what? How can she even *think* that she's pathetic? The fuck?

"Brianna, I've never seen you as pathetic. *You* are a goddamn warrior. Anyone would be lucky to bathe in the glow of your strength. I should have told you immediately after she asked me. I have no excuse for hiding that from you. I'm so sorry for feeding into that thought. I've always been amazed by your bravery. I've always been amazed by *you*."

Bri scans my face, looking for a lie I know she won't find. After a thorough, albeit anxiety-inducing assessment, Bri nods her head, and all the air whooshes from my lungs.

"Okay, but I need you to be honest with me. I...You've become an important person to me, and I need you to be open."

I cup her face in my hands before responding. "I promise to be honest with you. Full disclosure, Max also asked me to keep you company, too. And before you overthink things in that pretty head of yours, they just want to make sure you're okay. They love and care about you, Bri."

"I—Okay," Bri replies.

I don't fully believe her, but baby steps. "Now, back to the mirror thing. Do you trust me?" I await her answer with bated breath, hoping she'll say yes, but I'll understand if she doesn't.

Bri looks at me, and a soft smile plays at her lips before she utters four words that make my heart soar. "I trust you completely."

"Be ready tomorrow at twelve-thirty." I give her forehead a quick peck when someone knocks on the door. We adjust our positions so that we are cuddling on the couch instead of lying down.

"Are you planning on telling me what we're doing?"

"Hell no. It's a surprise. Do you need a ride home?" I ask, knowing she still doesn't have a car.

"Yes, please."

"Get everything ready and meet me at the bar when you're done." I place a chaste kiss against her mouth before walking out to help Gage with the closing duties. I'm at the door when I remember something she said earlier.

"Hey, Bri?"

"Yeah?"

"You really had a crush on me, huh?" That interaction I'd had with Max is all starting to make sense now. I'm about 99.9% sure that's what he had been about to say.

"Yes. Clearly, I haven't learned my lesson." Her response reminds me of the old Bri. The one who wasn't afraid of putting me in my place.

"The feeling was mutual, babe." I toss a wink in her direction before closing the door to the office.

Gage and I work in silence, but his gaze glances over in my direction from time to time. He's probably trying to assess the situation with Giselle. I could have called her out for her hateful rhetoric, but Bri needed me.

"You good, man?"

I huff out a sigh, eyes cast toward the ceiling. "I will be. I just, I don't get why Giselle had to tear into Bri like that."

"I'm about to say something that might piss you off. I need you to hear me out fully before you get mad." Gage waits for my curt nod before he continues.

"First, Giselle was way out of line. She shouldn't be saying shit like that to anyone, let alone Bri. She hasn't had it easy in life, and I think something about Bri triggers her."

"Fucking hell, Gage. How can you be defending her? You have sisters. You even have nieces and nephews. What the fuck?" How he's friends with her blows my mind. I never really asked him about it. But I have warned him that she's toxic as hell.

"Not defending, just...I understand her more than most. But, she was in the wrong, and I will be having a conversation with her. I'm not sure it'll do anything, but she and I *will* have words. I'm sorry for what she said. That woman in there," Gage nods to the office before continuing, "is fucking incredible. Giselle doesn't handle jealousy well. And your girl intimidates the shit out of her. I have your back, both of your backs, always."

I let out a long sigh before speaking. "I appreciate it, man. I know you have my back. You always do. Thanks for taking over the closing duties, I appreciate it."

Our exchange is interrupted when Bri comes out of the office, fully dressed and wearing a tired expression. A lot has happened within the last few hours, so her exhaustion makes sense. I take her hand in mine and walk her out to my car. Tomorrow can't come fast enough, and the plans I have for her and that damn body of hers have my dick itching to come out and play.

Brianna

If I let myself, I could fall head over heels for this man

I'VE BEEN STARING AT my computer screen for what seems like fifteen minutes. The more I scroll, the more overwhelmed I become. There are so many options for therapists out there; how are you supposed to know who is the right fit for you? A frustrated sigh leaves my lips, and I do what I've been putting off since the start of my search: text Cas.

> **Me: Hey, Cas. I was hoping you could help me with something.**

> **Cas: Yeah of course. What do ya need?**

> **Me: Got any good referrals for therapists?**

The three dots dance across my screen only for a few seconds, but it feels like minutes.

> **Cas: Yeah. I think you and Dr. Jacqui will be the perfect fit. You can call her at 735-555-5555.**

> **Me: Thank you, Cas, I appreciate it.**

I type the number into my phone and before I lose the courage, I hit dial.

"Thank you for calling Therapy Connections. This is Jacqui speaking, how can I help you?" Her voice instantly puts me at ease, making this decision ten times easier.

"Hi, my name is Brianna Montgomery and I, um, I need to set up an appointment for therapy."

"Hi, Brianna. Thank you for reaching out. Let me check my calendar." The sound of nails clacking on the keyboard echoes in my ear until it nearly shreds my nerves. My heart stampedes like wild horses inside my chest as I wait.

"Ah yes, here we go. I have Tuesdays at ten or eleven a.m. I also have some afternoon slots at one or two p.m. Which works best for you?"

"Um, ten a.m. works for me."

"Great. I just need a good contact number from you."

"Oh, of course. It's 312-444-4444."

"Perfect. I'll put you down for this upcoming Tuesday at ten. If you could come fifteen minutes prior to fill out the necessary paperwork, that would be great. Do you have a pen and paper handy?"

"I do, yeah." She rattles off the address and I write it down, along with adding an appointment reminder on my phone so I don't forget.

"Thank you so much." I'm glad this is a phone conversation so she can't see the sheer panic on my face.

"Of course, I look forward to meeting with you. Have a great day."

I'm scared shitless, but I also feel a sense of relief. I'm finally getting the help I should've gotten after the accident. My appointment is five days away, giving me enough time to prepare mentally and emotionally.

My doorbell rings, and when I glance at my phone, I see that it's twelve-thirty on the dot. Asher is nothing if not punctual. I'm curious about what he has planned for us today since he was being rather evasive last night. He didn't give me any specifics in regard to what I'm supposed to wear, so I'm in black leggings and the same oversized t-shirt from the night he stayed over after taking us home from the bar.

When I open the door, it's the first thing he notices. He eyes me like I'm his prey.

"You're lucky we have plans, otherwise I'd take you on your couch," Asher groans.

"You didn't tell me how to dress, so this is what you get."

I wasn't *trying* to seduce him. That was just an added bonus to me wanting to be comfortable. We walk up to his car, and when he opens my door, I'm floored at what I see. On the passenger seat is a pack of sour gummy worms.

"W-What are these for?" Emotion clogs my throat, making it sound like I swallowed sawdust.

"Well, I wasn't sure how you'd feel about being in a car, so I wanted to make sure you had your comfort snack just in case. I even have soothing music queued up on my phone for us to listen to."

I don't think, I just throw my arms around his neck, bringing my lips to his. I give him access to my mouth, allowing myself to become dizzy from the lack of oxygen. His tongue tangles with mine, and when I take it between my lips and suck, Asher grunts, and his hands grip my ass with a bruising intensity. I claw and pull at his hair, and he pulls me in so that my body is flush against his. His cock grinds against me and stars dance in my peripherals. Fuck, this man can kiss.

Asher is the one to break the kiss first, and I can only imagine how crazed we look.

"What was that for?" Asher pants.

"For being so thoughtful. For thinking of my comfort and making sure I feel safe."

"You always have a safe place with me. You're a once in a lifetime woman, Bri, and you deserve to be treated as such. And I'll make damn sure to tell you as often as you need."

My heart melts at his thoughtful words. I think of everything he's done for me, including that little reading confession, and I can't help but smile. If I let myself, I could fall head over heels for this man. Maybe I'm already falling. Would it be so bad?

Asher buckles me in my seat, and I immediately tear into the gummy worms, my mouth salivating as the sour sugar coats my tongue.

The moment Asher is in the driver's seat, he turns toward me holding a black, silky object in his hand.

"I didn't know you were into bondage."

"Relax, you dirty girl. I just want our destination to be a surprise. Can I?" Asher holds the blindfold out toward me, giving me the option to say no.

But something about this has my blood heating with desire. I nod my head before I feel the smooth fabric cover my eyes. He tugs at the tie in the back, but not enough to cause pain. The soft purr of the engine roars to life, only to be drowned out by his classical music playlist.

The blindfold feels glorious across my eyelids. I'm a happy woman. I have my soothing music, sour gummy worms in my lap, and a gorgeous man next to me. A man who has yet to let go of my hand. Asher's thumbs rub soothing circles on the back of my hand, and I melt into the seat.

The car comes to a sudden stop, and I assume we've reached our destination. I attempt to pull off the blindfold, but Asher stops me with his hand.

"Not until I get you out of the car. Patience, my dear Bri, patience." I can't see it, but when Asher's driver's side door opens and closes, I assume he's rounding the car to get me. Soon enough, I'm being pulled out, and he's walking me in some random direction.

"I'm going to take this off now. I need you to have an open mind when I do."

What on earth would I need to have an open mind for? But the second the fabric is removed from my eyes, it all makes sense.

"A lingerie store? A freaking lingerie store. How is this supposed to help me with my body image, Asher? I already struggle with what's underneath my clothes. But me in lingerie? Why would I wear less clothes to fix how I view myself?"

"It might not, but I have a feeling it might help you see what I see. What everyone sees. Will you do this for me? And if you hate everything you try on, we will walk away and never look back." Asher looks at me with a pleading expression, and I feel my resolve dissolving like a Listerine strip.

"Fine. But I don't have any money on me. I can't buy anything even if I want to."

"I'll take care of you. This is as much for me as it is for you. I've always been good at taking care of what's mine, and that includes you. So, let's go." Asher smacks my ass before dragging me into the shop.

The second I walk inside, I'm immediately overwhelmed. Every color of the rainbow is scattered across the store. Some pieces are more conservative, whereas others are basically ribbons tied together. The walls are a deep purple with a dark wood flooring, with about six enormous dressing rooms the size of walk-in closets. This place is fancy, and I'm struggling to feel like I belong.

"Welcome to The Madam's Boutique. My name is Jessica, how can I help you?"

"Hi, I'm Asher. We have an appointment."

Asher reaches out to shake Jessica's outstretched hand. She's a stunning woman in her mid-thirties with curves for days. Like, seriously, she's stunning. She has shoulder-length brown hair and the most beautiful brown eyes I have ever seen.

"Oh, yes. Bri, is it?" she asks while turning to me. I expect her to snarl at me, but her tone is nothing but welcoming.

"Yes, hi. It's nice to meet you." I go to shake her hand, but she's pulling me into a bone crushing hug.

"The pleasure is all mine. I'm excited to be styling you today. You are absolutely beautiful. Your boyfriend here has good taste to bring you here." Jessica winks at me.

"Oh, he's not—" I say at the same time Asher says, "That I do." *Well, that's something I'll have to unpack later.*

"Perfect, right this way. I need to take some measurements before giving you some pieces I think will work for you. Are there any colors that are an automatic no?"

"Um, I guess yellow and orange. I don't think either of those colors flatter me."

"Give her as much red as you can. She looks hot in red," Asher chimes in.

"We shall see what we come up with. Right this way, you two. Asher dear, you can sit on the chair outside the dressing room while we measure. Then once I pick everything, Bri can show you all the pieces we've picked out."

"H-He's going to see me in these?" I gulp at thought.

"Why, of course, sweetie. The man's seen you in less, so this should be a walk in the park." Jessica pulls me into the dressing room and has me dress down to my bra and panties while she measures me every which way.

The moment she finishes scribbling down my measurements, she turns to me with a face-splitting grin. "Okay, great. I have everything I need. Before I go pull some pieces I know you'll just *die* for, I do ask that the only undergarment that we require you to keep on is your underwear. Any questions?'

"Um, no. I-I think I'm good."

"Great, I will be right back with a few sets."

The door clicks softly shut behind her, leaving me and my insecurities locked in this medium sized room. As if my anxiety summoned him, a soft knock on the door sounds. The way my body melts and my worries vanish, I know it's Asher before he opens his mouth.

"How are we doing in there?"

"Um, okay. I'm currently avoiding the giant mirror behind me, but I'm getting anxious about having to look at myself."

"I'm so proud of you for doing this, baby. This is a huge step for you, and you are so goddamn beautiful when you push yourself. It's a total turn on for me, if I'm being honest."

"I could walk around in a garbage bag, and you'd probably still be sporting a hard on," I joke. Asher brings the real Bri out to play, and I am so thankful for it. I miss her, and whenever she pops up, I cling to her for as long as I can.

"You're not wrong. Oh, perfect timing, Jessica."

I'm standing in nothing but my panties now the second Jessica enters my dressing room with two armfuls of items. She places them delicately on the hooks before giving me two thumbs up and leaving me alone.

The first piece is a rose petal pink lace and silk slip dress. The material is soft to the touch and glides on like butter. It feels amazing against my skin. I shake away any lingering anxiety before I open the door to show Asher.

"Damn. You look amazing. Turn around for me?" I do a slow turn, giving him a full three-sixty view. "How do you feel in it?"

"It feels like heaven on me."

"It'll look like heaven on the floor, too," he practically growls, hooking his finger toward me. "Now, come here." Asher stands while holding out one of his hands to me. The second my hand links with his, he walks me over to the mirror and I breathe through the anxiety. I was expecting to hate everything about it, but when I see myself in the full length mirror, I gasp in shock.

"I-Is that really me?" I can't believe it. My hands cup my cheeks as I admire my reflection.

"It is, and you are breathtaking. This thing makes your thighs look incredible." My hands fall to my stomach as I turn left and right before coming back to center.

"I-I don't hate it. I...I look—"

"Stunning," Asher finishes for me. He gives my bare shoulder a soft peck before pushing me back into the dressing room to try on the next item.

The next piece Jessica chose for me is a matching bra and panty set in black lace with a matching waist garter belt with stockings. It slips on with ease. I chance a look at the mirror—needing to have this moment to myself. I deserve to look in the mirror and love what I see.

When I turn around, I can't help but blurt out, "Oh, fuck." The woman staring back at me isn't some disgusting, ugly woman. No. What I see is a powerful, sexy woman who's gone through the wringer and is still a damn warrior. I finally see myself as beautiful.

"What? What happened? Is everything okay?" I can hear Asher walk over to the door. The second he opens it, his jaw is on the floor, and I watch him adjust himself before clearing his throat.

"*Oh fuck* is right. You look like a goddess. A fucking queen. And I want to get on my knees and worship you properly."

"I still have one more item to try on, so off you go." I push him out the door with his tongue practically hanging out of his mouth. The last set is a silky, bright red—because of course—push up bra with a high waisted G-string thong bottom. This, too, slips on easily and fits like a glove. Okay, Asher is right. Red is my color. This set compliments my tanned skin and dark hair perfectly. I look like sin in this matching bra and panties, and there's only one man I want to sin with.

"I'm dressed, you can come in." I'm playing with fire, and I don't mind getting burned. I'm admiring myself in the mirror when I hear the door click shut behind me. The sound of the lock echoes throughout the room, and I toss a sultry smile over my shoulder.

"Bri, I've been a patient man, but you in red? That's my fucking kryptonite. You've been such a good girl stepping out of your comfort zone. And good girls need to be rewarded and celebrated. So, on your knees, baby."

Brianna

Crawl to me

ASHER STALKS TOWARD ME, but I hold my hand up to stop him. He's not in charge right now. I am.

"Today is about me, right?" I ask.

"Yes, of course it is."

"Then it's my turn to play. You said I'm a queen and you will praise me like one? So, get on your hands and knees and crawl to me," I demand.

Fuck, this feels good. Not many of my past hook-ups allowed me to be the dominant one. But the ones that did? Fuck, it's exhilarating.

Without hesitation, Asher drops to his knees, never breaking eye contact with me as he slowly crawls toward me on his hands and knees. He attempts to get up when he reaches me, but I push him back down. "Uh-uh. I never said you could get up. Take off my underwear. With your hands this time—we aren't total animals." Asher is very attuned to me and knows that this is what I need right now, so he listens to every demand I give him.

Asher sees me in a way no other man has. He somehow knows that sour gummy worms are my comfort food. He knows to play classical music to calm me down. Not sure *how* he knows exactly, seeing as how it's a piece of me not many people outside of Avery knows. Despite the distance I placed between the two of us over the years, he just...knows. Being seen so intimately is scary enough, but being seen by *Asher*? It feels like taking a bra off after a long day at work—freeing, refreshing.

Beneath the spotlight of Asher's gaze, I finally feel worthy enough to be loved. But most importantly, it gives me permission to love myself. Something I realize I've started to do ever since he knocked on my door a couple of weeks ago.

I'm standing in nothing but a bra as my panties are now at my feet. I use his shoulders to step out of them before I push him down so that he's sitting on his haunches. I throw one of my legs over his shoulder and smirk down at him before making my next demand.

"I want you to eat me out like it's a royal feast. I want to ride your face until your chin is dripping with my cum."

"As you wish, your highness." I catch a glimpse of his smile before his head dives in between my legs.

Asher wastes no time getting to work on my throbbing clit. His tongue swirls in that circular motion I like, and I toss my head back. Asher flattens his tongue, and the tiny grooves send electrical currents down my spine as I let out a loud whimper. He does it over and over again, and I can't help but grind against his face. My hands tangle in his sandy, blond hair, my nails scratching his scalp. The way his tongue spreads my pussy? I'd be a puddle on the floor if not for his firm grip on my ass. He licks me from my clit back down to my opening, coaxing a groan from my throat. I dig even further into his scalp until I'm sure he'll have bald spots when all is said and done.

"Oh, fuck. That's good. Holy shit, Asher, you eat my pussy so well. Like you were born to do it." Asher blows cool air on my pulsing clit and my knees buckle. His tight grip on my ass is the only thing that keeps me upright. I'm a hot, squirming mess, finding a rhythm that'll have me seeing stars.

"Do that thing with your tongue again." Asher, being as connected to me as he is, knows exactly what I'm asking for. He flattens his tongue and moves back and forth, slowly picking up his pace.

"Fuck me faster, Asher. I need to come. I'm so—oh, *fuuuck*," I whimper as he sucks my clit in between his teeth. I'm practically assaulting his face with my hips as I chase my orgasm. I ride out the remaining waves as I attempt to catch my breath.

"Oh my God. You're way too good at that. I should be jealous of all the women before me, but I want to send them fucking flowers."

My leg slips off his shoulders, and I barely have a second to process what's happening before Asher has me pinned to the wall, arms clasped in one of his hands, resting above my head.

His chin glistens with my cum, and I watch as he licks as much of myself off of him as he can. He takes one of his fingers to wipe off anything he missed before bringing it to my mouth.

"Be Daddy's good girl and suck." I obediently open my mouth and close around his finger the second it hits my tongue. My eyes roll back in my head and my back arches, searching for friction. Who knew tasting myself would be so hot?

And then Asher whispers five words that have me weak in the knees.

"It's my turn to play."

Asher

"You had your fun, now it's my turn. Does my dirty girl wanna play?" Bri nods her head frantically as her hips buck.

"Ah, my greedy little girl. Are you desperate for this cock?" Bri whimpers, and I can't help but chuckle. My dirty girl wants to be bad.

"Get on your knees." I let go of her arms, which fall limply at her sides. Bri does as I ask, and when she looks up at me underneath her lashes, I almost come on the spot. My cock swells until the head threatens to burst. I need to be inside my girl, and I need to be inside her fast.

A soft knock on the dressing room door startles us both. "Everything okay in there? How are the pieces fitting, Bri?" Jessica asks.

"Um, good, great, thank you. Everything's fine. I just needed Asher's help with something," Bri responds while gripping my dick over my jeans. I swallow down my groan, but my hips involuntarily thrust into her hand.

"Great. I have another client coming in in five minutes, so send Asher to come get me if you need anything." The sound of Jessica's heels clicking on the wood floor slowly begin to fade.

My attention is back on Bri, and she's grinning up at me with wicked intentions behind her eyes.

"I needed to help you with something, huh?" I grip her chin with my thumb and forefinger just tight enough, not to cause any pain.

"And you did an excellent job." Fuck, this girl will be the death of me.

"Now, where were we?" My thumb brushes across her lower lip, eliciting a sharp intake of breath from her sexy mouth.

"Oh, yeah, here's what's gonna happen. You're going to undo my pants and take my cock out. And then I'm going to fuck your pretty little mouth. It's going to look so good wrapped around my cock."

"Yes, sir." Bri works the button and zipper of my jeans, pulling my jeans and underwear down to my ankles in one fell swoop. My cock is pointing straight to her mouth, almost as if it knows where it wants to go. The tip is already leaking with pre-cum, and I watch as Bri's face morphs from desire into concern.

"What's the matter, baby?"

"I'm not sure it'll fit. Asher, that thing is way too big for my mouth."

"It'll fit, baby. Something tells me you can handle anything, and this cock is made for your mouth. So pretty, so plump, and so fuckable. Remember, you have a safe word. Use it if you need it, otherwise stop talking and open up." Shit, maybe that's taking it too far. It's seeing Bri on her knees for me that brings out the dominating side of me.

Bri does as she's told and opens for me. My hand is wrapped around my cock, and I tug it from base to tip, watching as she tracks the motion with parted lips.

"You want to suck this cock, Bri?" I ask.

"Yes." Bri's response is instantaneous.

"Then grab what you want and put it there yourself." The second her hand wraps around me, I almost lose it. My own hand will never be enough anymore. Only her hands. Bri teases the tip by flicking her tongue against it, licking up the pre-cum that's beaded there. Son of a bitch, that feels good.

"Motherfucker, Bri," I growl when she takes her flattened tongue and runs it along the underside once, twice before she takes all of me in her mouth. And damn, does it feel like heaven.

"Hold onto my thighs, baby, and tap out when you need to." She nods her head before I slowly push myself as far as her throat will allow and let her adjust for a moment. Her whimper gives me the green light, so I start off with slow thrusts so she can get used to everything. But if I'm being honest, it's mainly for me. I'd rather not blow my load this early on.

My pace begins to increase, and then before I know it, the animal in me takes over and I'm fucking her face. Bri moans and gags around my cock while I throw my head back and let out a silent roar.

"Shit. You suck my cock so well. Looking like my little slut on your knees for me." I freeze mid thrust and curse myself for calling her such a vulgar thing.

"Fuck. I'm sorry. I was wrapped up in the heat of things, and what I said was uncalled for." Bri lets me go with a soft pop, and what she says to me takes me by surprise.

"I liked it. I'll be your little slut for you anytime you want, Daddy," Bri says before taking my cock back in her mouth. I'm still frozen in place, but then Bri nods her head and looks up at me with *fuck me* eyes, and I lose any sliver of control I have left.

"Good fucking girl. My little slut on her knees for me, sucking me off like she's dying of thirst. I'm going to fuck your face fast and hard. I want tears streaming down your face and drool dripping down your chin. I want that tight little throat around my dick as I fill it with my cum. You'll drink every last drop like the good little slut you are. And if any of it escapes your mouth, I'm going to do it again. Tap once if you understand, or twice to use your safe word."

Bri taps my thigh once, and immediately my fingers are tugging at her scalp. I thrust my hips hard and fast, and she doesn't tap out. No, my dirty girl is taking everything like a champ. Bri lets out a soft moan as her eyes flutter closed.

"Eyes open. I want you to look at me while you're choking on my cock. I want to watch you take every damn inch of me." Bri's eyes remained closed, and I think she's doing it just to rile me up.

"Eyes on me or I stop. And we both know you're too greedy to stop sucking me off. You were meant to suck my cock, bear. So put those goddamn gorgeous eyes on me." She looks at me, and I can feel the tingle at the base of my spine.

"Oh, shit, I'm close. I hope you're ready to drink every last drop of me." Bri's hands travel up from my thighs, and just when I think she's about to tap out, she grabs my balls, and that's all it takes for me to detonate. I'm coming down her throat with an intensity like never before. Bri is just staring up at me, tears leaking down her face as she takes it all.

"That's right, baby. Be a good little cum slut and drink it all. I know you're thirsty for it." I watch her throat bob as she takes it all. I'm completely spent by the end of it, but Bri is running her hand up and down my shaft, milking everything she can before letting me go.

She barely has time to catch her breath as she stands before I'm slamming her into a wall and kissing the fuck out of her. That was one of the hottest things I've ever experienced. I pour every ounce of my feelings into this kiss, more specifically those three little words I shouldn't say yet. And maybe I'll never get to. She's still finding herself, and I can't take that away from her, no matter how badly I want her to love me back. I peck her lips a few times before pulling away.

"Fuck, you did so well. Are you okay?"

"Yeah, I'm good. Now we need to get out of here and go home. I could use a nap."

"I think it's safe to assume you want to take everything home?"

"I do, but Asher I said I don't—" I interrupt her with a chaste kiss on her lips.

"And I said I got you. I'll grab the other two sets, and you just get dressed. Then you can hand me the rest, and we'll check out." I gather the two pieces in my hand and give her some privacy while she gets herself situated. This girl makes everything feel right.

Bri opens the dressing room door and hands me the red number we christened. I hold her hand the entire way to the register. When everything is checked out, we head to the car, and I ask her if she wants the blindfold back on.

"No, I think I'm okay. I feel safe with you. I know you'd never let anything happen to me." Such simple words that pack a powerful punch to the heart.

"I'll always protect you. For as long as you'll have me." We fall into a comfortable silence on the drive home, and when Bri asks me to come inside, I decline. Not because I don't want to, but because after everything she did today, I want her to spend time with herself.

She's about to get out of the car before I stop her. "I want you to do something for me. I want you to go look at yourself in the mirror and just admire yourself. You are a masterpiece that should be admired and cherished, and I need you to start doing that for yourself."

"Okay. I will. Thank you for today, Asher. It's the first time in months that I looked into the mirror and felt beautiful, powerful. And I wouldn't have wanted to do it with anyone but you. Thank you for always seeing me even when I refused to see myself." She leans over and gives me a peck on the cheek before she hops out of the car. The heat of her kiss still lingers while her words swirl around in my mind.

I've always seen you, Bri.

Brianna

I am beautiful in any body

I'M DOING IT. I'M standing in front of the mirror, fully nude and just admiring myself, waiting for a panic attack that never comes. I tilt my head to left and right as my hands explore my body. I trace my ample curves and focus on changing the narrative in my mind.

I am worth more than my looks. I am beautiful in any body. I am worthy of all forms of love. I will learn to love and embrace the body I'm in.

I turn to the side and admire my ass. Damn. Okay, my ass is amazing. It's round and full, and I now see Asher's obsession. I turn to face the mirror again and trace intricate patterns woven across my thighs and stomach and force myself to accept them. Fake it 'til you make it, so I'm going to start making myself love them. They are just marks on my body. They tell the story of my trauma and what I'm still working through.

I love myself and all the marks on my skin. They don't define who I am. Only I do that.

My hands toy with my generous breasts. Like my ass, they are voluptuous, and I know I should be proud of them. Women pay lots of money to get what I have naturally. I pinch my nipples with my forefingers and let my head roll back as pleasure pulses throughout my body. I think of Asher and everything we did in that dressing room, and my clit throbs.

Who knew admiring myself in the mirror would be so arousing? I hurriedly rush to my bed when an idea strikes. I grab my tripod and set it up so that it can frame the part of me I'll be playing with. I switch the mode to video and grab the remote before laying on my bed.

I get myself in a comfortable position before pressing record. My legs spread as wide as they can and my hand slips between my legs. My finger slips inside my pussy, and I can feel how wet I am. I focus on the sensation of pumping my finger in and out, curling it against my inner walls.

"This is what you do to me, Asher. You've given a part of myself back. The part who enjoys sex again. You've turned me into a horny puddle all the time, and I want you to see what you do to me." My words come out breathless when I pinch my clit and my hips buck in response. I'm full on panting like a cat in heat now, my fingers swirling around my clit in slow, circular motions. My cunt is throbbing with arousal, and I need to slow it down.

"You make me feel sexy, beautiful. I feel worthy to be loved and to be worshiped. This is all because you made me look in the mirror. I'm fucking myself because I liked what I saw in the mirror. I'm a knockout, and my curves are to be celebrated and not shamed. You took me shopping and helped me own who I am. You brought me my comfort snack knowing I would be nervous about driving. You held my hand the entire drive. I like how you look at me. I like how you fuck me. I like how you understand me. You never ask me to change, and I can never find the words to say. So let me just do this instead."

I pinch my clit between my fingers before circling it with my thumb. I feel heat pooling at the base of my spine and my breathing picks up. My thumb works overtime as my orgasm begins to build.

"Fuck. Asher. Asher. Asher. You make me do this. You've ruined me for every other man. Oh my God, ASHER!" I scream his name as I come harder than I have by myself in a long time.

I mean, this is the first time I've masturbated in months. The thought of touching myself made me feel disgusted. I never thought the body I have now should be celebrated. Now? I plan to flaunt what I have—even if I'm not one hundred percent loving myself fully. I'm a lot further than I was months ago, so I'll take it.

My body is trembling as it comes down from my mind-blowing orgasm. I remove my finger from my pussy, and get up close to the camera before bringing my finger into my mouth and cleaning myself off. I swirl my tongue around my finger, and a soft moan escapes my lips. I stare into the camera before turning it off. Before I lose my confidence, I pull up Asher's number, attach the video, and hit send.

About thirty minutes later, I get a text from Asher.

Asher: *image*

It's a picture of Asher gripping his cock, a drop of pre-cum glistening at his tip. My mouth waters and visions of his cock in my mouth have me squirming on the spot.

> **Asher: Damn, baby, that was so fucking hot. Look at my girl owning her hotness. Sexy as fuck, bear.**

> **Asher: Is this what you wanted? Me pumping my cock, wishing it was your mouth instead?**

My entire body heats and my clit begins to throb.

> **Me: Well, I invited you inside, but you declined. So, I guess it's just you and your hand tonight.**

> **Asher: Fuck me. I'm really regretting that decision right now.**

> **Me: * laughing emoji* *kissy face emoji***

> **Asher: Oh it's funny, huh?**

> **Me: ...maybe**

> **Asher: I wonder if it'll be that funny when I'm shoving my cock so far down your throat you'll choke.**

> **Me: ...**

> **Asher: What, no smart remark? I'm disappointed, bear. But I'm so goddamn proud of you, baby. Seeing you learn to accept your body is hot as fuck.**

> **Me: You make me feel sexy.**

> **Asher: No, you are sexy all on your own. Now I need to take care of this situation you put me in. But Bri?**

Me: Yeah?

Asher: Just know it'll be your name that I'm yelling. And as I'm fucking my fist, I'm thinking of how it feels to call you mine. Night, Bri.

His.

The more I think about it, the more appealing it sounds. I think about sharing my life, my fears, my vulnerabilities with anyone else, and it feels wrong.

His.

I realize I want nothing more than to be his person. I put falling in love on my list, but maybe I need to make an amendment to that item. I don't want to fall in love with anyone but Asher Larson. Hell, I'm probably already halfway there.

Brianna

How is he here right now?

TODAY IS MY FIRST therapy session, and I'm beyond nervous. I take the cloudless sky as a good sign that I am on the right path. Well, that and there was zero traffic on the drive over. Ted, my Uber driver, was incredible. He could sense some nervousness and offered me control of the music, so naturally I put on comforting spa sounds. The theme of the day seems to be tranquility, because the moment we pulled into the parking lot, I knew this was where I needed to be. The soft brick exterior with vines crawling up the side is surrounded by a slew of trees—which I guess makes sense since nature can be quite therapeutic. Whoever chose this location had their patients in mind. To my right is a white, metal bench and over to the left is a bird feeder. I watch as robins flutter their wings while pecking at the bird feed.

I thought the outside was inviting, but it doesn't compare to the inside of the therapy office. The walls of the waiting room are a soft lilac blue, providing a sense of security and comfort. The hardwood flooring is deep gray, and scattered throughout the room are a mixture of velvet chairs and couches in dark gray and blue. I anxiously check my phone for the hundredth time, and that's when I see a text from Asher.

> **Asher:** Hey, bear. I wanted to say how proud I am of you for going to therapy. You are a headstrong, determined woman. If you need anything please let me know. You got this, baby ▢

> **Me:** Thank you. I'm so nervous but it's time.

> **Asher:** Curious, what therapy place did you end up choosing?

> **Me:** Therapy Connections. Cas gave me the recommendation and when I talked to the therapist on the phone, I instantly felt relief. I think this is a good fit.

> **Asher:** Yeah, that's where I went when I was dealing with everything with my brother. I'll let you go. Proud of you.

I'm smiling like a crazy person when I hear footsteps. I look up and the woman in front of me screams no-judgement.

Dr. Jacqui gives off a witchy vibe with a crystal necklace hanging from her neck. She's dressed in an off white sweater with a dark green, corduroy skirt. She has on lacy, black, pattern tights with black combat boots on. I internally shake my head. Cas *would* recommend this woman to me. Her brown hair is in soft waves that rest against her shoulders, and she has a cat in a witches hat pin on her sweater. Already, I feel at ease in her presence.

"Hello, Brianna. Welcome." She offers me a reassuring smile as I hand her the completed paperwork. "Oh, good, you've completed everything. You can follow me back to my office."

We enter her office, and it gives the same vibe as the waiting room. But instead of blue walls, they are a soft cream color, and the couch is forest green. I sit down and it feels like a hug from a friend. Dr. Jacqui goes over the rules of confidentiality and that I have complete control in what I choose to share.

"What brings you here to see me?" Dr. Jacqui asks.

Oh, okay, so we're jumping right in. I wring my hands in my lap, but the clamminess has them sliding around with ease. My mind races as I brace myself.

You need this, Bri. This is the start of healing. The start of being you again.

I suck in a deep breath and start out with words barely above a whisper.

"We were in an accident." I can't meet her eyes. Flashes of that night threaten to rip me from the present moment. I need to get this out before I lose all courage. I clear my throat, my grip against the plush couch grounding me to the here and now before continuing.

"My brother and I were on our way to an outing, and we got hit by a drunk driver who blew through a red light. I only had a minor concussion and a few scratches, but my brother, Max, suffered the most. He was in a coma and had to have multiple surgeries."

Jacqui's silence permeates the space, and I hate that I can't read her expression. My breath catches in my throat as I wait for the inevitable judgement.

"I am so sorry that you had to go through that. How painful that must have been both emotionally and physically. How are you coping with everything?" Her words feel like a hug from a friend, warm and inviting, giving me the courage to continue.

"In the beginning, I was really depressed. I couldn't leave my house or even take care of myself. It was a dark place for me. I've slowly started to live again, but I'm still struggling with a few things."

"Might I ask what those things would be?"

"Um, well, I've gained a lot of weight since everything, which, up until recently, I've had a hard time coming to terms with."

"What happened recently to shift your perspective?"

"Um, well, my brother's best friend, Asher, has been helping me. He's really been helping me push myself out of my comfort zone. He's been a lifesaver, really."

"Sounds like you found a great partner to help you through everything."

"Oh, no, we aren't together. He's more of a...um—"

"Friends with benefits?" Dr. Jacqui interrupts.

"Oh, no. I don't even know how to describe our relationship, but it feels like it's more than that."

"I see, well, whatever the relationship is between you two, I'm glad you have someone to support you."

"Yeah. My best friend, Avery, has also been a saint in this whole process. I ghosted her for a while when I was struggling, but she waited for me with open arms when I was ready to come back."

"That's wonderful to hear. How are you and Max?"

"That's where things get complicated. I, um, haven't seen him or my parents since my friend Avery's wedding." I look down, unwilling to meet the discernment that I assume will be on her face.

"May I ask why?" Her question has me breaking down. I'm falling apart on her couch.

"I feel guilty for everything. It's all my fault he was in the hospital in the first place. It's all because I wanted to go fucking axe throwing that this happened. My parents have been texting me asking how I've been, and

I'm ignoring them. I can't seem to face them knowing what I did and how they probably hate me. Anytime they'd look at me, I saw their pain. Pain I caused with my selfishness. It's all my fault. It's all my fault." I bury my head in my hands as shame sits like a heavy boulder on my chest. It feels good to spill my true feelings to a stranger, but I still feel awful.

"You are carrying a lot of unnecessary guilt. That's some heavy stuff you're holding onto. You have permission to feel all those feelings, but I feel like it's a lot to take on when the blame lies elsewhere. I understand it may feel like your family hates you. Our minds can be a powerful weapon, using our insecurities as their bullets. I'm glad you decided to come today, and I'm happy you're here. I want to give you some information on a type of therapy that I feel would be a good fit for you." She gets up to rifle through her desk as I look around the room for tissues.

Dr. Jacqui comes back with a small pamphlet in her hand and gives it to me. On the front are the words EMDR, or Eye Movement Desensitization and Reprocessing, with lots of words describing the process. From my understanding, it's a technique to help the brain reprocess trauma so it no longer impacts your life. It sounds intense and extremely invasive.

"Take that information home with you and let me know next session if you feel like it's a good fit for you." We spend the rest of my session working through some of my feelings, and it feels nice to spill everything that's been a massive burden in my heart. We set a date and time for next week, and by the time I'm walking out of the building to call a rideshare, I'm exhausted. I get as far as pulling up the app when I hear a familiar voice.

"Hi, baby." I snap up when I hear Asher's voice.

He's leaning against his door, hands in his pocket and one leg crossed over the other. How is he here right now? Why is he here? I don't give myself time to answer those questions because I'm running full force into his now outstretched arms. His arms wrap around me at the same time my legs wrap around him. Asher is spinning me in a circle while cradling the back of my head with his hand.

"You're here."

"I'm here. Where else would I be? I knew you'd need me, so I'm here."

"How are you real? Like, this is some book boyfriend level shit." I pull back so I can look at his face. "How did I get so lucky to have you?"

"Bear, you've always had me. I was yours long before you ever gave me the time of day. You aren't lucky to have me. I'm lucky to have you. You are worthy of someone who will make it their life's mission to make you happy." I bring my lips to his, but it's not a frantic kind of kiss. This kiss is slow, romantic, and has my nervous system aflutter.

"Wait, how did you know when I would be done? I don't think I told you the time."

"When you told me the place, I drove here immediately, well after making a few stops first. I've been here for over an hour."

"You're amazing. Thank you for always knowing what I need before I do." I hop down and Asher walks me around to the passenger side of the car. I let out a gasp the second he opens the door. Sitting on the seat is a bouquet of red roses with white baby's breath and a giant bag of sour gummy worms. My vision becomes blurry with tears.

"What's this?" I ask.

"You did something difficult today, so I needed to get you something as beautiful as you are. I wanted you to know that watching you heal is the most incredible thing I have ever experienced. Watching you find your light again is awe-inspiring. I want you to feel loved and treasured every second of every day."

Asher presses a lingering kiss to my forehead before rounding the car to get into the driver's side. I bring the flowers up to my nose, inhaling their sweet smell. I'm holding the flowers in one hand while my other is interlocked with Asher's. Asher's focus is on the road, while mine is trained on him. My heart feels full, and my head is dizzy with a flood of emotions.

I was already falling for this man, but now I'm head over heels, lost for the man sitting next to me.

Asher

Full of beauty, grace and wonder

I KNEW TODAY WAS going to be hard for Bri, so I knew I needed to do something. I called Avery earlier this morning to see if I could pick up her spare key so I could surprise Bri when she gets home. Of course, Avery wanted every single detail before she agreed to anything. Once I laid out my entire plan, she burst into tears, gushing at how sweet it was.

Avery also filled me in on other things Bri likes to do when she wants to relax. After picking up the key from Avery and Cas' house, I went to a few stores to gather everything I needed. I was setting everything up and making sure everything was in its place when I texted Bri about therapy and where she was going. I needed to pick her up. I knew she would need some support, so it was a no-brainer for me to be there.

Bri and I pull up to her house, and I bring out the blindfold from the lingerie store and hand it to her. I get out of the driver's side so that I can help her from the car to her house.

"Why am I wearing this thing again?" she huffs.

"Patience, bear. You'll find out soon enough." We walk to the house slowly so that she doesn't trip over anything.

"Wait, don't you need my key?"

"Nope, I have Avery's spare."

"Avery? What does she have to do with this?"

"You'll see." The key slips into the lock and the door creaks open. I bring her into the living room where everything is set up. My heart is beating as fast as a hummingbird's wings inside my chest. Everything has to go perfectly.

"Okay, you can take it off now." I hold my breath the entire time it takes her to slip the fabric from her eyes. Bri gasps while her eyes ping pong around the room.

"What...What did you do? How? Why?" Her questions come out in a rapid fire, and I know I did good.

"You did a hard thing today. Well, you've been doing hard things for months, and you deserve to have a self-care day. I called Avery about my plan so that I could use the spare you gave her, and she gave me all the insight I needed. As for why? I wanted to give you everything so I can pamper you. So, that's what I'm going to do." I press a soft kiss to her shoulder before giving her a little push to go explore.

Bri walks to the coffee table that's decorated with all her favorite snacks: sour gummy worms, mustard flavored pretzels, Reese's, and Twix. Rose petals and LED tea lights decorate the entire space, bathing the room in intimate lighting. And a self-care day wouldn't be complete without two face masks, something Avery told me that she loves to do. In the middle of the table is a single rose with a note attached to it.

Brianna,

You remind me of this flower. Full of beauty, grace, and wonder. Your light shines brighter than any woman I've ever met. But I know sometimes it's hard to shine when all you feel is darkness. So let me be your guiding light through your darkest of storms. Anytime you can't see how beautiful you are, I'll be there to tell you how incredible you are. And if you just can't see the light, then I'll sit with you in the dark, because wherever you are is where I want to be.

Yours, Asher

Bri's head is in her hands and she's sobbing. Fuck, I messed up. Maybe the letter was too much? *Shit*.

"Bri I'm—" But she throws her arms around me, causing me to stumble.

"I love it. Thank you, Asher."

"You're welcome. Why don't you go and check everything out? I have to do one more thing." I playfully swat her ass before heading upstairs to draw her a bath. I have a bucket of sparkling wine on ice, a bag of leftover petals, and her favorite bath salts. Avery informed me that Bri likes her bath scalding hot, so once the tub is filled about halfway, I sprinkle the salts in. I stop the faucet when the water is three quarters full and sprinkle in the remaining rose petals. I place some chocolate, red grapes, two wineglasses—in case she wants me to join—and some more tea lights on a wooden bath tray. The bucket of sparkling wine with a wine opener sits right next to the tub, and I go ahead and get two white, fuzzy robes and slippers to put on after the bath.

I step back to admire my work, tweaking things here and there. When I'm fully satisfied, I head downstairs to grab Bri. I enter the living room to see Bri sniffing the flower and rereading my note. Her skin glows in the soft lighting; she'll look even more amazing in the tub.

"Bri, I need you to come with me. You don't have to wear the blindfold, but I need you to close your eyes for me, love."

Bri gasps her surprise when I pick her up bridal style and carry her up the stairs. I made sure to dim the bathroom lights before I went to grab Bri.

"Where are we going?" Bri asks. My girl is impatient sometimes.

I lean down to place her back on her feet, her hands still interlocked behind my neck before I whisper in her ear, "We're here. Open your eyes."

Bri takes in the surroundings with a hand to her throat. "I—" She's at a loss for words. Exactly what I wanted.

"You did all this?" She turns toward me with a glassy look in her molten eyes. "For me?" The words fall from her plush lips like a prayer.

"I did. I heard that you happen to love baths. So, I figured I'd set one up for you. It has some more of your favorite snacks and some sparkling wine. I even put the lavender bath salts you love so much." I kiss her on top of her head before pointing to the door where the robes are.

"There are robes and slippers over there, and the water is hot enough to burn a layer of skin off. Enjoy." I lean in for a quick kiss before walking out. I don't get very far before her hand grabs my arm, stopping me.

"You wanna join me?"

I can't help the smirk that stretches across my face. "I thought you'd never ask."

This is the first time I'm seeing her fully naked, so I just sit back and admire her while she undresses. Fuck. Her body is ridiculous. Bri looks over her shoulder and winks at me.

"You gonna bathe in your clothes?"

I remove my clothes as quickly as humanly possible before stepping into her whirlpool tub. The second I sink my body into the water, I'm reaching for Bri's hand to pull her in. She wiggles around in an attempt to situate herself, which means she's rubbing against my hard cock.

My arm shoots around her stomach to hold her in place. "If you keep moving like that, water will end up everywhere because I'll be fucking you in the tub. Sit still." I groan when she wiggles a few more times.

"Would that be so bad?" Her fingers trace patterns across my forearms, and I can imagine the sultry look on her face.

"Normally I'd say no. But this isn't about that. Wine?" I make a grab for the bottle, and just as I'm about to pour it into the glasses I had set out, Bri is putting said glasses on the floor. As soon as the cork is free, Bri is making a grab for the bottle and chugging it like a champ. God, I love this woman.

"My kind of woman. My turn." I grab the bottle and take a long pull, feeling the bubbles slide down my throat.

"Can we try something? I've read about it in books, and I've been meaning to try it." Bri's words carry a hint of hesitation. She doesn't understand that I'll do and try anything she asks.

"Now I'm even more curious. What are you thinking?" Of all the things she could ask, I wasn't expecting this.

"Can you take a drink of the wine and spit it into my mouth? It's always so hot in books, and I want to see if I like it in real life." My brain needs to send a message to my throbbing cock to chill the fuck out.

I clear my throat before answering, "Uh, yeah, we can do that. Turn around and sit back on your heels." She's about to obey like the good girl she is when I stop her so I can remove the bath tray. Once that's done, she gets into position, and I hover over her on my knees.

I grab her throat and tilt it up toward me. "Open wide, baby." She does as I ask and I take a short pull from the bottle before leaning down and spitting it down her open throat. Bri gags a bit, but swallows like the good girl she is.

"Did that live up to the hype?" *I know it did for me.*

"Mmhmm. Thank you." She kisses my stomach before returning to her previous position. Water sloshes over the edge as I readjust my position and pull her into my arms. Both of us are content cuddling each other while eating the snacks and polishing off the bottle.

"Hey, bear?" I've been curious about something for a few weeks now. I'm not sure how she'll react. Will she get mad? Will she tell me the truth or flat out lie?

"Yes?"

"I'm curious about something. But before I ask the question, I want you to know you don't have to answer."

"Okay..." Bri sounds skeptical. I mean, I don't blame her. I would be, too.

"Have you gone to see Max at all since everything happened? Every time I go, he asks about you, so I'm just curious." I can feel her whole body tense, so I place the bottle on the floor and massage her shoulders, allowing her to melt into my touch.

"I haven't, actually. I haven't seen my parents, either." Bri sounds so heartbroken, so I press a soft kiss on her shoulder. I remain silent in case she wants to continue—which she does.

"I just feel bad for everything that happened. I feel like they hate me, like I let them down. I'm having a hard time facing them on my own."

"It breaks my heart knowing you feel like you're a disappointment. Would it help if I went with you to visit them? That way you have support if things—and that's a big *if*—go south?"

"But I don't want to drag you down with me." She sounds so small, almost childlike. I tilt her chin to meet my gaze.

"You wouldn't be dragging me down. Everyone needs support, and I'd be honored to be yours. So, if you'll have me, I'd love to help you overcome this next hurdle."

"Yes. I would." Bri's eyes shine with gratitude. Those three words sit on the tip of my tongue, but I bite them down. *Not yet.*

"You tell me when, and I'll be there." The once-hot water grows tepid, chilling out our bodies, so we pull the drain plug and put on our robes and slippers. We head downstairs to put on green, gooey face masks while gorging on snacks and watching *Where The Heart Is*—a personal fave of hers. I love having her in my arms. I could spend hours just cuddling with her.

"Hey, Asher?" Bri asks after pressing pause on the movie.

"Yeah?"

"I, um, want your help with something."

"Anything."

"Can you, um...Can you help me be more comfortable with driving? I don't want to keep relying on you or Ubers all the time. If I want to take back my life, I need to get over this fear of driving." My throat feels tight with so many emotions. Her vulnerability is a beautiful thing to watch. I turn her face to meet mine and place a kiss to her lips—face mask be damned.

"I would be honored to help you, thank you for trusting me with this."

"Thank you." Bri snuggles deeper into my arms as she plays the movie. We are halfway into the movie when I notice Bri's eyes become heavy and her breathing has slowed down.

"It's time for bed. Go upstairs and get ready while I clean everything up down here. I'll just let myself out when I'm done."

"Can you stay?"

"Is that what you want?"

"It's what I need."

"Then I'll stay. Go on up, I'll be there shortly."

Bri is halfway up the stairs when she turns around. "I'm glad you're in my life. It feels worth living again, like loving me is..." She swallows, tearing her eyes from mine. "Like loving me is easy."

Bri locks eyes with me before whispering words that would bring any man to his knees. "Thank you for being my person. For helping me see my worth apart from the shape of my body." Bri smiles at me before walking the rest of the way up the stairs.

Thank you for being my person. I clutch my chest, and my heart feels full. *You're my person, too, Bri.* Everything is put in its place in no time, and I all but run up the stairs.

After I wash off my mask, I head to the bedroom to find Bri already passed out, snoring softly, so I slip in carefully behind her, pulling her back to my front. I'm so glad she asked me to stay. I never want to wake up alone anymore. Once you wake up beside the love of your life, the loneliness of sleeping alone is ten times louder.

Brianna

Our new norm

"Have you given any thought to the pamphlet I gave you?" Dr. Jacqui asks. I've been seeing her for a few months now and so far, it's been working. She's given me an ample amount of resources on grief and how even though the stages are linear on paper, in real life they are anything but.

She also took the time to explain anxiety to me, and I now have a better understanding of what Avery goes through. Even Cas, too, with how he had to work through his trauma. I've been teetering around the idea of EMDR. It sounds really intense, but I've also watched countless YouTube videos of people swearing by it, saying it changed their lives.

"I have. I guess I'm concerned about how intense it's gonna be." I've been more honest with my thoughts and feelings, and it's refreshing. I was always a blunt, *say what's on my mind* type of girl. But guilt does crazy things to one's personality. I'm finally getting that back, and I don't plan to go backward.

"That fear is valid. This process can be a lot, but remember you are allowed to stop at any time. There is a whole protocol for this type of therapy, so I'd never throw you into it right away. Take some time to think about it more, and when you're ready, we can start. And if you aren't, then we go a different route, okay?" I adore my therapist. She never shames me for being hesitant about something, or needing to change the subject because it's too much to handle at that moment. She'll always circle back to it, but she usually switches up her approach which makes me grateful.

"Yeah, okay."

"Good. So, how has the list been working for you? I love that you came up with this idea. It takes some of my clients years to get there, and yet, you did that all on your own." After about my second or third session, I confessed that I made a list to find myself again, and she was so invested, we ended up talking about it our entire session. I love how she never forgets anything I say here. It makes me feel like I'm important to her.

"It's good. I actually had a realization the other day about one of the items."

"Oh?"

"So, I put it on my list to fall in love. I've always looked up to my parents and their relationship. They've always set a great example of how to treat the other, even if they were driving each other nuts. When I put that on my list, it was strictly to find someone who I could share my life with. But..."

"But?" Dr. Jacqui prompts.

"But I realized this entire time, that goal was meant for me to fall in love with myself."

"Ah. And have you fallen in love with yourself?"

"I'm starting to."

"Tell me more about that. What do you love about yourself, Bri?"

"I'm loud, and fun. I am full of life and energy, and I'm a great friend. I'm compassionate to those I care about and will do anything for them. But most importantly, I love my body. That one was the hardest for me. Going from slightly curvy to midsize hasn't been easy. I've been learning to embrace my newfound curves, and I can't imagine myself wanting to go back to who I used to be. It also doesn't hurt when you have a man who spends every waking second telling you how amazing your body is." I can feel my cheeks flush, especially when I think about everything we've done so far.

"Ah, yes, that does help. How are you and Asher?" It feels weird to admit this to my therapist before I tell him, but I need to talk it through.

"I'm in love with him."

"I can imagine how wonderful that feels. Tell me more about that."

"Well, he does whatever he can to make me happy. I mean, you remember what he did for me after my first therapy session. And then everything he did when we got to my place. He says the sweetest things to me, and he makes me feel important. He never judges me and offers to help carry my pain. He pays attention to me and loves on my body like his life depends on it. He even offered to help me with talking to my parents and Max when I'm ready."

"Sounds like you found someone who respects you, and that makes me happy. I'm assuming you haven't told him?"

"Not yet, but soon. I want to tackle things with my parents first before I do anything."

"Speaking of, are you ready to see and talk to them?" I ponder her question for a moment.

Am I ready to see them? Will they hate me for months of radio silence? Will they ignore me like I ignored them?

I close my eyes and think about all the unanswered texts I've gotten. The last one stopped months ago, and it set me back a little in my healing journey.

> **(February 12th, 2026) Mom: Hi, sweetie, I hope all is well. I don't know much about what's going on. I talked to Avery and she said to just give you time, so that's what your dad and I will do. We love you so much and it makes us hurt knowing you're in pain. We are always here. Whenever you're ready, we'll be here.**

> **(February 12th, 2026) Dad: What your mom said. We love you, bug. Take care of yourself.**

I've typed out at least a million responses in my notes app, never gathering the courage to send it. Until now. Until *him*. His endless patience and support have allowed me the room to shake myself out of my cocoon and into a beautiful butterfly. I haven't fully blossomed yet, but talking to my parents is the next step. Max will be harder to work up to, but I'll get there. I know I can.

"Yes. I think I am. I was actually thinking of texting them now, if that's okay? I'd really like the support."

"Yes, of course. Go right ahead." *Breathe in. Breathe out. You got this, Bri.*

> **Me: Hi, Mom. Hi, Dad. I'm sorry it took so long for me to reach out. I wasn't in the best place. I'm still working through a lot, but I'm a lot better now. I wanted to invite the both of you over for dinner at my place. I'm thinking this Saturday at six? I love you both so much, and thank you for giving me the space I need.**

Mom: SWEETIE, oh it's so good to hear from you. Your dad and I would love to have dinner with you. Please let us know if you want us to bring everything. I cannot wait to see you and hug you.

Dad: What Mom said. It's good to hear from you, kiddo. Love you and can't wait to see you.

Me: I love you guys, too. I should warn you, it won't be just me at dinner. Asher will be joining us.

Mom: Larson? Oh I hope so. I just love that boy.

Dad: He better treat my girl right.

Me: Dad...

Me: See you both on Saturday.

I look up at Dr. Jacqui and her face is blurry. My fingers touch my cheeks and that's when I realize I've been crying. Once I start, I can't seem to stop, and Dr. Jacqui just reaches out to squeeze my hand, allowing me to feel the emotions as they come.

Asher is waiting for me in the parking lot, and I've never been more grateful that he's his own boss. He wraps his arms around me and offers me silent comfort. When I get into the passenger seat, another set of flowers—daisies this time—are waiting for me. This has become our norm, and I wouldn't have it any other way.

"How did therapy go today?"

"Good. I had some realizations, but more importantly, I finally did it."

"Did what, bear?"

"I texted my parents and invited them over for dinner. They are coming at six on Saturday. Can you still come?" Saturdays are busy at the bar, so I won't blame him if he can't go.

"I'll be there. I can just head to the bar after. You're more than welcome to come hang, maybe we can have a repeat performance in the office." Asher grins his boyish grin while winking at me. There are so many other things I want to try with this man, but I just haven't worked up the courage yet. Maybe soon.

Clearly, today is the day for taking risks, because I'm placing my hand on his arm, stopping him from buckling his seatbelt.

"It's time." Asher blinks at me, and I watch as recognition flashes across his face.

"Are you sure?"

Am I sure? Well, a part of me still doesn't want to do it. I'm scared and nervous, but it's now or never.

"Yes, I'm sure." Asher leans over to place a bruising kiss to my lips before all but jumping out the car. I follow suit and place my hand in his outstretched one. I find myself being crushed in his arms while he repeats how proud of me he is.

Asher

Her laugh is like music to my ears

BRI IS SEXY AS fuck when she steps outside of her comfort zone. After gushing over how proud I am of her, I take her hand in mine and bring her over to the driver's side door. She looks at the handle like it has a poisonous snake wrapped around it.

I squeeze her shoulders before leaning down to whisper in her ear, "You can do this. I'm right here if you need me. We can take it one step at a time. I've got you." Her eyes lock on mine, and I watch as trust and something else shine in her eyes. Fuck, she's stunning.

"O-Okay. I-I can do this. I have to do this." Bri's hand wraps around the handle and I watch her take a slow, deep breath before pulling it open. I take a step back, but not far enough in case she needs me. Then I watch as she climbs into the driver's seat, and I swear my heart flips inside my chest.

"Look at you sitting in this car and owning it like the badass you are. Fuck, Bri, if we weren't in this parking lot and you weren't doing something so scary, I'd drag your ass to the backseat and fuck you senseless."

Bri's laugh is like music to my ears, and I watch as her hands white-knuckle the steering wheel. She's doing it. She's taking back the thing that threatened to destroy her.

"Asher. Look! I-I'm doing it. I'm sitting in the front seat. I know it's probably silly—"

I grip her chin with my fingers and turn her gaze to me. I must have an intense expression on my face because Bri inhales a sharp breath while she searches my face.

"Bri. It's not silly. You are doing something you never thought you'd do again. Seeing you stare your fear directly in the face is so fucking hot. So, I never want to hear you say this is silly when dealing with some tough shit. You hear me?"

"Y-Yes. It's not silly. I'm not ready to drive yet, but it feels nice to sit here."

"How are you feeling sitting behind the wheel?"

"Well, my heart is beating wickedly fast, and I feel like I want to throw up, but I'm here. And I feel...proud of myself for doing it."

"Damn right you feel proud. Now, look into my eyes and let's breathe together to see if we can get that heartrate down a little." I run my fingers through her hair and just focus on breathing nice and slow. Bri mimics my breathing, and I can see the tension begin to leave her body.

"Good girl. You're doing so well. Fear who? You're taking that fear and kicking it in the balls." That elicits a chuckle out of her, and soon enough she's jumped into my arms, her legs wrapped around my waist.

"Thank you, Asher."

"You don't have to thank me, baby. I got you. I'm always here. Are you ready to go home now?" Well, her home, but lately it's beginning to feel like mine. But if I'm being honest, home is staring into her soft, amber eyes.

"Yes. I could use a good nap with a strong pair of arms wrapped around me. Know anyone who's up for the task?" I love playful Bri.

"I think I could find someone." Instead of letting her go, I walk around to the passenger side and, after removing the flowers and snacks, place her in the seat before buckling her in.

"You know I could have walked." Bri laughs while smirking at me.

"I know, but I love having your sexy legs wrapped around me." I toss her a wink before rounding the car. The second I start the engine, I place a hand on her thigh and rub soothing circles the entire drive home. She starts to get out of the car, but I practically bark at her to stop. I decide to carry her bridal style into the house as visions of her dressed in all white flutter around in my brain.

Brianna

Over the next few days, I slowly learn to conquer my fear of driving—with the help of Asher. He's a fucking blessing, and I'm glad he showed up that day all those months ago. He was the push I needed to start living my life again. While I'm in the driver's seat of my own life—pun intended—he's been the perfect passenger, always encouraging me to be the best version of myself.

Each time I get into the car, I take a step toward owning my fear. So far, I've managed to turn the car on and allow the car to vibrate beneath my body. And every single time I move forward, Asher is there with endless praise and kisses. I often think how lucky I am to have him. I was hesitant to let him in, dead set on hating him forever. But Asher's overall goodness snuck past the last remaining defense I had. His empathy and affection thawed the ice around my heart when it came to him. And the fact that he still wants me despite every hateful thing I said to him isn't lost on me. He's been a godsend, helping me overcome my fears and reintroducing me to myself.

Today, I'm ready to actually put the car in drive. As I sit in my driveway, I notice my palms continually sliding off the steering wheel from how sweaty they are. Asher doesn't say a word, knowing I need this moment to collect myself. Instead, he has his hand on my thigh, letting me know that he's here.

You've got this, Bri. You can conquer anything. Look at all you've accomplished so far. You aren't going on the highway or anything. Just around the neighborhood. You can do this.

I let out a steady breath before moving the gear shift from park to reverse. I take all the necessary precautions: looking to make sure all of my mirrors are in place and glancing in my rearview to make sure no cars are coming. I slowly take the foot off the break, and when the car starts to move, I slam my foot back on the break, causing Asher and I to jolt.

"Hey. We can do this another day if you're not ready. We don't have to push ourselves. This isn't a race you need to win."

His words are exactly what I needed to remove my foot from the break again before stepping on the gas, and soon enough we're moving slowly down the driveway and turning onto the street. I feel like a teenager learning how to drive for the first time. Twenty miles an hour feels like fifty, but I keep going. Asher squeezes my thigh, offering his silent support. As I continue to drive, I force my death-like grip on the steering wheel to loosen. And the breath I must have been holding whooshes out of me.

The soothing sounds of spa music comes through the car speakers and every tense bone in my body relaxes. I glance quickly at Asher, offering him a grateful smile before turning my attention back onto the road.

What was meant to be a quick drive around the block has since turned into me driving around the neighborhood a few times.

I feel...good.

No, I feel great.

Am I still nervous? Hell yeah, but I'm better at managing my feelings thanks to my therapist and the man currently gripping my thigh. I'm getting better at fighting off the intrusive flashes from the accident, but sometimes, they slip through the cracks. Right now? Crickets—and I couldn't be happier.

The moment I pull into my driveway and turn the car off, Asher is unbuckling me and pulling me onto his lap. I barely have a moment to catch my breath before his lips are on mine. His hands might hold my face in a gentle manner, but his lips are anything but. Our tongues move together while our teeth clash. This kiss is frantic and desperate—and I'm loving every second of it. Asher only pulls away when my hips start to rock against his.

"As much as I want to do that right now, it's not the time. You did it. You drove the fucking car, Bri. I'm so fucking proud of you. You are taking your life back and I can't wait to see you continue to regain control of your life. You are a truly incredible woman."

"T-Thank you. Thank you for being by my side every step of the way. I may be an incredible woman, but you are a wonderful man."

"A man is only as wonderful as the woman who's by his side. You make me better just by being in my life. I can't wait to see how you handle dinner with your parents. I know that's a big step, and I'm honored you want me there with you."

"I wouldn't want anyone else there with me."

"Even Avery?"

"Even Avery. I love her dearly, but helping me with my journey back to me is a job only *you* can help me with. Now, I'm going to go inside to clean up and make the house look good for Saturday." I place a quick kiss on his lips before bolting inside the house, turning over my shoulder to watch him back out of the driveway. My heart and life feel full, and he's a huge reason for that.

Asher

I'm in love with her, sir

FRIDAY NIGHT IS ABSOLUTE madness at the bar, but I'm stuck in my office running the business side of things, gathering everything to send off to our accountant. Opening this bar has been a wild dream come true for me, but something still seems to be missing. My professional life feels like it's half full. And no matter how hard I think about it, nothing seems to give me that spark I'm searching for.

There's a soft knock on the door, a welcome reprieve from crunching numbers and filling out paperwork. "Come in." I'm still working on filling out these forms when I hear a throat clear.

When I look up, I'm staring directly at Max and Bri's parents, Colleen and Liam Montgomery. Colleen is a petite woman who could pass for Bri's twin. She has the same long, chestnut hair, but unlike Bri's, hers is pin straight. Her honey-like eyes have a softness to them that mirrors Max. Don't let her size fool you, though. The woman can pack a mean verbal punch when necessary.

I remember when Max and I were playing catch in their yard and accidentally broke a window. She burst through the front door real quick to give us a piece of her mind. Despite the fiery attitude, Colleen's face is etched with deep laugh lines and crow's feet from all the smiling and laughing she's done throughout the years. She also gives the best hugs.

As for their father, Liam, he has the same toffee-colored brown hair that has the same texture as Bri's. Liam and Max are similar: charming, funny, and always down for a good time. That has to be the secret to having zero grays. Well, that, or he goes to dye his hair whenever he spots one. Personally, I think it's the latter, but I'd never burst his bubble. He's roughly ten years older than Colleen, but he doesn't look a day over fifty. Liam's face is set into a permanent scowl, but that man turns into a complete puddle for those he cares for. When my brother was struggling, I found myself having many deep conversations with Max's father. He was actually the one who suggested therapy in the first place.

I walk around the desk just as Colleen is opening her arms for me. "Colleen. It's good to see you. Give any thought to leaving this old man and marrying me instead?" I wink at a running joke that started when Max and I first became friends in the seventh grade.

"Oh, Asher, you absolute charmer. But I'm afraid I'm happily married to this goon." She presses a kiss to my cheek while laughing. I turn to Liam, and for once, I can't get a read on him.

"Hi, Liam, it's good to—"

"What are your intentions with my daughter?" he interrupts. His wife smacks him on the arm while giving him a warning look.

"Liam—" she starts, but I put my hand up to stop her.

"No, it's okay. I'd be asking the same question if it was my kid," I reassure Colleen before turning to Liam. "I'm in love with her, sir. Have been since I was seventeen."

"Have you told her?"

"Not yet. She's still healing and I'm content with helping her grow. My love for her isn't going anywhere. In fact, I fall more in love with her every day. Her light, her laugh, her heart. She's it for me, and I hope that she sees it someday. If not, that doesn't change a damn thing. I'll be just her friend for the rest of our lives if that means I get to be near her."

Liam purses his lips, assessing my answer before he pulls me into a giant bear hug. "That's the answer I was hoping for. Take care of our girl. She may be strong, but she's way too hard on herself sometimes."

"I will."

"Good. We'll get out of your hair and leave you to whatever it is you were doing. We'll see you tomorrow at six."

"Stay awhile. Drinks are on me tonight, just let Gage know."

"Don't mind if we do. Thanks, Asher. Colleen is right. You are one of the good ones." They leave the way they came, and as I look down at my paperwork, I have zero desire to do any of it. I want a certain sassy brunette, and I don't think I'll be able to concentrate until I'm with her.

It's two hours until closing, and Gage and I have been running back and forth most of the night. The Montgomerys have since left, but I hardly had a chance to talk to them. People are demanding drinks left and right, and I'm exhausted.

I feel her before I see her. Our eyes lock onto each other immediately, and I couldn't be happier.

"Are we due for another porno tonight?" Gage smirks at me, just barely escaping the towel I throw in his direction.

"Fuck off."

"Hey, I get it. She's hot. I'll hold down the fort, you go hang out with your girl."

I walk around the bar and reach for her hand, pulling her into the office and locking the door. The second I turn around, her lips are on mine. Tongues are gliding, the sounds of our moans mixing together.

She's the first to break the kiss, and then she says something I didn't know I needed to hear. "I've missed you." Granted, we just saw each other the other day, but a day without Bri feels like a week.

"I've missed you too, baby. I've missed your face, your voice, your laugh. I've missed that sweet pussy of yours." I nuzzle her neck, my beard tickling her sensitive spot as she shrieks.

"Speaking of. There's something I've been wanting to try that I've been too scared to do. You have every right to say—"

"Yes," I growl, cutting her off. "Whatever it is, I say fuck yeah."

"But you don't know what I'm asking for."

"Don't care. If it involves any part of you naked, then I'm in. What do you wanna try?"

"I want to ride your face."

"Have you...Have you not done that before?" My voice is raspy as images of Bri sitting on my face play in my mind.

"I have, but not since...Well, not since being seventy pounds heavier. I've been too self-conscious to do it. I'm always afraid I'll suffocate my partner."

"And you want to try it with me?" Bri looks at me with sheer determination in her face.

"I *only* want to try it with you."

"Okay." I grab a pillow from the couch to put underneath my head, angling myself to give her a better experience. I lay down, but I stop her just as she begins to unbutton her jeans.

"Wait, hold up. Are you wearing jeans?" She's opened up to me about how uncomfortable they make her. Something about feeling like all her insecurities are on display.

"Oh, yeah. I got them today, actually. I was getting mad at myself for getting in my own way, so Aves and I went to the store, and I bought a few pairs. I even looked in the mirror and I felt good."

"I'm so proud of you. Now, take everything off, I want you completely naked when you sit on my face."

She does as I ask, but when she gets ready to lower herself onto me, Bri hovers over me.

"I said sit on my face, not hover."

"I don't want to hurt you."

"You won't, bear. Trust me. Ya know, that would make for a unique gravestone, don't you think? Here lies Asher, death by pussy. What a way to fucking go. Now sit your ass on my face and ride me like the dirty girl you are."

That's all it takes for Bri to be fully seated on me, and fuck it feels good. My tongue glides right through her arousal and she tastes so fucking sweet. I tongue fuck her pussy while gripping her ass. She begins to slowly rock back and forth, seeking the friction she desperately craves. I slip my finger inside her pussy, coating my finger with her arousal. I need as much lubrication as I can for what I want to do. I remove my finger only to circle the tight hole of her ass. I circle it a few times before inserting a finger into her. Her hips buck and she begins to pick up speed, riding my face even faster.

"Asher, holy fuck, do that again, please." *Ah, my girl likes that.*

"My girl begs so beautifully." I continue pushing my finger in and out of her while I take her clit in between my teeth and bite. Bri leans over me, her hips swirling as she chases her impending orgasm.

"Goddamn, *fuck.* Oh, yes, right there. I'm gonna come. Oh, fuck. Suck me harder, please baby." I do as she asks, my cheeks hollowing out with how hard I suck on her clit. I feel her begin to pulse around me.

"Come for me," I demand just before bringing her clit into my mouth again.

"YES!" Bri screams as she rides my face even faster while she finishes out her orgasm. She's fucking stunning when she comes.

"This is starting to become a new habit for us: fucking in your office," Bri says while she slides off of me, sitting on my chest. Both of us are catching our breath while we stare at each other. Then she says something I'm not expecting.

"I love you, Asher. I know it might seem like a post-orgasm high type of declaration, but it's true. I love you." I pull her mouth to mine, allowing her to taste her release on my tongue. I pull away even more breathless, and it has nothing to do with what we just did.

"I love you, too, Bri. I have for a while now. You're mine, and now that I have you, I'm never letting you go. Fuck, I love you so much, come here." I pull her down on top of me and wrap my arms around her.

"I love you, too. So much. You've been the best gift I've ever been given. You've seen every part of me. The good and the bad, and you're still here." I cup her cheeks, making sure she's looking into my eyes before I say my next few words.

"I've *always* seen you, Bri. Even when you thought I didn't notice you, I did. I notice everything about you. Every part of me loves every piece of you, and I will continue to do so for as long as you'll have me." We lay there in post orgasmic and emotional bliss, completely at ease. I tell her to hang out here while I finish up everything. I can't wait to lay next to her, cradling her in my arms, falling asleep to the person I know I'm meant to be with.

Brianna

We are gonna do a little experiment

"Bear, will you sit down? All your pacing is making me dizzy."

I'll be seeing my parents for the first time in *months*, and I've been a frantic mess all day. My body is buzzing with so much anxious energy, it could power a block-wide blackout. The joints in my fingers are sore, but I'm afraid if I stop fidgeting with them they'll begin to shake. I'm a goddamn mess, and no amount of deep breathing will help me. A soft grip on my shoulders stops me mid pace. Warm arms wrap around my middle, intoxicating my senses with leather and cinnamon. My head falls back against his chest as he sways our bodies from side to side, like you would a newborn child in search of comfort.

A heavy, nervous sigh slithers its way up my throat, slipping past my lips. Asher squeezes me harder while pressing a soft kiss on my shoulder. The warmth from his lips seeps into my skin, settling some of the anxiousness radiating throughout me.

"I need things to go smoothly. I've already disappointed them enough, so dinner needs to be just right."

"Everything is going to be fine. Your parents love you, and they're just excited to see you. Did they ever tell you point blank that you're a disappointment to them?"

"Well, no, but—"

"So then why are you still hanging onto that feeling? Does it make you feel better or worse? What happens if you were to let the disappointment go?"

"I...I don't know."

Asher has been working hard to help me combat the negative worm-hole of my mind, but I know I don't always make it easy. Once my mind latches onto an anxious thought, my body feels as if I've stepped on a glue mouse trap, rendering me immobile in my mind. I've brought this up to my therapist a few times, and she suggested I bring him to our next session so she can give him some pointers. When I brought it up to him, he crushed me into a hug similar to the one he has me in now, and said he'd be there. After attending a few sessions, he's gotten real good at challenging Patricia—the name I've given my anxiety.

"I guess I've been holding onto the feeling for so long, it's become my personal safety net. I'm not sure who I'll be without it."

"I get that, baby, I do. I just hate how it brings you down. You could never be a disappointment to anyone if you tried. I wanna try something with you, but we need to go upstairs. Do you trust me?"

"Of course I do—" The wind is knocked out of me when Asher tosses me over his shoulder like I weigh as light as a pile of feathers.

"Don't even *think* about saying anything about your weight right now. I deadlift, so this is nothing for me." Asher smacks me on my ass as he walks up the stairs.

Our eyes connect in the mirror before us, confusion painting my features as my breath catches in my chest.

"Why are we standing in front of a mirror?" His hands slither down my body, leaving fire in their wake.

"We're gonna do a little experiment. But first, I need to grab something from downstairs."

"We were just down there, and you didn't think to grab it then?"

"I was distracted by your fine ass. Sue me." Asher pecks me on the cheek before running downstairs to retrieve whatever he needs. Not even three minutes later, he's back with a dry erase marker in his hand.

"Why do you have that?" I point at the object in question.

"Here's what's gonna happen. You are going to write down everything wonderful about you on this mirror using this marker. Then I'm gonna tear off our clothes and fuck you right here while you stare at yourself in the mirror."

When did it get so hot in here? And fuck, just thinking about watching us fuck turns me on.

"Fuck me how, exactly?"

"You're gonna stand in front of me while I finally pound into your pussy from behind. I'm going to fuck you so hard, you won't be able to walk for days. Now, arms up," Asher demands.

I have no choice but to listen. Not that I would have objected, anyways. He slips my silk camisole off and I hear him curse when he sees I have no bra on. Just wait until he pulls my matching shorts down and finds no panties.

"Wait, I thought I was going to write things on the mirror before you stripped me naked?" Asher's hands are on my waist, so I spin around to meet his gaze.

"I changed my mind. Strip first, then write."

"You just want to see my bare ass when I bend over, don't you?"

"What can I say? It's a fine ass. Now, turn back around." His thumbs and pointer fingers slip into the waistband of my shorts, and he yanks them off.

"Are you fucking kidding me?"

"What?" I ask innocently, knowing exactly what he's referring to.

"You mean to tell me all morning you've been walking around in this tiny excuse for clothing with nothing underneath? And I'm just now finding out about it?"

"I like the way the silk feels against my bare skin. It had nothing to do with you. Greedy much?" I taunt him.

"Oh, you're asking for it now. Here, hurry up and write things down because I don't know how long I can wait."

I take the marker from his hand and turn toward the mirror. My first instinct is to write down everything that's wrong with me, but I resist that urge. So instead, I focus on the positives. *Brave, beautiful, compassionate, smart, creative, loving, great ass and tits.* I turn around to find Asher fisting his cock with a ravenous expression upon his face. I turn back to the mirror and continue. *Great friend, good sister and daughter, fantastic body, bold, daring, healing, in love.*

I've filled up most of the space, so I replace the cap on the marker and toss it on the floor. Within seconds, Asher is up behind me with his hand wrapped around my throat.

"Good girl. You know I love you, but right now I'm about to fuck you like I hate you. Fuck. I didn't bring any condoms."

"We don't need them. I'm on the pill."

"Shit. Okay, that's cool." Asher flounders, seemingly caught off guard.

"Great, now are you going to fuck me or not?"

The pressure around my throat tightens and my eyes roll back in my head from the pleasure.

"Eyes open, baby, or I'll walk away right now. I need you to watch me while I slam into you." Asher lets go of my neck. His eyes crawl across the room until landing on their target. With deft fingers, he shoves the ottoman from the foot of my bed closer to the mirror. His arms ripple with exertion and my thighs become slippery with raw, animalistic desire.

"Right leg up." I follow his command, too turned on to fight him.

Asher takes his position behind me, one hand gripping my throat and the other holding his cock. "Normally, I'd do more foreplay, making sure you're ready to take me." His fingers slip between my folds with ease, and I watch as a satisfied smirk plays across his face.

"But you're so goddamn wet already, my cock will slide home without any issues." Asher lines his dick up with my entrance and pushes the head in, letting me adjust.

"Is that all you got? I thought you were gonna fu—" The rest of the words fall out of me when I feel him fully seated inside me. My pussy clenches around him, desperate to keep him locked in place.

"You're pussy's so greedy for my cock, isn't it, bear? Doesn't want to let go." I don't have time to process that because he's slamming into me, upward thrust after upward thrust, hitting the spot inside me that has me seeing stars.

"Holy fuck. Yes, right there. Harder. I thought you wanted to fuck me like you hate me." Asher's hand around my throat tightens as his cock rams into me over and over again.

"Play with your tits. I want you to pinch and roll those sexy nipples between your fingers while I fuck your cunt." It takes longer than it normally would to bring up hands up to my breasts with how forcefully he's fucking me. It still doesn't feel hard and rough enough. Like he's holding back from going full beast mode. I pinch and circle my nipples with my hands while staring at us in the mirror. I watch where his cock disappears inside me, and my arousal begins to drip down my leg.

"My dirty girl likes watching me fuck her, doesn't she? This is what you do to me. You make me feel unhinged. All I want to do is own this cunt of yours every which way. I want to fuck you every morning with my cum dripping down your leg like my own personal branding." His thrusts become more aggressive. I move my raised leg from the middle of the bench to the end of it, giving him more access to my pussy.

"You take me so well. This pussy was made for me. Touch your clit, baby. I want to feel you come on my dick."

My fingers trail from my nipples to my clit. I alternate between pinching and circling the bud, and soon enough, the pressure begins to build with such an intensity that I know I'm going to come so hard.

"That's right. Come on Daddy's cock like a good little slut. You know you want to. Come for me," Asher growls into my ear, and I lose it.

"Asher, fuck. I'm coming." My pussy pulses around him and I hear an *oh fuck* from behind me.

"Can I come inside you? Because I'm so fucking close."

"Come inside me Daddy, fill me with your cum. And if it drips down my leg, I want you to push it back inside me or rub it into my skin. I want your cum all over my skin and inside my pussy."

"*Fuck*" is all he manages to say before he's coming inside me. Wet, hot liquid shoots into my pussy. "Take every last drop like the dirty girl you are. Your pussy is thirsty for my cum. Take. It. All." Asher thrusts into me a few more times before slipping out of me.

We're both spent, pulses racing and sweat dripping from every inch of our bodies. Asher takes his finger, wiping the remaining cum from my legs before painting my lips with it.

"Lick them clean," he demands, and I swear my now-sensitive clit throbs as I lick away the cum from my lips.

"Look into the mirror, bear. Do you believe the words now?"

"Hmm...I'm getting closer to believing them, but we may have to do this a few more times so that it sticks."

"I'd be happy to. Now, let's take a quick shower and a nap before your parents come in three hours. I don't want them to see you freshly fucked. I'd rather keep my balls attached to my body."

To my disappointment, the shower is just a shower. We wash each other's hair and bodies. We dry off before slipping into the bed, fully naked.

"I love you, Asher."

"I love you, too, bear. I'll set the alarm in about an hour so that we have time to get ready. Sweet dreams, baby." I snuggle against his back and fall asleep with a smile on my face. I could get used to this.

Brianna

She just had to have hammer pants

THE DOORBELL RINGS, AND I'm about to have a panic attack. I feel Asher's arms circle around my waist as he presses a kiss to my shoulder.

"You got this. I'm right here with you. I love you." I spin around in his arms and pull his lips to mine. Our lips move in a soft, slow rhythm, tongues dancing together in a graceful manner. I pour everything into this kiss, allowing my actions to speak for me.

"I love you, too." Okay, it's time. I move to the front door, stumbling around like a newborn deer. The second I open the door, my vision blurs.

"Mom. Dad," I blubber, and if their arms didn't wrap around me, I would have fallen to the floor. The three of us embrace each other while sobbing uncontrollably. I've missed them so much. The four of us have always been super close, practically doing everything together.

"I'm s-s-sorry. I'm so sorry. I let you both down, and I'm not sure how I'll forgive myself. Especially after the way you helped me financially after everything. I-I'm s-such a b-bad d-daughter." I'm full-on wailing now—I'm surprised they can even understand me at all.

"Sweetheart, no. You aren't a bad daughter, and you most definitely haven't let us down. We just want you to be okay. We love you regardless and we are just so happy you texted us back," my mom assures me.

"Bug, you've been going through a lot. We understand that you needed space. So we gave it to you. We're here now, that's all that matters," my dad adds.

"Hey, Bri. I'm gonna give you three some space. I'll finish setting up dinner, why don't you sit on the couch and let me handle everything else?"

"You don't have to—"

"I think you need this time with your parents. I'm just a room away." I nod, sending him my appreciation with my smile. My parents and I move over to the couch. It's time to share everything I've been feeling.

"I, um. I promise I wasn't trying to hurt you guys by shutting you out. I just couldn't face you."

"What do you mean by that?" my mom asks.

"I'm to blame for everything. If I hadn't begged Max to go axe throwing, then none of this would have happened. I fucked up and everything in my life feels like it's been flipped upside down. And then there's you two." I take a deep breath, trying to collect my thoughts. My emotions feel like they want to swallow me whole.

"What about us, bug?" my dad chimes in.

"You guys love Max. He's your baby boy and I hurt him. I'm the reason he was in the hospital. You guys should hate me." My voice cracks on the word *hate*, and my mom gets up from her spot on the couch to pull me into her arms, rocking me back and forth.

"Shhh, honey. It's okay. We don't hate you; we could never *ever* hate you. It breaks my heart that you've been holding onto all this guilt. You've been going through this all on your own?"

"In the beginning, yes. But then Asher came along, and he's been really helping me. I've also been seeing a therapist who's been really great with sorting through everything."

"Brianna, that's great. We also went to therapy right after everything happened. Your mom and I were struggling with each other for a while, so we decided talking to someone would be helpful." My dad throws a curveball my way. Problems? I'm really trying not to feel guilty about this, too.

"What problems?"

"Well, we could have lost two children that day. It doesn't matter that Max had more serious injuries, you got hurt, too. We weren't dealing with our pain in a healthy way, so we just needed to sort things out. It's not the first time we've been to couples counseling," my mom adds to the conversation. My head is spinning with all this new information being thrown at me.

"You've had issues before?" I ask.

"Oh, honey, we've had our fair share of moments. We aren't perfect, but we know that we love each other and there's no other option but for us to sort it out. We care about each other too much to walk away."

"Wow, you think you know someone." We're silent for a moment before we burst into manic laughter. I can feel my heart repairing itself just a little more.

"I just, I feel like I've just been a massive disappointment lately. I could barely get out of bed for months. I've lost a lot of myself in the process. I guess I didn't want you guys to see me like that. I was a mess, and I've just recently started to feel like myself again."

"You don't always have to be okay, bug. Sometimes we need to break in order to come back stronger. You never have, nor will you ever be, a disappointment. Your mom and I don't think so, and I can bet Asher doesn't think so, either. You take all the time you need to find yourself, and we'll be here for whatever you need." My dad gets up to sit on the other side of me and presses a kiss atop my head.

"I love you guys so much. Never again will I shut you out. It's been lonely."

"We love you too, bug. Even if you need space, we'll understand," my mom says.

"Thank you. I don't know about you, but I'm starved. Should we eat?" We get up and head to the table where everything is already set up. My eyes find Asher's immediately, and my heart swells with love for this man. I can't believe I held such a grudge against him all those years. All over some stupid shit Giselle pulled. He's the most amazing man.

Asher pulls out my chair and presses a quick kiss on my lips before taking his place beside me. Dinner goes smoothly and it doesn't feel like any time has passed between us. There's lots of talking and laughter. And, of course, some embarrassing stories about my childhood.

"We couldn't convince her otherwise. Brianna was obsessed with the *U Can't Touch This* video, and she just *had* to have a pair of the hammer pants. She even went as MC Hammer for Halloween." My mom's laughter is music to my ears.

"I was four. It's your fault for showing me the music video, so don't put it on me," I playfully scold my parents.

"Oh, Bri, you're so cute. I bet you wore the shit out of those pants," Asher says to me before turning to my mom. "Please tell me you have pictures. I need to blow one up to hang over our bed."

Our bed.

The words fall from his lips, detonating the chatter like a bomb. Silence pulls up a chair, making their presence known. Seconds feel like hours as I watch two sets of eyes blinking at me, pure astonishment written across their faces. My mom is the first to crack when I watch a smug smile tug at the corner of her lips. Tension seeps from my dad's shoulders as he relaxes even more, eyes crinkling with happiness.

Asher, whose jaw went slack at his own words, quickly recovers.

Our bed. Damn, I really like the sound of that. I can't wait to explore that later.

Dinner goes on for another hour, and I'm not looking forward to my parents leaving. I make a vow to myself that I will be better when it comes to making time for my parents.

We all say our goodbyes and make plans for next month for dinner at their house. After endless hugs, I close the door and walk right into Asher's arms.

"I love you so much and I'm so grateful for you. Thank you for being here for me, and not just tonight. Thank you for coming over that day and giving me what I needed."

"I'm happy you let me in. You are a kaleidoscope of colors, and I love getting to witness you fall in love with yourself." I offer him a watery chuckle before pressing my lips in a quick kiss.

Asher lets out a heavy sigh before bringing his forehead to meet mine. "I wish I didn't have to head to the bar, but I can't leave Gage on his own. We have a giant party scheduled for tonight and—"

"I know. I think I'm going to put on a face mask and crawl under the covers of *our* bed," I tease.

"You caught that, huh?"

"I sure did. Go handle business. I'll probably be passed out the second you leave. Oh, wait, hold on. I have something for you." I walk over to the designated junk drawer and pull out the house key I had made for him.

We haven't put a label on our relationship, so I'm curious as to where we stand, but I want him to have this. I flip over his hand so his palm is facing toward the ceiling before placing the object inside.

I see Asher's throat bob a few times before he looks up at me with pure adoration in his eyes. "A key to your place?"

"I like having you here. Now, you don't have to keep borrowing Avery's. This way, you can lock the door when you leave and won't have to break a window when you leave the bar."

"I...I...Thank you. But full confession, I returned Avery's key weeks ago. But not before I made a copy of it. Now I have two." His face is pure mischief, because of course he had a key made.

I playfully push his shoulders while rolling my eyes. "Get out of here. Go get people wasted. I'll be in our bed waiting for you." I mean to plant a quick kiss on his lips, but Asher takes it further by pulling me into him and coaxing my mouth open with his tongue.

All too soon he pulls away, leaving me dizzy and wanting. "Now I have a reason to shut the bar down sooner than later. Night, bear."

Asher

I'm in the mood for dessert

CRAZY ANIMAL MASKS SIT upon our faces, the perfect end to a long day. I have Bri curled up next to me in bed, her cold feet seeking warmth in between my legs. Soft spa music filters through my phone. This right here is what pure bliss feels like. My fingers paint imaginary patterns up and down her arm as I think to myself, *I could get used to this.* Lazy, relaxing evenings talking about our days or just bathing in the silence, content with just being in the presence of the other. If sixteen-year-old me could see me right now, he'd have a full-on conniption, jaw on the floor, constantly pinching himself thinking it was just an illusion. I feel the mask begin to bunch and shift as a smile stretches across my face when I look at the beautiful, incredible woman nestled beside me.

"What's a dream of yours?" I ask.

"A dream?"

"Yeah, what's something that you've always wanted to do? What's something you're passionate about?"

Bri's silent for a moment, her face mask bunching as her face contorts with concentration. Damn, she's sexy when she thinks.

"Well, remember when you helped me get rid of all my books?"

How could I forget? The torn, haunted look on her face is forever burned into my brain. I hated watching her box up her joy, her passion. Right now, said boxes are scattered throughout my tiny two-bedroom apartment above the bar collecting dust. There's a small chance that Bri might get angry with me for keeping them, but I couldn't bear to donate them. If I know my girl like I *think* I do, she's going to end up regretting getting rid of them. So for now, I've been holding onto them in hopes that she'll want them back.

"Yes, of course I do."

"Well, lately I've been regretting that decision." Sadness and regret pour out of her with the likeness of a fire hydrant test. I watch as her throat works while she tries to collect herself before continuing. Pain stings behind my eyes, but I blink it back. Now isn't about me. I remain silent, knowing sometimes she just needs a moment to collect her thoughts.

"It was a decision I made when emotions were a mess for me. Now that I've been working through things, I'm kicking myself. I miss reading. I miss getting lost in a book and falling in love with the characters."

"I'm sorry, baby. I wish there were something I could do about it."

Fuck. I hate lying to her, but I'm glad we're having this conversation. I feel a plan beginning to percolate in my mind, but I need to let it marinate some more before I move forward.

"It's okay. You asked me about a dream of mine. Ever since I was young I wanted to open my own bookstore. I love giving people recommendations, and when they come to me for more? It makes my heart happy."

"Why don't you do that? I know you love working at the salon, but if this is your passion then go for it."

"Honestly, this is something I've only shared with Max. He's even helped put together a blueprint of what it could look like. I was so excited to finally do it, but then everything happened with Max and I, and I don't know. Now it just feels like a silly daydream."

I whip my head in her direction so fast that the sheet mask slides down my face. Silly daydream? How can she think her dreams and goals are that insignificant? Face mask aside, I grip her chin in my hand and force her eyes to meet mine.

"Bear. I don't want to hear the word *silly* come out of that sexy mouth of yours when it comes to something you are passionate about. I think that dream of yours is perfect for you, and I hope you consider doing it."

My serious expression burns so fiercely that I bet if I peeled off her mask, she'd be blushing. Her vulnerability is infectious, and before I realize it, I'm blurting out what's been on my mind for a while, hoping it'll help her in some way.

"I know for me, I've been trying to figure out what's been missing from my life. Like, I love the bar and everything I do there, but I've been trying to search for something more."

"Maybe we should put our passions together. There's nothing like being booked and boozed."

My head snaps in her direction, and I feel that final piece click into place. She laughs it off, dismissing it as a far-off idea, but it feels right. *Booked and Boozed.* I let those two words rattle around inside my brain. The more I think about it, the more I feel like this is it. That this is what's been missing. My mind is reeling with ideas.

"Brianna, you are a genius. I'd kiss the fuck out of you right now if we didn't have these masks on. Booked 'N' Boozed. We can take books and pair them with cocktails. You can be in charge of the book recommendations, and I can create the drink that pairs with the book." Bri's face beams underneath her green face mask.

"I love that idea. Do you think you'll have enough time to do both?"

"I can step back from the bar a bit. Let Gage take over. We've been meaning to hire someone for a while. Let me talk to him about it, but I think we really need to do this."

Bri peels both of our masks off before kissing me on the lips and offering me an ear-splitting grin.

"Let's do it."

"You're sexy when you're excited about something. We need to hurry up and dry our faces off because I'm in the mood for dessert."

I rocket off the bed, bringing Bri with me into the bathroom. We discard the face masks and rinse ourselves clean. Bri's barely finished drying her face when I sling her over my shoulders, reveling in the feel of her body pressed against mine. The feel of her round, full ass in my hands has my cock twitching in my sweats.

I prowl to the bed, placing her down, taking a moment to appreciate the woman spread before me. Her chestnut hair spreads wildly against her blush sheets, making the perfect contrast of dark and light. I spend what feels like forever in between her thighs, lapping up her sweet honey. My own personal heaven. Bri will always be the balm that heals me every single time.

Brianna

Healing isn't linear

I've been so wrapped up in my Asher bubble that I haven't really hung out with my best friend. And I plan to rectify that ASAP.

> **Me: Hey Aves, you busy?**

> **Avery: Ah, so she is alive lol. I thought you had abandoned me for Asher.**

> **Me: Ugh shut up haha. Wanna grab lunch?**

> **Avery: Bristol Cafe?**

> **Me: See ya there.**

I PULL UP THE rideshare app and put my location in. Since I started taking baby steps toward driving again, stepping into a car doesn't make me all that nervous anymore. I'm at the restaurant within twenty minutes, and because it's not busy, I'm seated almost immediately. Five minutes later, Avery walks in, her skin radiant with her pregnancy glow.

I pull her into my arms, squeezing her with just enough force so I don't harm the baby. The moment we pull away, I bend down and talk to my future niece or nephew.

"Hello, little one. It's your auntie Bri. I love you so much."

Avery's eyes glisten with tears as she cradles her belly, a soft smile playing across her delicate features.

"How are we feeling?" I ask her.

"I'm good right now. I sometimes have nausea so bad I can barely leave my bed without the urge to vomit. But other than that, things are going okay. Doctor says the baby is doing well, and I'm antsy to know what we're having. How are you?"

"I'm good. Better than good, actually. I told Asher I loved him."

"Shut up! Oh my God, how do you feel?"

"I, well, it felt right. We just had sex—"

The sound of a throat clearing has our attention turning to the waitress standing by our table, notepad in hand.

"Um, what can I get y'all to drink?" She rushes the words out so fast that it takes us a moment to process what she says.

"Um, I'll have an unsweet tea with lemon," I respond, unable to meet her eyes.

"I'll have water, thank you." Avery beams up at her like we didn't just traumatize the poor woman.

She mutters a *got it* before speeding away from our table. Avery and I look at each other for all of two seconds before we burst out laughing.

"That poor woman. She looked mortified. Oh my God. I'll have to avoid this place now." My hands cover my eyes as laughter continues to shake my entire body.

"Eh, she'll be fine. But anyways, back to you. So...You told him you loved him. That's great, Bee. I'm so happy for you."

I pull my head from my hands, and I feel a smile stretch across my face. "Thanks. He said it back to me, too. I just, I'm still wrapping my head around it."

Avery's response is to roll her eyes. "Well, duh. That man has been in love with you for, like, ever. How do you feel?"

"I feel amazing. I like having him alongside me. He's just everything."

"That's great, Bri."

We're interrupted by our waitress dropping off our drinks with complimentary bread and butter before asking what we want to eat. I order the deluxe cowboy burger and Avery orders pretty much the entire menu. God, I've missed my girl. Avery and I sit in silence as we sip our drinks and eat our bread. I'm the first one to break the silence.

"So, I talked to Asher about the favor you asked of him."

"Oh?"

"Yup, he—"

"Ope, hold that thought. I gotta pee." Avery leaps out of her chair and shuffles off to the bathroom. Today's service is quicker than normal because our food comes before she gets back. My mouth waters as I look at the Cajun fries and burger. My stomach grumbles, and just as I'm about to take a bite, my phone pings with a notification. I'm as giddy as a teenager at the thought of a text from Asher.

> **Max: So, I just spoke to our parents, and they said they saw you. I don't understand why you haven't come by to see me? No one is telling me anything. And even if they did, it would hurt more because it didn't come from you.**

You are the worst. So selfish. Your brother hates you. Your family probably hates you, too. Everything they said was a lie.

My body feels as if I've been locked in a walk-in freezer, and my appetite is suddenly gone.

I jump up from my seat so fast the table moves. I don't care to apologize for causing a disturbance, and I bolt out the door. My lungs scream at me as I run out the door and far enough away from the restaurant to call for an Uber. I don't need Avery to try and convince me to stay.

My car arrives and I'm sure I look absolutely insane, but I can't seem to care.

My phone rings continuously as Avery's face flashes across my screen. I can't talk to her right now. I need to be alone. I deserve to be alone. The phone stops ringing only to ping with two incoming messages.

> **Avery: Bri? Where did you go? What happened?**

> **Avery: I love you. I'm not sure what happened. But please let me know you're okay.**

I leave her on read. The depression that always lingers around every corner pounces on me like a lion does its prey. It doesn't matter that I've finally managed to claw my way out of that black hole. The second the beast sniffs out a sliver of weakness, it welcomes the meal as if it's been starved.

My Uber drops me off at my house and I mutter out a curt *thanks* before I bolt up the stairs and into my room. I don't bother to change out of my clothes; I just put an oversized hoodie on. I crawl under my covers and fall back into the darkness that swallowed me whole before.

I've been holed up in my room for a two days, falling into old patterns. My brain pounds against my skull and my eyes have a permanent crust from crying myself to sleep every night. I've avoided my phone like the plague. Because if I look at their messages, I see *his*, and then I lose it. I've been in a perpetual state of sadness and shame, and I hate that I'm here again. I was doing so well, and I just can't face anyone knowing I've fallen back into my sorrow.

I'm startled when the other side of the bed dips with a heavy weight, and I inhale the uniquely distinct smell of leather and cinnamon.

Asher.

God, look at how pathetic you are. Asher is going to go running the second he sees how far you've fallen.

His arms wrap around my stomach, and I flinch. I make an attempt to remove his hand, but he tightens his grip.

"What happened, baby?"

"I-I don't. I c-can't."

Asher just pulls me closer into his body, and his arm around my body feels like a protective shield.

"It's okay, bear. You can tell me when you're ready." Asher presses a soft kiss on my shoulder, and I feel the heat through the layers of clothes. We lie there in silence, but it's not uncomfortable.

Do I let him in? Should I tell him what's been going on? Will he think differently of me?

My thoughts are flashing across my mind at the speed of light as Asher brushes soothing strokes up my arm. I've been determined to wallow in my own despair, locking everyone out of the world, but then I hear the sound of my therapist's voice.

You are deserving of love, Brianna. It's okay to lean on those whenever we need help.

"I, um, I went out to lunch with Avery. Everything was good and then—" My voice breaks and I feel his arms squeeze me even harder, providing me the support I need to continue.

Be strong, Bri. Don't let the negative thoughts win.

"Avery got up to use the bathroom and then I got a text from Max. And all the progress I've made so far combusted, leaving me in the destruction of my guilt. I just, I'm so fucking selfish. I should be able to talk to my brother. He's better now, and yet, I have been ignoring him still."

"Bear, you're still working on some really tough shit. Healing isn't linear, something I've had to learn myself. You'll talk to your brother when you're ready. You are the least selfish person I know. So, I'm gonna need you to stop talking about my girl that way."

"You're right. I know you're right, but sometimes it's hard. I was doing so well, and it just...It sucks to fall back a few steps."

"What you're doing isn't easy, but I'm so proud of you for continuing to work through some tough shit. You're inspiring."

"I—well, thank you. I'm glad you're here. Thank you for not giving up on me. And I'm sor—"

"No. Don't you dare apologize. You don't need to. And I'll always be here. You need me, I'll come running. Sounds like you've had a long day. Close your eyes and sleep. I'll be here holding you."

My eyelids are heavy with exhaustion. I snuggle deeper into his arms and fall asleep with a smile on my face. *Everything will be okay.*

Brianna

Drink every last drop

I WAKE UP FEELING a little more like how I've been these past few weeks. My arms stretch out only to find the other side of the bed empty. I feel my inner monsters trying to make something out of nothing, but I mentally push them off the cliff. I'm not going to give in to their demands today.

I pad over to my ensuite bathroom to wash my face and brush the knots from my hair. I give myself a onceover, and once I'm satisfied, I head downstairs. I don't know where Asher's gone, but I love having him here with me. There's something about waking up in the arms of the love of your life.

The moment I step into the kitchen, I see the familiar coffee shop logo and my heart stutters inside my chest. The closer I get to the table, I see a black, velvet, rectangular box, and I open it with giddy excitement. Inside is the most beautiful sterling silver chain with a book charm attached to the end. Next to the coffee is a single pink rose with a red bow wrapped around it and a note attached.

Drink every last drop, Bear - Asher

Fucking Christ. He just *had* to reference what he said to me when he fucked my face. And now I'm all hot and bothered. I grab my phone, put the straw in my mouth, and snap a picture to send him.

> **Me: *image* Thank you for the beautiful gifts. I love you.**

> **Asher: You're welcome, baby. I'll be home soon to take you somewhere. Love you, too.**

I puncture the top of the coffee with the straw before taking a long pull. The cold liquid rushes down my throat and I let out a happy sigh.

He's just so thoughtful. Between taking me to and from therapy and helping me become more comfortable driving, it's overwhelming how incredible he is to me.

Speaking of being more comfortable with driving, I've been able to drive around the block by myself without having a freak out. And now, I think it's time to get myself a car. I can't rely on Asher being my personal driver for the rest of my life, even though he's never once complained. This next step is necessary for me to get back to myself again.

Asher isn't here to take me car shopping, so I use the Carvana website, grateful that they deliver the car to you. I scroll through every make and model, looking for the perfect car for me. I end up getting a 2021 silver Nissan Rogue, and pick the three hour delivery option. I can't wait to see Asher's face when he sees what I've done.

Two hours later, my car is being delivered at the same time Asher pulls into the driveway. I watch with bated breath as his eyes rake over the shiny, silver sedan. He circles around it, looking up, down, left, and right like a mechanic would. Asher folds his arms over his chest, and when his eyes meet mine, he offers the most panty-dropping grin known to man.

"I'm so proud of you. And this is perfect for you."

His gaze darkens, flicking to the delivery guy waiting for my signature.

"I can't wait to christen the fuck out of this car."

My face heats at his words and a pulse throbs between my legs as I shove the papers back into the delivery guy's grip with shaking hands.

"You folks enjoy." He snickers as he saunters back to the truck.

"Asher!" I hiss as he pulls me into a happy dance, our bodies flushed together, not a single thing between us.

"Look at you kicking your list's ass."

I'm grinning like a fool while breaking out into a happy dance. *Look at me. Doing hard shit* and *taking my rediscovery list by the horns.* I'm in the middle of one of my many happy twirls when Asher grabs me by the hand and spins me in a circle before pulling my body flush against his. I let out an involuntary *oof* right before we begin to sway.

"What are you doing?"

"Dancing with my girl. I have a question to ask you, and it feels right to do so while holding you close."

"But there's no music."

"It doesn't matter. Music or no music, I want to dance with you."

"You're ridiculous, but I love it. I love you. What do you want to ask me?"

"We've been hanging out for some time now, and I don't think I'd want to do life without you. You've become one of the most, if not *the* most, important person in my life. I want to take the next step and ask you to be my girlfriend, officially."

"Took you long enough to ask, but yes. Of course I'll be your girlfriend. Wow, we sound so high school." Asher kisses and nips the sensitive spot on my neck, and I squeal.

"Well, I've wanted to do this since high school, so that tracks. Anyways, we have plans. Let's go." Asher drags me by the hand toward his car, and surprise, surprise, there's a bouquet of tulips.

"If you keep giving me flowers, I might need to open a greenhouse. They're lovely, thank you." I lean over the seat and kiss him. "Are you going to tell me what we're doing?"

"Nope. You'll see when we get there."

"No blindfold this time?" I ask just as he's pulling it out.

"Of course. It makes it more fun that way." I roll my eyes before placing the fabric over my eyes. The drive feels short, and I assume we've parked, because the car has stopped. Asher opens his door, and within seconds, the passenger door is opening and he's pulling me out of the car.

"Okay, you can take it off." When I do, I realize we're in the parking lot of our local independent bookstore.

"EEEK. Are you taking me book shopping?"

"Kinda. I have a challenge for us. When we get inside, we have ten minutes to search for a book for the other person. The only rule: it has to be the craziest, most insane book you can find. So, bear, are you up for the challenge?"

"Oh, hell yeah, I am. This is gonna be so much fun." We stand outside of the store and my body buzzes with excitement. I quickly glance at Asher before bolting inside. People look at me, but I don't seem to notice nor care. I am on a mission. I hear him call me a cheater behind me, and I can't help but laugh.

I'm already scouring the aisles when I get a text from Asher.

Asher: Choose wisely, bear.

> Me: You're talking to the queen of book recs. I got this...do you? *winky face*

Being in a bookstore again feels...right. It's my home away from home. My fingers brush across the smooth spines of a plethora of books. I see some of my favorites from Kennedy Ryan to Shantel Tessier to Lyla Sage. I *know* we're here to get a book for each other, but I'm struggling to not leave with at *least* five books...okay, ten. What can I say? Book buying is an addiction. Back in high school, whenever I wasn't in class, I could be found in the library, nose deep within the cream-colored pages, getting lost in a story.

A piece of my heart slots back into place while I stand amongst thousands of stories. I lost my love of reading while darkness held me captive. But now that I'm back? I'll be holding it within my clutches like a lifeline.

I'm scanning the aisles both for an idea as well as making sure Asher isn't close by. As I'm scouring my surroundings, something grabs my attention. My footsteps are muffled against the carpet as I make my way over to the cover that draws my attention. The moment my fingers grip the glossy cover, I feel my face stretch out in a wicked grin. This...This is perfect. I tuck the book under my arm in case I bump into Asher. I'm looking every which way, making sure he's not nearby. I make it to the checkout, and the moment the book is inside the bag, I walk outside and wait. I can't *wait* to see the look on his face when he sees what I picked out.

Asher

Did someone say robot erotica?

Bri thinks she's so slick…running ahead of me like that. But I'm determined to find the perfect book to give her. My mission? To find the most ridiculous book they have. I take the escalator up and make my way toward our go-to section when I get a text.

> **Bear: What's taking so long? *image attached***

BRI IS OUTSIDE WITH a giant grin on her face, her hair blowing in the soft breeze. She is stunning, and she looks…happy. My fingers pinch to zoom closer, and I scan every inch of her beautiful face. I allow myself a moment to bask in her radiance before returning to my mission. My eyes flicker across the signs from romantasy to fantasy to…wait, does that say what I think it says?

Monster Erotica. Yup. It sure does. My feet move with purpose over to that section as I glance at the spines. What in the actual fuck am I seeing? Some of these titles are…something. Among the shelves are alien romance, krampus romance, and there's even a Covid monster romance.

What the fuck? Why is that a thing?

Then I come across the most insane of the bunch: robot erotica. How does that even work?

I pick up the book and read the silly title: *Romancing the Thick Cocked Robot* by Chandler Kitty. The actual fuck? I let out a snort of laughter that has people's heads turning in my direction. I murmur my apologies before putting the book under my arm in case I run into Bri.

I ignore the looks from the cashier as I purchase the book. I take the bag and hightail it out of the store, only to come face to face with Bri.

"You finished before me?"

"Well, I did have a head start; pun intended." She winks at me while holding up her matching bag.

"You little minx. Okay, let's go. You cool if we stop by my place? I have something I need to pick up on the way to your house, and I need your help getting it." I can't wait to see the look on her face when she sees her books still in their boxes in my living room.

"Sure. Are we doing the book exchange at your place or mine?"

"We can do it at mine, if that's cool."

"Works for me. Now, let's go. I swear, I was getting some weird ass looks when I was shopping."

Twenty minutes later, we are pulling into the employee parking lot behind the bar. We have our bags in hand, and I'm suddenly very nervous.

What if she gets pissed at me? What if I overstepped a boundary and she ends our relationship?

I shove those thoughts away as we walk up the stairwell and into my apartment. The first room we'll enter is the living room, so my heart is beating like a drum inside my chest.

"I can't wait for you to see your—" Bri stops in her tracks, and the bag in her hand falls to the floor. "What is that?" I remain silent. I can't seem to find the words to say.

"Asher...What the fuck is that?" She points to the boxes.

"Um, they're your books. I knew you wanted to get rid of them, but I couldn't donate them. I just knew you'd want them back one day, so instead of bringing them to Goodwill, I brought them back to my place. I'm sorry if I crossed a line, I just—"

Words lodge in my throat as Bri stands there, jaw unhinged in complete silence.

Shit, I overstepped. I knew I shouldn't have kept this a secret from her. I should have—

My thoughts come to a screeching halt when Bri's body collides into mine. Kisses fall from her sweet lips onto my skin, peppering me in her affection.

Okay, so she's *not* mad, then.

"Oh my God!!" she practically screeches. "I can't believe you kept them!" Each word is punctuated with open mouthed kisses across my entire face. Every press of her lips sends electrical shocks throughout my system and blood rushing south. "This is the most thoughtful thing anyone's ever done for me!"

"This is so thoughtful. I can't believe you kept them. Oh my God." Bri's body shakes with tears, and I carry her to the couch, cradling her in my arms.

"Of course I kept them. They're a part of you, and I just couldn't bear to toss away something you love so deeply. We can load my car up and bring them back to your place, if you want."

"Our place." Her words catch me off guard.

"What?" I ask.

"I want you to move in with me. It's not home without you in it. I want you in every corner of my house. I want to make a home with you. I miss you like crazy when you're not with me, so do you want to?"

"Hell yeah, I do. Home is wherever you are. This place is just that, a place. I hate the days when I don't wake up next to you."

Bri straddles my lap before kissing me. I tilt her head back so I can deepen the kiss further. We're so lost in the moment that I forget about the books on the floor.

"Hold on, Bri. We have to do the book exchange."

"Oh, yeah. Although, with both bags being identical and on the floor, I don't know which is which."

"I guess we'll just have to pick whatever bag, and if we pick our own, we can just switch." Bri leaps off my lap to grab both bags. She hands me one before sitting next to me.

"On the count of three?" she suggests.

"One...two...three." We pull the books out simultaneously, and then I see we picked out the same book. We look at each other and keel over with laughter.

"Why doesn't this surprise me?" Bri asks.

"I guess we just know each other so well."

"We can buddy read it together now. Ah, this is so exciting. I've never had a boyfriend who likes to read. I can't wait to lay with each other and read this ridiculous book. I mean, robot sex? How does that even happen?"

"That's what I thought when I saw it. And how thick of a cock can a robot have? Make it make sense."

"Seriously, it's ridiculous. I think this book will look perfect on my shelf. Um." Bri shifts in her seat, tossing nervous glances toward the boxes that litter my floor. She looks uncomfortable, but I remain silent, knowing she'll say what's on her mind when she's ready. "So, this may sound like it's random, but I think it's time I talk to Max. I miss my brother so much, and I hate that I've kept him in the dark. He built me that bookshelf, and just thinking of putting the books back on my shelf has me thinking about my relationship with him."

"That's great, Bri. Do you want me to come with you? Or is this something you need to do on your own?"

"I'd really like you to be there. Maybe not in the same room when I'm having the conversation, but just knowing you'd be there makes me feel better about it."

"Then I'll be there. Oh, hey, I talked to Gage about possibly stepping back and starting a new venture. He's down with it, so let me know when you're ready to start planning everything."

"This is happening for real then, huh? It wasn't something you said because you thought it'd make me happy?"

"Of course it's real. I want to do this with you, and I'm not doing this just to make you happy. Doing this with you will make me happy, too."

"Well, I should probably formally quit my salon job before we do anything. My boss has been incredible with everything, letting me take leave while I recovered from everything. As long as you're doing it with me, then I'm all in."

"I can't wait to plan everything with you. This feels like it's been the missing piece for both of us, and the fact that we'll do it together? I can't even begin to express how happy I am."

"Well, then I say we stop talking. I've had another position that I've wanted to try with you."

"Oh? And what might that be?"

Bri leans in and whispers in my ear, "I want you on your back while I ride your cock like I'm in a rodeo."

"I think we can manage that." I stand up and toss Bri over my shoulder, bringing her into my bedroom. I toss her onto the bed where she bounces a few times. I hover over her, caging her head in between my forearms.

"I can't wait to see how you ride my cock, baby." I flip our positions so that I'm on my back and Bri is straddling my hips.

She whips off her shirt and unhooks her bra with a simple flick of her fingers. She leans down, her tits swinging in front of my face. I take one of her nipples in my mouth while pinching the other with my fingers. Bri's hips grind against mine and she lets out a long moan. I love how vocal she is during sex.

I bite her nipple before soothing it with my tongue.

"If you keep rocking those hips, I'm not gonna last long." Bri shimmies off of my lap so she can remove her leggings. Her eyes remain locked on mine as she makes a show of sliding the black fabric down her thighs. The moment she steps out of her pants, she saunters back over to me with an extra swish of her hips before climbing back on top of me.

"You aren't coming anywhere but inside of me."

Brianna

Temperature play? Yes please

ASHER KEPT MY BOOKS for me.

He. Kept. My books.

He *knew* I'd regret my choice to let them go. Seriously, how did I get so lucky to call this man mine? I crawl up his body, peppering quick kisses along the way. I grip his swollen cock in my hand, giving it a few firm tugs, and watch as his eyes roll back in his head. My tongue glides along the underside before licking the bit of pre-cum from the tip, savoring the salty taste that's pure Asher. As I line him up with my entrance, I feel powerful. I am in complete control here, and I allow myself a moment to revel in it as I tease myself by sliding his cock along my folds, coating himself in my arousal.

"I swear to fuck, bear. If you don't put my cock inside of you and ride me like the dirty girl you are, I—"

The rest of his sentence is cut off the moment I'm fully seated on him, circling my hips to quench my thirst for that delicious friction. Fuck, this feels good. My head falls back, and I circle my hips, reveling in the sensation of feeling full.

"You better start moving or I'm gonna flip you over and fuck your pretty pussy myself."

I lean down so that my full, supple tits are in direct view of his mouth. Asher licks his lips before blowing cold air onto my sensitive nipples. Lust-filled shivers race down my spine like raindrops on a car window. I lift my hips an inch or so off of him before slamming black down and rocking in a quick, feverish motion, chasing after the high of a blissful orgasm.

Lift. Slam. Rock.

The rhythm I've created has me seeing stars behind my eyelids.

"Eyes open, baby girl. I want to watch your pleasure play across your beautiful face."

My eyes snap open, locking with his raw, hungry eyes. I continue my rhythm, obsessed with the way his cock fills me to the brim. I am in charge of my own pleasure here, and it feels so damn incredible. I haven't even worried about my weight once. I think that insecurity of mine has been fucked out of me.

Asher brings my breasts into his hand, squeezing them firmly. The sensation has me picking up speed, chasing an orgasm that is on the horizon.

"Fuck, I love when you play with my tits." I lean down, and this new angle has me crying out. "Take one in your mouth. I want your tongue fucking my nipple while I'm fucking your cock."

Asher does exactly as he's told, and holy shit does it feel incredible. He flattens his tongue against one of my nipples and the friction sends an explosion of sensations throughout my body. He blows cold air against my nipple again, lighting up my nervous system like lightning across a darkened sky.

"Yes! Do that again!" I demand as I begin to rock my hips faster when he blows the cold air again. The cool air feels like heaven. My back arches and my toes curl so hard it borders on painful.

"You look gorgeous on top of me, baby. I could have you in this position every day and never tire of the view. Now, come on my cock like a good girl."

"AAAH. Oh my God!" I shout. It's the *good girl* that has me detonating. My rhythm goes from frantic to slow, riding out my orgasm for as long as I can. I'm completely spent when I slip off of him. I have every intention of snuggling with Asher, but he's now hovering over me with a wicked grin on his face.

"You thought we were done? It's my turn now, baby, but I need to grab a few things first." Asher presses a quick kiss to my lips before pushing himself off the bed. He comes back moments later with the famous black silk blindfold and a matching ribbon. His rough hands trace their way up my body, and I'm wriggling beneath him. He finds his way to my ear, tugging on the sensitive lobe with his teeth before whispering in my ear:

"How do you feel about being tied up and blindfolded?"

Oh. I wasn't expecting that to come from his mouth, but my mouth waters and my sensitive clit throbs with excitement.

"I'm up for anything. Tie me up, Daddy." Asher's grin is pure sex as he lifts the back of my head to place the silk over my eyes. He grabs my wrists in one of his as he places them over my head. Asher is tying some intricate knot, and when I try to wiggle them free, I'm met with resistance.

"Don't even think about it. It's my turn to use you. So, you're going to lay there like a good girl and take everything I give you."

"Yes, Daddy."

"Good, let's begin" is all Asher says before walking away.

Asher

I fill a bowl with ice cubes and grab the low-temperature candles I bought last week along with a lighter. I've always wanted to try temperature play, and Bri is the perfect person to do it with. As much as I didn't want to involve my brother, talking to Xander about spicing things up with Bri and I was the right move, even if he did get carried away with the suggestions.

I grab the toy I bought for us to try together, knowing her being blindfolded will make the experience more intense. *It's time to play.* I run up the stairs to see Bri squirming on the bed and rubbing her thighs together. Goddamn, she's a fucking masterpiece, body sprawled out before me with her hands tied together. She's vulnerable and at my mercy. A wicked smile tugs at the corners of my mouth as I think of how much fun this is gonna be.

"Asher?"

"It's me, baby. I brought some things with me, but before we continue, I want to make sure you understand what you're in for."

"I'll do whatever you want, just do something soon. I'm dying over here," Bri whines.

"Patience. Have you heard of temperature play?"

"W-What's that?" Her curiosity is so much of a turn on that I have to tell my dick to chill out.

"It involves the use of hot and cold on your body. You hear this?" I shake the bowl and watch as she purses her lips in confusion before nodding her head.

"That's a bowl of ice cubes, ready and waiting to glide across your body, paying close attention to those nipples of yours." I pinch the perky bud between my fingers for emphasis, causing her back to arch, pushing her luscious breasts further into my hand. I grab the unlit candle and glide it across her stomach, leaving goosebumps in their wake.

"Then there are these candles I bought. I want to watch the warm wax pool from the top of the candle onto your smooth skin. I want to hear you gasp and moan while the wax hardens against your skin. All your senses are at my mercy. Does this feel like something you'd like to try?" Bri lets out a whimper before nodding her head.

"Words, baby. Use them."

"Yes, I want that."

"Good girl. I also bought us a vibrator that's specifically meant to suck that pretty clit of yours. As I fuck your cunt with my fingers, I want to use the toy at the same time. Yes or no?"

"Y-Yes." *Thank fuck I charged the toy earlier today.*

"I was hoping you'd say that." I grab two ice cubes and rub them over her mouth.

"Open up and lick it as if it were my cock." Bri does as she's told and her tongue swirls and flicks the ice cube, making my cock twitch.

"Look at you licking the ice like the dirty girl you are." Bri responds with a moan as she arches her neck as she begins to suck the ice cube into her mouth. Her tongue accidentally brushes against my fingers, and I'm tempted to shove them down her throat and gag her. *Not the time, Asher.*

The ice cube leaves her mouth with a soft pop, and I glide it down her chin and her neck before circling it around her nipple. She sucks in a sharp breath, but I don't give her time to process everything because I have an ice cube on each of her nipples.

"AAHHH, Asher, holy fuck!" Bri screams while pushing her tits into the ice.

I let the ice cubes melt, and I lean down and blow on each nipple as she squirms beneath me. I make a grab for the vibrator and turn it on.

"Open those sexy legs of yours and show me that pussy." Her legs fall open, and I let out a curse when I see how wet she is.

"Damn, is that all for me?"

"Yes..." Her response comes out breathless.

"Look at how wet you are, baby. I think I need a taste." I bend down, using my tongue to lick up her slit. She tries to clamp her thighs around my head, but I hold her steady. I click the button on the vibrator, and the sound of buzzing is music to my ears.

I give her zero warning before I press the toy against her clit, starting it off on the lowest setting. Bri's hips jerk and her back arches as she lets out a string of curses.

"Shit. Fuck. Oh my God fucking goddamn it, yes!"

Bri's body swivels her hips, chasing after her own pleasure. The second the toy reaches the highest setting, Bri's back arches off the bed, her scream threatening to shatter my eardrums. Her grinding picks up speed, and her body quivers with an impending orgasm.

"Ride it out. Fuck the toy like a good little slut. That's it. Such a good girl. You fuck this toy so good." The praise sends her over the edge, and she screams my name.

"Asher, Asher, Asher, oh *God*."

"That's it, let go. Come for me," I growl at her, pushing the vibrator even harder against her. I bury my face inside her cunt and lap up her come like a dehydrated man.

"You taste so damn good." I toss the toy on the floor, and Bri's chest is heaving and her legs lay limp on the bed.

"I'm nowhere near done with you. I'm gonna light these candles and drip hot wax all over your sexy as sin body. And then I'm going to flip you on your stomach and fuck you from behind."

"Asher, I can't come ag—" I stop her mid-sentence by smacking her pussy.

"You can and you will. You'll take it all and you'll take it well, understand?"

"Yes, Daddy." I light the candles and let them hover over her body. The ice cubes have long since melted. When I see the wax start to pool around the top of the candle, I walk around the bed so the wax can drip over her nipples.

I bring the candle closer to her breasts. I tip it over and watch the wax drip onto her perky nipple. I hear Bri's sharp inhale, and her body writhes against the bed. I let a few more drops fall before walking around to the other side of the bed to give the same treatment to her other breast.

"Mmmm, that feels good." Bri enjoying herself has my cock itching to be inside her. I move the candle down her body. Wax drips in between her chest and down her stomach, stopping before her pussy. I blow out the candle and place it in the holder it came with. I wait for the wax to dry before I flip her over.

"Time to flip you over, baby. The blindfold and ties stay on."

I lower her arms and flip her over so that they're trapped beneath her. I position her so that her ass is in the air. I smack her cheeks a few times all while stroking my painfully hard cock.

"My cock is ready for your cunt. I know you're gonna take it so well. Your pussy hugs my dick like it belongs there."

Again, I don't warn her before slamming into her. I pound into her with enough force to shake the bed. I'll be surprised if we don't make a hole in the wall.

"My dirty fucking girl. Look at your pussy gripping my cock so well. Fucking hell. You're such a good girl for me."

"Asher, don't stop. Oh, yes, right there. Feels so fucking good." Bri's words are choppy with how hard I'm fucking her.

"I never want to stop. I want to fuck this cunt all the time, and it still won't be enough. I'm going to come inside this pussy, and you're going to like it."

"Yes. Come inside me. I love having your come in me," Bri whimpers. The base of my spine begins to tingle with an impending orgasm.

"I love you so fucking much, bear," I grunt while I continue thrusting.

"I love you, too. Holy shit, I'm coming," Bri howls.

"I'm coming, too." This is the first time we've come together, and it's an experience I definitely want to repeat. Within seconds, I'm spilling into her, and my thrusts begin to slow. I press a kiss to her lower back before pulling out of her.

"I'll be right back." I kiss her ass before going to grab a towel to clean her up. I come back with a warm, damp towel and clean up our mess. I toss the towel into my hamper in the corner before I remove the blindfold and the ties around her wrists before sliding in beside her.

Bri shifts in my arms so that we are face to face, and I'm taken back by her beauty.

"Why are you looking at me like that?"

"You're just so goddamn beautiful, Bri. Everything about you is incredible. You're the most amazing woman I've ever met."

"You're pretty incredible yourself. I often wonder how lucky I am that you chose me."

"Choosing you has been the easiest thing I've ever done in my life. I choose you always, and I will choose you for the rest of my life—or as long as you'll have me." She wiggles her way into my chest, pressing a kiss on my chest.

"You saved me," Bri whispers before sleep takes her.

"You never needed saving, Bri. You've always been a damn warrior." I pull the covers over us, and I'm out moments later.

Brianna

Tell me your dick is small without telling me your dick is small

"Tell me, how have you been since our last session?" Dr. Jacqui asks.

"I've been good. Everything with my parents went well. Sharing everything with them felt freeing. I went into it afraid they'd judge and hate me, but none of that happened."

"That's fantastic, Bri. Expressing your feelings isn't easy, and you did it anyway. You really seem to be taking charge of your life again. It's wonderful to witness. Have you talked to your brother yet?"

"No. I'm still working up to that one, but I drove myself to therapy today."

"Is this the first time you've driven since the incident?"

"It's my first time driving myself to therapy, but it's not my first time behind the wheel. Another thing that Asher has been helping me with."

I explain how Asher has been working with me to overcome my fear of driving and how extremely patient he's been with me. I'm sure my cheeks are hella red with how much I gush about him. But what's not to swoon over? The man is a literal book boyfriend. After years of pinning after imaginary men, I found myself a real one.

"That's wonderful. It sounds like you are choosing to not let fear control you anymore. How does that feel?" she asks.

"It's amazing. The initial shock has worn off, but it's still nerve-wracking at times. It's something I'm continually trying to bulldoze my way through. Asher just makes it even better."

"I love this for you. Now, what's your plan with Max?"

Ugh, she always brings it back to the topic at hand. I mean, am I surprised? That's what therapy is for.

"I'm still trying to figure that out, but Asher promised to come with me for extra support."

"That's wonderful. I know we've been working on preparing you for phase three of EMDR. You're doing a lot of the heavy lifting already, and I'm so proud of all the work you've put in already."

I made the decision to try EMDR a few sessions ago. The more research I did, the more I felt like this was the final step in healing for me. I don't want what happened to me to take over my entire life. I've learned a lot about myself during this whole experience. Things that have opened my eyes to issues that I never really thought about before.

I have always been someone who thrives off control. I tend to gravitate toward the role of the leader. I just never really understood why. If things didn't go a certain way, that's when my imposter syndrome kicked in. In order to avoid that, I always made sure everything was planned out. And then when everything happened, my entire world was flipped upside down. Nothing in my life was mine anymore, and trying to come to terms with that has been hard to wrap my head around.

"Yeah, it's been exhausting...this healing thing," I joke, which makes my therapist laugh.

"Yeah, it's definitely not easy. How are you coping with everything? What are you doing for self-care?"

"I've been reading again," I say, my eyes flicking to my hands fidgeting in my lap.

"It's something me and Asher have been doing together every night, actually." I pause, sucking in a breath, knowing the bomb I am about to drop.

"We lay with each other every night. He kept the books I donated months ago and..." *Just say it, Bri. SAY IT!*

"And I even asked him to move in with me."

Butterflies erupt in my stomach, taking flight and bringing every loving emotion with them.

"Bri," she begins. I wait for her to scold me, judge me, tell me it's too soon. "That's amazing. I am so happy for you."

She reaches over and squeezes my hand, and for the first time in ages, I feel light as a feather.

Who knew having a partner who reads alongside you could carry as many benefits as it does? I've always had a CVS receipt-sized list of things I've wanted to try that I read about in my smutty books. And with Asher, a fellow avid reader, I get to explore an even kinkier side of me. Plus, it doesn't hurt that he highlights the things in his books that he wants to try with me. Thinking about the first time we ever brought a fictional scene to life has me squirming in my seat.

My mock fireplace is turned on. Fuzzy gray socks decorate my feet, keeping them nice and toasty. A beach-scented candle provides a soft glow throughout the room, bathing the space in sea salt and orange blossom.

A cozy, soft, blue crochet blanket is draped over our laps as I'm curled up against Asher while we read. This has become a staple in our Sunday evening ritual, and there's no place I'd rather be. Normally, we try to read the same book—it's more fun that way. But I've had the latest Ari Wright book on my Kindle for ages, and I just couldn't wait any longer. And boy, am I glad I did. It takes every cell of my being not to squirm on the couch—especially with Asher sitting next to me. We've tried out so many different positions. Some that still have me blushing whenever I think about it. Despite how much he loves to worship my body, I can't gather up the courage to play out a particular fantasy of mine.

Any romance reader will tell you that there are some scenes in books they want to recreate in reality. But not the dark romance ones, because green flags in those books are walking red flags in real life. I like a little pain, but I don't think I can stomach the shit that goes down in those books.

Anyway, as an avid reader of romance, I have had a few sections in books annotated with the hope that one day, I'd find a partner who'd want to reenact it with me. I've been shot down many times—by many different men. Something about how it's unrealistic of me to have those expectations. Like, tell me your dick is small without telling me it's small. So, since Asher and I got together, the request has been sitting on the tip of my tongue. I've just never had the courage to do something about it. Asher's body shifts next to me as he places his book on the coffee table before us.

"Bri, I can practically hear you thinking out loud. Care to share your thoughts?"

I pull my bottom lip in between my teeth as I contemplate whether or not I ask him. I glance down at the page I've been rereading before glancing into his gorgeous blue eyes. I can do this. The worst he can say is no, but somehow, I highly doubt he will.

"I've been wanting to try something. And before you say no, I just want you to hear me out, okay?"

"Bear, you could ask me to walk on a pile of Legos barefoot, and I'd do it."

"That's a tad dramatic, but okay. Well, I know you read spicy books like me, and I've always wanted to try and maybe...you know, recreate a scene. I don't know...it's just an idea."

My face flushes with embarrassment, and I refuse to look at his face. I check my nailbeds, which are in desperate need of some TLC. I pick invisible lint off of my leggings. I'm determined to keep my eyes fixated on my lap, but a warm hand cups my cheek, forcing me to meet his eyes.

It's there that I see blown-out pupils and a rapid pulse fluttering at the base of his neck. All telltale signs of a man turned on. I open my mouth to speak, but Asher beats me to the punch, uttering words I didn't know I needed until now.

"I thought you'd never ask." I all but throw myself on his lap before crushing my lips to his, my Kindle tumbling to the floor with a soft thump. Asher's hands are on my hips, preventing me from seeking the friction I crave, and it's him who breaks the kiss first.

"As much as I love watching you get yourself off, you asked me to do something. Let me see the scene you want to recreate."

Grinning like a madwoman, I grab my e-reader off the floor and pull up the scene I was just reading. I watch as his eyes rapidly flicker over the Kindle, reading the scene where the MMC takes his girl's throat ruthlessly while controlling her pussy with a vibrator. There's something sexy about watching a man you love reading a dirty sex scene. What's even hotter is knowing he's about to do said ungodly things to you.

Asher practically growls the second he shuts the Kindle off before tossing it on the couch. I let out a loud squeal when he flips our position—with me underneath him. He looks at me with such intensity that I could come right now.

"Give me a few minutes. But when I come back, you better be naked and on your knees for me like the dirty girl you are."

The second he leaves the room, my clothes practically fly off me. Just knowing that he's going to get my favorite vibrator—the one that he can control—has me so wound up it borders on painful. It sounds like a stampede with how fast and hard Asher is running down the stairs, and when he looks at my current position, his smirk almost does me in. Almost.

He tosses the vibrator at me, and I waste no time inserting it inside of me, relishing in the delicious pressure it gives. All the while, Asher is practically ripping the seams of his sweats with how fast he yanks them down his body. He fists his cock, pumping up and down, and my mouth waters. Fuck.

Asher saunters over to me, cock in one hand, remote control in the other. I stare at the bead of pre-cum that shines at his tip, and I want to lap it up so fucking bad. He must sense this because his cock is now a paintbrush—my lips the canvas. There's no mirror here, but I'm sure my lips are wet with his arousal.

"Lick your lips."

A simple, yet arousal-inducing request. A request I waste no time completing. The saltiness hits my tongue, and the vibrator shifts with how fucking slick I am. I have zero time to process anything because Asher has turned my vibrator on to its lowest setting. The delicious buzzing sensation lights my body up like the Fourth of July.

"Good girl. You're about to suck my cock while I control your pussy, aren't you?"

I moan in response, which isn't good enough for him because he's upped the intensity. So much so that my hips involuntarily buck forward.

"Use your words, baby."

"Ye-Yes."

"Good girl, now open up and let me in. I'm gonna fuck you until your throat is raw before coating it with my cum." A shiver runs down my spine. I glance up at him underneath my lashes and open as wide as I can. The moment my lips wrap around him, I hum, knowing he loves it when I do that. I guess this is the right move because he begins to fuck my face just the way I like it: fast, rough, and dirty.

"Look at you. Sitting pretty on your knees for me. Such a good girl." I make that humming noise again and am rewarded with the vibrator hitting my favorite setting. Buzzing sounds mixed with hips thrusting and the occasional gagging are the perfect soundtrack for this moment. Fuck. I should have asked to do something like this sooner because damn, it's hot.

My hips begin to rock as I chase the impending orgasm that I feel bubbling at the base of my spine. When I look up at Asher, his head is thrown back in complete bliss—his face contorted in a familiar way. He's close to coming. I'm close to coming. I reach out to cup his balls, and his fingers accidentally—maybe not so accidentally—push the remote to the highest level it can go. Soon, salty, hot liquid is spilling down my throat while I scream around Asher's cock.

His hips jerk a few times before he pulls out of me. I barely have the vibrator out of me when he's pulling me up by my neck and pushing me onto the couch. He gets down on his knees, forcing my legs apart, and he shoots me a wicked grin before diving between my legs. He laps up my arousal like a thirsty dog. My already sensitive clit is throbbing, and when he pulls it between his teeth, I find myself experiencing another mind-numbing, earth-shattering orgasm.

I'm a sweaty, panting mess by the time he removes himself from my legs.

"W-What was that for?"

"Your cum is mine. And I'd rather die than let a single drop of it be wasted on anything other than my tongue."

I pull him into me for a bruising kiss, mixing both of our arousals together. The taste of us is pure, raw, and incredible. A perfect cocktail.

"*There. Now our tastes are intertwined.*" *My grin is probably cheesy, but I couldn't care less.*

Asher's wicked grin has my sensitive core pulsing. The feel of his lips trailing along my jawline has my skin breaking out in thousands of goose-bumps. I suck in a sharp gasp at the delicious pain of him nipping at my earlobe before whispering in my ear:

"*I think we found our new Sunday tradition.*"

Damn it.

Now I'm so fucking turned on, *in therapy,* and it's borderline painful.

Deep breaths, Bri. Look at where you are. There's a time and a place to think dirty thoughts, and your therapist's office isn't one of them. Wait, what were we talking about? Oh, right. Books. Asher helping me. Me asking him to move in. Focus, Bri, focus.

I allow my mind to focus on the words my therapist is saying and *not* on the dirty replaying of that fantasy.

"You're making some big life changes, are you ready for all that?" Out of all the decisions that I've made, this one is the easiest. I like who I am with him. Asher brings out the parts of me I love, parts I thought I'd forever lost. He's become such an important part of my life, and I don't know who I'd be without him.

"I am. He's been an integral part of my healing journey, and I can't imagine doing life without him."

"That's great. So, how are we feeling about diving into some of the memory stuff? We've been teetering between phases one and two for a while, and I think you're ready to start reprocessing. Before we begin, I want to check in with you to see where you are."

"I'm ready. The accident won't be erased from my mind, but I don't want to be within its chokehold any longer."

"That's understandable, so let's plan to start next week. Until then, keep doing what you're doing, and I'll see you next week."

I leave the parking lot with a smile on my face and a raging pulsing sensation between my legs. I know just the person for the job.

Brianna

I winked at you after I said it

THE USUAL EXHAUSTION THAT immediately follows a therapy session is over-powered by my arousal. I hyperfocus on the road before me while my thighs aggressively rub together, my clit thirsty for the friction as if she's in the middle of a drought. Since Asher, I don't know if I'll ever *not* be wet. Just looking at the man has me weak in the knees. After today's revisit to fantasy's past, I am antsy to take out my horniness on his oh so willing cock.

On the drive home, I stop to get my favorite iced vanilla latte as a reward for doing hard shit in therapy, because damn it, I deserve it. My body is buzzing with excess energy and horniness at surprising Asher at work later.

I'm pulling into my driveway about ten minutes later. Surprise blooms throughout my body like flowers on the first day of spring when I see Avery sitting on my front porch.

"Hey, Aves, what are you doing here?" Avery's gaze meets mine, and my iced coffee falls out of my hand when I see tears.

"Aves, what's the matter? Is the baby okay? Is it Cas?"

"No, Bri, everything's good. Cas and the baby are fine. Can we go inside?" Panic threatens to claw its way up my throat as I help her up. We walk through the front door and make our way to the couch. The silence is killing me.

"Aves, this no talking thing mixed with the tears is scaring me. What's going on?" Avery pulls a white envelope out of her purse and hands it to me.

"Open it." My fingers trail over the envelope's seal before opening it.

I let out a gasp before I scream. "Are you for real?"

"Yes. It's real. I'm having a little girl. Cas is losing his mind and is already threatening to murder any man who comes within a five mile radius of her. I'm having a girl, Bri." I get up from my spot on the couch and throw my arms around her. I'm so ecstatic for my best friend.

"I'm going to have a niece! I'm so happy for you guys."

"Thanks, babes. She's going to have the best life and even better people around her. You are going to play such an important role in this girl's life, Bri. I know she already loves you so much."

I place my hand on her growing belly and whisper, "You're so loved, baby girl. I can't wait to meet you. Oh, and your parents are total horn-dogs, so be prepared to be grossed out."

"Bee, stop that."

"What? Am I wrong? All you have to do is walk around the house and Cas is practically drooling over you." Avery snort-laughs and just shrugs her shoulders.

"I could say the same about you and Asher. You two go at it like rabbits."

I flip my hair over my shoulder and toss her an innocent look. "I have no idea what you're talking about."

"Really? Does candle wax ring any bells for you?"

My face turns beet red, and I shift in my seat just thinking about that night. I called Avery the following day and gave her a summary of what happened.

"Oh, that? That was nothing."

"Nothing, huh? Then why are you squeezing your thighs together and your pupils are blown?"

"I hate you." I mock glare at her.

"You love me. Admit it, you two are just as big of horndogs as Cas and I."

"Fine, you win."

"Speaking of, how *are* you and Asher?" She waggles her eyebrows at me, and I playfully push her shoulder.

"We're good. He's slowly starting to move his things in, and the sex? Avery, it's out of this world. The way he pays attention to my body? It's like he's committing it to memory so that he never forgets a single detail. I'm actually planning to surprise him later at work. I bought this silky, black wrap dress, and I plan to do my hair in big curls and wear absolutely nothing underneath." I see Avery roll her eyes at me.

"Thanks for the details, Bri. I don't think I'd survive without them."

"Shut up. But seriously, though, Aves. I'm so happy. He makes me happy."

"I'm so happy for you. You're such an amazing, wonderful human and you deserve the world. I feel like I should threaten to chop his balls off if he hurts you. Ya know, like you did with Cas."

"I still live by that threat, but go for it. Fair is fair."

Avery and I scour Pinterest, creating endless boards of inspiration for her baby shower. My best friend isn't one for extravagant things, so I offer to take as much of the load off her shoulders as I can. I *love* planning shit like this, always have. And it feels even more special because it's for my future niece.

I'm still reeling with the news that my bestie is having a girl. I'm putting together yet another Pinterest board when I realize it's almost time for me to surprise Asher. I hop in the shower, making sure to wash and exfoliate every inch of me. By the time I step out of my scalding hot shower that even Satan himself wouldn't be able to withstand, my skin is pink, but every inch of me feels as smooth as silk.

My body is thoroughly moisturized, my hair and makeup are on point, and I feel my body pulse with anticipation knowing my pussy is about to get destroyed by the man my heart can't stop thinking about.

Who knew I'd be as into office sex as I am?

Well, okay. Office sex with *Asher*, specifically. This man has reignited my sex drive, and for that I'll be forever grateful. Plus, this will be the first time I'm actually driving myself to the bar. What better way to celebrate that milestone than to have my man pound into me relentlessly? Everything seems to be falling into place, and I'm ready for what happens next.

Asher

I've been by to see Max multiple times, but this time is different. When Bri talks to her brother, I don't want our relationship to override the conversation. I brought this up to Bri and she gave me the okay to talk to him about us.

Us.

It's surreal to think that Bri and I are an *us* now. When I walk into Max's room, I'm surprised to see Cas.

"Hey, man, what're you doing here?" I ask Cas.

"Well, Asher. Max and I are friends. And when you're friends with someone, you hang out with them." Cas smirks at me. *Bastard.*

"Fuck off, Cas," I retort before turning to Max.

Max's strength continuously astounds me. And I'm not just talking about his physical strength, but mental and emotional, too. Anyone could have taken the cards he's been dealt and let it run their lives.

Not Max, though.

He's showed up for PT every day, ready to make it his bitch.

Watching him go from limp and lifeless to being able to walk on his own has been truly incredible to witness. He's nowhere near one hundred percent, as he still has faint twinges of pain in his arm and shoulder, but he's here. He's alive. And that's what matters. I notice the boot he once relied heavily on sitting in the corner, and I know without a doubt that his mom is the reason it's still there. His doctor has given him the all clear to go back to work with some slight restrictions, but anytime someone brings it up to him, he changes the subject. He says he's content with office management stuff at his company, but I call bullshit. Well, I silently call it.

"Hey, buddy, how're things going?"

"Good. Shit has been a lot better. I no longer have to do as much PT now, and I'm able to walk up and down the stairs without feeling like I need to take a break."

"That's good. I'm happy for you, man."

I don't think Max is gonna give two shits that I'm dating his sister. But there's a sliver of doubt lingering in my mind that has me second guessing myself.

Max, Bri, and I have been in each other's lives for years. We'd spend every summer going on trips with each other's families or just hanging out at each other's houses. There has always been this unspoken, intense connection between Bri and I. There had been many nights tossing and turning as visions of Bri flooded my brain. Her laughter was the perfect lullaby, guiding me to sleep. Well, that and the endless amount of Bri-induced orgasms. I'd chalked it up to teenage hormones and *not* because of how incredible she was. During the daytime, I'd drown in my own denial. And at night, I let my imagination run wild as I pictured Bri's pretty lips wrapped around my cock. It wasn't until her name slipped through my lips after a mind-numbing orgasm that I realized the truth.

I was hopelessly, stupidly in love with my best friend's sister. A confession I'd take with me to the grave as a kid since Max was extremely protective of his sister. Hell, he warned our entire baseball team off from dating his sister. And since I was both his best friend *and* teammate, I was double fucked. So, I kept my feelings for her under lock and key, planning to never tell a soul how I felt. The only time I came close to saying fuck it was when she threw herself at me during that party.

Now that I have her, I refuse to give her up for anyone or anything. Even if that means my relationship with Max isn't the same. Because Bri deserves to be loved out loud. And no one, not even my best friend, will stop that from happening.

"Asher?" Max interrupts my inner monologue.

When I look up at him, it's clear he's been talking to me, and I wasn't paying attention.

"Hmm?"

"I was asking how Bri was doing? She still hasn't been by to see me or texted me back. I just want to know she's okay."

"She's doing a lot better. She wants to come see you and she will when she's ready. Speaking of Bri, I have something I need to say."

"Finally!" Max shouts, causing me to jump out of my seat.

"Finally? What do you mean finally?" *What the fuck?*

"Well, I'm assuming you two are together?" Max raises his brow, wearing his signature crooked smile.

"We are. I'm sorry I didn't ask for your permission to—" Max interrupts me.

"Permission? Like Bri would give a shit if I said yes or no. Either way, I'm happy for you guys. It's been obvious you two liked each other for years. I know you'll treat her right, so I'm fully behind it."

"Thanks, man. I didn't know how you'd act, honestly. I mean, you warned our entire baseball team not to fuck with her. What did you expect me to think?"

"Fucking hell, man. I winked at you after I said it. That was me telling you the rules didn't apply to you, dumbass."

"Fuck. You did, didn't you? Goddamn it, so we could have been together this whole time. Asshole. As far as Bri not giving a shit about your thoughts? You're wrong. She values your opinion a lot. I think that's why she hasn't been to see you. Your opinion of her matters."

Max isn't an overly emotional person, but as soon as the words escape my lips, Max's eyes fill with sadness. I watch an entire life of pure sibling love flash before me as his gaze swims with unshed tears begging to be freed. His head falls into his hands, and I watch as emotion rattles his entire body like an earthquake. With Bri, I'd pull her into my arms. But with Max, he just needs the space to feel. So Cas and I sit next to him in silence, offering our support just by being here.

"I've held everything in for so long and I can't take it anymore. I am a complete mess, and I feel like I'm losing my mind. That accident fucked me up, and I miss my sister. She was my first ever friend, and the fact that she hasn't been by to see me hurts. I understand she's going through her own shit, too, I just wish she would come to me."

Well, damn. I guess all that waiting for Max to express himself paid off. I've always had a solid connection with my gut instinct, and it told me to wait him out. Max will come to you when he's ready. I just wish I knew how bad it was, because seeing my best friend shatter before me? Truly heartbreaking.

"She wants to. She's just been dealing with some heavy shit. Give her time, she'll come around."

"I just feel like she hates me. Either that, or she's mad at me or something. We've never gone this long without talking to each other. It feels like a piece of me is missing."

"Hey. Trust me when I say this, she doesn't hate you. I think you both need to talk to each other and when you do, things will make sense. Do you..." I pause, unsure if I want to ask this type of question. Not everyone is pro-therapy. As much as Max has been supportive of me and my therapy journey, I'm not sure where his thoughts lie on the matter. "Listen, man, please don't take this the wrong way, but are you planning to go to therapy to deal with your trauma?"

"Yeah. I think I need to. I have it on my list of things to do, but I'm not ready yet."

"I get it. It took me a while to work my way up to therapy. Shit like this isn't easy to work through. You have to be ready to tackle your shit," Cas adds.

If anyone knows about healing from grief, it's Cas. He's a recovering addict who is still processing and healing from his childhood trauma. I give him a shit ton of credit. It's not easy to turn your life around, and yet, he did it.

"Yeah, I guess so. And I'm not even close to being prepared to have the difficult conversations. Anyway, enough about me. How's dad to be?"

"Good. Avery and the baby are doing well. We found out what we're having." Cas looks down at his feet, but his smile is as wide as can be.

"So, are you going to stop there? Or are you planning to tell us the news?"

"We're having a little girl." Cas' eyes begin to water, and his smile widens even more.

"Watch out future partners, this little girl has three men in her life who will kick their ass if they hurt her," Max jokes around.

"Don't even get me started on that. She's not allowed to date until she's forty."

"You aren't gonna be able to stop her. With a woman like Avery, that girl is destined to be beautiful. Men, and or women, will flock to her like bees to honey."

"Fuck," Cas curses while throwing his head back.

Max and I can't help but laugh. Poor Cas, he has his work cut out for him.

"So, Bri and I are planning on going into business together," I blurt out. Cas and Max look at me with matching surprised expressions.

"What?" Max asks

"Yeah, she told me she's always wanted to open her own bookstore, and I've been wanting to do something more with my life. So, the two of us are going to pair certain cocktails with books and call it 'Booked 'N' Boozed.'"

"I like that. I think the two of you will work well together, especially with the things Avery tells me." Cas winks at me.

Max covers his ears and shouts, "I don't wanna know! That's my sister."

We spend the rest of the time laughing, and they share their opinions on cocktail names. We talk until I have to leave for the bar.

Brianna

Are you gonna feed me that cherry?

I PULL INTO ACES, and I thank my lucky stars no one's here yet. They don't open for another hour, but not even Gage's motorcycle is in the employee's only lot. I glance around and when I spot Asher's car, I walk up to the back door and knock. My original plan was to wear my black wrap dress, but then I had a ballsy idea. So, underneath my long, brown trench is the red lingerie set that Asher bought me during our shopping trip. Inside my bag is the dress so that I can hang out with him while he works. He's sexy as hell behind the bar.

"Hi, bear, what are you doing here?" He leans in and presses a quick kiss to my lips before pulling me inside.

"I love watching you work." I trail a finger up and down his arm, and I watch as the pulse in his neck quickens. "It also helps that watching you shake up a cocktail is total forearm porn for me. So, I figured I could hang out before it gets crazy."

"I'm glad you're here. I told Max about us, and he wasn't even surprised. Can you believe that?" Asher is prepping behind the bar, so his back is to me. I strip my coat off and toss it on the floor and climb on top of the bar top. Asher has yet to pay attention to me, his attention focused on preparing the garnishes.

"I'm not surprised. Max has always given me shit for liking you—even when I didn't like you at the time. Well, if I'm being honest, I think I was in denial."

"Really? Max can be a real dick sometimes, huh?" I frown at his back because he *still* hasn't turned around. I have to get creative with my methods here.

"Hey, Ash? Can I have a cherry?"

"Yeah, here." He hands me the bowl without looking at me. *Gah...men.*

"I want you to feed it to me." There, he'll have to look at me now.

"Why do you want...*Fuck.*" Asher finally turns around, his eyes scanning my body.

"Took you long enough. Now, are you gonna feed me the cherry?" I lean over the bar, breasts spilling over the lacey top. Asher places the cherry on my tongue, and before he can pull the stem off, I pop the entire thing in my mouth. I work the stem into a knot before grabbing Asher's hand and spitting it into his palm.

"Motherfucker. Is this the outfit from the dressing room?"

"It sure is."

"I'm curious. What was your plan for all this?" Asher waves his hand over my outfit.

"You're a smart man, take a guess."

"My dirty girl, you want to be fucked in the office again, don't you?"

"Mmm, nope. Try again."

"Did you wear this just to tease me?"

"I'm not *that* cruel. I'll give you one more try. Make it count, because if you get it wrong, I leave." Asher narrows his eyes at me, cocking his head to the side while he thinks. My pulse begins to race when I see recognition cross his face.

"You want to be fucked in this bar, don't you?"

"Look at you using your upstairs head." I attempt to pat him on his shoulder, but Asher grabs me by the back of my neck and brings his lips to mine. Greedy tongues tangle with each other while moans and grunts fill the silent space.

"Are you fucking serious?" We break apart at the sound of Gage's voice. He's off to the side, tattooed arms crossed over his chest with a smirk on his face.

"Leave, Gage," Asher demands, but the fact of getting caught turns me on.

"Don't have to tell me twice. I'll be back in thirty minutes. Wipe that shit down when you're done." Gage sends a wink in our direction before turning and walking out the door. Asher follows closely behind him to lock the door.

The second he turns around, he's ordering me around. "Bottoms off, legs spread out, baby."

"What about my heels?"

"Leave them on. I want them digging into my back when your pretty legs wrap around my waist as I fuck you on this stool. Now, do what I said." I slip the bottoms off before tossing them at Asher, who puts them in his pocket.

"You're not gonna get these back. Now, let me see how wet you are for me."

I slip a finger inside of me, gathering my arousal on the tip before extending it out toward Asher. His lips wrap around my finger, licking it clean.

"Mmm, so fucking good. Now scoot down a little bit, you're gonna lay back while I fuck you with my cock." My upper back comes in contact with the edge of the bar top with my ass on the edge of the smooth, leather chair. I squirm in the chair as Asher unzips his pants and fists his cock.

I lean up on my elbows, watching him while licking my lips. He has such a nice dick, and I love when he's inside of me.

"You like what you see, Bri?"

"You know I do. Now, why are you standing there holding your cock and not—" Asher slams into me, stopping me mid-sentence. My eyes roll into the back of my head, my legs wrapping around his waist.

"Look at you sucking my cock inside your pussy. Hold onto the edge of the bar, baby." That's all the warning he gives me before he's pulling out and ramming back into me. Over and over again, he fucks me like he owns me. I mean, he pretty much does at this point. I'm an independent woman, but the way this man possesses me? I'm living for it.

Asher lifts my hips which changes the angle, and I feel him hit that special spot.

"Oh, fuck. Yes, Asher. That's the spot. Right there."

"Fuck, you take me so well. You are mine. You taste like mine, and you feel like mine. No one will ever fuck you again. Do you hear me?"

"No one, Asher, only you. Ahh shit, I'm close."

"I know you want to come on this cock, so fucking give it to me." Asher rotates his hips before he slams into me.

"Oh, fuck, I'm coming. Asher!" I scream.

"That's right, baby. Milk Daddy's cock like the greedy girl you are." Within seconds, Asher is coming inside me, and I'm biting my lip so hard that I'm sure I draw blood.

Asher pulls out of me only to put his head between my legs, cleaning up the mess we made with his tongue. My clit pulses, but I'm just completely spent.

"I'll never be able to look at this bar the same way again."

"Me neither. I guess I should get dressed and let you finish opening." I unwrap my legs from his waist, and he grabs my hands to help me off the bar.

"You don't have to leave. You can hang here while I open."

"Oh, I wasn't going anywhere. I'm gonna get dressed and then hang out with you while you work." Asher's smile is infectious, and he presses a kiss to my forehead.

"I love that idea. Now, go get dressed before people start banging on the door."

Asher looks fucking sexy as hell making drinks. I watch as his forearms flex when he's shaking up a mixed drink for one of the patrons. Every so often, his eyes find mine from across the bar and he smiles. Sometimes, he'll look at the spot he fucked me on earlier before winking at me, making me squirm in my chair.

I've been nursing my cherry Coke for about thirty minutes when I feel a presence sitting down next to me. I'm ready to tell the person I'm not interested, but when I look over, I groan. *Giselle.* What the hell does she want?

"Can I help you?" I don't look at her while I ask the question. Maybe she'll get the hint and walk away. Of course, she doesn't.

"I think it's cute how you think you and Asher will last. Men like him," she nods her head in his direction before continuing, "go for a specific type of woman. And I hate to break it to you, *Bri,* but you aren't it."

"What the fuck is that supposed to mean?"

"I mean, a year ago maybe, but since you've uh…gained weight, he won't stay. Plus size ain't a cute look. I'm only saying this because I don't want to see you get your heart broken. I care about my friend."

"Giselle, we haven't been friends since we were thirteen. Ever since you cut me out of your life. Or did you forget that?" A flicker of what I assume is yearning flashes across Giselle's face before her bitchy mask slips into place. It's a rare moment when I get a glimpse of my former friend.

"You hooked up with my boyfriend!"

"Giselle, I never hooked up with him. He came onto me, then lied to you, saying we had sex. I've *never* touched that asshole. Unlike you, I care about my friends. So, with all the love I can muster, fuck off."

"You're always fucking everything up. I mean, look at what you did to Max. You put him in the hospital. Everything you touch turns to dust. I wonder how long it'll take for you to fuck Asher over."

Giselle starts off with a mock pout, but then a flash of guilt crosses her face. She goes to open her mouth, but I'm not focused on her anymore. My eyes sting and my heart feels like it's going one hundred miles an hour in my chest. The walls begin to close around me, and my face and arms feel hot. I *need to get out of here.* I look for Asher to make sure he can't see me. I don't want him to see me this upset when he's so busy. My gaze locks with Gage, and he must see the need to escape, because he just gives me a nod.

I grab my bag and bolt out the door, desperately needing air. I should call a rideshare because I'm in no condition to drive, but I can't risk waiting for it to arrive and Asher finding me. I'm practically running to my car and peeling out of the parking lot.

I'm not paying attention to where I'm going, so I don't realize that it's *the* intersection before it's too late. My breaths are erratic, and my heart is racing at the speed of light. I can't get myself to slow down. Honking surrounds me, but I'm frozen. The light has since turned green, but I can't move. I'm back at the scene of the accident, and my ears fill with the sounds of shattering glass and tires squealing. Somehow, I manage to grab my phone and hit dial.

Black dots dance across my vision, and it feels like I'm about to pass out. I'm not sure how long I've been sitting in this spot, but a knock on my window has me jumping out of my skin.

Asher

Sleep well, little warrior

I FEEL HER ABSENCE before I look up to where she was sitting to find her no longer there. Where could she have gone? And why didn't she say goodbye? A flash of blonde hair crosses my path, and I internally curse.

"What the fuck do you want, Giselle?"

"What does she have that I don't?" I'm surprised at the vulnerability in her tone. When I look up, she genuinely looks upset.

"She's everything to me. She has been since I was seventeen. She's kind, and loving, and she's funny as hell. She's adventurous and courageous, and I love her."

Giselle is eerily quiet, so when I give her my full attention, she nervously fiddles with her fingers and chews on her bottom lip.

"Spit it out, Giselle."

"I said some things to Bri, and she ran off." She may look guilty, but my blood is boiling.

"What did you say to her?"

"I said she's the reason Max was in the hospital and that it won't be long until she screws you over. I...I'm sorry." Giselle is full-on crying now.

"Goddamn it, Giselle. You just have to exploit everyone's insecurities, don't you? Why are you like this? With an ugly heart like yours, it's no surprise you're always alone!" I shout at her, not giving a shit about the looks I'm getting from our customers.

"Ash—" Gage tries to soothe the tension, but my murderous look shuts him up real quick.

"I-I—" she stutters with a panicked look on her face.

This time when Gage intervenes, I let him. "Asher, man, step back. Take care of your girl and I'll take care of everything else."

Just that second, my phone rings and Bri's name flashes across my screen.

"Bear?"

"Asher..." The fear in her voice has my blood freezing. My mind wanders with endless possibilities.

"Are you okay? Are you hurt? Where are you?"

"I-I...Can you come get me?" Shit, she's having a panic attack. She's having a panic attack and I'm not there.

"Send me your location. I'm on my way."

"O-Okay. I-I can't do this." *Shit.*

"Hold on, baby, I'm coming for you. I love you, I'll be there soon." I reluctantly hang up, but I need to call an Uber so I can drive her home. Something tells me she won't be able to do much in the state she's in.

My phone pings with her location. "Fuck," I curse while slamming my hand against the bar.

"What's up?" Gage asks.

"She's at the same intersection where the accident happened and she's fucking panicking. Goddamn it. I should have checked on her throughout the night. I should have—" I'm stopped mid-sentence by Giselle.

"I'll take you." She's settling her tab with Gage while gathering her things.

"No. You've done enough. I hope you're fucking happy with what you've done. Go find someone else's life to ruin."

"I—" Giselle starts, but I'm already moving past her, phone in hand pulling up the Uber app.

Five minutes away. Fuck. *I'm coming, bear. I'll be there soon.* I'm pacing the parking lot looking like a madman when a midnight blue sedan pulls up. A quick glance at the license plate confirms it's my ride. I'm jumping in the car, and after three failed attempts to get my seatbelt on, I'm finally buckled in.

"I will triple your tip if you step on it."

It's dark outside, so I can't really see the driver's profile, but their eyes meet mine in the rearview mirror. They must see the urgency in my expression, because they nod curtly before stepping on it. It's only a five minute drive, but it feels like hours. I have the driver drop me off at the gas station near the intersection. He's barely pulling to a stop before I'm out of the car and running, eager to get my arms around her. I'm out of breath, but I don't give a fuck. I'm knocking on her window, and when she jumps, I jump. Her eyes are bloodshot, and she looks like she's seconds away from crumbling to the ground.

People honk at me, but I don't care. I aggressively wave at them, telling them to go around us. My focus is on my girl, frozen in her seat.

"Can you unlock the door, sweetheart?" She looks like a zombie, but her hand moves to unlock the door. The second I hear the clicking sound, I'm opening the door and flicking the hazards on. I pull her into my arms, her body soft against mine as I sit with her in my lap, rocking her in the driver's seat as sobs wrack her body. She clings to me like a koala, my fingers tangled in her wild mane in a desperate attempt to ground the both of us.

"I got you. I'm here and you're safe. You're okay."

"T-Thank you for coming."

"You call, I come. Always. Let it out, baby. You can cry on my shoulder." That's all it takes for her to break down all over again. Bri's crying so hard that she chokes on her sobs. Her body vibrates with emotion, and I just let her cry. We don't talk about what happened. We don't need to; she'll talk about it when she's ready.

I press a kiss to her temple and squeeze her tighter against my chest. I rock her in my arms while murmuring in her ear, "I love you. And you're safe now."

"Can you t-take me h-home?" Bri's voice sounds so small that I have to bury the rage down.

"Of course, go ahead and crawl over to the passenger seat. I'll drive you home."

"H-How did you get here?"

"I ordered an Uber immediately after we got off the phone. I had them step on it so I could get to you."

"Y-You did?"

"Of course I did. You needed me, so I came. Best seventy-five bucks I've spent."

Bri's eyes widen in shock at the astronomical amount. I cup her face in my hands, wiping away any tears that fall before leaning in to kiss her forehead. "Let's not worry about that now. Let's get you home and in bed."

"Okay." Bri climbs over to the passenger seat, and I buckle her in. She reaches for my hand, and I interlock our fingers together. The light turns green, and I look both ways before driving through the intersection.

Bri is passed out by the time we pull into her driveway, so I'm carrying her through the house bridal style. As I'm tucking her in bed, she whispers something that I wasn't expecting her to say after everything.

"I-I know I-I said I wanted to talk to Max, but I-I'm n-not r-ready y-yet," Bri stammers before turning over, and then she's out like a light. My little warrior just went through a scary experience, and now she wants to tackle a difficult conversation with her brother.

"You're stronger than you know, bear. We'll do it when you're ready." I lean down, pressing a kiss to her temple before whispering in her ear, "I love you, baby. Sleep well, little warrior." I turn off the lights before slipping in behind her. Her strength is a beautiful thing.

Brianna

My life has felt like an endless thunderstorm

MY HEAD IS POUNDING when I wake. After the night I had, it doesn't come as a surprise to me. What does shock me is waking up alone. Asher's side of the bed is cool to the touch, alerting me that he's been up for some time. The sound of crinkling paper has me turning over, and that's when I see it. A piece of paper with Asher's familiar scrawl.

Good morning, beautiful. Head downstairs when you wake up—Asher

Warmth spreads throughout my body like that first sip of morning coffee. I toss the blanket to the side and run to my closet. The feel of the silk pajama set glides across my skin like a swimmer in water. My eyes flick to the pair of sweats I used to live in, and pride radiates inside my chest at how far I've come. The gray sweats represent a time in my life when my world was void of all color. When everything was crashing down around me, cloaking my world in complete darkness.

I hug the fabric against my chest, thanking them for their love and support before placing them in their designated spot. The closet door closes with a soft click, and I slip my feet into my fuzzy slippers before walking downstairs. The smell of vanilla waffles assaults my nose. I turn the corner into the kitchen and my breath hitches. Spread out before me are all my favorites. There's the main dish, the vanilla waffles, but next to it is a bowl of the juiciest, most ripe looking watermelon I've ever seen.

My favorite iced coffee sits on the other side, and I watch as drips of condensation race down the plastic cup. The sound of sizzling has my attention snapping to the oven where a shirtless Asher is cooking. I should be concerned about the potential burns he might get, but I can't help but ogle him. Seriously, the man is fucking built. He's the perfect amount of muscular—not too bulky but not too skinny. Avery may like her men skinny, but when I touch a man, I want something to grab onto. And Asher has plenty of muscles for me to explore. I watch, completely mesmerized as his back muscles ripple like fresh raindrops on a crystal lake while he flips whatever he's making. Asher's skin glows underneath the sun's rays, illuminating the most delicious back dimples that I want to sink my teeth into.

Great. Now I'm horny *and* hungry—which seems to be a permanent feat with him around. I glide over toward him and feel his muscles tense when I press a kiss against his back. I wrap my arms around his middle, letting the heat from his skin soak into mine. My face is buried into his back, and I inhale the now familiar scent of cinnamon and leather. My mouth waters, and not from the smell of turkey bacon and hashbrowns crackling in the pan.

The burners click off, and Asher transfers everything from frying pan to plate. He turns around, lifting me up and plopping me onto the counter next to the stove. The cold countertop shocks my system with the same intensity as stepping into an ice cold pool. Asher steps in between my legs as my arms wrap around his neck.

Our lips meet, the kiss languid and sensual. Our tongues intimately dance together as soft moans fill the space. Asher is the first to pull back, tucking a few strands of hair behind my ears. His eyes scan my face and when his gaze meets mine, I see the love there.

"Good morning."

"Good morning. How long have you been up? I woke up and you weren't there." My fingers scratch his scalp and Asher's eyes flutter closed while leaning into my touch.

"I've been up for a while, planning some things for you."

"For me?"

"Yeah, last night was a lot for you, so I thought you'd need a reset day." I pull my hands out of his hair, my arms falling limp against my sides.

Yesterday started off amazing, especially before the bar opened. But then Giselle had to open her damn mouth and started pelting pitches at me that I had a hard time dodging. Insecurity after insecurity was hurled at me, and the armor that I've spent so much time rebuilding cracked.

While my shield didn't shatter completely, it fractured just enough to let the panic attack slither its way in. And then I came up to the scene of the accident, and the small grip I had on my feelings combusted.

"Thank you for coming to help me."

"Bri, you don't have to thank me for something I'd do in a heartbeat. You needed me, so I came. End of story. How are we feeling?"

How am I feeling?

I sit in silence, processing everything that's transpired within the last nine or so hours. If he had asked me the question last night, my answer would have been that I felt broken and hurt. Now? I feel a sense of determination looming over the horizon like a sunrise. I meant what I said last night. I think it's time for me to talk to my brother. I'm no longer a puppet on a string, controlled by the hands of my depression. I've been reintroduced to myself, and I love who I see. She's beautifully bold and has learned to fall in love with herself again. She's accepted herself as is—which includes embracing every inch of her body. She's learning to regain control over her life and taking risks. She's beautifully me, and a big reason for it is the man standing in front of me.

"I think I'm okay. Yeah, last night was rough, and had you asked me yesterday, I would have had a completely different answer. Giselle is a miserable human who thrives off exploiting people's insecurities, and honestly? I think she did me a favor. I've been succumbing to my fears and anxieties for way too long. And the only way for me to let them go is to face them head on. I've been avoiding Max for way too long. He's the only person who can shut those fears down for good."

"Bri, you are inspiring. I hope you know that. You've taken something traumatic and turned it into something beautiful. Sure, in the beginning you were struggling, a woman stranded in the middle of the ocean with nothing to cling to. Instead of letting yourself drown, you created your own life preserver and saved yourself. You are your own hero, Bri."

Asher's words rob me of breath and my eyes sting with unshed tears. Of all the things he's said to me, this one hits different. I press rewind on everything that's happened since Avery decided to crawl under the covers and hold me in her arms. I've credited a lot of my progress to her and Asher. Now, I'm looking at each scene through a new lens, and I see what Asher sees. True, they may have helped me heal, but the common theme in every image that flashes through my mind is *me*. I asked for help. I stepped out of my comfort zone. *Me*. I did it. My body shakes with happy tears.

"Baby," Asher says before pulling me into his arms.

"I did it. I did this. I-I'm the reason I am who I am today. It's all because of me." My words and tears are free flowing out of me.

My life has felt like an endless thunderstorm, one after another flooding my entire life with pain and heartbreak. Now, in this moment, I see the rainbow peeking through, and its colors are intense and vibrant.

"You did it. I'm so proud of you." Asher rubs soothing circles across my back, providing similar comfort to a mother rocking an infant to sleep.

"I'm proud of myself, too," I admit, which has both of us laughing.

"I think we should probably eat breakfast now. Most of it is probably cold now, lukewarm at best." Asher pulls out of my arms to grab plates on the counter to bring them over to the table. I hop off the counter to join him. Sounds of silverware clanking against plates fill the open kitchen in surround sound.

"So, I had an idea that I wanted to run by you," I say in between bites.

"Lay it on me," Asher replies before bringing a mug of steaming hot coffee to his lips. I'm momentarily distracted by watching his throat work as the liquid glides down his throat. I squeeze my legs together as I think about another warm thing sliding down my throat. Asher clears his throat, and my face heats.

"What are you thinking about?" Asher's smirk tells me he knows exactly what I'm thinking about.

"Oh, nothing. Anyway, my idea. One of my goals was to take more risks and regain control of my life. I feel like I've started to do that. But I've been putting something off for a while. An experience I'm in desperate need of a redo." Asher turns in his chair, giving me his undivided attention.

"I'm listening."

"I want to go axe throwing. According to my parents, they told the place about the accident, and I have, like, a credit, I guess. All I have to do is tell them my name and I can come in whenever. I was supposed to do this with Max, but I want to experience this with you. So, would you go axe throwing with me?"

Asher rises from his chair and crouches down in front of me, the press of his hands on my thighs sending electrical currents throughout my body.

"I would be honored to go with you. Mind if I invite my brother and his wife? They've been dying to meet you."

"Yes, of course. I'll make a reservation for this Sunday?"

"That should work, let me text my brother to make sure he's down." Asher types away on his phone, and the reply is instantaneous.

"He says they're in." I lean down and press a chaste kiss to his lips before returning to my breakfast. I can't wait to share a lifetime of breakfasts with this man.

Asher

A splash of orange juice with champagne

"I'll be right back."

I leave a confused Bri to finish her breakfast so I can prepare the rest of her self-care day. I begin to draw her a bath, adding in rose scented bubbles. Over on the counter I had placed a bamboo bath tray and covered it with all of her favorites: two face masks, champagne glasses filled to the brim with mimosas, and our current read. I'd say it was a bit presumptuous of me to assume that she'd want me to join her, but I'm banking on knowing my bear. She'll want to spend this time with me.

When I notice the water hit the halfway mark, I shut off the faucet and move to the bedroom where I've scattered a few fall-scented candles throughout the room. Soon it'll smell like we stepped into a fall Hallmark movie, one of Bri's guilty pleasures. I'll admit, they aren't all bad. I mean, sure, the plot is pretty much the same, but I think that's the appeal.

I make my way over to the window to open it just enough to let the crisp autumn air permeate the room. Two silk robes—one in a soft lilac and the other in a charcoal grey—lay across the bed. Massage oils in every size bottle are littered across her cherry wood dresser along with a tube of blood red nail polish.

"What is all this?" The sound of Bri's voice startles me.

"You weren't supposed to see this yet. But since you're here, it's your own personal spa day. I have a bath drawn up for us with your version of what a mimosa is."

"A splash of orange juice with champagne?" she asks while she cocks her head to the side.

"Is there any other way to make one?"

"Nope. But what is all that?" Her eyes flick to the rest of the room, taking inventory. She has no idea what I have in store for her tonight.

"All part of your relaxation day, now get your fine ass in the bathroom."

We strip down and carefully step into the bath. The sheet masks are barely on our faces before I feel her body molding against mine, her head resting in the crook of my neck. As I'm reading the moment where the enemies finally become lovers, Bri sips her drink as a soft, contented sigh slips past her lips.

Bliss. This is what pure, uninterrupted bliss feels like.

"Don't think I missed your assumption that I'd let you join me in the bath."

"Bear, it wasn't an assumption. It was a fact. I knew you wouldn't tell me no. You love me too much. Plus, if you said no, I wouldn't be able to do this." I softly toss the book I was reading onto the floor as far away from the tub as possible, but not before ensuring her page is marked.

Can't have my girl losing her spot

"Hey, you were just getting to the good oh—" Her words are cut off when my finger slips inside of her, my thumb finding her clit swollen and waiting.

"My girl liked that scene, huh? Tell me, who were you thinking of while reading the words?"

A soft moan escapes from the back of her throat while the pad of my thumb moves in soft circles against her core.

"I was picturing him and m—" I pinch her clit, pressing down with just enough pressure to skirt the line between pleasure and pain.

"Wrong. Answer." I pinch down even harder, feeling her squirm on top of me before letting go. I remove my fingers from inside of her only to paint circles on her inner thighs.

"Cruel. That was cruel." Her words come out breathless and choppy. I mean, if I was played with like this, I'd be the same way.

"You want my fingers, Bri?"

"Y-Yes."

"Then answer the question correctly. Who were you thinking of?"

"You. Always you."

"That's my good girl."

I don't give her time to process much before I'm sliding two fingers inside her pussy, pumping in and out. The sounds of her arousal mixed with her whimpers fill the space like a beautifully evocative aria.

The moment I insert a third finger, Bri's body contorts, limbs softening, muscles relaxing as she chases her pleasure. Pleasure I'm purposely keeping from her. Just as quickly as my fingers were thrusted into her, I pull them out. Her frustrated groan escapes her pouty lips, and the sound has me chuckling into the nape of her neck. I drag my nose slowly up the side of her smooth skin as her intoxicating, saccharine scent infiltrates my system, threatening to short circuit my brain.

"What do you want, Bri?" How I manage to form a coherent sentence is beyond me.

"I-I want..." Her stuttering is the highest compliment. I have her exactly where I want her...at my mercy.

"Say it. What. Do. You. Want?"

"I want to come." The raspy tone of her voice sends a signal to my dick, but it's not the time for that. Right now, it's all about Bri.

"And?"

"And what?"

"Beg for it."

The water threatens to slosh over the side as Bri shifts her body to face me, a sinful smirk decorating her face.

"Please. Fuck me with your fingers. Play with me. Tease me. Do whatever you want, just make me come."

"That's my girl."

Before Bri can turn her head, I crash my mouth onto hers, my tongue demanding entry in between her soft, supple lips. Tongues brush and tangle together as my fingers slip back inside her, allowing me to swallow her gasp. My pace starts out torturously slow, thriving in her squirming body. Our lips are still locked as I make a grab for the champagne flute with my other hand. The moment my fingers wrap around the stem, I'm breaking apart from the kiss, my fingers once again removed from inside of her.

"Open for me, baby." Bri's head tilts back, her mouth open as wide as it can go. I take a long pull, allowing the bubbly sensation to sit on my tongue for a few seconds before leaning down and spitting it into her awaiting mouth. My move is deliberate, knowing this is bound to make her even slicker. I watch as she swallows, wishing it was my cock instead. Her whiskey eyes lock with mine, demanding to finish what I started.

I've had enough playing around.

"Eyes on me. I want that pretty face as you come."

Just as I suspected, she's more soaked than she was before. My finger slips in with even more ease and I begin to rub her clit in fast, circular motions, picking up speed and pressure as I go.

"Oh. Asher. More. I need more. Please."

I do exactly as I'm told, pressing more firmly on her bundle of nerves, finding the perfect speed that I know will have her coming fast and hard.

Her fast, panting breaths match my pace and soon enough, water is thrashing over the edge of the tub as she comes with my name on her mouth.

"You're so sexy when you come. Let's dry off so we can keep going."

"Keep going? I don't know if I can handle any more."

I lean down and nip at her shoulder, enough to leave a mark before gripping her jaw in my hand and forcing her to look at me.

"You can and you will," I growl the words in her ear. "Now, let's go. I have plans for that body."

Asher

Open wide, baby

BRI'S HUNGRY GAZE PROVES her a liar. She wants more, and I plan to give it to her.

I take in her naked form, and I feel my heart beat wildly in my chest. I now understand the temptation between Adam and Eve, because staring at a naked Bri has me wanting to toss my plan out the window and fuck her senseless.

Chill the fuck out, Asher. Continue with the plan. I clear my throat and shake the dirty thoughts from my mind.

"Have you ever had a massage?" Well, that's one way to ease into the next activity.

"I have. Alex really had a way with his hands. I left the place a complete puddle."

Bri's grin is wicked and purposeful. She knows exactly what she's doing when she mentions a man massaging her. I growl before stalking up to her, gripping her by the neck.

"I don't give a fuck about Alex. I'm going to ask you again if you've had a massage, and your answer better be a no. Have you ever had a massage before?" Jealousy is a power surge through my body. It makes zero sense, but the thought of another man's hands on her has me seeing red.

"And if I say yes instead of no?" Bri taunts.

"Then I'm going to toss you on this bed and fuck the memory of that asshole out of your brain." Bri's eyes flash with desire, and I know what her answer will be before she opens her mouth.

"Yes. I have. Alex's hands were—" Bri's words end in a squeal when I throw her down on the bed. My grip on her thighs is so tight that it's bound to leave marks, but she doesn't seem to mind.

My fingers dance along her collarbone before I'm wrapping my hand around her throat and squeezing. Her eyes begin to bulge, but when I look, there's no fear there. She licks her lips and her back arches, her hips seeking out my cock.

"My dirty girl wants to be fucked, doesn't she?" Bri just stares at me, so I loosen my hold on her neck. "Answer me."

"Yes. I want your cock inside me. Fuck Alex—" I grip her pussy in my hand and squeeze as tight as I can.

"There is no Alex. His name will not leave your lips if you want my cock, bear. If you say his name again, I'll shove my dick so far down your throat that you'll gag."

Bri looks me dead in the eyes with a daring look before whispering, "Alex."

I move around to the side of the bed, dragging her body to the edge. I wrap her hair around my fist and yank her head back. Bri lets out a whimper, but her mouth opens in the most perfect O.

"Open wide, baby." When she does, I insert my cock into her mouth and start off with slow thrusts before I begin to pick up speed. Bri gags around my cock when I hit the back of her throat, but her eyes roll in the back of her head as she lets out a moan.

"My girl loves it rough, doesn't she? She fucking craves it, loving when I take charge like this, huh?" Bri nods around my dick as drool drips down her chin.

"You're gonna swallow my cum like a good girl, aren't you?"

"Mmmm," Bri hums around my cock, and the vibration has me exploding down her throat. Her throat works as she swallows every last drop. Damn, I love when she does that.

"Fuck, look at you sucking me off. Such a good fucking girl." I pull out, allowing Bri to gasp for air. Some of my cum leaks down her chin, and I watch as she traces the remnants of my release with her tongue.

"So much for that massage." I let out a satisfied sigh.

"We can still do it. You took such good care of me. Let me return the favor."

Bri gets up from the bed and saunters over to the oils while I run to the bathroom to grab the forgotten towels to lay on the bed. The plan was to massage her, releasing all the tension from last night. But like always, things with her took a left turn.

"Lay down, Asher. Let me make you feel good." Bri's words reek of double meaning, but I just want to feel her hands on me. I go to lay on my stomach, but Bri's hand on my arm stops me.

"No. I want you on your back." I grin up at her as I situate myself on my back.

"My body is all yours, baby." The feel of Bri's thighs squeezing my hips has me rethinking the plan. My cock twitches, and the look on her face says she notices.

I watch as massage oil drips like molasses from the bottle onto Bri's hands. The sound of the cap clicking shut reverberates around the room. Bri's eyes lock with mine while she rubs her hands together, warming the oil in her palms. My heart skips with anticipation, and my throat feels like I swallowed a handful of sand. Goosebumps spread like wildfire on my skin the second her hands connect with my chest.

Bri massages my chest and shoulders with firm pressure all while maintaining eye contact. Her hips wiggle around my waist, and my fists clench with the need to touch her. Bri knows *exactly* what she's doing to me by rubbing my shoulders while she begins to rock her hips back and forth. My stomach muscles tense when her hands work their way down, and I suck in a breath when her hands fan out across my abs.

Focus, Asher. She's in control now. You have to chill the fuck out.

It's hard to remain still when all I want to do is flip her over and fuck her. But I resist the urge...barely.

"Bri. Keep rocking your hips like that and the sliver of control I'm clinging to will snap."

"Hmm..." Bri's hands stop what they're doing to lift herself up just enough to glance at my angry, hard cock.

"Aww, poor baby. Looks like someone needs some relief, huh?" she teases me. I look at the spot she's hovering over, and my skin is glistening. I can't tell if it's from the oil or her arousal.

"Bear," I grunt when her hands trail over my hip bone. This woman will be the death of me.

"Maybe I can help. Would you like some help, Asher?"

"Fuck, I don't think I've ever rebounded this quickly. I should be concerned that my dick is still hard, but then I look at you and it makes sense. You, Bri, are dicknip."

Bri giggles before rolling her hips and leaning forward. Her wild hair falls like a curtain around my face, tickling my neck. I groan while she smirks. She knows the spot is a sensitive spot for me. "Is that a yes?"

"I...fuck. Yes." My voice is raspy, but I don't have time to clear my throat to try again. Bri's hands wrap around my cock, giving it a few tugs before she's guiding it toward her entrance. She winks at me before I'm fully seated inside her.

"I love how full I feel when you're inside me," Bri moans as she tosses her head back, chasing her pleasure by slowly rocking her hips. Her hands are on my chest, and when she picks up her pace, she drags her fingernails down my body, leaving angry, red marks in their wake.

"That's right, baby. Scratch and claw at me. I'll gladly wear these marks on my chest. Let people know who owns my body. Take all the pleasure you need. My body is at your disposal."

"Oh, God. *Asher.*" Bri's whimper has a sultry undertone to it as she picks up her pace. She lifts her hips up and down, slamming her pussy down on my cock.

"Oh. Oh. Fuck, that feels so good!" Bri shouts. She's working herself up, and I can feel her pussy grip my cock even tighter, her walls beginning to flutter around me. She's close, and I need to feel her come on my cock like I need to breathe.

"That's it. Come like the good girl you are. Soak my cock with your slick." She slams down onto me and rocks her hips even faster now, her breaths coming out in staccato pants.

"Yes, yes, YES. Asher, AAH." The sound of my name leaving her mouth when she comes is music to my ears. Bri shatters around me and rides out her orgasm before collapsing against my chest, me pulsing inside her from my own release.

"I think I really like massages." Bri grins while pressing a kiss to my cheek. She rolls off me and nestles herself into my arms.

"I will never be able to look at massage oil the same way again." My response has both of us shaking with laughter.

We sit in comfortable silence, Bri tracing patterns on my chest with her fingers and me combing my fingers through her hair.

"I love you, Asher." Bri's whispered confession breaks the silence.

"I love you, too, Bri."

The room grows heavy with silence, nothing but the sound of even breathing and precious heartbeats between us. As if the world itself is holding its breath, Bri is fast asleep against my chest.

Bri's soft snores fill the space, so I slip out of her hold to blow out the candles and drain the forgotten water in the tub. I let her nap knowing she needs the rest, so I head downstairs and clean up the mess from breakfast. The smile I'm sporting seems to be a permanent fixture, and I wouldn't have it any other way.

Brianna

I thought you were a figment of his imagination

TODAY IS AXE THROWING day, and fear holds my body captive, offering unrealistic demands. My legs shake aggressively as I white knuckle the steering wheel. Asher sits in the passenger seat, a comforting hand on my thigh, offering me the silence I didn't know I needed. Asher can read me like an open book, often assessing my needs before I even have time to process. At first, it scared the fuck out of me. I'd find any flaw to hyper-fixate on. The moment that seed was planted in my head, I firmly believed Asher saw it, too. Avery called it my self-deprecating prophecy. Now, having someone see me—all of me—and love every inch is exhilarating.

Despite our time slot being at seven and it's only a fifteen minute drive away, we left at six. When I asked if we could leave early, Asher agreed with a smile before planting a soft kiss on the tip of my nose. I knew this was going to be hard for me, so I planned it out so I'd have enough time to prepare.

I've been sitting in my driveway for fifteen minutes, calming music blasting through the speakers. I focus on the slow inhale and exhale of my breath, imagining my heart slowing down with each outbreath.

You will be okay, Bri. Just because it happened once, doesn't mean it'll happen again. You have overcome a lot since the accident. You have Asher sitting next to you. You're safe. Nothing bad will happen to you. You got this.

I press my foot on the brake before throwing the car in reverse. I repeat the mantra *I got this* in my head all the way to our destination. When I come across *the* intersection, Asher reaches for my hand, squeezing it like his life depends on it. He squeezes my hand three times, and on some instinctive level, I know he's telling me he loves me. I flip my hand over, interlocking our fingers and repeating the gesture back to him.

Like Asher did that one night when the light turned green, I look both ways before sailing through the intersection. I hold onto my breath before I reach the other side where it comes out in a *whoosh*.

I did it!

I made it through without having a panic attack.

"Pull over," Asher demands.

I quickly glance at him before returning my attention to the road. "What?"

"Pull over," he repeats. I look behind me before turning my signal on and pulling off to the side. The moment I put the car in park, Asher is rounding the car and unbuckling my seat.

I'm having a hard time processing what's happening when I find myself out of the car and pressed up against the cold metal door as Asher leans down to crash his mouth against mine. His lips assault mine with enough force that I'm sure they'll be permanently swollen. His tongue demands entry into my mouth, tangling with mine in a possessive manner only Asher is capable of. Cars are zooming by, but my head is spinning with the feel of his lips on mine. Asher pulls back only to rest his forehead against mine.

"I'm so fucking proud of you, Bri. You took that intersection and made it your bitch. You did that. Not me. Not Avery. You. You did it, baby, and if we didn't have anywhere to be, I'd take you in the back seat and eat you out. But knowing my brother and his wife, they're already in the parking lot waiting. But seeing you conquer your fears like a boss? Hot as fuck." Asher's face nuzzles my neck, his stubble tickling my sensitive skin.

Asher opens my door for me, and I climb back into the seat. Once he's buckled in, we're back on the road.

"Any questions on how to throw the axe?" Silas, our guide, asks. He'll be hanging around us, making sure we're following the rules and that no one gets hurt.

We all shake our heads, so Silas gives us the go ahead. Asher and Xander argue over who's going first while Amber and I hang back and observe.

"You're good for him, Bri."

Amber is a beautiful, curvy woman with long, black hair and the most striking, green cat-like eyes I've ever seen. I liked her from the moment I met her. She greeted me with a giant grin on her face and pulled me into a hug. It appears the Larson men like their women curvy, because Amber is very similar to me in size. She oozes confidence, and she has this ability to make anyone within her orbit feel comfortable.

"He's good for me, too," I reply, my tone laced with affection.

"I'm glad to finally meet you. I'm not gonna lie, for the longest time I thought you were a figment of his imagination. He'd always talk about this Bri person, and Xander and I always went along with it. He didn't do your body justice, though. Girl, your curves are banging. If I wasn't so in love with my husband, I might make a pass at ya." Amber winks at me.

"I heard that," Xander and Asher say at the same time.

"My curves? Girl, your ass is out of this world," I reply, ignoring the guys' comment.

"Damn right it is," Xander says while smacking his wife's ass before kissing her cheek.

Asher's arms snake their way around my waist, and he kisses the sensitive spot underneath my neck. "I'm glad we're doing this."

"Me too. Did y'all figure out the order?"

The order goes as follows: Amber, Xander, me, and then Asher. Amber hits the bullseye every time, whereas I always miss by a mile. Silas tries to give me tips and tricks, but they're completely useless. I suck. Xander is just as bad as I am, so we bond over our mutual suckiness.

Meanwhile, Asher hits the spot every time, tossing me knowing looks over his shoulder. He knows exactly what he's doing to me, as my face turns a soft fuchsia and the pulse between my legs becomes almost unbearable.

The man is good at everything he does. *The bastard.* The hot, good with his...everything, kind, incredible bastard.

Asher and Amber are battling it out to see who can get the most bullseyes in a row while Xander and I sit at the table eating snacks.

"So, Asher told me you're an architect. What got you into that line of work?" I ask in between chowing down on garlic fries.

"Well, I'm sure Asher told you I struggled with alcohol for years. When I started to change my life for the better, my therapist suggested I find a hobby. I didn't know who I was outside of drinking, so it took a while to find what felt like me. Then I started drawing, and for the first time in my life, my brain was quiet, and I felt at ease. It started off with rough landscape sketches, and when I showed them to my therapist, she suggested I look into art professionally." Xander takes a moment to eat some fries and wash them down with some water before continuing.

"I spent hours scouring the internet before stumbling upon architecture. Something about designing something from scratch and watching it become real was thrilling to me. So, I went to school, and years later I opened my own firm where I met Amber. And for the first time in forever, things fell into place for me."

"That's amazing. I know Asher is extremely proud of you. It's not easy rising from the ashes."

An idea begins to circulate in my brain. Asher and I haven't done much planning in regard to our business idea. A big part of it is because I haven't felt ready to move forward yet. Max and I created a binder with ideas for the store when I first proposed my idea to him. Right now, that binder is collecting dust on the top shelf in my closet. I haven't even shown it to Asher yet. It feels like something I should look through with Max before I share it with him. But with my brother being a carpenter and Xander being an architect, I wonder if the two can work together to make Booked 'N' Boozed come to life.

I turn in my seat to face Xander head-on before speaking. "I have a business proposal for you."

"I'm all ears." Xander listens as I share the plan Asher and I came up with. I let him know that while my brother is still healing, he can help with the construction of the business. While I talk, I can see the wheels turning in Xander's head.

"I'm down." Xander extends his hand out toward me while grinning like a maniac.

"But I haven't even shown you my ideas yet."

Xander shakes his head while shifting his gaze to his younger brother. "It doesn't matter. If it makes Asher happy, I'll do it in a heartbeat. He's a good guy, Bri. But since you, he's been the best version of himself. So, if you both want to do this, then I'm in."

"You'll do what?" Asher asks as he throws his arm over my shoulder.

"Xander agreed to help us with our business idea."

"We're still doing that? You haven't brought it up in a minute, so I wasn't sure if we were moving forward."

"Babe, let's go get some pretzel bites and let them talk," Amber says to Xander before dragging him behind her.

I turn back around and look into Asher's questioning gaze. "I want to do it. I, um, well, because it's something I shared with Max, I wanted to go over the plan with him. I didn't tell you this, but we created this binder of ideas years ago. I wanted to talk about it with him first before we followed through with anything. I know it probably makes zero sense, but—" Asher stops me mid-sentence by tilting my chin up.

"I get it. This is something you've shared together, and you want him to feel included. I should confess that I already mentioned it to him, and he seems excited. So, you just let me know when you want to move forward with the plan, and I'll be right beside you."

"He wasn't mad at me that I didn't tell him about it?" I ask, my throat feeling like I swallowed sludge.

"Absolutely not, Bri. That man would never be mad at you. Is that why you've held off with the plans?"

"Yeah, I guess so. I didn't want him to think that because we're together that I'm replacing him in any way."

"I can see that, but I can assure you he's happy for you, for us. Talk to Max first, and if you still want to go through with the plan, then we'll do it."

"Okay. I think Max and Xander will do well together. Thank you for being so patient with me." I rise up on my tiptoes to kiss his lips.

"Get a room, you two," Xander teases while mock gagging.

"Fuck off," Asher retorts while flipping him off. Our time slot is coming to a close, and I'm beaming with pride. I did it. I took charge of something my trauma tried to take away from me. I'm still glowing as we say our goodbyes, and Amber and I make plans to have dinner with Avery. I have a feeling those two are gonna hit it off.

"Hey, Asher, can you drive? I just want to relax."

"Sure. You did good today."

My eyes flutter closed, and I feel the corners of my mouth pulling into a soft smile. The car's vibration purrs beneath me and soft, soothing sounds from my go-to playlist bathe my body in serenity. I did it. I took something that nearly destroyed me and, in Asher's words, made it my bitch.

The rough, almost sandpaper feel of a thumb rubbing soothing circles along my hand has a contented sigh slipping past my lips.

Asher.

He's a huge reason I was able to do this today. True, I've rediscovered my strength, but without an anchor, I'd be lost at sea. His presence alone is a balm to my soul. He's your favorite hoodie fresh out the dryer. He's my everything.

I turn my hand so that our fingers interlock before bringing our joint hands to my lips and pressing a soft kiss against his wrist.

"Thank you for today."

"Bear, you don't have to thank me. I'd do anything for you, always."

"I know, but it means a lot to me. You knew today would be hard given who I was supposed to do this with. Yet, you helped take a tainted memory and turn it into something beautiful."

Everything around me halts, the words a reality slap in the face. I wasn't tainted, but I felt broken, lost. Energy was wasted searching for pieces of me that were never missing. They were tucked away waiting to be set free. Waiting for the right person to set them ablaze.

Asher.

Somehow, my soul knew it was always meant to be him. He saw me—all of me—and cherished every inch like a precious gem.

"You're worth going above and beyond for, Bri."

Asher squeezes my hand a few times before I feel the softness of his lips linger at the pulse point on my wrist.

We spend the rest of the drive home, hands interlocked, silence blanketing us in what could only be described as the purest love that's ever caressed my skin.

We're pulling into my driveway, and just as I'm stepping out of the car, Asher tosses me over his shoulder, speed walking to the front door.

"Asher! What are you doing?"

"You did a hard thing today. I think that deserves a reward."

He slaps my ass, which has me squealing and laughing all the way to the bedroom. All humor slips off my face as I see the intensity of his gaze locked on mine. Asher scans my body like a man starved.

"It's time to play."

Asher

We pulled an uno reverse

"Will you go on a date with me?" I blurt out the words when she's in the middle of washing her face. The question lingers in the air. Bri blinks up at me, the steady stream of water filling the space while suds still effervesce on her skin. After our evening out with my brother and his wife, I realized we haven't been on an official date.

"Huh?" Bri asks as she lathers her face in some sort of cream.

"A date. Will you go on a date with me? I realized we've done pretty much everything but go out on a date. So, I was asking if you want to."

Bri looks me up and down before laughing. "You've already gotten in my pants, Asher. Why do you want to go out on a date?"

"Because you're too beautiful not to show off. We kind of went about things differently. Normally, you date for a while before hooking up. We pulled an Uno reverse card, so now I want to take you out. I want us to dress up and go somewhere fancy. I want us to eat, laugh, and maybe dance together. I want the world to know I'm with you. So, Bri, will you go on a date with me?"

A soft expression crosses her face before she wraps her arms around me. Her smile is so bright it's practically blinding.

"I would love to go on a date with you. When and where?"

"Tonight at seven, and let me worry about where we're going. I'm going to do it right and pick you up, so I'm gonna leave so I can get ready for tonight."

She tries to kiss my lips, but I pull back.

"Uh-uh. What kind of man do you take me for? I am more than my hot body, Brianna." She rolls her eyes at me before playfully pushing me away. "Be ready at seven. I'll see you soon."

I grab my phone from my back pocket and text Cas asking for his help.

> **Me: Hey, man, you free?**

> **Cas: I'm happily married, Asher, but I appreciate the flattery.**

> **Me: Hah. No, I'm going on my first date with Bri and I need some help planning it out. Think you can help?**

> **Cas: You two have been going at it like bunnies and you're just *now* going on a date?**

> **Me: Yeah. I know. Can you help?**

> **Cas: Sure.**

> **Me: I'll meet you at your place.**

> **Cas: ⊠**

I arrive at Cas and Avery's house in thirty minutes, and I have my hand raised into a knock before the door is opened. I'm greeted by a glowing and very pregnant Avery.

"If I wasn't so in love with your best friend, I'd steal you away for myself. Cas be damned." Avery throws her head back and laughs; she knows my teasing is just that. Teasing. "But seriously, Aves, carrying Cas' kid looks good on you."

"I heard that. And Avery is stuck with me for life. Come on in." Cas walks toward the living room, so I follow. Cas leans in, pressing a loving, lingering kiss against Avery's lips before leaning down to whisper adorations against her belly. I look away, feeling as if I'm intruding on an intimate moment that's meant to be private.

"So, what's your plan for said best friend?" Avery asks while waddling in.

"Honestly, I have no idea. We already did a bookstore adventure, so I can't do that. I was thinking of taking her to a fancy restaurant, but that feels too basic."

"Ooh, what about a cooking class? She has always wanted to take one of those."

I remember Bri mentioning that once or twice one summer during our childhood. I had completely forgotten that was one of her bucket list items up until Avery mentioned it.

"I could do that, but do you think it's too late to have a cooking class? Our date is tonight at seven, and it's currently ten-thirty in the morning."

"Nah. I know a guy who owes me a favor for mentoring his grandson. I'll call him to set it up."

Cas excuses himself to make the call while I turn toward Avery to get more ideas.

"Do you know any other items she's always wanted to cross off her list?"

"Hmmm, well, she already has floor-to-ceiling bookshelves alongside one of the walls in her office library, but I know she's always wanted a reading chair."

Avery pulls out her phone and scrolls through Amazon to find the chair Bri wants. She shifts in her seat, showing me a light purple, velvet LITA lazy chair with a matching ottoman. It screams Brianna. I add it to my cart and request same-day delivery.

"Done. I had it delivered to this address. Do you think Cas can put it together while we're out?"

"Yeah, I'm sure he can. Oh, you know what else she's been wanting?"

"What's that?"

"She's been obsessed with this special edition collection of her favorite book series. Here, let me pull up the website and show you."

I watch as Avery pulls her computer from the coffee table onto her lap. As soon as she has the website open, she hands me the laptop, and I place the order immediately. The earliest it can get to Bri's house is with two-day delivery, so I click on that option without even blinking an eye at the ridiculous price. If it brings a smile to her face, then it's worth it. I print off the confirmation email before folding up the paper and putting it in my pocket. While I can't give her the gift now, I can at least show her that they're on their way.

"You really do love her, don't you?"

Avery looks at me with such adoration in her eyes. It's clear she wants her best friend to be happy.

"With every fiber of my being. My heart beats for that woman, and I'll do just about anything for her. Is there anything else I should cross off her list?"

"Well, I know she's always wanted to sleep outside underneath the stars. She may be tough on the outside, but she's a gooey romantic on the inside."

"I can do that. Thanks, Aves. How are we feeling?" I gesture toward her belly.

"I'm tired with zero control over my bladder and she's kicking me like crazy, but I love every second of it."

"Have you two come up with a name yet?"

"I did, but I haven't told Cas yet. I asked his grandparents if it was okay to name her after their daughter, Cas' mom. I got their approval, so I plan on telling him tonight."

"He's going to love that." She smiles at me and Cas picks this time to re-enter the room.

"You're all set for tonight at Lagoon. Chef Marnie will take care of y'all." Cas presses a kiss on the crown of Avery's head before sitting next to her. They exchange a heated look, and I take it as my cue to leave.

"Thanks guys for all the help. I'm gonna leave. Y'all are sending each other *fuck me* eyes, and I'd rather not see any of that."

I stop at Target on the way to my apartment to get a blowup mattress, some snacks, and a bottle of sparkling wine. I hold off on the flowers until I'm on my way to her. Instead, I get her the entire Elle Kennedy series she's been dying to read. Well, I get two copies of each—thank you Target BOGO deal—since we now spend our Sundays reading the same book. And if she wants to reenact a scene or two? Well, who am I to stop her? I still have hours to go before I see her, so I text Amber to see if she can take Bri out to find an outfit for tonight.

> **Me: Hey, Amber. I'm taking Bri on our first date and I was hoping you could take her shopping for an outfit for tonight.**

> **Amber: First date? Y'all have been hooking up for months and you're just going on a date *now*?**

Me: Yeah, I know we did things backwards. Will you help me?

Amber: I got you, little brother.

Me: Ignoring the little brother dig and saying thank you. Here is her address.

Brianna

Fuck, it's hot in here

WHEN I OPEN THE door, the last person I expect to see standing on the other side is Amber.

"Uh, hi. What are you doing here?"

"Hey, girl. Asher told me about your date tonight. I'm here to take you shopping. So, get your shoes on and let's go."

"Okay. Wait, what?" Confusion grips me as I gawk at her, a playful grin playing across her face.

"I'm taking you shopping. We gotta pick out an outfit so hot, Asher will foam at the mouth."

"You don't have to. I was just gonna grab something from my closet."

By the look on Amber's face, you'd think I personally offended her, with her hands on her hips and her eyebrow cocked.

"Hell, no. New date...new outfit. Plus, it gives me an excuse to get some new clothes, too. Do you have any idea what y'all are doing?"

I look at her with a *what do you think* face, which has her full-on belly laughing as we walk to the car.

"Typical. Why do men do this? I swear, Xander does the same. Then they pull the *you look good in anything you wear* card. I swear, one day I'm going to dress in a unicorn onesie the next time Xander says to dress nice." I laugh so hard that I accidentally snort.

"Oh, I like you. You and my best friend, Avery, will get along great." We swap stories about the brothers while we drive to the mall. I used to hate shopping for clothes since I've gained weight. Now? I embrace who I am. Plus, it helps to have a man like Asher who loves every inch of your body.

"Okay, what are we thinking?" Amber asks as we walk into one of the department stores.

"Well, I want to look fancy, but I also want Asher's eyes to bug out of his head. He likes me in red, so I'm thinking of something body-hugging in a deep red, like merlot or mahogany in color."

"Yes, girl. Do you trust me?"

Ya know, for just meeting the girl, I feel a sense of safety around her. Her personality screams genuine. I know I can lay my trust and faith in her hands, and she'll handle them like they're glass.

"I do."

"Great. It looks like we're the same size, but just in case I'm wrong, I'll do a size up and then down with each item. Now, off you go to the dressing room, and I'll hand you things I find."

I head in the direction of the dressing room, and my mind thinks back to one of the last times I was in one of these. With Asher's tongue in my pussy like his life depended on it.

Fuck, it's hot in here.

Amber is back in minutes, tossing garment after garment over the top. The first is a velvet number that's a deep, red wine color. It's floor length with a slit that stops mid-thigh with a gap in between the top of the dress and the skirt, showing off a little skin. I love the feel of it on my body, but it doesn't feel like *the dress*.

The next option is a knee-length bodycon dress in mahogany with a similar triangular cut-out in the front. The cut on the back of the dress is so low my entire backside is on display. I have three more dresses to try on, but I feel like this is the one. It's silky, and compliments all my curves. It also doesn't hurt that it makes my tits and ass look damn good. I step out of the dressing room door and Amber gasps. She twirls her finger in the air, gesturing for me to spin. I have a winner. Both of us agree. We find a pair of strappy, gold heels that complement the dress perfectly.

She convinces me to stop in a lingerie store because according to Amber, a first date requires sexy new underwear. I have zero say because she's dragging my ass inside the store. We settle on a hot pink lace bra and panty set that's practically see-through.

We stop for an iced coffee before we're headed back to my house.

We're pulling into my driveway when I ask, "Do you want to help me get ready?"

"Oh my God, yes! Let's have a whole mini spa day."

Spa day...The last time I had one of those, it turned into something completely different. Thoughts of Asher creep into every crevice of my being, leaving me feeling hot and flustered. I guess that's what happens when you spend as much time together as we do.

Amber and I have face masks on while we paint each other's toes. I'm hopping in the shower to wash and scrub every inch of me while Amber talks to her husband. I'm in a tank top and a pair of sleep shorts when she sits me down to do my hair and makeup. I'm facing away from my mirror so that everything will be a surprise.

Her words, not mine.

About an hour later, she's putting the finishing touches on me, and when I turn around, I gasp.

"Holy shit, Amber, you're good. Ever thought about doing this professionally? Cuz damn, you did amazing."

"Yeah, I have my license and all, but I haven't found a place that I want to work at, so I do it out of my home for now." That's when an idea strikes.

"I work at a salon. Well, not currently, as I've chosen to step back and heal after the accident. Since I'm most likely opening up my own bookstore with Asher, I won't need to go back. I could put in a good word for you."

"You'd do that?" Amber's eyes shine with emotion, her hands clasped in front of her chest.

"Yeah, you're talented. Your work deserves to be appreciated."

"Ah, thank you. Okay, I'm going to go before I start crying. You look hot and I can't wait to hear all about it. Here's my number, let's hang out without our men orchestrating it." I type her number into my phone and give her a hug goodbye. I glance at the clock, and I see that there's an hour left until Asher picks me up. Nerves and excitement swirl together like a cotton candy machine. I haven't been on a date in so long.

I'm putting on the finishing touches to my outfit when the doorbell rings. My shoes are in my hand as I hurry down the stairs. The second the door opens, the flowers in Asher's hand fall to the ground, his jaw practically on the floor.

Asher

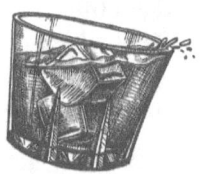

There's more?

Fᴜᴄᴋ. Mᴇ.

Bri is fucking gorgeous in anything she wears, but this dress? I promised to take her out, but jealousy is a power surge circulating throughout my body, knowing everyone with a pulse will be looking at her.

The velvet hugs every inch of her curves, worshiping every inch like a lover. Her warm, earth-tone colored hair falls wildly down her back. My fingers ache to wrap it around my fist and kiss her stupid. She's a goddamn vision.

"You, Bri, are breathtaking. I hope you have bail money because I can't be held accountable if any man looks at you."

"So dramatic. Can you help me put my heels on? I didn't want to trip down the stairs." Bri extends the hand with her shoes toward me. I squat down in front of her, her arms resting on my shoulders.

I barely resist the urge to nip at her ankles, but we have a reservation to get to. The second shoe is on, and I pick up the fallen bouquet of calla lilies. After my Target run and getting ready, I had plenty of time to stop and get her flowers.

"These are different. Normally it's roses."

"I asked the florist what flowers represent beauty, and she recommended these."

"Oh" is all Bri gasps, her face alight with awe and appreciation.

She brings the flowers against her chest, her whiskey eyes shimmering with love and appreciation. She is magnificent, and I can't wait until she figures out our plans for the evening.

"Ready to go?"

"Yes, let me put these in a vase and we can head out."

Her heels click against the vinyl flooring. When she makes her way back to me, I hold out my hand to interlock our fingers together. I brush a kiss across her knuckles before tucking her arm underneath mine.

I open the car door for her and buckle her in before heading to the driver's side. As soon as I start the car, she's already asking questions.

"Are you going to tell me where we're going? Am I dressed okay?"

"We are going to Lagoon for a special dinner, and yes, you are dressed perfectly. You always look good, bear."

"What strings did you pull to get in there?"

"Cas helped me," I admit.

"Thank you, Cas."

"For real. Hey, Bri, if you could have any bookish item in the world, what would you choose?" I already know the answer, but I want to make sure nothing's changed.

"Oh, that's easy. I love the *Twisted* series by Ana Huang. Have you *seen* those special editions? My heart would swoon. One day, I'll have them." She lets out a wistful sigh, and the piece of paper is burning a hole in my pocket.

We pull into the beachfront restaurant and the valet approaches my car within seconds. We walk up to the hostess stand and when I give her my name, she asks us to follow her. The restaurant isn't super busy. I'm not sure if this is Cas' doing, or if it's just a slower night.

"Wait, where are we going?" Bri asks.

"Patience, bear." I squeeze her hand and throw a wink over my shoulder.

"Chef Marnie, Asher and his date have arrived," the hostess informs the chef before turning and walking away.

Chef Marnie turns around and offers us a warm smile. Wisdom and happiness are etched across her face in the form of laugh lines and crow's feet, evidence of a well-lived, happy life. Although her hair is covered by her chef's hat, loose, gray, curly tendrils frame her face.

"Well, hello. It's so nice to meet you. Are you ready for your cooking lesson?"

Bri whips her head to me with a surprised expression on her face. "Are you serious? This has been on my—"

"Bucket list. I know, I remember."

"Y-You remember that? That was over ten years ago."

"I remember everything about you, Bri. Are you ready to cook?"

"Yes." Bri does a little happy dance in her heels and my heart melts.

Chef Marnie walks us through the dish we're gonna make: chicken marsala. We have matching off-white aprons and hats to protect our clothes. Bri is in charge of chopping and stirring things, as I prepare our chicken. We listen to Marnie's instructions, and we sip our complimentary champagne while the chicken cooks, occasionally flipping the meat around in the pan so it doesn't burn on one side.

The smell of oregano and mushrooms permeates the room, making my mouth water. We wash our hands and have been instructed to walk through the way we came in, and the hostess will take us to a private table. We are guided to a secluded area with cobblestone pavement, and a pergola hangs over our heads with vines twisted along the columns. Fairy lights are strung throughout the place, and scattered across the ground are black, metal tables. The hostess guides us to a table that has a bottle of wine chilling on ice. I pull Bri's chair out for her before walking around to the other side.

"This is incredible, Asher. The view is breathtaking."

"It really is." She's looking around, but my eyes are trained on her. Brianna is stunning, her skin twinkling underneath the glow of the lights. She takes my breath away every single time I see her.

Our food arrives ten minutes later, and we focus on eating what we created. Damn, we did good. We make small conversation in between bites and sips of wine. Classical music begins to play over the speakers. I wipe my face with my napkin before getting up.

I extend my hand toward her. "May I have this dance?"

Bri places her hand in mine, face beaming so bright the stars look on with envy. I spin her once, twice, three times before we begin to sway, hearts colliding in a rhythm uniquely ours. Having her in my arms with a look of pure awe and trust shimmering up at me is my paradise.

"This is the most amazing date I've ever been on. You have your work cut out for you for our future dates."

"This is only just the beginning."

"What? There's more?" she asks, pure wonder in her voice.

"Mmhmm," I feel my lips curl in a playful smirk, "now, what do you say we get out of here and head to the next place?"

I settle our bill, and the valet has our car ready by the time we get to the front entrance. Bri's hand stays locked in mine as we make our way to the car.

I'm barely out of the parking lot before I pull off to the side of the road. My excitement to give her the gift is overwhelming.

"Wait, why are we stopping?"

"I was planning to give you this at the house, but I just can't wait." I reach into my pocket and pull out the black, silk envelope—another Target find—and hand it over to her.

"W-What's this?" Bri fingers along the envelope's flap, a frown stretched across her face.

"Open it and find out." I don't have to tell her twice. Bri not so gracefully tears open the envelope. When she opens the piece of paper, her gaze flickers between me and the content printed across it. She blinks once, twice, three times before letting out an ear-piercing squeal. Her entire body dances in the seat. Well, as best as one can while still being strapped in.

"ASHER! I—How did you...Why did you...How?"

"Avery—"

"Oh, my. I...I can't believe you'd do this for me. That's why you asked about what bookish thing I wanted. Oh, you're good, Mr. Larson. I...Thank you."

"Anything for you." Bri sniffles, and I notice tears falling like shimmering diamonds down her face.

"Damn it, Asher. My makeup is flawless, and you're ruining it with your generosity."

"And you'd look gorgeous with makeup smeared down your face. Ready to go? We have one more thing to tick off the list for tonight."

"There's *more*? I'm not sure I can handle anything else."

"Trust me, you'll love what I have planned next."

Ten minutes later, we're pulling into our driveway. And Bri has yet to look away from the piece of paper clutched in her grasp.

"Bri, we're home. Go ahead and put comfy clothes on, and I'll meet you in the backyard."

And just like that, she's off like a rocket. I have already moved most of my stuff into Bri's, so I don't have to go home to get a change of clothes. As she gets unready, I gather everything I need to bring outside.

I texted Cas earlier to blow up the air mattress after he set up Bri's new reading chair. I had her new books from Target on the kitchen table and asked if he could put them on her chair. And from the loud squeal that comes from upstairs, I assume she's found it. It'll only be a matter of minutes before she charges downstairs and sees everything I've set up.

Brianna

You aren't a bare minimum kind of woman

HOW DID HE...WHY DID he...*What?* As I stare at my new reading chair, I can't seem to form a coherent thought or question. But it's not just the reading chair, because Asher doesn't do anything halfway.

No.

Sitting on top of the chair is the *entire Off-Campus* series. A series that I remember mentioning to him in passing. Moisture sliding down my face alerts me that I'm crying. The thoughtfulness of this man alone is enough to have my heart soaring like an eagle taking flight.

My fingers trail along the fuzzy purple chair, the soft plushness feeling like heaven against my fingertips. Visions of lazy Saturday mornings curled up in this chair reading with sunlight streaming through the open window as birds sing their hellos to the world flash through my mind.

Asher is truly everything I could have ever wanted in a partner. He continues to surprise me every day. Speaking of surprises, he has another one waiting outside for me. The fall weather has me leaning toward warmth and comfort over sexy and revealing. I reach for my gray sweats and hoodie, wanting to replace a sad memory with a happy one. The moment I step outside, my hands fly to my face, momentarily stunned at what I see.

Asher is there with his hands inside the pockets of his checkered sweats wearing a sweet smile on his face. Behind him is a blue blow-up mattress with a shit ton of pillows and blankets piled on top. In front of the mattress is a gray tub filled with ice, two wineglasses, and a wine bottle. Snacks are scattered across the bed, and my feet become unstuck as I launch myself at him. Thank God for his calves of steel, because he's able to keep us upright.

"This is incredible, thank you." I press a smacking kiss to his lips before hopping down.

I carefully plop down on the mattress and grab the mint Oreos. There's every snack imaginable here: sweet spicy chili Doritos, pistachios, Red Vines. Seriously, Asher thought of everything. While I unwrap the snacks, Asher is pouring the wine into the glasses he brought out. I've been so distracted by everything he set up out here that I forgot about the reading chair upstairs.

"Thank you for my reading chair and the books. I can't believe you remembered those were the ones I wanted."

"I remember everything about you."

Asher's fingers brush a runaway curl off my face, and my face nuzzles against his hand like a cat marking their scent.

Mine.

"As for the chair, well, I had help from Avery and Cas. I was thinking of ordering myself one so that way we can read together side by side."

Seriously, how did I get so lucky to have a man like Asher in my life? Not only does he do shit like this, but he wants to get his own chair just so he can be near me? My heart threatens to jump out of my chest at the thought of spending weekends in our reading den together. He isn't afraid to read romance books. In fact, that's a majority of what he reads.

"Hey, Asher?" I ask.

"Yeah?"

"I know you like to read romance books, but I don't think I ever asked why." He confessed he got into reading as a way to talk to me, but I'm curious as to why he continues with romance.

"I know you love them, and you're always talking about this book boyfriend and that book boyfriend. I was curious, so I started picking them up. At first, it was to have any excuse to talk to you—one I was too scared to follow through on. Then I started taking mental notes on reasons why you liked that character. I guess I hoped that if we ever got together, I'd know how you'd want to be treated—"

"You did all that for me? Why?"

"You deserve to be treated like the women in those books do. You aren't a bare minimum kind of woman. These male characters go above and beyond for their girl, so that's why I read them—well, started reading them. Somewhere along the way, I began to enjoy what I was reading.

My Amazon book recommendations haven't been the same since. But if it meant you and I were connected on some level—even if you had no idea—then I'd happily sacrifice my search history."

I'm completely stunned. I mean, I guess I'm not really surprised, but the fact that he's taking notes on how to treat a woman right? If I wasn't already so in love with this man, my heart would have dropped at his feet right this second—alongside my panties. I remove the glasses from his hand and place them on the ground gently before straddling his lap.

"That has to be one of the hottest and sweetest things you've ever said to me."

I caress his cheeks with my hands before our mouths meet. There is no rush with this kiss, we just take our time and explore each other's mouths. The slow, lazy meeting of tongues heats our bodies against the cold, fall evening. There's nothing inherently sexual about this moment, just Asher and I conveying our love through a kiss.

It's Asher who pulls back first, pressing kisses to both of my cheeks before resting his forehead against mine. I snuggle closer to him, my head lying against his chest, listening to the strong, steady beating of his heart.

Just two individual souls twining together to create something beautiful. Something uniquely ours. Just being around him silences my worries, doubts, and fears. His calm energy soothes my chaos. I love this man with my entire being, and I'm glad we've chosen each other.

I find myself pulling back to admire the beautiful man that is Asher Larson. I watch his features soften with love and admiration, and I feel my face relaxing with what I assume is a matching look. He's everything I've ever wanted.

I know I wanted to fall in love, but I hadn't expected to do it twice—once with myself, and the other with the beautiful man in front of me.

"I love you, Asher. Thank you for loving every inch of me before I could learn to love myself."

"I love you, too, Bri. You've always been a fighter, and watching you love yourself, flaws and all, is breathtaking." I curl up into his arms, my head resting on his chest and his chin atop my head.

We remain silent, allowing nature's soundtrack to fill the space. Somewhere in the distance, there's a frog croaking. Cars are rushing by, and crickets call out to each other. The sky sparkles with millions of stars, not a single cloud in sight.

"Bri?" Asher's fingers massage my scalp, and I let out a soft sigh.

"Hmmm?"

"Can I ask why you've never gotten that book set? I mean, I totally love spoiling the shit out of you, but I'm just curious."

"I always said I'd buy it, but then every time they restocked, it sold out within seconds. I always thought that if it was meant to be, it would. And then life got away and while the books were always in the back of my mind, I just forgot about getting them. You got lucky that they weren't sold out when you ordered them."

"They're that popular, huh?"

"Oh, yeah. Remember when I made you crawl to me that one time?"

"Yeah."

"Well, I borrowed that scene from the second book in the series. So, I guess we were role-playing spicy book scenes before it became our thing."

"Damn, I need to read that book. Cuz fuck, if that wasn't one of the hottest things of my life. Hey, when we open our store, do you want to see if we could offer special editions? Maybe we can do a spotlight special for one each month?"

"You'd do that?" Asher does these little things that catch me off guard.

"Yeah. It's important to you, so I want to make sure we make all your bookish dreams come true. Well, all of your dreams, really."

"I fucking love you. I'm so happy to be doing this with you."

"I wouldn't want to do this with anyone but you."

"You really are the best. All my other boyfriends have nothing on—" I squeal when Asher tickles my sides.

"Other boyfriends, huh? Tell me, Bri, when do you have time for these other boyfriends?" My laughter comes out wheezy while squirming beneath his fingers.

"I-I can't breathe, Asher." His fingers stop what they're doing only to lift the hem of my hoodie up. Fireworks shoot off in my body when his lips press on my lower stomach.

"I asked you a question, bear. When do you have time for these boyfriends?"

"I-I meant past boyfriends. I, um—*oooh*." His fingers slip beneath the waistband of my sweats. The cool air hits my bare thighs as Asher slips the cotton fabric down my legs. I mentally high five myself for having the tall, earthy colored fence posts installed when I moved in. Last thing I want, or need, is my neighbors watching my every move. They might hear things...but they don't need to see everything that's about to happen.

"Tell me something. Have I successfully helped you fall in love with sex?" His gravelly tone sends desire right to my core.

"Mmmm...I don't know. I might need more practice."

The look on his face tells me everything I need to know. He *knows* I'm lying and being a brat. We've crossed off that item on my list forever ago. I just like having him between my legs.

"Well, then I guess I'm not doing my job well. Lift your hips for me, baby." I silently thank my lucky stars I chose not to wear underwear.

"Fuck. You've been bare under these sweats this entire time?" Asher's nose nuzzles my hip bone.

"Y-Yes. I didn't feel like putting them on." My confession comes out breathy.

"Easy access then." Asher's hot breath fans across my pussy before sliding my pants off my legs. He takes my legs and wraps them around his head before inserting his tongue inside me.

"Holy shit, Asher," I gasp. His tongue laps up my arousal. The friction from his flattened tongue has the eyes rolling in the back of my head. My hands shoot out to grip his hair when he takes my clit between his lips and sucks...*hard.*

"That's it. Ride my face. Soak my face with your cum," Asher growls as my hips pick up speed. Asher inserts two fingers inside me, and when he crooks them in the spot he knows I like, lights flash behind my eyelids. Everything begins to explode around me.

"Yes. There, right there," I moan, and Asher nips on my sensitive clit before flicking it with his tongue, all while curling his fingers inside me. The pressure building at the base of my spine is so overpowering, I might combust if I don't come soon. Hips rocking, tongue flicking, fingers curling. That's all it takes for me to come like I haven't before.

"Asher, oh fuck. It's too much," I whimper.

"Don't you dare stop. I want my chin drenched in your cum. Come for me, baby." My vision blurs and a metallic taste fills my mouth from biting down on my lip too hard. Asher's paying attention to my clit like there'll be a test and he needs to ace it. His tongue swipes up and down my slit a few times before removing himself between my legs. His chin glistens with my cum, just like he wanted.

"You do so well with me between your legs. Such a good girl for me." He kisses both of my cheeks before planting a lingering one to my forehead. Asher slides my sweats up my body before pulling me into him. Well, that's one way to replace the bad memory these sweats hold for me. That's the last thought I think about before I drift off into a peaceful sleep.

Asher

You're too sexy to resist

BRI'S DEFLATING THE AIR mattress while I pack away the snacks from last night and prepare breakfast. I'd call last night a success, and not just because I ended our date with my head between her legs. Sleeping with Bri under the stars is an experience we'll be repeating. She absolutely loved it; her entire being glowed with happiness.

I'm flipping our pancakes when I feel Bri's arms wrap around me. She smells like apple crisp and vanilla ice cream, and I want to say fuck breakfast and devour her whole. But Xander is due any second now to go over the plans he drew up for our bookstore.

Our bookstore.

I can't get over the fact that this is about to become reality. A dream I didn't realize I wanted until Bri shared hers with me. I love creating new drink recipes—I have since college. When I moved from the dorm to a shared apartment with my roommates, our place was party central. And not because we were these frat boys who loved to party. Word got around that I could make one hell of a drink, and once the news spread, we became the go to.

After Gage and I dropped out of college, we took a few mixology classes and loved them. It's there that I learned I had a special skill. I'm able to look at a person and find them the perfect drink. For Bri? Anytime I look at her, I see her as a bourbon cherry old fashioned. Her personality is bold and spicy. Mixed with the tangy cherry taste, and it's perfect for her. Her eyes light up when she gives people a book recommendation. Mine light up watching them take the first sip of their drink with a satisfied smile. The fact that Bri and I are taking both of our passions and combining them? I just know we're gonna be unstoppable.

"Good morning," I can feel the zing from Bri's lips through my t-shirt.

"Good morning. Your iced coffee is sitting in the fridge along with a banana nut muffin."

"Keep treating me like this, and you may end up waking up with my lips wrapped around your cock every morning." Bri chuckles, the vibration floating from her chest through my back.

"I wouldn't be opposed to that. Sounds like a kickass way to wake up. Don't let me hold you back, bear."

Bri's head is buried in my back, and I hear her slow, deep inhale. "How do you smell so good all the time? Like cinnamon and leather. It makes me want to buy all the candles with those scents just so I can smell it all the time."

I let out a laugh before squeezing one of her hands in mine. "I could say the same thing. You smell like dessert, and I just want to eat you whole."

"Nothing's stopping you. I love when you eat me out. Best feeling ever!"

"Annnnd I've lost my appetite," Xander exclaims from the back door. I could be in a room full of people, but if Bri's with me, everyone fades into the background. This isn't the only time my brother has walked in on a conversation like this.

"Ever heard of knocking?"

"Dude. I rang the doorbell three times before walking around the back of the house. It's not my fault you left both the gate and back door open." He turns to Bri to greet her. "Morning, Bri. You look extra glowy this morning." I toss a glare at my brother just in time to see him winking at her.

"Fuck off, Xander."

"Love ya, too, bro. I have the plans drawn up if you want to see them, but I can come back later if y'all wanna have some alone time." I love my brother to pieces, but sometimes, I wouldn't mind strangling the bastard. This is definitely one of those times.

"Oh, you have them drawn up already? I feel like I just asked you about it." Bri squeals while she goes to hug my brother.

"Once I heard you guys talk about what you wanted to do, my mind couldn't let it go. Ideas and visions about what it could look like flooded my mind, so I ended up drawing it out. I have, like, seven drawings in this folder." Xander pulls a red folder from his briefcase.

Sometimes, it's hard to come to terms with the man who's in front of me. For years, he was a complete asshole, lost in his own addictions. I enabled him for far longer than I should have, which only made our relationship worse. We had a huge falling out and didn't end up talking to each other for years. I spent a lot of time working through my own thoughts and feelings in therapy. Honestly, without therapy, I don't think I'd be where I am today. And I sure as hell wouldn't be working behind a bar, let alone owning one. I was so afraid that I'd turn out like my brother if I touched a drop of liquor. I guess a part of me still holds onto that fear because I haven't been drunk in years—not since college. It's the only way I can maintain a healthy relationship with alcohol.

When my brother got sober, things weren't magically fixed. We had to work through a lot of anger and resentment in order to get to where we are now. And seeing him with a passion for something other than drinking is amazing. He went from having a bottle as an accessory to a briefcase, and I couldn't be more proud.

"Ah, I'm so excited. Let me get changed and I'll meet you at the table. Asher, make sure your brother has a plate of food, too. I don't want to be rude and eat in front of him." She kisses my cheek before hightailing it up the stairs.

"Yeah, brother. Don't be a dick and eat in front of me." I roll my eyes, and before he has a chance to head to the table, I grab his arm.

"Hey. I'm proud of you, man. I know working through your shit isn't easy, but I admire how you work just a little harder every day. You've come a long way in the last few years, and I just want you to know that I'm happy for you."

"Thanks, man, I appreciate it. Yeah, being sober isn't for the faint of heart. It's still a struggle every day. While I still can't trust myself to go into a bar, I'm excited to help you with this project. Yeah, you'll have alcohol there, but it's the setting that's different. I'm proud of you, too, ya know. You didn't let my mistakes turn you bitter or ugly. You also didn't fall into the same trap I did. You're a better man than most, Ash."

"I wouldn't say that, but thanks, man. I'm glad I have you as a brother. Even though I didn't get a choice."

"Yeah, I begged Mom and Dad to return your ass, but I'm glad they didn't. Life without you is pretty dull. Oh, hey, speaking of life. Amber and I are trying." I almost burn my hand on the stove at the news.

"Trying? As in trying for a family?"

"No, trying to win the lottery. Of course for a family, dumbass. It's been a little challenging so far with my fertility issues. Had I known my alcoholism could affect my chances of starting a family, I'd never pick up the damn bottle. Had I known that someone like Amber was somewhere out there waiting for me, I'd have never let drinking overcome me like it did. It's a struggle I'm having a hard time overcoming. We're gonna give it a year before we seek out a specialist. Meanwhile, I'm back in therapy to work through some of my regret and guilt. If I can't give my wife a family…" Xander's words come out shaky. This isn't easy for him, and while he's the reason for this issue now, he doesn't deserve to be struggling like this.

"I'm sorry, man. I know that's not enough, but I am. You'll get your family. I just know it."

Bri walks down the stairs in a hunter green sweater dress that falls just below her knees. Her hair is tied up in a messy bun and the expression on her face is pure bliss. God, I love this woman.

Bri claps her hands together before walking to the table. "I'm ready to see the designs, Xander. Asher, will you bring the food to the table when it's ready? I'm too excited to wait."

"Of course, bear. I'm flipping the last pancake as we speak. Go sit down, I'm right behind you." I smack her ass when she walks past me, ignoring the smirk on my brother's face.

I'm carrying our breakfast over bit by bit, and I just watch as Bri dances in her chair, sipping her iced coffee. I put the plate down, yank her head back by her bun, and kiss her senseless. Xander be damned. My girl looks hot, and any chance I get to kiss her, I'll take it.

"What was that for?" Bri asks, chest heaving.

"You're too sexy to resist." I turn and walk back to the kitchen to grab the remaining plates and dishes. The table is decked out buffet style, with turkey bacon and sausage, a huge stack of pancakes, butter, syrup, and a bowl of mixed berries.

We spend a moment putting food onto our plates and passing dishes to each other. We sit in silence; the only sounds are utensils scraping plates and chewing. Bri is bouncing with so much excited energy, she's practically inhaling her food.

"Okay, I can't take it anymore. Let's see the drawings." Bri has her arms out in a gimme gesture that has both Xander and myself chuckling.

Xander pulls out the folder and Bri all but snatches it out of his hand like a toddler receiving a sucker from a grocery store. I scoot closer to her so that we can look at the sketches together. I'm completely blown away by my brother's talent. Who knew he could draw this well? We flip through sketch after sketch, and when we reach the fifth drawing, our eyes lock together, and we know. This is it. This is our future store. I have the biggest grin on my face while Bri's eyes shine with emotion. Hell, even my throat feels tight.

"Xander, I can't thank you enough for doing this. These sketches? They're incredible. Your talent is out of this world." Bri wipes her tears while I rub her back. She picks up the drawing we both have fallen in love with to show Xander.

"This is the one. I can feel it in my bones." Xander takes a sip from his coffee before taking a closer look at the paper in her hand, a smile slowly spreading across his face.

"I was hoping you'd pick that one. It's my favorite. I'm glad you asked me to do this. And I can't wait to work with you guys on bringing your baby to life."

"Seriously, thanks, man. This is just incredible." This piece of paper right here makes everything that more real.

We finish eating breakfast, talking about this and that. Xander opens up to Bri about him and his wife's struggles with getting pregnant. Bri, being the wonderful human that she is, gets up from her chair to hug him. The way she cares for people, listens to them. She's astounding.

Xander has long since left, leaving Bri and I to clean up our meal. We've gotten into a routine of I wash the dishes and she dries. Then Bri says something that has my heart doing somersaults in my chest.

"I'm ready to talk to my brother now." The resilience of this woman. I reassure her that I'll still come if she wants me to, which she says yes to. My little warrior is about to tackle her biggest demon, and I won't be anywhere else than next to her, holding her hand.

Brianna

The blue was my guiding light, my savior

My body is drowning in a sea of panic. My screams fall silent, and I'm so paralyzed with fear that I can't seem to move.

It's just your brother, Bri. Try and relax. You have nothing to worry about.

But I do. I do have things to worry about. I've been putting this off for months, involved in a toxic relationship with shame and guilt. If I thought talking to my parents was anxiety inducing, it's nothing compared to talking to my brother. He was in the car with me that night, they weren't. I've grown so much in the last few months, but of course my brain loves to be a bitch...fucking Patricia. I'm suddenly pulled back to the scene of the accident.

So many cop cars, bathing the scene in blue and red. Blood and glass cover every inch of the scene. I know I'm being harassed with a million and one questions, but I cannot seem to speak. My mind and body are still in my

now totaled car, the sound of squealing threatening to burst my ear drums. My heart beats manically inside my chest and my breath comes in quick, frantic pants.

Breathe. I. Can't. Breathe.

A deep, smooth voice whispers in the distance. I know this voice, but as I search the scene, I can't seem to find where it's coming from. Tears blur my vision, and my head feels dizzy and light. I press my hands to my head, and a loud, shrill sound pierces the air.

Where is that coming from?

Why is it so loud?

The deep voice from earlier is more frantic and desperate. The sound feels closer now. I allow the soothing sound to wrap around me like my favorite blanket. Warm hands grip my shoulders, jolting me out of this nightmare.

"Bear? Can you hear me?" Asher's voice is muffled, and some part of me feels his hands on my face. Asher pulls me into his arms, wrapping me tight. The pressure is a welcome sensation, like a weighted hoodie.

"Just follow my breathing. Focus on the rise and fall of my chest." So that's what I do. Asher knows telling me to breathe won't work, so he has me focus on his breath. My ear is pressed against his chest, and I listen to the steady drumming of his heartbeat. It pulls me into a state of calmness like a lullaby does to a newborn baby.

Thump. Thump. Thump.

With each beat of his heart, I feel my frantic pace begin to slow. My mind continues to race, but everything around me begins to slow down. My heartbeat becomes the harmony to his, creating a symphony that steadies my entire being.

"That's it, baby. Keep focusing on my breath. I'm right here with you. The sun is shining, the wind is blowing, and you are safe. Max is just inside waiting for you to run into his arms. You're about to do a very hard thing, but everything will be okay. I know it." If feathers had a voice, they'd sound like Asher, soft and smooth. My last deep breath comes out shaky, almost as if the fear is leaving my body.

When I pull back to look at him, I see love, support, and empathy swirling behind those beautiful, baby blue eyes. I've been in the dark for so long. Lost in a sea of endless gray until I saw a flash of blue over the horizon. The pull was too strong to ignore. Little did I know that bright blue color was pulling me out of the stormy sea and onto the shore, where for the first time in forever, I could breathe. The gray threatened to swallow me whole, but the blue was my guiding light, my savior.

I stare into those same blue eyes that saved me all those months ago, and I'm overcome with gratitude. It's a warm light that spreads from the top of my head to the tips of my toes. Asher is my saving grace, my hero, my everything.

I pull his lips to meet mine, pouring my heart and soul into the kiss. I've finally come to terms with everything that's happened, and talking to Max is the final chapter of a book I'm ready to close and put back on my shelf. This book is one of many in the story of my life, and while this book was harder to get through, I did it. I not only survived, but I thrived.

I'm so wrapped up in Asher that I don't realize his voice until a second later.

"Get a room, why don't ya." I pull away from Asher, and my eyes immediately fill with tears.

"Maxie…" His childhood nickname comes out in a whisper.

"Breezy." Max's voice comes out raspy.

"Say it again," I plead, yearning to hear the sound of my childhood nickname. Thousands of sibling memories play out in my mind like a home movie, showcasing my favorite moments beneath a grainy, muted lens.

"Breezy…" I want to run into his arms, but I'm not sure if anything still causes him pain, and I'd rather not risk reinjury. Instead, I power walk toward him, wrapping my arms around him as tight as I can.

"Hi, Max."

"Hi, Bri. Hey, Asher." Oops, I forget he's here for a minute, but being the supportive boyfriend he is, he doesn't mind.

"Hey, Max," Asher says, offering a nod of acknowledgement before turning to me. "I'll be in the car. Text me if you need me." I nod, and Asher turns around and walks to the car.

Max and I head inside and move toward his couch. Nothing has changed. His walls are the same dark gray as before, with a dark cherry hardwood flooring. His massive TV is the main focus of the living room, with a fireplace made of stone with family pictures along the mantel.

I'm staring at one of the two of us the night he graduated from high school. We decided to go hiking—his request, not mine. I remember that night like it was yesterday. We shared our dreams and aspirations while being content with just being in each other's presence.

"Ah, that's one of my favorite photos of us. You gave me so much shit for growing old. We'll have to go hiking there again soon."

And now I'm losing it, head in my hands, body shaking uncontrollably.

"Breez, hey, come here." Max opens his arms, and I launch myself at him.

"I-I'm so sorry. It's all my fault that you were in this situation in the first place. If I hadn't convinced you to—" I'm surprised he's able to understand what I'm saying with how hard I'm crying. Max stops me mid-sentence by pulling me into his arms.

"You are *not* to blame for this. The only person who deserves the blame is the one who decided to drive drunk. I may have given you shit about going axe throwing, but I wanted to go. It was just more fun to fuck around. I'm sorry I made you feel like you had to force me."

"I—You did? You wanted to go?"

"Hell yeah. Throwing axes while hanging with you? No brainer." I feel the guilt slowly evaporate from my body like a rain puddle on a hot day.

"I just hate that you're in pain when all I got was a minor concussion and a few scratches. You were in a coma, Max. How could I *not* feel guilty for that?"

"Did you force that woman to get behind the car while intoxicated?"

"Well, no, but—"

"Did you tell her to run through the red light?"

"NO, b—"

"Did you break my leg, arm, and shoulder all by yourself?" I can't help but laugh at his ridiculousness.

"You know I didn't, Max. But I'm the reason we were in the car in the first place."

"You're right, you were. But I also got in the car willingly. We can't predict what's going to happen, Breezy, but we're here and we're alive."

"You always have to be right, don't you?" I ask. The familiar teasing feels like coming home from a week-long trip, comforting and familiar.

"Did you expect anything less? Um...Can we sit down? My leg is feeling a bit stiff, and we have a lot to talk about."

"Oh, yes, of course. I'm sorry."

We make our way over to the couch and I feel his eyes boring into the side of my face. This conversation is long overdue, but I'm fucking terrified.

"I'm so sorry, Max. I—"

"Can I go first?" Max asks, his voice wavering a little.

"Oh...S-Sure."

"First, I'm going to tell you how much I love you. I need you to not only hear that, but accept it. You mean the world to me. You're my best friend and I need to get this off my chest." Max pauses to collect his thoughts before continuing.

"It hurt me when you cut me out. I-I understand that you were hurting, but I needed my sister. You didn't answer any of my texts, and I couldn't help but think I did something wrong."

Max's pain is a direct hit to my heart. And my tears are cascading down my face at a rapid pace. I reach out to grab my brother's hand, squeezing it a few times so I can collect myself before I respond.

"No, Max. Never. This was all on me. You did absolutely nothing wrong. I wanted to reach out so many times, but I was so frozen in my own despair that I didn't know how. I didn't think you'd want to see me. I had somehow convinced myself that *you* hated *me*."

"I could never hate you, Bri. You're one of the most important people in my life. I felt so...so lost and empty without you. It was like I was floating in space, unable to latch onto anything. I just...I missed you, you little asshole." Max's watery chuckle breaks some of the tension.

"It takes an asshole to know an asshole." I rest my head on his shoulder and inhale a deep, shaky breath. "I'm sorry I cut you out. I cut everyone out. Well, except for Asher. He kinda refused to leave me alone. But I have both you and Avery to thank for that with y'all asking him to babysit my ass."

Max flinches beneath my weight. "I'd say I was sorry...but it looks like it worked out in your favor. So...you and Asher, huh?"

"Yup. You cool with it?" I ask.

"Yeah, it was only a matter of time before you two got together. But if he breaks your heart, I'll break his face. If you break his, I won't speak to you for, like, a week," Max jokes.

"I missed you, big brother." I rest my head on his good shoulder.

"I missed you more, little sister." Max presses a kiss to my head. We stay in this position for what feels like hours, catching each other up with what's been happening.

"Oh, so I know Asher talked to you about our business idea?"

"He did, and I think it's a fantastic plan."

"Well, his brother Xander drew up a plan for what the building might look like, and I was wondering if you'd help build it when you're up for it?"

"Fuck yeah. I'd be honored. I'm, um, I'm not sure I can do much physical labor for, um, a while yet. But I do great work at the desk in our office, and I can put my bossiness skills to good use. I have a fantastic team to help me with everything else."

Something seems...off with Max. When we originally talked about my desire to open up a bookstore, he was all over it, creating a very intricate plan. But the Max who sits next to me is stuttering and his smile is too bright—signs that he's keeping something from me. I'm not sure what, but his lack of enthusiasm to be involved in every aspect of *building* the store is concerning.

"Don't you want to do more than bossing people around? I mean, Max, you helped me come up with this plan."

"Nah, I'm cool with being the boss." He shrugs his shoulders.

"Are...Are you okay? You don't seem as excited—"

"Bri, I'm good. I can't wait to see your dream come to fruition."

I want to push, but something in his tone tells me to hold off.

"Thanks, Maxie. I'm glad it's finally happening and that we can do this together."

Max and I are practically glued to each other's side for hours as we animatedly talk about the plans for the bookstore. Emotional exhaustion from our reunion is threatening to pull me under, so I say my goodbyes while I cling to him like a koala to a eucalyptus tree. I breathe in his cedar scent, and I'm reminded of all the times I ran to him for solace after a boy broke my heart—or I got a bad grade on a test I studied for. His arms were my safety net, and now that I've moved past my guilt, I'll never go too long without a hug from my best friend, my brother. We make plans for the following weekend before I'm out the door. When I walk out, Asher is standing there, flowers in one hand and an iced coffee in the other.

"I really might have to open that greenhouse now," I say as I walk toward him.

"Then we'll build you the best greenhouse there is, because I don't plan on stopping with the flowers. How did it go?"

"Good, very good. My heart feels full and happy. But I noticed Max was weird with when I asked him about helping build our store. He looked excited, but something felt off. I get this feeling he's hiding behind his desk. Did he say anything to you?"

"Yeah, I think he's struggling with some shit. I suggested therapy, and I think he'll do it when he's ready. We just gotta give him time, bear." The empathy that radiates from this man is truly awe-inspiring. He genuinely doesn't have a mean bone in his body. Well, except for when people are assholes to those he loves—then the gloves come off. Asher is sweet, kind, patient, and boy does he know what to do with that mouth of his. Despite the way he makes me feel physically, emotionally and mentally I know I'm safe with him. I always have been.

I lean in and press a quick peck on his lips. "I love you, Asher Larson. I hope you know just how much you mean to me."

"I love you, too, Bri bear. Always have, always will. You've had a long day. Let's go home and take a nice, long bath before you take a much deserved nap." Asher hands me the coffee and flowers before opening my door. As we drive home, I listen to my heart put the final missing piece back together.

Asher

Don't you think it's a little too early for a beer?

GAGE AND I HAVE been interviewing for my replacement for weeks, but no one fits. With Bri and I going into business together, it'll be difficult to work both jobs. I plan to remain a silent partner, helping when absolutely necessary. Gage will be taking over all my previous duties. The bar has been closed since we've gotten back to back interviews, and we are nowhere near close to finding someone. Case in point, the curvy blonde in front of us with the world's lowest cut shirt possible and a nauseating amount of perfume on. It's clear she doesn't want to actually work by how hard she's eye fucking Gage right now.

"We have a few more candidates to interview before we make our decision. Thank you for taking time out of your day, we'll be in touch." I shake the woman's hand, ignoring the lingering looks she's giving me. She swings her hips with dramatic flair when she walks out the door.

"Thoughts?" I ask, turning to my business partner and future owner of Aces.

"No." One simple word, but it's very on brand for Gage.

"I need a break, let me know when the next candidate arrives. I'm headed to the back." I need a moment. This endless interviewing has been exhausting. I'm shuffling papers around when I hear a high pitched voice interacting with Gage.

Curiosity gets the better of me, so I quietly open the door and watch for as long as I can before I'm spotted.

"What can I do ya for?" Gage is leaned over the counter, fully engaged in the conversation with a smile on his face.

"I would like one beer, please." The voice has to belong to a girl no more than five or six years old.

"Beer, huh? It's only eleven a.m. Don't you think it's a little too early for a beer?" This is a new side to Gage. He's soft and playful with this little girl.

"Nope. My mama lets me drink beer all the time." The girl wiggles in her seat, her grin showing she's missing one of her bottom teeth. Her blonde, curly hair is in two pigtails, and she's wearing a long sleeve, white shirt under a maroon, velvet dress. She has whiskey brown eyes and freckles scattered across her nose.

"Mama lets ya drink, huh?"

"Yup. And she gives me suckers and candy. My mama is the best." Gage throws his head back and lets out a loud laugh. Moments later, a woman with long, blond hair with the same whiskey brown eyes and dressed in a brown, cropped sweater and dark jeans with suede boots rushes into the bar. She's a subtle sort of pretty, and the little girl on the bar stool is her spitting image. That must make her the mother.

"Cora Rose, what did I tell you about running off?" She has her hands on her hips, but her eyes scream fear.

"I'm sorry, Mama. You were talking to that lady, and I was thirsty for beer."

"Your daughter has been asking me for a beer for the last five minutes." Gage's expression completely changes. His shoulders are tense. I watch him analyze the woman with weariness and another emotion I can't pinpoint. And just like that, a mask of indifference slips over Gage's features as he busies himself with cleaning the already spotless bar top.

"Oh, yeah, the girl loves her root beer," she addresses Gage before turning to Cora. "Sweet baby girl, you scared your mama. I know you wanted something to drink, but running off is scary. Something could have happened to you, and I need to keep you safe. Do you understand?"

"I'm sorry, Mama. I won't do it again." Goddamn, this kid is cute.

"What lady were you talking to?" Gage asks.

"Oh, um, I just moved to town and I was asking if anyone was hiring. I haven't been lucky so far. Let's go, Cora bug." She reaches for her daughter's hand, and Cora's face falls with disappointment.

"She hasn't had her beer yet," Gage blurts at the woman. But the second he looks at Cora, his expression turns soft. "You thirsty, little one?"

"Mmmhmm. Mama, can I have a beer?" Cora turns to her mom with a puppy dog face.

"Are you looking for work?" I finally insert myself into conversation, and Gage shoots me a look.

"I am. Are you hiring?" she asks with a pleading expression.

"Do you have any serving or bartending experience?"

"Yes, I—Yes, I have experience."

I look at Gage, sending him a wicked grin before turning to the woman and offering my hand to her.

"Hi, I'm Asher, and the grump over there serving your cute, sweet little girl is Gage."

"Kennedy, it's nice to meet you," Kennedy says while shaking my hand.

"Where are you moving from?"

I notice Kennedy begins to tense up. She takes a breath and forces herself to relax before she answers. "Indiana. I wanted a fresh start for my daughter and I. I can give you references if you'd like. I'm bubbly, and fun, and a quick learner. I'm great with people and handling money."

"No need. When can you start?"

"Oh, are you serious?"

"Sure am. I even have a place up for rent if you need a place to stay. It's right above the bar. It's not big, but it has two bedrooms. One for you and one for your daughter. It's yours if you want it."

"Oh, um..." Something akin to skepticism crawls across her features, and I watch as a storm brews beneath the surface. Kennedy glances to her daughter, who remains blissfully unaware of the tension rolling off her mom. The moment Cora grins up at her, I see the gears switch in her mind, and it's made up before she turns to me. "I don't want to take advantage."

"You aren't. It'll make it easier for you to get to work if you live upstairs."

"Well, if you really don't mind, then thank you. I—we would appreciate that."

Gratitude and relief replace her hesitation as tension evaporates from her body. Kennedy turns toward Gage, and I press my lips together when I see her reaction to him. There's a warrior beneath the skittish exterior when she rolls her shoulders back and extends a hand out to my partner.

"Hi, I'm Kennedy." A soft, shy smile tugs at her lips, but her expression shifts into something I can't quite read.

Gage's large hand engulfs her petite one. I watch his jaw tic with what I *assume* is... annoyance? One can't be sure with Gage. His hand lingers for a moment before something snaps him out of whatever daze he was in. Whatever spell he was under has been broken, and his face morphs into a disinterested look.

"Gage. I'll see you next Monday, and we'll start your training. Don't be late." His curt tone, while unsurprising, seems to be a tad extra than his normal demeanor. Gage turns toward Cora and his entire demeanor softens. He's always had a soft spot for kids, being surrounded by his nieces and nephews.

"Nice to meet you, Cora. Enjoy your beer." He offers her a smile and a wink before turning around and walking off.

"Don't worry about him. He's a grump. It takes time for him to get used to someone. Congrats and welcome to the Aces family."

"Thank you, thank you, thank you. Cora Rose, finish your drink and let's go."

"You can move your stuff this weekend. I'll be fully moved into my girlfriend's house by then. Swing by the bar Friday night, and I'll give you a key. Where are you guys staying right now?"

"We have a room at a motel for the next few days, so the timing is perfect. Thank you, Asher. I'm so excited." Cora slurps the rest of her drink before hopping off the stool and walking toward her mom.

"Bye, bye, Mr. Asher." Cora waves at me the entire way out the door.

Gage comes out minutes later, grumpy as ever.

"So...Thoughts?" I ask.

"She'll do," Gage replies nonchalantly.

"I have a good feeling about Kennedy. I think there's more to the story about her moving. So, do me a favor, and don't be a total dick to her."

"Me? A dick? Never." Gage winks before turning his attention to preparing for work tonight, but he's moving slower than normal.

"Wait, what do you mean there's more to the story?" Gage is wearing his signature frown, but I can tell he cares. He just doesn't want to admit it. Which, given his history with women—one in particular—I understand the reservation.

"I don't know, but she tensed up when I asked where she was from. Just a feeling in my gut." Gage's response is a curt nod, and I can't help but smile. I have a feeling Gage has met his match—in more ways than one.

Brianna

She has blossomed into a beautiful butterfly

I'M STANDING OUT IN the parking lot of the salon I've called a second home for years.

The weather has a bite to it, and the weatherman predicted we'll be getting a crazy snowstorm later. But knowing Chicago weather, the "snowstorm" will be a light dusting. Gotta love midwestern weather, where the weather is nipple-hardening cold in the morning and sweltering hot in the daytime—especially in the fall/wintertime. I texted my boss earlier about wanting to talk to her. She called me immediately, shouting and screaming with how happy she was to hear my voice. I've been gone for so long, so I can only assume she thinks this is my inevitable return to work.

As I think about the last five or so years, I remember them fondly. I truly love and adore these girls. I started here as a receptionist when I first started beauty school. I slowly worked my way up to master stylist, and my clientele list was about a mile long. I hate to let them go, but it's time to move forward.

My future is with the bookstore with Asher. Xander and Max have been working tirelessly to create the foundation of what our place is going to look like. The more it comes together, the more excited I become. Everything in my life has fallen into place, and for the first time in a long time, I feel secure. In myself, in my stage in life, and with my relationship with Asher.

Okay, Bri. It's now or never.

I take a few steadying breaths, watching the puffs of air dissipate before my eyes. I make my way up to the salon with my heart hammering inside my chest. I'm not sure what I was expecting, but it wasn't a full blown welcome back party. *Well, shit.* This might be a tad awkward. Regardless of my plans to leave, it's nice to feel so welcome.

One by one, my coworkers all give me bone crushing hugs and share how much they've missed me. The last to greet me is my spunky, spitfire boss, Alison.

"Brianna, oh, it's so good to see your face. How are you? How's Max?"

"I'm good, we both are. It's so good to see your face as well. Can we, um. Can we go to the office to talk?" If she suspects anything, she doesn't give it away.

"Yes, yes of course. Come on back."

I follow Alison to her office and take in the chaotic space. The walls are matte black, with one of them being a chalkboard wall where everyone can write uplifting, positive messages. Her desk is also black, and her chairs are a bright purple. Then there's a fake fern named Alan in the corner. This office screams Alison.

Alison takes a long look at my face before recognition crosses hers. "You're here to quit, aren't you?" There is no hostility in her tone, just curiosity.

"I am. I'm sorry to be throwing this at you."

"Oh, honey, no. There's no need to be sorry. What are you going to be doing now?" I tell her my plans for the bookstore as well as my relationship with Asher and how he plays into everything.

"My Brianna has blossomed into a beautiful butterfly. I'm so proud of you. You'll have to let me know when you guys open. The girls and I would love to celebrate with you. Damn, now I have to figure out how to replace you. Not that you are replaceable, you are one in a million, Brianna."

"I'm glad you mentioned that. I have a friend named Amber who has been looking for a salon job. She's talented. She did my hair and makeup for my date with Asher." I pull my phone out and show her. Then I pull up Amber's Instagram feed to show Alison her work.

"Wow, she is super talented. I just *know* my clients will love her." My heart begins to beat fast while Alison scrolls through Amber's photos.

"And you can vouch for her?" Alison asks while glancing up from my phone.

"Yes, one hundred percent. Not only is she extremely talented, but she's an amazing woman. She's kind, fun, and she's very personable."

"Well, then tell her she's hired." Alison hands me my phone back, and it takes me a minute to process what she just said.

"Wait, what? Are you serious?"

"Yes. If you trust her, then so do I. We'll miss having you around here. You better visit us from time to time. I'll even give you the employee discount whenever you get your hair done here."

"Thank you, Alison. I'll miss you guys, too. Y'all took me on when I was just starting, and I'll be eternally grateful for every opportunity you've given me." Alison stands up and walks around her desk to pull me into a hug.

"Love you, kid."

"Love you, too." My welcome back party turns into a goodbye party. I'm going to miss these girls, but I know I'm making the right step.

About an hour later, I'm walking into the house I now fully share with Asher. He's sitting on the couch reading the book I recommended to him. The second he sees me, he puts the book down and opens his arms for me. I crawl into his lap and press a kiss to his neck.

"How'd it go?"

"It was sad, but good at the same time. I'm ready for this next adventure in my life—in our life."

"I can't wait for our store to open. We're gonna do good things, Bri." Asher and I cuddle together on the couch, and he talks about hiring his replacement and the tension that seems to be emanating between Gage and Kennedy. That'll be interesting to watch unfold.

"Love you, Asher. Thank you for knocking on my door all those months ago."

"Love you too, Bri bear."

Brianna

You're my little warrior, my Bear

It's finally time. Months of blood, sweat, and tears, and it's finally opening day for our store. The second I stepped into the store this morning, I fell to the ground. Xander has been working tirelessly to bring the vision Asher and I had to life.

Max has been extremely helpful in his own way. Getting him to be open with what he's going through feels impossible. I know he's struggling because his use of humor has been more excessive than usual. That, and he's still insisting that the doctor has these weightlifting restrictions still in place. I mean, I don't know much about healing from multiple surgeries, but something feels off. Still, having him delegate tasks to his team makes him happy. And he still gets to be a part of this process, so I'm not pushing him on it. Well, not pushing as hard as I want to, if I'm being honest. I know it killed Max not to have more of an active role in the creation of Booked 'N' Boozed. But his fingerprints are throughout this store, and for now, that's enough.

Avery is in the corner, feeding her baby girl while Cas and Asher run around the room putting up last minute touches. I walk over to Avery and coo over her gorgeous baby, Paisley.

"I still can't believe you're a mom. She's literally your spitting image, Aves. How's motherhood treating you?"

"I'm exhausted and cranky, but I wouldn't change it for the world. Being a mother is truly a gift I didn't know I needed." I brush my fingers over her dark curls, admiring the freckles on her cheek.

"How are you feeling about today?" Isn't that a loaded question. Today has been a whirlwind, but Avery insisted on getting my hair, makeup, and nails done for today. She told me it was necessary for tonight and that I'd hate myself if I looked like a crazy person in my photos.

"I'm overwhelmed and anxious, but excited. We've been working so hard these last few months, so now that it's finally here? It's surreal."

"Well, at least you look good."

"Well, yeah. My best friend forced me to get ready with her. Of course I look good."

I feel Asher's arms wrap around me, swaying our bodies back and forth.

"Hey, baby. Today's the day. Are you ready?" I turn around to peck his lips.

"Hey. Yeah, I'm more than ready. Are you?"

"I've been ready for years." *Years?* That's weird since we haven't been planning this for that long. Whatever, I have other things to think about.

"Well, everyone's here. You want to give your speech now?" Asher asks.

"More than ever." I give him another quick kiss before removing myself from his arms.

Asher and I walk up hand in hand to the front of the shop, and I loudly clear my throat to gather everyone's attention.

"Hi, everyone. Thank you for coming to the opening of Booked 'N' Boozed." I pause, taking in the loud applause and cheering. "We're so happy you decided to join us in the celebration. First, I wanted to shout out to my partner, Asher. If it wasn't for you pushing and encouraging me to be the best version of myself I can be, I wouldn't be who I am now. Thank you for always being the man I needed and helping me see the woman I was—especially when I couldn't see it myself. You are truly the best man I could ever share a life with." Asher kisses my cheek and squeezes my hand.

"To Max and Xander. The store would still be an idea in our heads if it wasn't for your creative genius. The both of you worked tirelessly to make our dream a reality, and for that, we are eternally grateful."

"To Avery and Cas for supporting me through thick and thin. I wouldn't be the woman I am today without you two by my side." I turn to mine and Asher's parents for the final thanks.

"To our parents, thank you for being the best role models. You've taught us everything we know, and we both love you guys so much. With all that said, stick around, buy a book, and get a drink from Asher. Thank you again for coming, and have fun."

Asher

The box that's in my pocket feels like it weighs a thousand pounds.

It's now or never.

I glance around the room, and I'm overwhelmed with how many people showed up for us. Bri's parents are over in the corner talking to mine, and when Colleen catches my gaze, she winks at me. Avery and Cas are in the designated rocking chair in the corner—a feature we put it for breastfeeding mothers, so they don't have to feel like they need to excuse themselves to the restroom. The space is secluded enough from the public space, allowing the mother and child to have the privacy they need. To my left, I see Kennedy with her little girl, Cora, in her lap reading a children's book. And who should be hovering over them but none other than Gage. ·

Kennedy is so focused on her girl that she has no idea how the man standing next to her is looking at her. I've known him for years, and I've *never* seen that look on his face. He must sense my gaze on him, because when his eyes meet mine, he takes a giant step back from her and gives me his normal Gage-like scowl.

Yeah…Something's happening there.

And if not yet, soon. I squeeze the pocket with the ring inside and clear my throat loud enough to get everyone's attention.

"If I could have everyone's attention for a minute." Bri gives me a questioning look.

"Bri, you are the most incredible woman I've ever met. I knocked on your door over a year ago hoping to provide friendship and support. What I didn't expect was for you to become the most important person in my life. You're strong, resilient, and beautiful inside and out. You're my little warrior, my bear."

"Oh my God." Bri's eyes tear up and her hands shoot up to her face.

"I loved watching you blossom. Watching you on your journey to finding yourself has been the greatest gift one could ever receive. You've always been the woman who stands before me today, and watching you be reintroduced was everything."

"Asher, oh my God." Bri's hands are flapping in front of her face.

I pull the ring from my pocket and get down on one knee. "Brianna Mae Montgomery, will you do me the honor of becoming my wife?"

"Yes. One thousand times, yes." Bri launches herself at me, assaulting my mouth with hers. Someone clears their throat, forcing us apart. I slide the ring on her finger. A perfect fit for a perfect woman.

"I love you, bear."

"I love you, too, future hubby."

Epilogue

Asher

My dirty wife

"Where are Asher and Bri? We needed to cut the cake, like, ten minutes ago." The sound of Avery's voice has us frozen in place. My dick is pulsing inside her, and my hand suddenly covers her mouth.

"Shh. Don't make a sound," I demand.

Eventually, Avery's footsteps begin to fade. The second they do, I'm back to pounding my cock into my wife.

My wife.

I can't believe I get to call her that.

"Look at my dirty wife taking her husband's cock like a good girl." My thrusts are hard and rough, just how she likes it.

"Asher. Oh my God, don't stop," Bri whimpers.

"I wouldn't dream of it, wife," I growl into her ear. My fingers flutter around her neck before I squeeze. Bri's eyes roll back into her head, and I feel her pussy grip my cock even harder. The harder I squeeze her throat, the more she responds.

"Does Mrs. Larson like being choked out?" Her response is to nod her head and whine.

"Are you gonna come on my cock like a good little wife?" I grunt in between thrusts.

"Y-Yes," Bri chokes out. I unwrap my fingers from around her throat and pull her up into a sitting position.

"I want you to watch me fuck this cunt of yours. I want you to watch as my cock rams into you over and over again. Are you off birth control?"

"Y-Yes."

"Good girl, I'm gonna come inside you, filling you to the brim. Anything that leaks out, I'll stuff it back inside you. Do you understand?"

"Yes, Daddy. I u-understand." Her voice comes out in staccato pants.

"Good, now watch me fuck your pussy. I want you to see what you do to me." Bri and I watch where our bodies connect, both of us mesmerized by how fast and hard my cock disappears into her pussy.

"A-Asher, oh right there. D-Don't stop. I-I'm close." Bri's legs that are wrapped around my waist tighten their hold. Her inner walls begin to flutter around me, and our breathing is erratic.

"Come for me, wife."

"AHHH Asher, oh," Bri screams my name, but I'm not fully satisfied.

"Use my other name, baby."

"I'm coming, my husband. You fuck me so good, come inside me." Bri calling me *her husband* has me fully feral.

Bri unravels on my cock, and seconds later I spill inside her, filling her to the brim. My thrusts begin to slow, and I bring my forehead to hers. We allow for our breathing to regulate before I pull out of her and tuck myself back into my pants.

"My dirty little wife likes it rough, doesn't she?"

"Only for you." My life has been a whirlwind, in the best way possible. I tuck a few strands of Bri's hair into whatever updo she has for the wedding day. We both fix our attire before I lift her off the table.

The second we said I *do*, Bri whispered into my ear that she wanted me, so we both snuck off into a closet to take care of things. What a way to christen our new marriage.

"Are you ready to go out there, Mrs. Larson?

"Why yes, yes I am, Mr. Larson."

We walk out hand in hand, and the first person we see is Avery, who looks at Bri, then to me, and then rolls her eyes. Clearly, no amount of adjusting things could hide what we just did.

Later in the evening, I dance with my beautiful wife, and emotion clogs my throat.

Bri is radiant with a dark merlot colored lip, a mix of browns and golds dusted across her eyelids, and she's wearing what they call *dramatic lashes*. Her natural curls are in a low ponytail with white beads scattered throughout. I have to give Amber her props, because she took my wife's natural beauty and amplified it. Her makeup is one thing, but this dress? Hot damn, just looking at how the off-white silk hugs her ample curves has me wanting to drop to my knees and devour her pussy right here...wedding guests be damned.

And it seems that the back of the dress is missing, but you don't see me complaining. It allows me to trail my fingertips up and down her spine—which is foreplay for her.

Is it rude to leave the wedding to go back to the room for round two?

When I look into her golden-brown eyes, I see my whole life staring back at me. Our bodies are so close that she reaches down to grip my cock before helping me adjust myself. God, I fucking love this woman.

I press a quick kiss to her lips before leaning in to whisper, "I love you, my wife."

"I love you, too, my husband."

The rest of the night is spent dancing under the stars and mingling with all our loved ones. Everything couldn't have gone more perfectly. I have the most incredible woman by my side, and I can't wait to do life with her by my side.

Bonus Chapter

Book recs & big O's

Asher

I'M ROOTED IN PLACE at the front of Booked N' Boozed as I watch Bri help a customer find their perfect book. I'm always in awe whenever I'm in Bri's presence, but watching her in her element? I'm mesmerized, awestruck. Fucking enchanted. It's been a few months since we opened our store, and I never tire of watching Bri recommend books to fellow readers. She brightens every room she enters, but right now, she's liquid sunshine.

My forearms are braced on the edge of the counter while I shamelessly check her out. I mean, can you blame me? She's a walking wet dream with curves for days and an ass I want to sink my teeth into. The way Bri's dress hugs her like an eager lover has jealousy licking up my spine. I'm fully aware I'm jealous of a fucking *dress*, but all rational thinking fled my brain the moment she walked downstairs. It's form-fitting and reaches mid-thigh, the color reminding me of the blush that creeps across her cheeks when she comes. That soft mauve color is forever tattooed in my brain.

As if she senses my gaze, Bri whips her head around, a knowing smirk decorating her stunning features. It's an *I know what you're thinking* kind of look. And because my bear likes to play, she fingers the hem of her dress. Bri glances at the sign above the customer's head, then back at me with a raised brow. She does this as her fingers flirt with the bottom of her dress.

The moment my eyes connect with the dark romance sign, hundreds of images assault my senses. Me, dressed in all black with a mask on my face, chasing Bri through the woods behind the cabin we rented. Bri sprawled out on the edge of a hot tub from said cabin while I ate her cunt out. Bri on her knees, sucking me off while I mixed custom drinks for a book club meeting. It doesn't matter how long we've been together, we still want each other with the same intensity as a new couple.

Our gazes reconnect, and my face stretches into a sinister smirk. I swear I can hear Bri's soft gasp from across the space. Her attention may have returned to the woman in front of her, but I can tell she's turned the fuck on. Bri squirms and her ass flexes, letting me know she's squeezing her thighs together, chasing after the friction she craves. My smile only widens when I think about what's currently between her thick, glorious thighs. She gasped and had my shoulders in a death grip when I inserted the toy inside her earlier. When she asked me what I was doing, I just leaned forward to kiss the outside of her pussy before whispering, "Payback."

I clear my throat a few times under the guise of something going down the wrong pipe, but Bri's spine straightens. And if I had to guess, her body is decorated in goosebumps. My dirty girl is trying to get the relief she's desperate for, but I'm in control now.

Alright, bear, let's see just how quiet you can be for me.

I reach into my pocket and pull out my phone. The soft click of my screen unlocking echoes across the quiet space, and Bri's hands clench into fists. *Looks like my girl is on edge. It's okay, bear. I'll take real good care of you.* I swipe through the many apps until I pull up the one I need. Ever since the book club incident, I've been scouring for a way to, let's say, *repay the favor.* After hours of scouring many adult toy stores, I came across a toy that I can control through an app on my phone. And because consent is sexy, and I don't want her to do anything that would make her uncomfortable, I showed her the toy and asked her thoughts. It's safe to say that that night will go down as one of the most intense sexual experiences we've had. My girl just loves a good submission kink.

I stalk her from the corner of the store like she's my prey, waiting for the perfect moment to catch her off guard. I know she's expecting something to happen. I mean, she has the toy tucked inside that sweet little pussy of hers, but I never said when, let alone *if* I'd be using it on her. The glow from my phone screen illuminates my face, my finger hovering over the screen as I wait to catch Bri off guard, which isn't hard to do whenever she talks about books with a fellow book nerd. The woman asks Bri for a personal rec, and after she scans the shelf for the perfect book, I know I have her right where I want her.

The second Bri reaches toward the top shelf, I press the button. Her entire body jolts, and the book falls to the floor with a loud thump. Bri's thighs clamp together, and I track a shiver that rolls down her spine.

"Oh my gosh, are you okay?" the customer asks while bending down to pick up what Bri dropped.

"Y-Yes. I'm so sorry, I don't know what ha—" Bri squeals after I dial up the intensity level. Okay, maybe two. She takes a moment to collect herself, but if I pay close attention, I can hear her panting. And if I know my Bri, her arousal is slowly dripping down her thick thighs. And if we don't hurry this customer along, Bri will surely make a mess of herself all over the damn floor.

"Damn, I'm sorry. I'm not sure what happened, but I'm fine. Are there any other books you're looking for?" Bri looks over her shoulder, half-heartedly shooting daggers at me. She loves this just as much as I do. But because she decided to give me sass, my finger *accidentally* slipped, upping the intensity even more. *Keep quiet, bear. You don't want her to know I'm fucking your cunt with a pretty little toy, now do you?*

"I, well...I was hoping for a hockey romance book. I've been in my sports romance era, and hockey romances just hit, ya know?"

I dial back the vibrations to a softer pulsing sensation so that she can walk the poor, unsuspecting woman toward the sports romance section. Bri's hands are clenched in fists at her sides, and a bead of sweat glides down her neck. My mouth waters, and I desperately want to trace the path with my tongue before sinking my teeth into her supple flesh. *Goddamn, this lady needs to leave. I need to fuck my girl right here.*

It feels like she's been talking to this woman for hours, when in reality it's been five, maybe ten minutes? But my cock is painfully hard and all but demanding to fuck her fast and hard. Great, now *I'm* shifting from foot to foot, trying to distract myself from how my cock presses against my jeans. *Fuck. No. Bad decision.* The friction from the movement has me biting back a groan, and so I take my frustration out on the counter. My knuckles are so white they're translucent, my grip is painful. The moment this person leaves the store, it'll be Bri's hips I'm gripping with enough force to leave marks.

After another painful five minutes, I'm checking out the customer and all but pushing her out the door. The moment she leaves, I'm stomping toward the door to lock it, flip the sign to *closed*, and slam the blinds shut.

"Dress off and bend over the table with your ass in the air," I demand without looking at her. I don't bother to see if she's following directions because I'm focused on closing the remaining blinds and double-checking to make sure the door is locked. When everything is in place, I turn around only to see a fully dressed Bri with a hand on her cocked hip.

Ah, so Bri wants to play out this type of fantasy, then. Well, one demanding asshole coming up.

"What the fuck did I tell you to do?" I growl.

"Hmm, I'm not sure. I wasn't listening." Bri cocks her head to the side, biting her lip to prevent herself from smiling. But the glint in her eyes gives her away. When she first asked me to roleplay as one of her beloved *alphaholes*, I had a hard time. I'm not that type of guy. Yeah, I love to degrade her from time to time, but being domineering and borderline cruel? I really didn't know how I felt about treating her like that. But Bri was persistent and kept insisting she'd love it. After many promises to use her safe word if she didn't like it, I caved. And fuck, was I glad I did. My cock still remembers how hard her pussy shattered around me the first time we did.

I stalk toward her, wrap her ponytail around my fist, and yank her head back. She yelps, but I only tug harder. "You heard what the fuck I said. Now, why aren't you bent over the table with that pretty cunt in the air for me to use, hmm? Do I need to push you down and just take it?"

Her whiskey eyes darken, and a blush creeps up her delicate neck, painting her entire face. She loves all forms of sex with me, but my bear *loves* being dominated. A soft whimper escapes past her plump, berry-stained lips, and it's all the invitation I need to fuse our mouths together. I don't wait to slip my tongue into her mouth, demanding entry like it's my God-given right. My teeth bite down on her bottom lip, just hard enough to fill my mouth with a metallic taste. I lick the wound, soothing the sting. Our tongues crash together like waves during a storm; rough, dangerous, and intense. Everything about this kiss screams ownership. My scalp tingles as Bri grabs at the root in a desperate attempt to keep her from getting lost in the storm we are creating.

I somehow manage to walk us back toward the table. We haven't found a clever name for it yet, but it's a long, rectangular, mahogany table with all of Bri's personal faves. Bri gasps, ripping her mouth from mine the moment her ass hits the table. But I give her any time to process what's happening before I'm spinning her around and bending her over the table. I push the dress up her body, and mutter a curse when I see her lacy, black thong. I lean down, pull the pathetic excuse of a string between my teeth, and yank. Bri lets out a strangled cry as her back arches from the pleasure. I give her panties another tug before a loud tearing sound cracks through the air like a whip.

"Did you just rip my—ooh...."

My knee slips between her legs, forcing her to widen her stance. She's so dazed from the kiss that she does it without fighting me. But she's far from forgiven for her bratty behavior. My girl might be wet, but when I'm through with her, she'll be absolutely fucking drenched. I rub my palm across one ass cheek before lifting my palm and smacking her...*hard*. Her cry of pleasure is an erotic symphony, and I don't even like the fucking opera. I continue the pattern: *rub, lift, smack, repeat*. Over and over, alternating cheeks until there's a visible handprint on each.

Mine.

"That's what you get for being a fucking brat. I should leave you here, needy and wanting like the greedy little slut you are. But I'm feeling selfish as fuck right now. So here's how this is gonna go," I lean down and press a kiss to the base of her spine before continuing. "I'm gonna remove that toy, and not only are you gonna lick it clean, but you're gonna have it in that pretty mouth of yours while I fuck my pussy. Do you understand?"

Stunned speechless, Bri just nods. Well, as best as she can with my hand still wrapped around her hair in a tight grip. I press another kiss to her spine before whispering, "That's my good girl." My fingers trace up and down her spine, eliciting a full-body shiver from her. My hands glide across her smooth skin before reaching into her pussy and pulling out the soaked toy.

Bri whimpers at the loss, but before she can verbalize her protest, I'm pulling her up by the neck and growling in her ear. "Arms up, baby. It's time I take what I'm owed, no?"

Bri eagerly complies, and I yank her dress off before discarding it on the floor.

"Damn, that pretty dress looks damn good on the floor, don't ya think?"

"Y-Yes," Bri moans.

"Now, open up and suck your toy like a good girl."

Bri's mouth forms the perfect O, and I pop the toy in between her plush lips. Her cheeks hollow out as she sucks and licks around the toy covered in her own juices. I look on with lust and admiration for my strong, beautiful Bri. Even after everything she's been through, her strength never wavered. She might have lost touch with it for a while, but she powered through and came out even stronger than ever. My goddamn fucking warrior.

The moment she shifts her attention to me, offering herself up to me on a silver platter, I push her forward. Bri's cheek rests against a stack of Rina Kent books, her ass mere inches from my cock.

"Grab the end of the table, bear," I demand. One hand is in her hair while the other is fumbling with my jeans. After a few failed attempts due to my hands shaking from the adrenaline, I pull them and my boxers down and let them pool at my feet. I don't bother to shuck them off because I need to be inside her. Now. I grip my length and tug from base to tip a few times before slamming into her in one go.

"FUCK!" Bri's scream is muffled around the toy in her mouth. As much as I want her to be gagged by her own arousal, I love hearing her scream my name more. I reach around to remove the toy from her mouth while pounding into her with reckless abandon as Bri's grip on the edge of the table tightens.

"Shit, you're so fucking wet and warm. My pussy feels so good." Moans, grunts, and the sound of skin slapping against skin fill the space like it's surround sound. Who needs the *Fifty Shades* soundtrack when I have Bri's moans and screams to satisfy me?

"Asher, oh god yes! Right there I—*fuuuck*." Bri's pants match my grunts.

"You take me so good. You were made for my cock, baby." Liquid heat pools at the base of my spine, and I know I'm seconds away from detonating.

"A-Asher, I'm so close. Harder!" Bri shouts.

I pick up in speed and intensity, and the second I slip my finger around her pussy to pinch her clit, Bri explodes and screams so loud that I'm shocked the windows didn't shatter.

I pump one, two, three more times before I'm spilling inside her. I let out a roar almost loud enough to drown out the creaking sound from the table. I ride out my orgasm even faster, unable to stop myself because she feels so fucking good. I pound and pound and pound into her, and that's when it happens.

That creaking sound I heard earlier? It was the table attempting to alert us to the abuse it was currently taking. The sound of a loud *crack* shatters the moment, and I grab Bri as fast as I can before we topple over alongside the books now mimicking snow off an avalanche.

Thud. Thud. Thud.

Bri and I stare at the splintered wood and books littering the floor with a dazed expression. Did that seriously just happen? After the initial shock wears off, we look at each other, and that's all it takes to lose our shit. Bri is bent over, clutching her stomach and cackling. I stare at her in amazement, absolutely baffled that this beautiful woman is mine.

Bri eventually collects herself, and the grin falls from her face when she meets my serious expression.

"Why are you staring at me like that?"

I grab her by the waist and pull her into my arms. Her arms naturally wrap around my neck, and I press my forehead to hers.

"I'm just so fucking amazed by you. Everything you are is everything I've always needed. And now I get to have you forever and always."

"I love you, Asher."

"I love you, too, bear," I whisper before pulling back to survey the mess.

"Bri?" I ask.

"Yeah?"

"We're gonna need a sturdier table."

Bri tosses her head back and laughs with every ounce of her soul. I quickly joined in, adding a mental note to replace the romance books we absolutely demolished during our *real* love making.

Playlist

Dua Lipa-Training season

Rachel Platten-Fight Song

Alessia Cara-Scars to your beautiful

John Harvie-Beauty in the bad things

MAX feat Jay from ENHYPEN-Love insane

Evanescence- Bring me to life

Zayn-Pillow talk

Jason Derulo-It Girl

Alex Warren-Ordinary

Ed Sheeran feat. Arjit Singh-Saphire

Rita Ora feat Liam Payne-For Ya

Acknowledgements

Hello again, my lovelies. I hope you enjoyed Bri and Asher's story. This one was definitely more personal than my first novel. As someone who's struggled with her weight most of her life, I wanted to write a plus-size girlie and represent all of my beautiful curvy humans out there. When writing Bri, I was able to heal parts of myself that I found unlovable and not good enough. While I'm still working on loving every inch of myself, I've grown so much, and I hope that readers will be able to connect with pieces of this story.

This story has been touched by many hands, and without them, Be Your Forever wouldn't be the book that it is today. Thank you to my critique partners, Caty Lee & Mia Gray, for always pushing me to be the best writer I can be. You've helped me grow immensely, and I am forever grateful to the both of you. To my writing partner in crime, Delaine, you are just the best. I cannot thank you enough for always letting me vent to you about the struggles and anxieties of my writing process. You are a goddamn rockstar. To my Beta readers, I truly love and appreciate the hell out of y'all –I'm also scared to name everyone because I am *notorious* for forgetting people on accident. But without y'all, I'd still be pulling out my hair trying to make everything just right.

A million thank you's to my editor and proofreader at @englishpropereditingservices for being the real MVP–of answering my many, *many* messages and just being the best editor/proofreader I know.

To my cover designer, Sam Palencia (@inkandlaurel), YOU CRUSHED IT AGAIN! Like, the cover is hot AF, and I cannot get over how incredible everything is.

Shout out to the indie bookstores that have taken a chance on me and helped support me. The Last Chapter Bookshop, Hello Darling Books & Beyond, Plot Twist Books, & Love Stories OKC. Indie bookstores rock and y'all are truly some of the most amazingly wonderful people around.

To my smutty bitches–again–y'all are just the best. I love you to a million pieces and thank you for always being my cheerleaders.

To my @saltedcaramelmadams, I cannot thank y'all enough for being there for me through my ups and downs. Your support means the world to me.

To my friends and family, thank you for always being in my corner, and I'm so happy to have your support in my life.

To all my thick, curvy, baddies...you will ALWAYS be enough.

About the author

Natalie Knolls is a trauma therapist by day, contemporary romance author by night. She has two cats, Kringle & Chestnut, that she's obsessed with. When she isn't writing, you can find her with either a book in her hand reading, or with a microphone beating out tunes at your local Karaoke bar. Writing has always been a passion of hers and she is inspired by raw, emotional stories that feature real people. Check out her debut novel, BE YOUR SOMEBODY, out now.

You can find Natalie on Instagram and TikTok @authornatalieknolls.

Also by

BE YOUR SOMEBODY

A friends to lovers story filled with emotion and heart (and a guaranteed HEA)

COMING SOON:

Gage & Kennedy's story